# HELL COMES AGAIN

## T. W. Manes

This book is a work of fiction, but Part 1 is based on actual happenings and facts the author has either experienced, participated in, seen with his own eyes, or was related to him. These have been combined into one central fictionalized character named Jim Cooley. All names throughout the book have been changed to protect the identity of any/all real person(s), and any resemblance to any actual persons, living or dead, are part of the author's imagination or are used fictitiously. Any resemblance to any actuals events, locales, organizations, or persons, in Part 2 & 3 are entirely coincidental and are not to be construed as real persons, organizations, events, or locales.

# Dedication

This book is dedicated to everyone who has ever had the unfortunate experience of going through the *'flames of hell'* in any manner whatsoever. But, a special dedication and sincere thanks goes out to all former "combat brothers" who have experienced the horrors of war known to them as **HELL**! Those who have survived the flames of hell once can usually be counted on to go through the flames again if *Hell Comes Again.*

Please know that everyone in our great nation owes all who have survived the flames of hell, a great and heartfelt appreciation!

*"Beloved, think it not strange concerning the fiery trial which is to try you, as though some strange thing happened unto you" 1st Peter 4:12 KJV*

# Part 1
# Chapter 1
# First Journey through the Flames of Hell

"Jim, get your head down! Find some cover, man, and get under it! This one sounds like it's coming right on top of us! Man, I'm telling you, we're gonna be right in the middle of its killing zone! We're gonna be burnt toast, man, without a doubt!"

My name is Jim Cooley. Mike Stanley is my best friend and my combat brother. He doesn't want me to die so he's screaming at me right now, "You've already been hit in your head once, Jim! You can't afford to lose anymore brain cells than you already have! You're already crazy enough for the rear-echelon, desk-hugging, panty wearing, sissified butt sniffers and lickers, to make you spend the rest of your life in a round rubber room! So find some cover man, and get your head down!"

In the 'real world' the date is sometime in April, 1971. Mike, me, and the rest of our combat brothers are a part of the 1st Brigade, 5th Mechanized Infantry Division, 5th Battalion, 4th Artillery of the United States Army. We're part of "Charlie Battery" of the 4th Artillery. We shoot big 2 foot tall bullets that weigh 95 lb. out of our 155-mm self-propelled artillery guns.

Mike is yelling at me because *we're in 'Hell'!* Yep! That's right! This is exactly where we are right now! Without a doubt, we're definitely smack dab right in the very middle of the burning fiery hot flames of *'Hell'!* And at this exact moment, we're trying our best to keep these scalding hot raging flames that's surrounding us from burning us to a roasted crisp!

Today, we're trying to stay alive for just one more day in the midst of these flames just like we've been doing for the last two and a half months. We're part of a huge military operation called Lam Son 719 that's been disastrous from the very start. This ill-conceived and totally dysfunctional operation is taking place in the lush, green; jungle covered Annamite Mountains along the western border of Quang Tri Province, South Vietnam, and the godforsaken country of Laos.

But what is so amazing to us is how these absolutely beautiful, green-forested jungle enclosed mountains, which rise anywhere from 4000' feet in elevation upwards to 8000' feet can be the actual fiery domain of the demonic god of hell! But they are! These mountains really are the home of Satan and all of his demons! *This place really is Hell!* So far there's been hundreds of human sacrifices laid on top of top of his blood drenched sacrificial altar!


Quang Tri Province is the northernmost province in South Vietnam. It borders the beautiful South China Sea on the east, Laos on the west, and the most worthless name of a place ever given to anything in the entire world called, *The Demilitarized Zone*, on the north.

The reason we're here in hell is because several of the United States' former and present deluded leaders believed that we needed to stop the evil spread of communism in this godforsaken part of the world.

*"Yeah! I know!* That's why I used the word, *'deluded'!"*

This area is a faraway little patch of ground three-quarters of the way around the world from the United States. All of it combined, North and South Vietnam, is smaller than the single US state of California. It's actually smaller than the state of Montana in square miles but is more reminiscent of California in looks by having a long extended shoreline.

So why should this little rice-growing patch of water-logged ground be a concern of ours? Most of the rice farmers don't really care who is in charge of their country as long as it isn't some foreign occupying power like the French who held Vietnam as a colonial possession for many years while draining it of its natural resources. The Vietnamese wanted the French out and took up arms against them. They called themselves the Viet Minh. The Viet Minh continued opposing the French for years and years before World War Two. During World War Two, they opposed the occupying forces of the Imperial Japanese military. They did this with our ~ the United States ~ help and supplies. But after WWII when the French wanted to reoccupy Vietnam again, they picked up arms once more against the French. War raged in the little country!

Eventually, in an attempt to stop all of the fighting and aggression, a demarcated line was established that separated Vietnam and divided it into two countries, North Vietnam and South Vietnam. The Viet Minh were concentrated in higher numbers in the more industrialized north while the French were hanging on by a thread in the south where the rubber plantations and other such natural resources abounded that France desired to milk until there was nothing left. But the Viet Minh never accepted the humiliation of having their country divided into two parts by outside imperialistic powers.

Since we had turned our backs on the Viet Minh after WW II, the Viet Minh asked Russia and China for help in driving the French out. But one of the perquisites of North Vietnam receiving aid from these communist countries was that they had to turn to communism, too.

Eventually, through the efforts of the Viet Minh who had taken to guerrilla warfare in the south by being farmers during the day and jungle fighters by the night, the French were defeated and kicked out of the country yelping like little yellow defeated dogs with their tails tucked between their legs.

After the French were defeated, the Viet Minh wanted to once again, unify their country under one government. But, once the people of South Vietnam had tasted the sweet delicious taste of freedom that comes from living under a democracy, they didn't want to be under anything that resembled a choking smothering government controlled totalitarian dictatorship.

Why did the US care about any of this? And why did the US

turn its back on the Viet Minh who had been allies with us during WW II? Why did we allow France to again reclaim its slave country after WW II? And more important than that, why did we ever send troops into the country to fight against our former allies?

These questions need just one answer, the French asked us to help them instead of helping the Viet Minh. Unfortunately, our deluded leaders in the US considered France a much better friend and ally than a little rice producing backwards country three-quarters of the way around the world from us.

But since the North turned to communism and accepted Russian and Chinese help, South Vietnam asked us to help them stand against the communists who wanted to reunify the country. As I said before, our deluded leaders believed that we needed to stop the spread of communism. Our leaders called it, the *domino effect*. They believed that if one country fell under the alluring sway of government supplied 'everything', then more and more countries would fall, just like 'dominoes', under that same tempting sway.

But my god, man, all our country needed to do was just wait it out! Yeah! Wait it out! When power-hungry narcissistic individuals who believe that it takes a 'village' to raise your own child take over a 'government' that then takes complete control of society, it isn't long before that 'government' begins to collapse onto its own self!

You see, it doesn't take any more knowledge than plain old common sense to realize that when a 'government' assumes complete control over all of the gross domestic product a society produces, and then supposedly divides the GDP up equally between all of the workers in that society, it will be just a matter of time before all of the workers in that society realize that it doesn't matter how 'much' or how 'little' work they produce, they are still going to get the same as their lazy, no-good-for-nothing, dope smoking, beer drinking, woman chasing, pill-popping worthless neighbor who sleeps most of the day and produces nothing to give to society but is still going to get his full equal share. People, it does not take a genius to realize that as soon as the workers in society realize that these no-good neighbors are getting the same amount of 'everything' as them, they will then slow their production down, too.

Then, as more and more people slow their production down, the GDP goes down to where 'everything' suddenly becomes, *a few things'* instead. And then one day it happens, 'a few things' suddenly becomes 'nothing' *and it's over!* The Berlin Wall falls! Communism bites the dust except for dinosaurs like Castro in Cuba and Mao Tse Tung in China.

Anyway, our deluded leaders wanted to make nicey nice with France and help them save face, so our deluded leaders sent 'advisors' into South Vietnam to 'advise' them how to fire weapons and teach them how to fight a war. Unfortunately, *for us,* most of the South Vietnamese didn't want to be 'advised', so our deluded leaders decided they needed to send 'fighting' men instead of just 'advisors' to *'show'* the South Vietnamese how to fight'. *Show* them how it's done!

But then, the South Vietnamese realized just like communist 'workers' did, that if someone else was doing all of the *fighting* for them, then why should they do any? So, they stood and watched as the 'fighters' got their rear-ends shot off.

So our deluded leaders said we need to send *'more'* fighting men into the killing zone to keep the few fighters we have from getting their rear-ends shot off! And as more deluded leaders came into office and the intoxicating allure of almighty American political power consumed them, along with the tempting siren of the immortality of recognition being forever foisted upon them by being the one leader who had won the war, the system went on and on and on and on by sending more and more fighting men from the United States at the same time as there was less and less fighting coming from the South Vietnamese.

The North Vietnamese had a lot of common sense and saw what was happening. They quickly realized that all they needed to do was leave the South Vietnamese alone and concentrate on shooting the rear-ends off all of the Americans and the lazy

South Vietnamese who were relying on the Americans to protect them, would capitulate in a massive show of cowardice in a short matter of time!

So my friends, that's why I'm here in *HELL* right now! My deluded leader, *"I'm not a crook"*, Richard Nixon, sent me here as a 'fighting' man and along with Mike and the rest of my combat brothers, we're trying our best to keep our rear-ends from being shot off!

But I'm telling you again, man, this is not a country. It's not a province! Nor is it even a place. It's *'Hell'*, man! Plain and simple, *'Hell'!* 'And the flames are raging 'hot'! Before this ill-conceived and fatally flawed operation is over, every one of us will be burned to a blackened crisp! Even if we somehow manage to survive our journey through these flames, the scars from the burns will be with us forever! Without a doubt!

Right now at this moment, all forty-nine of us in Charlie Battery are trying to find some kind of cover that hopefully, will protect us from all of the mortars, rockets, RPGs, artillery rounds, and AK-47 small arms fire that the insanely dedicated little serial killers from North Vietnam ~ North Hell ~ are continuously shooting at us. Even though it's only been about two and a half months of normal time ~ the kind of time that takes place in the real world ~ since we started out on this operation, it seems like it's been an eternity. And during this eternity, it's been a constant, life or death battles with these ferocious, evil, demonic, little serial killers who gladly do the god of hell's killing for him, and who then pile their human sacrifices at his feet on his sacrificial altar in complete obedience!

By this point, all of us in my unit are already way past caring anymore whether we live or die. If we live, we have to stay in these flames for the rest of our eternities, however long those are. For both Mike and me, it's somewhere around six and a half more months before our sentence will be commuted and our journey through these flames of Hell will come to an end. Although, again, the terrible burns we are suffering in these scalding fires will never heal. They go too deep! The scars too ripe! These are not just physical burns; they're mental burns too.

So far, for most of us in my unit, these flames have not burned our bodies too badly, thank God. But our minds are seared. They'll never be the same! Never be normal again! But that's only if we continue to live! If we were to die, that may be a way for us to escape these fires of Hell. At least, it would give us an opportunity to finally get some sleep, even if it would be 'permanent sleep'. Our only prayer is that if we do die, "Please let us take some of these communistic, godless, evil serial killers with us. Don't let us die before allowing us to rid the earth of some of these demonic, stomach curdling, blood drinking vampires!"

As of today at whatever time it is in the real world ~ time doesn't exist here in Hell. It stands still! Never changes! One day blends into the next! Different horrors! Different terrors! But same color of blood! Always same color of blood! *'Red!!!'* Bright 'red'!!! Never changes! Just like time! ~ it's now been eight days since any of us have been able to even close our eyes for five minutes to try to get some sleep.

*"No!* Not sleep!" That's another foreign concept here in Hell. I should have said, 'rest'. But, rest does not exist here in Hell, either! It, too, is a foreign concept! The bottom line is I don't know how we're still even standing on our feet, much less being able to function as we're supposed to do!

It must be nothing but instinct. Maybe it's the will to survive at all costs, the survival of the fittest ... I don't know and can't tell you what it is. But this I do know, we're no longer human beings!

We're no longer at the top of the food chain! In fact, we no longer have any civilized emotions whatsoever. We eat cold food out of dented up old cans with our dirty bare hands. We empty our bladders on the ground and watch it blend in with the constant, unceasing rain that does nothing to dampen these fires of hell. We empty our bowels in a deep muddy hole we've dug then hope and pray that we don't step in it later on. We haven't had a bath or a shower, other than standing out in the cold rain and soaping up for over a month now. And to do that, you're risking the chance that some kind of enemy killing projectile is going to bury itself deep into your heart or your head!

The only thing I can think of to describe us is that we have now turned into full-fledged zombie vampires! That's it! That's what we've become! It's because, 'we want blood! Enemy blood! *North Vietnamese enemy blood!!!!*'

That's the only way we will ever be able to escape out of these raging flames of Hell that's burning all around us. We have to drain the blood out of all of those North Vietnamese serial killers before they can drain our own blood! If we can do that, maybe then we can escape out of this Hell we're living in!

The reason we've been awake and in a constant battle to stay alive is because, eight days ago in human real world terms, our so-called South Vietnamese allies that supposedly have been fighting alongside of us to keep their country free from the North Vietnamese; in a massive display of hysterical panic, showed their true, yellow, cowardly colors, and actually threw their American supplied weapons down onto the ground. Then, by individuals, by platoons, by companies, by batteries, by full battalions, even by entire divisions, they all actually began running away from these very well trained and extremely dedicated North Vietnamese blood sucking serial killers! They have now abandoned us and left us here all alone in Hell so the demons from North Hell can suck our blood dry.

These serial killers from North Hell are not just trying to kill all of the South Vietnamese they come in contact with, but they're trying even harder to kill all of us Americans, too! But, we're not running away from them. We're not throwing our guns down and high-tailing it out of here like screaming little crying cowards. This is not even our country, and it shouldn't even be our fight, but again, we're not running. We're going toe to toe and face to face with these poisonous, two-stepping spiting snakes! And by the grace of God and with His help, we will survive! We will come out of this Hell!

Actually, the South Vietnamese cowering cowards have been throwing their weapons down and running away from the North Vietnamese almost every time they have come into contact with the demons of North Hell during this entire operation so far.

The crying cowards have totally refused to fight! That's now been somewhere around six or eight weeks before this day if you could measure time here in Hell. It's just that the last of them finally left and abandoned us eight days ago.

Nine days ago, a South Vietnamese 155-mm artillery unit exactly like ours, except their guns were very nice, clean, and shiny because they hadn't been used in a long time, pulled in right next to where we're set up ~ we're only about five miles from the border of Laos ~ but while we stayed awake all night long firing support missions, never once did they even fire one shot! Not once! Then, just as the sun was coming up, they packed up and pulled out of here, heading back to the safe rear area of the city of Quang Tri that sits next to the beautiful azure blue waters and white sandy beaches of the South China Sea!

*"Miserable little crying cowards!! That's what they are! All of 'em'!"*

So for the last eight days; since there's no more of the South Vietnamese cowering cowards for the North Vietnamese to kill, or to even yell "BOO" at and scare off, the little blood sucking serial killing demons from the north have turned all of their deadly attention on us Americans. They're now trying their best to kill all of us! But to their great annoyance and extreme displeasure, we won't run from them, even though this stinking, smelling, godforsaken, hellhole of a place is not our country and this shouldn't even be our fight.

Without a doubt, these North Vietnamese sub-human hell-born demons are blood sucking vampires, too, just like us. And they, too, want blood! Human blood! But most of all right now, they want our good ole pure D bright red American blood! From wherever they are and from whatever rocks they've crawled out from under, they can smell our blood; the same as we can smell theirs! And, they're every bit as thirsty for that thick, red, thirst-quenching liquid as we are!

# Chapter 2

A couple of days ago in normal human real world time, we began running low on ammunition. At that time, the rear echelon, sissified, big-butted, desk-hugging, panty-wearing, brown-nosed, butt-kissers who keep track of those kind of things, told us to stand-down for a couple of hours. Didn't mean we could just take a nap or sit down and rest somewhere, though. There were too many exploding enemy projectiles constantly coming in on us to be able to do that!

But, I was trying anyways to get just a minute or two of rest by leaning my worn out, mindless, rest deprived, almost lifeless body, against the side of my artillery gun. I was using it as a crutch to hold me up; to keep me on my feet.

I had to keep standing up. My men depended on it. I was their leader, their gun sergeant. If I collapsed, all of my brothers would soon follow and then, we would all die in just a matter of minutes. Those blood-sucking North Vietnamese leaches and maggots would fall upon us and suck every drop of blood out of our bodies before we could even force our eyes open again!

As I stood there propped up, I guess I just kind of blanked out for a minute or two. I wasn't out of it for very long, though. I quickly came back to reality when Mike's, very irritatingly loud voice, broke through my rest, slumber, and oh, so quiet peace.

"Jim, quit leaning against your gun and get under it, at least! Wake up, man! Get under your gun! We have a ton of rounds constantly coming in on us! One of them is gonna get you if you don't get under some cover!"

I eventually replied to him, "Okay, okay! I will. . . . . But man, Mike, I just don't have the energy ... or the mental strength . . . to even care anymore. . . . Sometimes, I think I just want to go ahead and get it over with and die! ... I'm just beat, man."

"I know! So am I! We all are! But, man, you don't wanna die here in Hell, man! Not here in Hell! So, as long as I'm still here, you're gonna be here, too. We've survived this Hell together for six months now. And we're gonna survive it for another six. That's all we gotta do. Just six more to go, man! We can do it! We're almost on the downward side of it now. You hear me? So get you head down, *'now'!"*

Mike was right, I couldn't die in Hell. If I did, I'd never get out of it. I'd never escape from its clutches. My eternity in Hell would last forever!

I began to slowly turn around, but, it wasn't by choice that I was turning slowly. In my mind, I was on target to run a sub four-minute mile going towards the back of my 155-mm self-propelled artillery gun so I could crawl under it. This big tubed monstrous man-killing machine some articulate hero had long ago very aptly named, *"Cap't Crunch"*, weighs 25 tons, and it should give me a lot of protection. That is, unless it were to take a direct hit from an enemy artillery round. In that case, I would be a goner faster than you can blink your eyes! I would be screaming, "That's one gigantic leap for mankind", and begin dancing on the moon with Neil Armstrong and Buzz Aldrin!

But just then, as I was still in the process of turning around and before I even had a chance to take another step, an enemy mortar round suddenly flew in out of the thick, dark, 99% percent humidity filled, rain drenched, overcast sky, and exploded close enough to send me rocking back and forth like I was standing on top of a rocking chair by the force of the exploding concussion. I was later told that I looked just like Joe Frazier getting his over-weight, fat butt, whooped but good by Muhammad Ali.

Man, I hadn't even heard the mortar coming in before it exploded. So, I didn't even have time to react to it! But that's not unusual; most of us artillery guys don't hear mortar rounds while they're flying through the air. They aren't too big, and they don't disturb the air too much, so they don't make much noise. They're not like big, heavy, artillery rounds that make a gawd-awful amount of noise as they come in on you. Those dastardly things sound just like real thunder; or a runaway freight train; or a seriously deranged, long-haired hippy drummer, who in his chemically induced paranoia and hyperactivity, is continuously pounding over and over again on a huge pair of symphonic concussion drums, as they blast their way through the air, ripping and tearing the atmosphere apart!

One, or more, of those big monsters is why Mike was yelling for me to find some protection. He apparently didn't hear the mortar round coming in, either, or he would have been yelling about that instead of the artillery round. But again, that's not unusual for all of us cannon-cocking artillery guys because, by now, we are so hard of hearing that we usually either communicate with each other by hand signs, or screaming at the top of our voices like Mike is doing.

So, neither Mike, nor anyone else in my unit, heard the mortar coming in until it exploded. As it did, though, in addition to rocking me back and forth in a Muhammad Ali imitation of his best rope-a-dope routine, a large chunk of broken, jagged, burning hot flaming metal about the size of a baseball exploded from the shattered shell, and then flew up and hit me on the left side of my helmet! Thank God it was only a glancing blow and didn't hit me straight on! My turning to go towards the back of my artillery gun is what made it hit me with a glancing blow instead of straight on, and that's what saved my miserable life.

But for several minutes afterward, I lay unconscious, flat on my back, moaning and groaning just like a knocked out drunken sailor on shore leave who had just been stupid enough to mess with an Army dude! I lay there face up, doing a perfect imitation of Joe Frazier with his big butt whooped flat on the canvas. But instead of being on a nice soft canvas, I was lying in a water drenched, mud-filled, urine containing enemy bomb crater, where the Rock of Gibraltar sized piece of shrapnel had knocked me silly.

Eventually, though, my jagged brain, which was acting totally and completely against my wants and wishes, began to regain some form of consciousness. As it did, the first jumbled and scrambled thought that entered my mind was, I somehow remembered that I had heard the explosion. That could only mean one thing. "I was still alive!" That's the old saying in combat, "if you hear the explosion, and then you remember that you heard the explosion after you wake up, that means you are still alive. If you don't remember the explosion, it probably means you're 'dead'!"

The next jumbled thought that went wobbling through my mind was, I began wondering if I could shout hallelujah because I had just gotten the golden gift of a major injury that would be enough for me to escape out of the clutches of this Hell and allow me to go back to the fairy-tale land of the deluded real world! But, sadly to say, within another few minutes, as a little more coherency slowly returned and I was able to look around some; even if my vision was still a little fuzzy, I realized it was not to be. I knew I was not injured bad enough to escape out of these clutches of Hell. It's just like the fiery old preacher of my youth used to say, "Hell is truly a place with no escape!"

I couldn't help but chuckle as that thought entered into my mind. 'In my youth', I thought. 'How old am I now? I'm only twenty. But what an eternity it's been since I was sitting in a church at the tender age of eighteen, until now. Back then I was just a little bed-wetting, know-it-all, whiny little, rosy-cheeked child. I thought I knew everything about everything. But, I was so totally and completely ignorant about this great big mean old world that's surrounding me right now. Without a doubt now, after what I've seen and heard and suffered through so far, I'm so old inside I'll never be young again. There are so many burns on my body that I'll be scarred ugly forever!'

One time back then in my bed-wetting youth, I had been sitting in a church listening to a preacher preach about 'Hell', a place he knew very little about because he had never been in the place. Sure, he had read about it and probably studied it, but he had never been there. So how could he say with true conviction what Hell was really like?

But I can tell you what it's like! I have been there. And, I'm still 'here' right in the middle of it 'now'! He's right about one thing, though. 'There is no escape from this place!'

After I regained enough consciousness to be able to think almost rationally, I immediately began thanking God that I had been wearing my steel helmet on my head, instead of my bush-hat that I wore almost all of the other time. I was only wearing the steel helmet because it was raining and the helmet helped to keep the rain out of my face. I was also wearing the fiberglass inner-helmet underneath of my steel helmet like you're supposed to do. If I hadn't been wearing both of them, I wouldn't be alive right now. The shrapnel put a huge dent in the steel helmet, while at the same time; it made a big, jagged, splintered, star-burst type of a mess in the fiberglass one.

To put it bluntly, it totally ruined both of them. If I can find a way to manage it, I'm gonna save both of them and take them home with me for a souvenir. It will be something I can show to my grand-kids when I get old; 'if' I get old! But first, I have to somehow get a reprieve to get out of this Hell so I can eventually get married and then have kids, who will then have to have kids of their own.

So today, Mike is yelling at me with such urgency right now because I no longer have a steel helmet to wear. Those are some of the things the Army doesn't keep spares of. At least, not out in the middle of a raging field of fire. I guess the Army assumes that if you get hit in the head hard enough to ruin your helmet, then you wouldn't be around to need a spare one anyway. And, as usual, the Army is wrong again! I'm living proof that a new helmet is very much needed.

But, even if I were to get a new helmet right away, it wouldn't fit my head at this time. I wouldn't even be able to put it on. You see, I have a huge new appendage growing out of the side of my head just above my left ear where the shrapnel hit me.

That jagged chuck of shrapnel gave me a bad concussion and a terrible headache, in addition to knocking me stone cold silly for several minutes. Some people around me may have said that I didn't need to get hit in the head to already be that way. But be that as it may, besides killing a lot of the few remaining brain cells I had left; it also put a huge knot on the side of my head that would fit perfectly inside of a woman's 36-DD bra cup!

Yeah, I know! The guys on my artillery gun crew started telling me right after I regained consciousness that I had a real nice looking tit growing out of the side of my head.

Yes, there's no doubt they all think they're the world's funniest comedians! But, you can't blame them for trying to inject some humor into our very deadly situation. When you spend all of your terrifying days and nightmarish nights trying your hardest to kill other human beings, and then with your enemies trying their very hardest to kill you before you can kill them, you do and say a lot of different things to try to ease the macabre atmosphere surrounding you! We all, including me, found this new tit growing out of my head to be very humorous; even though it was very painful to even smile.

In a small way, though, I was a little bit disappointed. That old jagged piece of flaming metal might have given me a few minutes of rest and relaxation by knocking me silly, and it also blessed me with a new tit, but it didn't even break the skin on the side of my head. Therefore, to me, I didn't qualify for a Purple Heart Medal, or anything else like that. To me, you gotta bleed to receive! *(I know, that's totally unlike a 'swift boat' navy fish down in the Delta who believes that even if you just 'see', you receive. Therefore, at last count, he has 'seen' three things so he has received three medals.)* Because of this, some of my guys wanted to puncture the 'tit' with the tips of their bayonets to make it bleed so I could receive. But, no way, *MAN!* That just wasn't gonna happen!

Getting hit with flaming exploding shrapnel is what can happen when you're in the middle of a killing zone like we are. In fact, the odds are that is exactly what is going to happen to you!

What you have to do though, after you get knocked down, is you have to climb back up onto your feet. Then, you have to somehow reach further down inside of yourself to find some way to try harder, and with even more gusto, to kill those reptilian slant-eyed, flared-necked, spitting cobras that had just tried to kill you! That's what you do! And, you do it before they have another shot at killing you! That's the way this deadly game is played! *'It is kill, or be killed'!*

Mike and I have been playing this deadly game for a long time now, and if I do say so myself, we have gotten very good at it. That's why we're still alive right now. Mike wants to keep it that way. I'm Mike's good-luck charm, and he's mine. We arrived on the same exact day into this Hell, and we both want to make sure that we leave, while still alive, on the same exact day. That's why he's screaming at me right now to find some kind of cover and to get my oddly shaped, helmet-less, tit-growing, head down!

# Chapter 3

I was told I was being sent to 'Hell' on September 30, 1970. I arrived there two weeks later on October 13, 1970. The mode of transportation that took me to Hell was a Flying Tigers, Boeing 707 airliner. The location in 'Hell' that the airliner landed was a place called Cam Rahn Bay, South Vietnam.

Cam Rahn Bay is a huge military base. It's located a little ways north of Saigon and right next to the warm, majestic, beautiful, alluring, azure blue waters of the South China Sea.

At the time I was flying into Vietnam, I was an insignificant, very disposable myopic little creature with the lofty rank of Private First Class. I was also a very scared, frightened, and terrified member of the mean green fighting machine of the United States Army.

As we were on final approach to Cam Rahn Bay, I looked out the window of the airplane to get my first view of what the fires of Hell would look like. But, I was stunned! I didn't see any fires, or even any flames! There wasn't even any smoke! What I did see below me for as far as my eye could see, were beautiful white sandy beaches with a beautiful blue ocean gently rolling and lapping up onto them. And in many places along those stretches of white sandy beaches were a lot of people sunbathing, playing volleyball, throwing footballs, or just enjoying themselves in other ways. There also seemed to be a lot of swimmers and surfers enjoying the clear blue warm water, too.

I thought to myself, in any other place and at any other time, because of the astounding beauty of this place, one could almost make-believe they were arriving at a South Pacific paradise! It was definitely not that, though. It's still a part of Vietnam, and thus, Hell, although, it's a beautiful part of Hell.

Cam Rahn Bay was nothing like what I had expected it to be. I had expected that as soon as the airplane landed, I would have to immediately run for my life into some kind of a bunker or a defensive location and begin shooting at the 'Charlie Cong'!

But, I was assured this would not happen by an old Army Staff Sergeant, who was actually coming back to Hell for his third journey through it. He kept telling me I would be happily surprised. And just as the Staff Sergeant had said, it was nothing at all like I had expected it to be. In fact, after I landed in Cam Rahn Bay, I walked down the stairs that were pressed up against the plane, down onto the tarmac, and into an airport terminal that could have been located in "Anytown", USA!

That is, I eventually walked down the stairs after I, and everyone else on-board our plane, eventually recovered from passing out due to a completely unexpected, poisonous gas attack that totally overwhelmed all of us on the plane! After we landed and as the door up near the front of the plane swung open, in that same instant, an awful stench that smelled worse than a million rotten eggs, a ton of cow-manure, a broken natural gas pipeline, a sulfur mine, and a guy I know named Latham, instantly swept through the entire plane!

"All right, who's the wise guy?" someone managed to yell before he suddenly lost consciousness.

"It's not any of us!" someone else up near the front of the plane managed to gasp out, "It's this country! *WOW!!! It stinks!*" before he, too, suddenly passed out!

"Don't worry, you'll get used to it," the big Army Staff Sergeant yelled through his tightly clenched teeth before he joined the rest of us and passed out, too!

Eventually, though, all of us somehow managed to regain consciousness from this sudden onslaught of what Hell smells like. None of us had been expecting that! None of us, other than the old Staff Sergeant, had expected to be greeted with a poisonous gas attack like we were exposed to! This gas attack just added that much more to our already being scared to death and to our insecurity! This was my first impression of Vietnam. It looked beautiful from the air, but it smelled like you were swimming naked underwater in the semi-solid sludge of a sewage treatment plant!

While trying not to puke on our buddy in front of us, we stumbled down the stairs and made our way into the airport terminal that again, could have been located in "Anytown", USA! It was a modern place with food courts, ice cream parlors, and *flushing toilets!* It should be a nice modern place; it handled thousands of Hell-bound passengers every year. As the Good Book says, ***"for wide is the gate, and broad is the way, that leadeth to destruction and many there be which go in there at"! KJV***

As I was slowly walking through the terminal taking in the sights, I was thinking, *'Vietnam might not be so bad after all! That is, if that Staff Sergeant wasn't lying about getting used to the smell.'* But, just a few minutes later, I soon found out that no matter what Vietnam looked like, it was still Hell! I ambled on outside of the terminal and walked straight into blazing, 100 degree heat with 99.999% humidity. It was so hot and miserable that it was literally pouring down rain. But before the rain could hit the ground, it would dry up and evaporate because of the hellishly hot heat! Combine that heat and humidity with the dirty butt, raw sewage smell of the entire country, and I knew immediately that instead of arriving in a South Pacific paradise, I really had just descended into the very pits of Satan's abode!

I hurriedly walked over and climbed onto a U.S. Air Force blue colored bus. Shortly after that, the bus pulled out and we were quickly transported over to a huge compound. This compound had two, nearly identical sections to it. It was divided right down the middle; one side was for the Newbies coming into the country, and the other for the 'Survivors' going back to the 'World'. On the Newbie side were probably four or five hundred pieces of new, *"enemy bait and target-practicing fodder."*

After walking inside the Newbies side of the compound to get checked in-country, I literally, spent hours upon hours standing in lines until both of my legs turned into solid stone, and until the cows came home, the chickens roosted, the sun came up, and ... ... ... ... until the Army's vaunted, world famous, paper shuffling mechanism finally decided to inch forward.

Eventually though, before my year long sentence to Hell came to an end, I finally stood in front of the last little green-clad, pencil-sharpening, paper-shuffling, puckered-up, panty-wearing, gum-chewing, rear-echelon Army clerk. As I did, he looked up at me with his trademark, 3/4" inch thick, coke bottom bottle prescription glasses, and said to me, "Hey, Newbie bait and target-practicing fodder, we're having a party down at the beach tonight around sundown. You're invited if you want to come."

I glanced up at him with astonishment written all over my face. Finally, I managed to reply, "You mean, it's okay to go down to the beach? I mean what about enemy frogmen, or something? I mean, I haven't even been given a weapon yet. What do I do if we're attacked?"

He laughed, "Yeah man, it's okay to go to the beach! Nothing to worry about! In fact, we have trained dolphins swimming out in the bay. They have been trained to kill any gooks that are stupid enough to try something like that. As I said, there's nothing to worry about! Come on down and enjoy your stay here while it lasts. I guarantee you there will be some very good stuff waiting for you down there."

"What are you talking about? What kind of stuff?" I replied.

He laughed again. "Man, you are a real piece of bait, aren't you?! Stuff, man! You know, the smoking kind of 'stuff'. Haven't you ever partaken in the divine pleasures of smoking 'stuff'?"

I suddenly realized what he meant. "Oh, 'stuff'! Yeah, man, I know what you mean. 'Stuff'! Sure! Is it any good?"

But as those words barely had time to leave my mouth, his eyes instantly got so big that I almost jumped back from the table! They came zooming out of those 3/4" inch thick lenses and straight towards me looking just like 3-dimensional bugged out frog eyes! I honestly thought they were going to pop right out of the thick lenses and splatter themselves all over my face like two huge insects!

Finally though, with much effort, he regained enough of his composure to say, "Man, this is the Golden Triangle! You ever hear of it? This is where we have the best of every kind of stuff in the world, whether you want to smoke the stuff or you want to shoot the stuff! This is Vietnam, man! Corner piece of the 'Triangle'!"

My guess right then was that he wasn't smart enough to know that a triangle has three corners to it! Either that or he was already partaking in the pleasures of the 'stuff' today.

"Hey, I'll tell you what, I'll see you down on the beach and turn you on to some Cambodian Red, okay?" he said, "I guarantee you'll see god after smoking one of those righteous things!"

So, around 7:30 p.m. local time on my first night in Hell, I went out the door of the barracks and began wandering on down towards the beach. At the same time, another new piece of enemy bait and target-practicing fodder had come out of another barracks and was ambling on down towards the beach, too. As we both came from opposite directions around a corner, we almost bumped into each other. But after saying our apologies, we continued going towards the beach together and talking as we went. I introduced myself to him as Jim, and he told me his name was Mike. This is where Mike Stanley and I first met.

When we got down to the beach, I stopped a little ways away from everyone else and eased my way down on to the sand. Other than my new friend, Mike, I didn't know anyone and I just kind of wanted to be alone to think for a while. As I sat down on the soft silky sand I put my hands behind my head and lay down backwards. The warm dampness began to seep in around and absorb me. It felt so good I squeezed my eyes closed, and in that instant, I was somehow transported back through the portals of time to when I had been a little kid and was floating on my Grand-Mother's old feather-bed she had resting inside of her screened-in back porch.

A large smile instantly wrapped all the way around and across my face as my old grandma and her feather-bed popped into my memory. She had passed away several years ago, but I still carried a lot of good memories of being out at her house when I was a little kid. The last time I had laid down on that old feather-bed was probably when I was around ten or eleven years old.

As these thoughts were wrapping their slow way through me, my mind drifted into the first sense of peace I had felt since I had first gotten my orders to go to Hell. As I quickly settled into this new-found nirvana I let my eyes slowly drift upward.

*"Wow!"* I thought! Above me was an exquisite, black velvet heavenly canvas of an enormously large and beautiful diamond filled sky. It was literally covered with millions upon millions of brightly shinning little sparkling diamonds floating serenely in the bonnet of God. There were more brightly shining little diamonds floating above me at that moment than I had seen in a lot of years. You just don't see that many stars while living in a big city like Phoenix, Arizona; which is my home town back in the real world. There's too much light pollution.

I slowly moved my gaze down and let me eyes drift way out beyond the white sandy shore to where the ocean suddenly blended in and became one with the horizon. The golden expanse of a beautiful quarter moon was slowly rising up out of the water into the majestic, diamond filled sky. As it did, it was reflecting its golden image back down onto the dark black almost smooth water. As I let my imagination go, it suddenly looked like a huge, almost round, shiny golden wedding ring!

Somehow, I knew that this awesome mind boggling portal of astounding beauty along with the softly alluring sounds of cascading water that I was basking in could only have been created by a Supreme, Supernatural, and Almighty God! Atheists can say all they want about there not being a God, but put them on the sandy shore of hell where in a day or two they are going to come face to face with a bunch of very dedicated and well trained serial killers that want nothing more than to mutilate and kill you, then, ask them again after that what their views are! I would be very surprised if they were to remain the same!

The beautiful diamond filled sky above and the symphonic sounds emanating below as the gently cascading waves curled and rolled onto the soft sandy shore could only have been created by the Master Painter and Master Musical Director of the entire universe! And, what was so great to me at that moment was that He was allowing me to bask in this astounding phenomenon of nature on the same night as I had just descended into the very clutches of the fiery flames of Hell! With my entire mind and body fully and completely wrapped in total admiration, I couldn't help but just lie there basking in the beautiful symphonic performance that almighty God had created this night for my pleasure and enjoyment! I don't know, and didn't care, if anyone else was enjoying it, but I sure was!

But then, as it so often happens, right in the midst of all of that beauty and peace and good feelings, an evil darkness rapidly began seeping into my mind! It immediately began to cast an enlarging and enveloping shadow over my entire being; and in that very instant, my mind suddenly brought me jarringly back to the realization of just exactly where I was! I was in the midst of a war zone! A place I would soon find out to be filled with the fiery raging flames of Hell that desired to completely consume me!!!

As I lay there, I couldn't help but wonder what tomorrow would bring . . . or the next day ... or the day after that ... or the next... ... ... *if I happened to be so blessed.* Right then, in the very midst of God's astounding beauty and majesty, a tremendous, stomach knotting, almost paralyzing fear, suddenly entered into my entire being and began to consume my mind and body! And just that quickly, I went from basking in the magnificent presence of the awesome wonders of the almighty Creator of the entire universe, to suddenly wallowing in the total darkness of complete unimaginable terror! As I lay there, I was consumed with wondering just how many tomorrow's, if any, I might have left!

A dreaded terror that I had never before come close to experiencing, or even thought was possible in the short life I had lived up to this point, was consuming every pore, membrane, and cell of my entire being! And as this terror descended down over me threatening to smother me, warm wet mists quickly welled up and covered my eyes! At the same time, my body began shaking almost uncontrollably!

As this was happening, I silently began praying to God. Unashamedly, I asked Him to allow me to live. I didn't want to die! I didn't care what anyone else may say! They may claim what I was doing was committing a foxhole, or more likely, a deathbed confession. I didn't care! I really don't want to die. Not now! Not tomorrow! Not the next day! ... ... *Not for a long time!* There are so many things I want to do in my life as I get older. I have always been a dreamer and I had dreamed of a lot of things I want to do in my life. Now, here I am in Vietnam---which is just another name for Hell---facing a completely unknown future, and I'm almost paralyzed with fear!

Just then, at that very moment, as if things couldn't get any worse, the paper shuffler from the processing center came staggering up to where I was laying. To me, he looked like some kind of a demonic, ugly, malformed alien being wearing space goggles!

As I glanced up at him, I could see that he had definitely, already been partaking of the deceiving pleasures of the 'stuff'! His frog like, big bugged, coke bottle enclosed eyes were glowing with red blood drenched weariness in them! At the instant I saw him and the state of mind I was in at that moment, I almost jumped right out of my entire skin and left it laying on the ground just like a snake sheds his and leaves it behind! In my fragile mental state and with the low level of light only coming from the small quarter moon, I honestly thought a demonic evil creature had somehow escaped from the very pits of hell and had come to take me back with him!

With extreme difficulty ~ he had long ago lost any ability to have any sense of coordinated motion ~ he leaned over close to me, and then in a slurred and strained voice, said, "Hey man, you look like you could use one of these. It's a Cambodian Red, man. It means it has opium mixed with the grass. You smoke it, and man, I tell you, you'll hallucinate! You'll see colors that you've never seen before, man! I swear to you, you'll see god, man! I swear this to you! I really do! You'll see god! Here, take one!"

I looked at him for a moment. By now, my initial fright had somewhat receded and I was really tempted to take it from him. It had been a long time since I had refused a joint! In fact, I don't think it had ever happened before that I had refused one. Even though, on many occasions, just like some silver-spooned sex-crazed draft-dodgers have claimed to do, I tried my best not to inhale any smoke from them. *Yeah right, man!*

But, for some reason right at that particular moment, I just wanted to be left alone with a clear head to see if I could somehow, someway, reestablish contact with my own God on my own terms. I didn't want some kind of a hallucinated god to appear to me that comes from an opium soaked marijuana cigarette! And, I really didn't believe my chances of seeing my own God would be greatly enhanced by smoking some stupid dope. So I said, "No thanks, man. Not now. Maybe later, OK?"

Instantaneously, it was like he had been touched by a faith healer and suddenly cured of all his ailments! He stopped the moving and jerking spasmodic movements he had been making and suddenly stood perfectly still. A look of incredulity suddenly swept across his face! His ears began tingling so bad you could actually see them vibrating! His bottom lip suddenly dropped so far down it was dragging on the sandy beach! And at the same time, his eyes suddenly popped so far out of his face that I thought two surface-to-air bloody red missiles had just been launched at me!

He could not believe what he had just heard! I guess no one had ever refused one of his Cambodian Reds before and it was just a tremendous shock to his system! Eventually, though, with great difficulty, he regained enough of his smoke choked voice to proclaim, "Yeah man, no sweat. Just look me up later if you want some. In fact, if you want anything, you know, like LSD, Cambodian Reds, Thai Sticks, Reds, hashish, amphetamines, even 90% pure heroin, just let me know, man, I'll hook you up!"

"OK, man, sure, maybe I'll do that!" His shoulders were stooped and slumped like the Hunchback of Norte Dame! His face was total devastation! His gait was like a ninety year old man! All as he turned slowly around and began to stumble away from me!

I turned to watch him shuffle back down the sandy beach. I knew by what I had said to him that I had totally and completely ruined the high he was experiencing! From the look of him, my refusal had probably totally brought him back to reality, or whatever sphere of reality it was that he lived and existed in!

But as I watched the poor, demonically possessed, satanically inspired, deluded little dude stumble away from me, I leaned back down, closed my eyes and tried once more to contact my own God. Unfortunately, it didn't happen! When the deluded little dude had come up to me, God had disappeared!

# Chapter 4

In the middle of the courtyard in front of this scenic, bed and breakfast compound, where I was staying with free room and board on a government paid expense account, was a huge map of all of Vietnam, including both South and North Vietnam. The map was about three feet wide and stood about ten feet tall.

Every morning, all of us Newbie pieces of enemy bait and target-practicing fodder would have to stand in a horseshoe ('U') formation with the map in front of us. In what would become a ritual, an Army Captain would stand next to this map and read off a couple hundred names. Then, he would call the people whose names he had yelled out of formation to get their new transfer orders.

After that, all of these Newbies would go over to the map and look at it until they could find where they were being transferred to. Most of them were going to places around Saigon, the capital of South Vietnam. Or, they were going down to the Delta, which was further south of Saigon. Or, some even went to Na Trang, which was a little ways north of Cam Rahn Bay. Very few received orders to go as far north as Da Nang, which was probably around five and one half feet up on this map, or almost two-thirds of the way up from the bottom of South Vietnam.

But here's the thing, 'two-thirds' of the entire United States' Army is made up of rear echelon company clerks, supply enablers, transportation specialists, or whatever other job they have been assigned to by the paper-shuffling, shake and bake, scared witless, so-called army officers who pick and choose who is going to survive, and who is going to have to fight to stay alive. This mostly assures that the 'fortunate ones', who make up the two-thirds majority, will be kept far from the 'fires and flames' of Hell! For these 'fortunate ones' who have been chosen by the misguided desk-hugging wide-bottom army officers, South Vietnam is not Hell! To them, it's a South Sea Tropical Paradise full of native 'Girl-Sans' who are willing to do, and be, anything they want them to do, and be!

But for the other one-third who have been chosen by these lap-dogging, desk-hugging, wide-load sign-bearing, big-butted army officers to be enemy bait and target practicing fodder, it's definitely "Hell"!! So, that's the reason why I'm now in Hell, instead of rollicking in the surf with a girl-San on each arm like these other rear-echelon dope smoking posers are doing! I'm a part of the chosen one-third who is expected to go fight, and then probably 'die' in this place called Hell!

I had been trained by the Army to become a menace to society. They had put a lot of effort, time, and money; plus a tremendous amount of yelling and screaming, in turning me from a meek, mild mannered southern Texas gentleman, into a ferocious fighting machine. So, naturally, believing they had accomplished their goals, I became a highly disposable part of the chosen one-third who was really going to get the opportunity to earn that whole extra $25 dollars a month of combat associated pay! I was a valuable, but very expendable, piece of new ripe bait to be used as enemy target-practicing fodder!

After a few days, I eventually received my transfer orders. I saw that I was being ordered to report to the 5th Mechanized Infantry Division Headquarters at a place called Quang Tri Firebase for further additional orders.

# Chapter 5

I said goodbye to Mike believing that I would never see him again. Then, I caught a big, 4-propeller, C-130 transport plane that was flying up to Da Nang. From there, I would catch another flight on up to Quang Tri Firebase.

I arrived at Da Nang at around five o'clock in the afternoon and walked into the building that served as the terminal. It was nothing like the one at Cam Rahn Bay. This was a completely bare-bones place that didn't even have indoor toilets. They had a set of two, *"two-holers"*, out back. (If you don't know what a 'two-holers' is, ask your grandma.)

I spotted the check-in counter and hurried over to it. An ugly, gnarly, old Air Force Corporal was checking people's orders and directing them where to go. I finally made my way up to him and handed him my orders. After looking at them, he glanced up at me with a huge evil grin flowing across his face ~ he knew I was a Newbie ~ then exclaimed, "Listen, I don't have any more flights heading up in that direction today. You're going to have to spend the night and fly out of here first thing tomorrow morning. Look at it this way, man, you get one more night to live!" he said, grinning from ear to ear.

"Okay! That's cool, man. Where do I find a place to sleep?" I innocently asked.

A shocked look instantly appeared all over his face! "Where do you think, man? Does this look like a hotel to you? Do we have any bell hops? You want a valet? ... You sleep right over there on the concrete floor, man!"

"Oh, this is just great!" I muttered under my breath. I grabbed my papers out of his hand and went over to try to find some kind of a bench, or chair, or something horizontal to spend a long, lonely night on. It was now about six o'clock in the evening.

I had never been to the airport at Da Nang before. So, I wandered around the small airport terminal for what seemed like hours. Eventually, I found an old, worn, rough, splintered, wooden bench that no one was sitting on.

I grabbed it, placed my duffel bag on one end of the bench, and then laid down using my bag for a pillow. But, my feet were sticking out over the other end of the bench by about a foot. Within thirty minutes of lying down, both of my feet and half way up my calves were totally numb. "This is nuts!" I muttered.

I sat up, grabbed my duffel bag and threw it down onto the floor. I then lay down on the cold moist old concrete to try to finally get some sleep. Before long, though, the dampness and cold of the concrete slowly began to work its way through my entire body. I knew if I stayed there for too long, I would probably wind up sick.

"Oh well, maybe it will keep me from getting killed if I am in the hospital!" I thought. Anyway, it was better than the bench because I could stretch all the way out.

As I was lying there, young Vietnamese men dressed in nice, clean, green, Army uniforms, would occasionally walk by. I had no clue as to their identity or whether they were for us or against us. I was petrified to fall asleep, wondering that if I did, would they come over and slit my throat or something? I still had not been issued any weapon of any kind. So, I tried to stay awake the best I could. But, the tensions flowing through my body and the absolute feelings of fear filling every pore finally caused me to nod off somewhere around three o'clock in the morning or so.

But shortly after falling asleep, I suddenly felt something crawling across my face! *It was a big, huge snake!* My eyes popped wide open, but I dared not even take a breath! I could feel this snake right next to my head.

I was terrified! I didn't know what to do. I had heard stories before coming to Vietnam about a species of snake nicknamed, *'The Two Stepper.'* The word about it was if it bit you, you could only take about two more steps before you died. That's how poisonous it was!

I lay there completely petrified, afraid to even twitch! But then, I heard it slide off the backside of my duffel bag. In that instant, I jumped straight up into the air and landed on top of the bench. At the same time, I was screaming like a quivering banshee, "Snake! Snake! Snake!"

One of the young Vietnamese men came running over. As he got up next to me, he pulled out a pistol and began waving it around in the air very menacingly! "Oh God," I cried! "If it isn't one thing, it's another! First, the snake! Now, I'm going to be killed by a Vietcong infiltrator!"

I could tell that this enemy infiltrator was getting ready to shoot, so I ducked my head and wrapped both of my arms around it. At the same, I fell down into a squatting position on top of the bench. "Oh Jesus, please don't let it hurt!" I prayed! With my eyes clenched as tight as I could get them to close, an ear ringing deafening explosion rang out right next to my head!

... ... For the next instant, there was nothing but complete silence except for the ringing in my ears. But I hadn't felt anything! There was no pain! No blood! Nothing! I hadn't even collapsed off the bench! But, I was too scared to open my eyes to look around. I was petrified of what I would see.

Finally, though, I had no other choice than to open my eyes. Even though I was trembling all over I finally forced them to creep partially open. As they were coming open I was totally and completely expecting to see the same slimy, filthy snake that had originally deceived Eve in the Garden of Eden; that old serpent himself, Satan, staring right back at me!

But, I didn't see Satan after all! What I did see though, was almost as terrifying as that sight would have been! I saw this young man holding up in front of him a hideous looking creature that had to have come straight out of the very lowest, nastiest, pits of Hell!

In sheer terror, I instinctively recoiled back! The hideous creature had a huge mouth on it, probably able to swallow a man's arm in full! And, it was full of long, razor sharp teeth. It's body was about twenty-four inches long with a tail that was at least another three feet long! What I had thought was a snake had been its tail slithering across my face!

The young Vietnamese man who had shot the creature had a huge grin on his face stretching from ear to ear. This grin was showing off his green, beetle-nut stained and impacted teeth. Then, he looked straight at me and began speaking in halting, pidgin, English. He said, "Rat! Big 'rat'! Make good soup, huh GI?"

Immediately, as those words entered into my tortured and tormented mind, huge involuntary shivers and silver-dollar sized goose bumps began racing all over my body; especially up and down my spine! At the same time, an almost uncontrollable shaking began consuming me! Then, within mere milliseconds after that, this poor skinny white boy from the dusty deserts of Arizona suddenly jumped off the bench and then accomplished the impossible. I invented Hip Hop dancing about twenty years before it would become popular in the United States! And at the same time, I began doing the Michael Jackson 'moonwalk' all over that airport terminal floor, years before he made it popular!

Eventually, though, I was able to gather myself back together enough to glance up at the Vietnamese man. Then in a loud, incredulous voice, I exclaimed, "You're going to cook that hideous thing? You're going to eat it?"

"Oh yes, GI! It make good soup! Very good soup with very good meat!" he said, again with a big grin on his face.

Right then, at that moment, I didn't know if I was doing the moonwalk, combined with a lot of hip hop moves, mixed with some Native American Indian ceremonial hoop dancing, because of the fear that I had felt at first in believing it was a snake! Or, I didn't know if I was doing the moonwalk and these other things because of the fear of believing I was going to be shot! Or, I didn't know if I was doing the moonwalk and other things from the revulsion of hearing him say, "Make good soup, very good meat!"

Anyway, there was 'No Way' I was going to fall back to sleep for the rest of that night! When I eventually was able to regain control over my legs and was finally able to stop my feet from involuntarily sliding back and forth across the floor in that ridiculous backward moving fashion they had been doing, I picked up my duffel bag and again placed it on the seat of the bench. Then, I climbed up on top of it and sat down. I wanted to be as far off that dangerous, man-eating creature filled floor as I could possibly get.

Eventually, though, just as it has done ever since time immortal, the sun finally slid up into the sky from its hidden dark berth somewhere below the horizon. Not long after that, the old grizzled Corporal showed back up and took his place behind the counter. Weaving and dizzy from lack of sleep and weak from lack of food, I wobbled over to him to find out about the earliest flight I could get out of there.

Right then, I didn't care if I flew straight up to Hanoi, the capital of North Hell! I just wanted out of that place!

As I almost collapsed on top of the counter, he took one look at me, and with a grin plastered from ear to ear across his ugly pockmarked face, said, "You're still here, Newbie? I thought you would have gone across the street over to the Air Force transfer hooches and slept on one of their comfortable beds. You know, the ones with real mattresses and springs on them. And, you know, I also heard they had served some real cow steaks and baked potatoes with real sour cream for dinner last night. Really man, I didn't expect to see you until around 9:00 or 10:00 o'clock this morning."

As soon as I heard this, I glared at him with pure hatred in my eyes! If it were possible for looks to kill, he would have been 'history'! Honestly, I firmly believe that if I would have had a weapon in my possession, I would have shot him right then! This is probably the reason why they didn't issue any guns to us until we got to our regular units.

My voice was dripping with pure acid, along with a glare that could have cut him to pieces. I stared right into his face, then said, "Hey puke face, let me tell you something, if you want to continue to breathe this putrid air and stay around to live in this god-forsaken place for another day, I would suggest that you place me on the next plane out of here! *You got it, man?!!!*"

With a grin a mile wide, he pointed, "There's your ride right there, partner."

# Chapter 6

After about an hour of flying, I looked out the window and spotted a small military post. A few minutes later, we made a rough landing onto the runway at Quang Tri Firebase. I reached over, picked up my duffel bag, and then walked through the back door ramp of the plane.

A crewman from the plane ambled over to me and then pointed towards a Quonset hut. He told me that is where I needed to go to process in. I wasn't for sure if I should believe him or not. But, I hurried over to the hut, running the whole way in a bent over zigzagging position. Inside of the small building were six of the little green clad, paper shuffling, army men. All of them were wearing their trademark coke bottle bottom glasses. But, oh man, right then at that moment, I can't describe to you my joy at seeing those guys! I mean, if they were there, then I must still be safe!

Let me emphatically state this, combat soldiers in the Army are totally expendable! This is the absolute truth! Us combat soldiers who actually have to do the fighting are supposed to stay alive as long as we possibly can, but eventually, we are destined to die according to the Army. For every type of combat soldier, the Army has already determined "kill ratios," "acceptable losses," and "life expectancies." Infantry soldiers have a life expectancy of approximately one week. Artillery soldiers ~ like I am ~ have a life expectancy of approximately three weeks. And acceptable losses for both, infantry and artillery, are *"ALL OF US!"* But, I swear to you, if the Army were to ever lose even a single one of its paper shufflers, it would cease to exist!

I knew that the Army would never put one of its paper shufflers in harm's way, so as I opened the door and saw all of these shufflers sitting at their desks and peering up at me through their thick glasses, I wanted to run over and throw my arms around each one and give them a great big hug! "Safe at last, I'm safe at last!" I screamed!

For the first time since I had been forcefully inducted into the Army, I actually enjoyed standing in line while I was getting all ninety-five copies of my orders shuffled around and stamped.

After that, I headed over to a transfer hooch. I would be staying there until I got new orders to wherever my next stop on this miserable journey through the bowels of hell would take me. The transfer hooch was a half-round corrugated metal Quonset hut. As I walked inside, it was like walking into an oven, or better yet, a kiln! It had to be around 150 degrees! But, I was totally exhausted. After hardly getting any sleep the night before, I moved over to one of the bunk-beds located along the sides of both walls and lay down. The next thing I heard was at 6 a.m. the following morning when an old sergeant around thirty years old burst into the room. "Everyone up!" he yelled. "Hit the floor!"

I opened my eyes to see just who this rude person was that had completely ruined a dream I was having of a little blonde girl I had left behind back home. It had not even been a full week since I arrived in Vietnam, and yet, it was already becoming hard for me to even remember what she looked like.

*"You worthless Newbies; you female single-parent dogs; you enemy bait and target practicing fodder, get your worthless rat's rear-ends out of those beds and get outside, now!"* the old sergeant screamed!

I hurriedly jumped up, got dressed and went outside. Unbeknown to me, while I had been sleeping, several more guys had come into the hooch and spent the night there. The old Sargent told all of us to get into a formation. Once we accomplished that task, he said that after breakfast, we were going out on a patrol. He said a platoon of North Vietnamese soldiers had been spotted last night probing our perimeter and we needed to go flush them out and eliminate them. "We're going on a search and destroy mission and kill all of those communistic, atheistic, illegitimate, single-parent, hairless dogs!" he proclaimed.

Immediately, a tremendous, mind numbing, almost paralyzing fear once again hit me in the stomach and almost bowled me over. All of us ~ there were now eight of us Newbies in the group ~ went pale with fear. The old Sargent looked at us, noticing our apparent fear and anguish; then said, "Don't worry! I'll be with you and you'll be getting an M-16 with two clips of ammunition."

He marched us over to the mess hall for breakfast. We all knew this would be the last meal we would ever eat while still alive on this earth, so we tried to savor every morsel of the food. Along with scrambled eggs were some small pieces of red stringy meat. As I looked at the tiny red pieces, I wondered if it might be 'rat' meat. Glancing up at one of the cooks, I asked, "Hey, what kind of meat is this?"

The cook quickly glanced over, looked at the meat; then said, "Water Buffalo! What do you expect?"

I had no idea what Water Buffalo meat might taste like, but I walked over to the table where the other guys were and sat down. Each one of us picked up one small little piece of the red morsel and slowly placed it in our mouths. Without any verbal communication between us, we all figured that if we took about two hours to finish breakfast that might give the enemy time to slitter back across the border into North Vietnam.

The old Sargent just sat there grinning the whole time. Eventually though, his patience began to wear thin and he finally said, "That's enough. Come on! We need to go kill some Commies!"

He led us outside and marched us over to a building that was surrounded by barbwire. Inside of it were the M-16 rifles and the two clips of ammunition for us to use to go "kill the Charlie Cong!" The old Sargent passed out a 'weapon' and two clips of ammo to each of us as he said, "Do not insert a clip into your weapons until we get outside the base."

Once we got outside the gate, he began organizing us into a single line by our height and size. The first guy in line had been the center on his high school basketball team. He stood six feet six inches tall. After him in descending height and size, he organized us all the way down to the Sargent and me who both stood an average size of five feet eleven inches tall. He put me at the back end of the line in front of him.

He then looked at this big ex-basketball center and said, "You take the point at the front. We'll follow you!"

But before the Sargent's words even had a chance to fade away, an extremely loud explosive sound suddenly roared throughout the calm still air and almost ruptured our eardrums! Our first impulse was that the enemy had somehow just dropped a two-thousand pound bomb on top of us! Then, even before our reflexes and instincts had a chance to react, the vibrating concussion of the explosion hit us smack in our faces and sent us rocking back and forth like a bunch of bobble-head dolls sitting in the rear-view window of a 57' Chevy!

Still before our reflexes reacted, a totally egregious smell swarmed around and covered us! In that instant, the nice clean air we were breathing changed into a thick layer of poisonous green colored sewer gases! The smell was even worse than when we had first arrived at Cam Rahn Bay and they had opened the airplane door, if that could be possible!

At first, we were so shocked and stunned that we didn't know what had happened. One of the guys yelled over the ringing and deafness in his ears, "What was that? It sounded just like a Whoopee Cushion exploded!"

The Sargent was furious, though! He knew exactly what had happened! He screamed, *"Oh, don't mess your pants! That's a sure give-away to the enemy! They will now smell us coming from a mile away!"*

With utter, total, complete embarrassment, the big guy chosen to be point man muttered in a sound just above a hoarse whisper, "I'm sorry. I'm so sorry."

I quickly looked over at the Sargent, trying to get his attention away from the big embarrassed guy. I leaned over and whispered, "Why do you have all of the big guys up in front?"

He glanced at me as if I were stupid or something. Then, "Because; since they are all taller than us, the enemy will have to shoot all of them first before they can get a straight shot at us.

It's the benefits of being in charge."

Just then, in those very rare instances where Einstein type revelation suddenly hits you smack dab in the frontal lobe of your brain and you instantly go from a blabbering idiot to being the world's smartest genius, I made up my mind right then and there that I was going to be *"in charge"* of every situation just as soon as I could.

The Sargent told us to load a clip of ammunition into our weapons and to chamber a round into the barrel. "But, make sure you have the safety on." Then, he began to march us off down a trail to go "seek and destroy" Charlie Cong. But as we marched, a smell just like a million gallons of open sewer wafted out behind us, along with a pale, greenish colored cloud hovering in the dry still air above us.

The further along the trail we went, the vegetation began getting larger and thicker. In fact, it began to get so thick in places that it completely covered over the trail. We had to hack our way through it with machetes. And to me, even in my inexperienced Newbie enemy bait and target practicing fodder state, it began to look like a perfect place for the enemy to set up an ambush!

But then, the trail suddenly opened up into a small clearing that was about fifteen feet square, but it was still surrounded by thick foliage all around it. As we entered into the opening the Sargent quietly said, "Halt! Come here closer to me so you can all hear." We quickly gathered around him in a close circle.

He began, "I don't like the looks of this. I got a real bad feeling for some reason. I tell you, I can *'feel'* them out there!" At that, we all began to slowly die inside. An empty, hollow, nauseated feeling filled my entire being; ugly foul-tasting yellow bile rose up into my throat, and my head suddenly felt like a balloon filled with helium!

"Listen up! I'm going to throw a grenade up ahead to make sure no one is hiding in there. So, keep your heads down!"

He reached up on his fatigue shirt and pulled a grenade off. It was about the same size of a baseball except it was green colored with yellow letters on it. He pulled the pin out of the grenade and then reached his arm back behind his head. But as his arm began to come forward in a throwing motion, the grenade suddenly slipped out of his hand and fell right smack down in the middle of all of us right at our feet.

*"OOOOOOH!!!!! SWEET JESUS, HELP US ALL!!!"* I screamed! And even if I do say so myself, it was the best imitation of a duet with Smokey Robinson and James Brown that has ever been performed!!!

We all knew we had only three short seconds before eternity was going to carry us all straight to Hell ~ the real one! So, we fell, knocked, scrambled, and trampled each other trying to get away from there! One of the big guys ran smack into me and knocked me flat on my face onto the ground! Then, in his panic, he stepped directly on my back which caused his feet to fly out from under him, which then made him crash right down on top of me with the force of a twenty-five ton tank. It totally knocked the wind completely out of me! I couldn't even move a muscle! I might have been able to twitch my eyes but I just don't know for sure even about that.

For what seemed an eternity I lay there waiting for the explosion that would be the last thing I would ever hear on this earth! . . . But, nothing was happening! The 3-second long eternity finally passed and my reflexes suddenly began to take over. I began gasping for air, and as the first small amounts finally reached my lungs, I began screaming! "Get off me! Get off! Get off!!!"

Slowly, the rest of the guys all began stirring, too. The Sargent whispered that apparently, the grenade was a dud. He said to be very careful, and slowly move away from it. But just then, in that very instant, the Sargent screamed, "Gooks! Gooks!"

He grabbed his M-16 and began firing into the foliage surrounding us! A rustling noise was coming from it! Suddenly, four "gooks" broke out of the green tangled vines and bushes and began rushing towards us! In that second, all of us became the ultimate inspiration for Rambo and began firing  from the hip, shoulder, side, and even between the legs! We expended the first clips in three point two seconds flat! (An M-16 rifle, fired from the fully automatic position, will have three more bullets already fired 'before' the first bullet ever leaves the barrel. That is how fast it shoots.) With fumbling hands and shaking bodies, all of us reloaded in another three point two seconds with new clips.

At that, I looked up and saw one of the Charlie Cong running straight toward me. He was no more than five feet away when I know I put at least half a clip into him! That is ten bullets! But, he stopped and just stood there looking at me after I had run out of ammunition! In fact, in absolute terror, being completely helpless with no more ammunition, all of us quickly looked around at all four of the Charlie Cong still standing there in front of us! There wasn't a single one of them lying down in a pool of blood. In fact, we didn't see any blood on them at all! Neither on them, nor on us! None of us had any wounds, either.

"Something was wrong here! Totally wrong!" I began thinking, 'There were nine of us and each clip of ours held twenty rounds. Twenty rounds times two clips equal forty rounds. Forty rounds times nine equal 'three-hundred and sixty' rounds! And not one of our rounds had even hit a single one of the enemy!' *Amazing!* I thought. None of them even had as little as a scratch on them!

"This is terrible! I know I'm a better shot than that and I didn't even touch a single one! Man, if all of us Americans are this bad at hitting our targets, we don't stand a chance over here!" I thought.

All of the enemy soldiers were wearing bandannas to cover their faces just like the outlaws in the old western movies I used to watch as a kid. But as we were staring at them wondering what was going to happen next, one of them began to shake, and soon after that his shoulders began to heave, and finally, the biggest laugh you have ever heard exploded out of him!

At that same time, all of them began laughing hysterically! Some even fell to the ground, holding their stomachs and kicking their legs up into the air! In Basic Training, we had learned that this position this enemy fool was in was called, 'the dying cockroach position'! Most of us had learned that first-hand and had the opportunity to practice it many times over! But I had to admit that these guys were good at it, too.

All of us Americans were lying on the ground where we had either fallen or slipped or fell when the shooting had started. I had never even had time to stand up after the fat boy climbed off me. But right then, we didn't know what to do! We just looked at each other! "What is going on here?" we wondered!

Just then, the old Sargent also began howling with laughter! Before long, he even had tears rolling down his face! Then, it slowly began to dawn on us. This was all just a setup! None of it was real! The grenade had been a dud on purpose and the Sargent had purposely dropped it! The "rounds" we had been firing were blanks, and the rounds the Charlie Cong had been firing back at us, had also been blanks! Finally, the 'enemy' guys reached up and pulled the bandannas off their faces! And surprise, surprise, surprise, they all had round eyes!


None of us said a word as we were walking back to the firebase. Our mouths were tightly sealed. Our jaws locked tighter than a vise! There was such an overwhelming feeling of relief inside of us, but at the same time, we really wanted to *'kill'* the Sargent and the rest of those 'enemy' guys with *'real' bullets!*

The Sargent was the only one talking. He was trying to explain that this was the Army's way of seeing how we would react under pressure and under enemy fire. He said we all performed excellent and he was proud of us. He then said we could be dismissed for the rest of the day so we could take showers and get cleaned up.

As we marched, an even more awful stench was blasting our nostrils and burning our eyes that caused the air to have a very dark green colored cloud hanging like a thick London fog all around us. I looked up ahead and saw three guys walking kind of bow-legged and leaning forward on their toes just like a toddler with a dirty diaper does!

# Chapter 7

A couple of days later, the Sargent again ventured into our hooch. He said transfer orders had come through for some of us. He began calling out some names. For those whose names he called, he said we needed to get our gear and report over to the processing hooch to pick the orders up. The first name on the list was mine!

I gathered my duffel bag and headed over to the processing hooch. Once I received my new orders, I saw that my next stop on this journey through Hell was to a place called Dong Ha! One of the paper shufflers told me that a re-supply truck was going to leave within the next thirty minutes going to Dong Ha and that I could catch a ride with it.

I ambled back out into heavy drizzling rain that had begun falling and began searching until I found the truck. There were two rear-echelon truck drivers standing beside the truck. Glancing up as I ambled over towards them, one of them said, "Are you the Newbie going to Dong Ha?" I shook my head up and down. "Then get in the back, shut up, and hold on. Got it?"

But as I was getting on the truck, I suddenly saw Mike, again. He had been transferred up to Quang Tri Firebase the day after I had already gotten there but we had been assigned to separate areas of the base. Lucky him, he didn't have to go through the grenade and fake enemy "training" like we had done.

Mike was going to catch a ride on the truck, too. But, instead of being transferred to Bravo Battery at Dong Ha, he was being transferred on up to a place called Firebase Charlie 2. The road going to Charlie 2 from Quang Tri runs through Dong Ha.

On the way over to Dong Ha, we raised the rear flap covering over where a rear window would have been in the cab if it would have had one. Mike leaned in and asked the guys if they knew anything about what Charlie 2 was like.

The guy riding in the passenger's seat turned around and replied, "Yeah, man! It's Hell, man! Every day sometime between

12 p.m. and 3 p.m., they get enemy rockets, and or, artillery rounds fired in on them. Man, why do you think you're being sent up there anyways? It's to replace the guys who get killed up there every day, man! That's why! I'm telling you man, we'll be lucky to get out of there ourselves without getting killed! And, you, Newbie bait and target practicing fodder, have to stay after we leave!

"Listen, the whole Firebase is constructed underground! You will actually live in underground bunkers up there, man! You'll live just like cavemen! I mean, that is only as long as you 'live', that is! Listen, just keep your head down, you hear? Firebase Charlie 2 is less than a mile and a half below the DMZ! Just keep your head down! You hear?"

He didn't say anything else, and Mike was too afraid to ask anything more! But his glowing Triple AAA 4-Diamond recommendation of the place just added to Mike's intense agony and fear.

Not long after that, we arrived at the sprawling little firebase of Dong Ha! The truck rambled through the front guard gates and eventually stopped next to Bravo Battery Artillery Headquarters. I jumped off, turned around and said, "See you later, Mike", then went inside of the headquarters where two paper shufflers were working steadily shuffling their papers.

I was dripping wet! The truck didn't have a cover over the top so Mike and I had ridden all of the way to Dong Ha completely exposed to the rain and cold! One of the shufflers took one look at me, grabbed a towel and handed it to me. Then, trying his best not to laugh, he said, "You must be the new guy they said was on his way here. Come on in and get signed in. Then, I'll show you where to put your stuff. You will be here by yourself until tomorrow, though. All six of the guns are out in the field right now. They've been gone for the last three weeks but they're due back in tomorrow."

I signed in. Then one of them took me over to a building that had sandbags stacked all around the base of it. In fact, everywhere I looked, all of the buildings had sandbags stacked around them going from the ground up to about 3' feet high. As we walked inside the building, the shuffler told me to grab an empty bunk and put my gear away. I began to do what he had said to do, but I turned around and asked him, "Do you get shot at a lot here? I mean, why all of the sandbags stacked against the buildings?"

"It's called, 'incoming'! Yeah, we get quite a bit of incoming around here, several times a month. It's mostly just harassment mortars coming in, though. Also, it doesn't happen too often, but sometimes we get a few Russian made rockets coming in, too. There have only been a few casualties from the incoming, though. It's mostly just damage to some buildings.

"But, watch yourself. If you hear anything that might seem out of the ordinary, *'Do Not'* be afraid to hit the ground! Some of the new guys come here and try to show how brave they are. They try to not flinch, or run, or hide when an enemy round comes in. But they're very stupid! They are the ones that keep the plastics industry back home very busy making body bags. I promise you, if you flinch, or even if you dive to the ground, even if it's not a mortar or a rocket, no one will laugh at you here.

"But hey listen, I have to get back over to my hooch. I'm on duty until chow time. If you want, when I get off, I'll show you all around our beautiful firebase of 'Dong Ha!'"

"Yeah! That would be great." I said.

He turned and walked out. As he did, I stood there and began looking around the place. Then, I began shaking my head from side to side. Finally, I burst out, "God, every place you have sent me has gotten progressively worse! Look at this place! This hooch has dirt floors! What's next, God?" I demanded! *"I don't know how much worse you could make it on me than this, God!!!"*

In just a short period of time, though, the awful answer to that extremely stupid remark would slap me right smack in the middle of my face! It would soon be getting progressively worse than anything I could have ever imagined, even in my worst nightmares!

The guns came back in from the field the next day. When they got set back up and ready to fire again, I was formally assigned to a gun crew. I was the only Newbie. But, I was made to feel welcomed by every one of the guys.

All 'Combat Soldiers' have a special brotherhood between them. Even a Newbie like me, who had never even seen any combat yet, was immediately brought into the brotherhood and made to feel welcomed.

The guys on my crew were friendly but they told me I needed to lose my 'newness'. They said I needed to get all of my new green fatigues and then wash all of the starch out of them. Then, they told me to take a metal file and scrape all of the black polish off my boots. And finally, they told me to go through my bag of toiletries and throw out all of my cologne and after-shave lotion.

"Why?" I asked. I was stunned at these orders.

"You can't have anything that smells out in the field. A gook can smell after-shave lotion, or even shoe polish, from at least a mile away. And they can see the bright glare shining off polished boots from the same distance. Most of the time, we have to go on patrols out in the bush to secure our own perimeter, and if you want to stay alive, man, you have to smell just like Vietnam!"

Oh man, 'that' thought almost gagged me!


After one week at Dong Ha, the word came down to head back out into the field. By now, at least in looks and smell, I fit right in. No one could tell I was a Newbie except by my nervousness. In that, I had a long ways to go.

Anyway, with me sitting on top of the gun next to the turret, we pulled out, turned west and headed in the direction of the absolutely beautiful, triple canopied jungle-covered mountains of Vietnam. But as Dong Ha began to fade into the distance, a knot the size of a cantaloupe began growing inside of my gut and I thought I was going to puke at any second!

For more than half a day, we traveled up to a mountainous region that was covered with trees and large clumps of thick green undergrowth. We then pulled off the rugged, washboard like trail that was supposed to be a road, and into an area that had at one time, a long time ago, been the temporary home of another artillery unit. But, man, this place looked very similar to a stinking, smelling, trash strewn garbage dump.

After pulling in, the first order of business was to get our big cannons set up and ready to fire. Without them being set up, we were basically helpless targets in an enemy shooting gallery! It was again pouring down huge sheets of rain as we were doing this. All of us were wearing green, plastic poncho covers and had put on big rubber boots that came half way up our calves, but we were still soaked completely down to the bone, and the mud was so deep in places that it came all the way up over the top of the rubber boots.

After we got the guns set up, we began walking around the dump trying to find anything we could use to try to cover the roof on some old dug-out bunkers that were still there. We needed something that would keep the rain out. Suddenly, we spotted some old pieces of plywood that were lying half buried in the muck and debris. One of the guys on my gun crew was a fellow from Phoenix, Arizona, like me. In high school he had been a star football player but had flunked out of college, so Uncle Sam drafted him. He stood about six feet, two inches tall and weighed about two hundred and ten pounds.

As soon as he spotted the plywood, he ran over to grab one of the pieces before anyone else could beat him to it. Once there, he reached down and grabbed a hold of the end of a piece. Then, with all of his strength, he began pulling it up out of the ground.

But as the piece finally burst loose and came up, about one million little hungry mice and rats began scurrying everywhere in every direction! There were so many of them that about a thousand of them jumped on him and began running all the way up his body! Then, some of them began to run across his shoulders and on up to the top of his head before finally jumping off onto the ground.

Oh man, this was such a pure pleasure for me to see someone as big as he was; who had as much rhythm as he did, and also at the same time, could sing in tenor notes so high that it almost burst your ears! I tell you, God has really blessed certain people with those inner qualities of dance and singing! But shortly thereafter, God decided to pay me back for the way I had been laughing at the poor fellow. In fact, I was laughing so hard that I had fallen down onto the ground and was wallowing around in the mud holding onto my stomach with my legs up in the air! The dying cockroach position!

Eventually, I managed to get myself back under control. As I did, I spotted a metal can about the same size as a large coffee can setting on the ground upside down. For some unknown reason, I had the urge to go up and kick the can like a field goal kicker would kick a football. But, just as soon as my foot made contact and the can went flying into the air, about one million tiny, slimy, little snakes of all different colors began scurrying all over the place, including all over my feet and legs! After that, several of the guys in my gun crew wanted the big guy and me to form a dance and singing duo. They said we would be fabulous! Since the big guy was black and I was white, they said we could call ourselves, "The Oreos"! Anyway, *Bad* Billy Powers and I became very good friends after that!

Later on that night I had my first contact with the enemy. Some of our infantry brothers were about a mile out in front of our unit on a, seek and destroy mission, when they encountered some North Vietnamese soldiers.

Our infantry guys quickly radioed in for artillery support. As soon as the word came over the radio to us, four guys on my gun crew quickly ran over to our cannon while the rest of us hurried to take up positions around our perimeter to watch for anything suspicious.

Within just a few minutes after that, one guy about twenty to thirty yards away from me began shooting his M-16 rifle. He also began to yell, "Gooks in the wire! Gooks in the wire!" which meant that enemy soldiers were probing our perimeter.

With no further warning, we also opened up with our M-16s blazing in the direction he was shooting. But as soon as we did, enemy bullets began whizzing around our heads along with green tracer rounds hitting the ground and smashing into the sandbags right next to us.

Eventually though, after about fifteen to twenty minutes, all of the shooting stopped! Even the cannons stopped firing! Soon, a call came in over the radio from the infantry guys that we had a confirmed kill of six enemy soldiers. Also, the next morning, we went out through the wire we had set up around our perimeter so we could search for any signs of the enemy we had been shooting at. In several locations, there were stained pools of blood and long drag marks where the enemy survivors had pulled their comrades back into the bush.

As I saw this, I began to wonder how I should feel. Several of the pools of blood and the drag marks were from the exact areas I had been firing my M-16 at. So, I knew that it was very possible, even probable, that I was responsible for that blood and those marks. In other words, I knew that I had probably killed some enemy soldiers last night!

"Should I feel remorse? Should there be a pang of guilt inside of me? How should I feel?" I wondered. Because, I didn't feel any of those things! In fact, there was almost a certain gleefulness inside of me. It almost made me feel light-headed! I had survived, my combat brothers had survived, and that was all that mattered to me!

For the next few weeks after this, we had several more skirmishes with the enemy. Following these, I knew I was really changing inside. The intense fear that had been my constant companion ever since arriving in-country, was quickly disappearing. Now, a certain part of me almost looked forward to a skirmish with the enemy! Part of me actually wanted it to happen! There is no higher high that mankind can experience than a high that comes from facing death head on and surviving!

But, I also began to notice that as the fear was disappearing, it was being replaced by hate! I was beginning to hate the enemy with everything inside of me because of them trying to kill my buddies and me! I could see the hate in the mirror when I glanced into one, but I could feel it even more as it was deeply embedding itself inside of my entire being! I was transforming into the basic angry animal that only war can do to a man! My instincts began to be what I was living on! Basic survival instincts, which means survival of the fittest! Yes, all of the cliques known to man, I was quickly becoming!

Trying to survive fighting a war in the province of Hell does that to a man! You quickly lose your humanity! Before you even know it, you have transformed from a civilized human being into an animalistic serial killer who thrives on your enemy's blood! And, it doesn't take long for this transformation to happen!

We stayed in that part of Hell for about a month and a half. Then, the word came down for us to go back to Dong Ha. This meant we were going to be able to take a cold shower and eat hot food for the first time in more than a month. It also meant we would be able to sleep on cots inside of a building instead of on the cold muddy ground in wet sleeping bags.

After this, other than for a few overnight excursions back out into the bush, we stayed on the firebase until Christmas. On Christmas Eve night, though, I was assigned to pull perimeter guard duty. This consists of sitting on top of one of the sandbagged bunkers that surrounds the entire base approximately fifty yards apart from each other. You're up there to keep an eye out for any movement from the enemy. A temporary cease-fire had been proclaimed by both sides but, our Top Dog ~ our Captain ~ told us to be prepared nevertheless.

I had the last shift of the night, the 3 a.m. until daylight shift. As I was sitting on top of that lonely old sandbag bunker very early on Christmas morning, I was so cold and miserable. But it wasn't just from the elements, or even where I was that was making me miserable. There was something missing in my life, and I had a good idea of what it was.

I was sitting there trying to my best to stay warm with my field jacket zipped up tight and my sleeping bag wrapped around my shoulders. But, I was also thinking about what Christmas really means. I knew it was much more than just a day of giving gifts. It's also much more than a gaily-lit Christmas tree and a warm, glowing fire in the fireplace. I knew it's much more than Santa Claus and his magic reindeer; that it's much more than happy holiday songs and lively music. You see, I knew what Christmas really is, "It's the day we celebrate the birth of the Savior of mankind, Jesus Christ!"

Where I was on a small artillery firebase in Dong Ha, Quang Tri Province, Republic of South Vietnam ~ otherwise known as Hell ~ we didn't have any gifts to give to each other, other than the gift of fighting together as combat brothers to stay alive. We didn't have a Christmas Tree or a fireplace to light a fire in. We didn't have any examples of Santa Claus. And, we were certainly not in the mood to sing happy holiday songs. So, the true meaning of Christmas was easy for me to see and understand! There was no 'clutter' to distract my mind!

As I sat there, I began thinking about Jesus coming to earth to be the ultimate blood sacrifice so the sins of mankind could be forgiven if they were to so choose. But what is so amazing is that He didn't have to do that! He could have stayed in Heaven surrounded in extreme luxury! But because He loved me personally ~ along with everyone else in the entire world ~ He willingly 'chose' to give up His riches in heaven and come to earth so He could reconcile me ~ us ~ to Him!

As I sat on top of that old, cold bunker, I knew exactly why I was so miserable. I didn't have a relationship with God! And without a relationship with God, there is emptiness inside of you; an open empty hole! Why? Because, God made us to be His own children; sons and daughters of His in direct relationship with Him! When that relationship is not there, God hurts and so do we! There is loneliness inside; a complete feeling of total emptiness because God is not living inside of us! The 'void' has not been filled!

All of these things were running through my mind. I really, really wanted to accept God's free Gift to me, Jesus Christ, but I knew what would be going on later throughout all of the units assigned to Dong Ha Firebase.

Since a temporary cease-fire had been called and there was only a minimal chance that we would be called to action, there would be some guys on the firebase smoking dope. There would be some guys dropping acid, or LSD, as it is called. There would be some guys smoking or snorting heroin. There would be some guys that would have snuck some Girl-Sans from the village of Dong Ha into a room and would be selling their bodies to other guys. And, being the absolute gutless wonder that I was, I did not have the inner fortitude to take a stand for God! I wanted to commit my life to Him! I wanted to have a relationship with God! But, I did not have the courage to stand up under peer pressure for God!

# Chapter 8

Two days after Christmas, my gun Sergeant came over to me. "Hey Jim, I need to talk to you."

"Okay, Sarge, what's on your mind?"

He hesitated . . . finally, he continued, "Jim, you know I like you a lot?"

I shook my head up and down.

"Well man, I got some bad news to tell you. You see, you're being transferred up to Charlie 2. They had a bunch of guys killed and wounded a couple of days ago in a rocket attack. I tell you, Jim, they get rockets, mortars and artillery coming in on them *every day* up there. There's some mountains over in the supposedly Demilitarized Zone called Rocket Ridge. Well, every day the gooks shoot mean nasty stuff in on the guys up there.

"Like I said, several guys got killed and wounded so they're really short-handed right now. And since you're the newest guy in our unit, you have to go."

"But Sarge . . . " I tried to interrupt.

"Look man, I did everything I could to keep you from going. We're not exactly overstocked with guys right now ourselves. In fact, every one of our guns are understaffed by at least one guy and two or three on others. But up at Charlie 2, they're running their guns with three or four guys only. . . . I'm sorry, man. I did what I could, but . . . you gotta go."

My first thoughts after the shock quickly wore off went to Mike. I knew he was at Charlie 2. *"Oh God, please don't let it be him!"* I prayed.

I didn't know exactly where Charlie 2 was located. "Sarge, where exactly is Charlie 2?"

He said, "It's right up next to the DMZ! Just three kilometers below the Zone! Just a little more than a mile and a half below it!"

He continued, "You know, Jim, in one way, it will be better up there. Whereas we here at Bravo Battery are a 'mobile' unit constantly going out into the field, Charlie Battery hardly ever leaves their firebase. They're needed up there to protect the 'Z' from being overrun. But, if the enemy ever decides to launch a major ground offensive, it will be one of the first places the enemy will attack.

"But look at the good side of it, man, at least you will have a cot to sleep on every night instead of the cold hard wet ground." he chuckled. Then, he added, again, "Look man, I'm telling you this for your own good, keep your head down up there, okay? They get in-coming every single day up there. Harassment fire! Rockets, mortars, even artillery comes in on the guys up there, *every single day*! So man, again, I'm telling you this because I like you, 'keep your head down'!"

Before the words were even finished coming out of the Sarge's mouth, an icy cold shocking shiver of fear went shooting up and down my spine and I could actually feel the hair on my neck beginning to stand straight up! This was the first time in quite a while that I had felt real fear inside of me again! 'Enemy Artillery Fire coming in on us!' I thought! Man, I didn't mind us being the ones shooting artillery out towards the enemy but I certainly did not like the idea of some of that nasty, man-killing flaming hot metal coming back in on me!

Before leaving, I shook hands with some of the guys, while the ones who were part of my gun crew, I hugged their necks! My very good buddy, the other half of the Oreos singing and dancing duo, Bad Billy Powers, almost started to cry. I saw his eyes water up and mine instantly began doing the same! We hugged each other for a long time, then promised we would see each other again back in the real world in Phoenix, Arizona.

As I was standing next to the gate on the road that would take me to Charlie 2, a US Army M-80 tank came rumbling up. I lifted my arm high into the air and waved for it to stop. I then asked the driver where he was heading. He said they were going home to Firebase Charlie 2.

"Great!" I replied. "Can I hitch a ride with you? I just got transferred up there." They waved me on up.

I climbed up on top of the tank and sat down next to the turret. Then, I decided to chamber a round into the barrel of my M-16 just to be ready for anything that might happen.

We headed out of the gate and traveled for several miles going west on Hwy. 9. We eventually came to a place where a rutted dirt road trail veers off going north towards North Vietnam. I had gone past this old trail several times before with Bravo Battery heading out into the field!

At the northeast corner of this intersection is a single Buddhist grave. It is out in the absolute middle of nowhere. Tall elephant grass, flowering bushes, and several short, stubby trees cover the landscape. It's an area of mostly rolling plains. The old Buddhist must have been someone special, though. The grave consists of a big mound of dirt about three feet high. Surrounding this big pile of dirt going all of the way around it is an eighteen inch high, old faded stucco fence. It also has a large weathered headstone sticking out of the ground on the east side of it.

After turning onto the trail going north and leaving the grave behind us, we continued on up in the direction of Firebase Charlie 2. After traveling for a while we came to a little village. This was a surprise to me. For some reason, I didn't think there would be any civilians up near the border with North Vietnam.

In the middle of the village was a center square. In the middle of the square was the village chief's house. In front of his house was a large South Vietnamese flag hanging on a tall flagpole, billowing slightly in what little breeze there was. Next to the flagpole were several shorter poles sticking out of the ground. But to my complete horror and amazement, hanging on two of the other poles were the first actual dead bodies I had witnessed in Vietnam up to that point.

I had participated in several firefights and had pulled the lanyard on our gun that had killed several of the enemy, but up to that point, I had not actually 'seen' any dead enemy soldiers, nor had any of my buddies suffered any wounds and died. But, tied to two of the poles were two naked male bodies hanging there!

My eyes were fixated on this unbelievable and horridly macabre scene! I didn't know how long the bodies had been hanging there, but there were maggots, flies, and even small mice crawling in and out of their body cavities. I was completely horrified and shocked by this extremely gruesome scene. I couldn't take my eyes off what I was seeing.

At the same time, I got light-headed and really nauseated. Suddenly, my morning breakfast started flowing upwards toward my throat. I couldn't help it! With a loud explosion, I leaned over the side of the tank and let it fly!

The battle-hardened Sergeant who commanded the tank began to laugh. Then, he yelled. "Hey! If you got anything on my tank, you're going to wash this thing when we get home! Understand? ... Hey Kid, how long you been here in Hell, anyway?"

Not long after passing through the village, I saw a brownish-red colored, barren circle of ground only about one-half of a mile in diameter. I also noticed a lot of very large mounds of dirt sticking up out of the ground all over the place. I would soon find out that one of those mounds would actually be my new place to live; a big mound of 'dirt'! Yeah! Dirt floors, dirt walls, and dirt ceilings! In fact, almost everything on Firebase Charlie 2 was underground and covered by huge mounds of dirt! The entire firebase looked like huge Buddhist graves!

As the tank clambered through the gate and finally came to a stop, I turned and thanked the guys for being my chauffeur. I also checked to make sure there was no partially digested morning breakfast on the side of his tank! As my feet touched the dirty dusty old ground, I turned around to look at Firebase Charlie 2.

As I did, all I could do was stand there shaking my head from side to side! I was now so close to North Vietnam that I could practically reach my hand out and touch the enemy!

Firebase Charlie 2 is an old firebase. It dates all the way back to when the French controlled Vietnam. Being that it had been a firebase for a long, long time; a minefield surrounds the entire base. In addition, there are numerous other explosive devices set with trip wires that would blow the enemy to smithereens if they tried to come through them. And just like at all the other firebases, there are guard bunkers setting approximately fifty yards apart surrounding the perimeter of the base.

Every so often, we would be assigned to pull guard duty on one of these perimeter bunkers. This was like an assignment from heaven. We felt pretty safe sitting up there on top of the bunker.

Shortly after I arrived at Charlie 2, I was assigned to pull day guard. This means sitting on top of one of those bunkers during the daylight hours. This was considered extremely divine duty! Almost nothing ever happens during the day time, so you can catch up a lot on your reading while improving your tan at the same time. But as I was sitting there, I suddenly spotted a farmer from the village down below ambling up the road. He was coming towards our firebase herding six cows in front of him. I was just casually watching him, wondering where he was going.

I soon found out. When he got next to our minefield, he took the stick he was carrying in his hand and began beating the air with it. He also began screaming at the cows. Naturally, all six cows immediately took off stampeding . . . directly into the middle of our minefield! For a brief second I was too stunned to react. I sat there watching in amazement, especially since not a single cow had yet stepped on a mine! But then, I quickly picked up the field phone that connects to the command bunker and began telling the C/O ~ Top Dog ~ about this incursion. By now, it had become apparent the old farmer was trying to find out how well protected our firebase was with our minefield. My C/O immediately ordered me to shoot the cows before they allowed the enemy to know that there were not too many mines left out there. I was also told to kill the farmer, too. I had to! He was a spy! I could not allow him to live and then tell the enemy where his cows had gone, and how far into the minefield they had been able to penetrate without stepping on a mine So, I began blasting away with the 60-caliber machine-gun! With short three-round bursts, I quickly shot all six cows first. Then, I aimed right at the old farmer's heart. Without any hesitation, I put another short, three-round burst straight into it. He didn't suffer! He was dead before he ever hit the ground!

I hadn't needed to get my Top Dog's approval to do this. Our minefield was considered a 'free-fire-zone'. This meant that we had standing orders to shoot to kill *'anything'* that moved inside of the borders of that minefield. But, it was wise on my part to cover my own rear-end! Not long after this, I found out it was going to cost the US Government $500 dollars for each cow I had killed. I was also told it was going to cost the government a whole $75 dollars for killing the old farmer since he was a South Vietnamese citizen. That equals to $3000 for the cows and $75 for the old man! Human life was pretty cheap compared to certain animals. The payments were reparations given to the village down below to try to keep them on our side. But, after being told that, I was glad I had gotten the C/Os okay to shoot that day.

# Chapter 9

Toward the end of January 1971, we heard through the grapevine that something really big was about to happen. After that, the adrenaline really began pumping through our veins! Our imaginations began running wild! With a mixture of both fear and excitement, we just knew that President Nixon had given the go ahead for us to invade North Vietnam so we could finally put an end to this insane war!

But, our feelings of excitement and anxiety soon came crashing down! Instead of being able to put a stop to this crazy war, we found out we would be moving up to the border of Laos, instead. Our orders were to move up and secure the entire area. But while we're doing this, the entire South Vietnamese Army is going on an extended stand-down. This means they are basically going to take a South Pacific Paradise Vacation while us Americans take the battle to the enemy. This odd arrangement is because the US Government wants the South Vietnamese Army completely rested up and raring to go before they enter into this fray.

After we're able to secure the area, we are then to stay and act as protectors for the South Vietnamese while they actually go across the border into Laos after coming off stand-down. Their job is to go across and stop the rampant flow of enemy supplies running freely down the Ho Chi Ming Trail from reaching more enemy forces further down in South Vietnam. Without supplies, the enemy will have to cease hostilities, or that was the plan anyway.

This operation is a major undertaking ~ one of the largest and most important of the entire Vietnam War! One that will have far ranging consequences whether it is successful or not! This operation involves US military units from all over South Vietnam coming up to help in this. Our Top Dog told us that the ferocity and intensity of this operation is expected to cause a casualty rate of 75% percent!

That means that 'Seven-Five Percent' of all American combat soldiers involved in this operation along the Laotian border are expected to either die or be wounded!

With extreme anticipation and excitement, the day finally arrived when we began to move out. As expected, my unit was the first artillery unit to move out. We drove out of the south gate of Charlie 2 and then on down through the civilian village past the skeletons ~ white bleached bones and dried ligaments were the only things left of the two bodies still hanging there. Then, we moved on down to the junction of the road where the Buddhist grave was. After that, we turned west on Hwy 9 heading towards Laos. We traveled on Hwy 9 for about the next three hours until we pulled over to set up our guns so we could shoot support for Bravo Battery to leapfrog up ahead of us.

By leapfrogging like this, we began to get closer and closer to Laos. Eventually, we were told to stop. Engineer units then went to work and cleared a big area out of the jungle for us to set up our guns. This area is where we will provide support for the South Vietnamese Army as they make their move into Laos. But we had to give it a code-name for the higher-ups to know where we were. A couple of very astute guys in our unit suggested we code-name it, "LZ Woodstock". It seemed like a good name because we planned on doing a lot of rocking and rolling with our huge cannons.

LZ Woodstock is only about five miles from the border of Laos, and thus, within a short distance of the Ho Chi Ming Trail. But for some unknown reason during this whole time of us moving into the area, we have not faced one bit of resistance. Not even one bullet was fired at us! Apparently, we had taken the North Vietnamese by complete surprise. Or, they were gathering their troops and waiting!!!

# Chapter 10

A little over two weeks after we got set up at LZ Woodstock, the South Vietnamese Army finally stopped their partying and began to reluctantly move. The South Vietnamese Army was far better equipped than their counterparts in the North! They were far better trained! They had all of the weapons of war that we Americans and our allies provided for them! They had a large Air Force consisting of helicopters and airplanes that we gave to them and trained them on! Plus in addition, this was supplemented by our own huge military air forces of every sort! They also had a vast numerical superiority in fighting personnel! Finally, they had the huge advantage of fighting this war on their own turf instead of having the logistical nightmares associated with being in a foreign country! But yet, by this time in the war, the majority of the South Vietnamese Army did not have the desire, courage, heart, and/or will, to fight for their own country! At least, this described most of the ones we encountered on this vast operation, which was code named, Lam Son 719! Because of this lack of dedication on the part of the South Vietnamese Army, Lam Son 719 quickly turned into a total "MUBAR"---Messed Up Beyond All Repair!

In the 'reality' of the circumstances of South Vietnam at this time, this operation had no chance of working! It just plain came down to the fact that the South Vietnamese military was not going to fight for their own country! All the South Vietnamese soldiers wanted to do was to go back to a complete stand-down status so they could continue partying hardy all day long while us Americans continued to do all of the fighting for them! There was no way the South Vietnamese were going to engage the North Vietnamese mano a mano! No way at all! Because of this, our unit got ordered to leave LZ Woodstock and move up to the border of Laos.

Before moving out, though, our unit was told that under no circumstance at all ~ no matter what might happen ~ absolutely 'no' American soldiers are to go across the border and enter into

Laos. *'But'*, if we do have to go across the border for a reason only the upper ranked rear-echelon, well-hidden butt-kissers stationed way back in the safe areas would know about, *'and'*, if we were to either get killed or wounded while inside of Laos and for some unforeseen reason our guys were unable to get our bodies out of there, then we would be listed forevermore as **"MISSING"** in action, instead of **"KILLED"** in action, even though our government would know differently!

Let me explain this just a little more.

1. First of all: we were definitely told that *'no'* American soldiers would be going into Laos under any circumstance whatsoever!

2. Second: *'but'* if a circumstance did happen that required it, we would then go across the border!

3. Finally: but if we were to get killed while in Laos, and for some reason, our guys were not able to get our dead bodies out and had to leave them inside Laos, then, our own government would make sure that we would not be listed as KILLED in action, and thus, our families notified of that dire consequence, but we would be listed as *MISSING* in action, instead!!

By now, though, on three separate occasions so far, *the 'but' if a circumstance did happen that required it, we would then go across the border,* has happened! But, it has not been to fight alongside of the South Vietnamese who were supposed to be over there fighting to block the trail! They aren't doing any fighting at all! All they are doing is running away from the enemy!

Let me tell you something, by this time, we didn't care one iota about the South Vietnamese. In fact, we hated them as much as we hated the North Vietnamese! In fact, on those three occasions we had to go into Laos, several guys in my unit were so fed up and disgusted with the little cowards that they opened fire on them trying to make them stay and fight!

The reason we had to go across the border was to help save our own brave American combat brothers who had been forced to go across and engage the North Vietnamese in deadly combat because the *South Vietnamese refused to do so!!* Our American infantry troops were forced to go into Laos to engage the North Vietnamese in deadly combat solely to give the cowardly South Vietnamese time to run out of Laos in disgrace. My unit was sent into Laos to engage the North Vietnamese in artillery duels to try to give protection to our American infantry troops!

All of this was so the South Vietnamese had time to run away! This left our own American brothers vastly out-numbered and in severe danger because of the chaos the South Vietnamese created by actually running away from the enemy! As we all said at the time; neither our infantry brothers, nor us artillery cannon-cockers, none of us at all, knew who was the enemy and who wasn't! So, if they were wearing different uniforms than ours, we fired our weapons on them!

Thank God, though, no one in my unit was hurt or killed during those missions into Laos! But, without a doubt, there were many, many American combat soldiers who did die inside of Laos and their bodies were left over there to rot! And, for all time forevermore, they will be listed as "missing in action" even though the military and the government know they are dead!

We couldn't help but wonder why this order was ever made? What could possibly be the reason behind such a huge government lie and cover-up? Who came up with it? And why? What about the harm this will cause to the surviving family members? I am sure that many, many moms and dads, wives and children, relatives and friends, may hold out hope forevermore that their son, husband, dad, and companion will eventually come home if they're listed as missing, even though our own government already knows they are dead!

And what about the monetary consequences of this order, in-addition to the emotional distress it will bring? It normally takes seven years for a missing person to be declared legally dead. Will this 'dead' soldier, who has instead been listed as 'missing' in a huge monumental lie, still receive his normal pay during this time? Or, will the government withhold this, along with his family not being able to file for life insurance proceeds until the seven years pass? In discussing this, we made a decision among ourselves that if any of us were to get killed inside of Laos and the rest of us couldn't get our bodies out, then when we got home, we would use every means we possibly could to let the families, and the rest of our country, know about this insane order!

We eventually found out where this order came from. This insane decision originated inside of, and was then put into effect by an official decree, solely and completely by the morally corrupted and criminally paranoid mind of the man that had been entrusted to the highest office in the land of the United States; the Commander in Chief of our armed forces, President Richard Nixon! And ***this insane, uncaring and deceitful order was solely and completely formulated without any regard whatsoever for the emotional concerns of surviving family members or any thought about the monetary relief that a life insurance policy could provide to the surviving members of the family!***

This totally insane and morally corrupted action was made for one reason only, and that reason was strictly to protect President Richard Nixon's criminally and morally corrupted, rosy-red, saggy, lying and conniving, rear-end! In the demonically deranged mind of this lying and conniving president, there was no way he was going to allow the American public to think that 'he' had extended the war in Vietnam over into another country, especially after 'he' had already sent our bombers and troops into Cambodia, which caused riots all over the US!

To this lying criminal who had been trusted by the American populace to be our country's top elected leader, the emotions and concerns of the relatives of the soldiers who will be classified as "missing", instead of "killed", does not matter to him even one iota!!! I am positive that he will lay his head on his pillow every night, and never once give even one thought about the emotional and financial distresses his paranoid actions have brought to many families! The only thing that does matter to him is that his own lying and conniving rear-end is protected! And what is really sad is that I wanted this man to be our president!

# Chapter 11

We've again been ordered to go into Laos. We loaded up all of our equipment and moved out in the direction that would take us toward the border of Laos. After traveling for approximately ten miles, we finally stopped. Because LZ Woodstock is approximately only five miles from the Laotian border, by us traveling about ten miles means that we are now somewhere in the neighborhood of being at least five miles inside of the country of Laos! Unknown to the American public, American military troops have again crossed into another sovereign country with the sole intent of bringing mayhem and death!

On our way, though, we passed scores of South Vietnamese so-called soldiers running away from the battle. We have had to come across the border once again to try to save our own American infantry brothers who have had to go across and engage the North Vietnamese in deadly combat because the South Vietnamese won't!

After getting our guns set up, we quickly began shooting support for our brothers; which we continued to do for the next two days straight, day and night, almost none stop! At this time, we only have four guys on our gun crew. That meant none of us got any rest, sleep, or even a five-minute break from the constant fighting!

By the time we finally got the word to return back to LZ Woodstock, every man in Charlie Battery was operating strictly on adrenalin and instinct. We were no longer well trained, battle hardened, human fighting machines! No! We were more like zombie robots! Our minds were not functioning properly and our movements were slow and uncoordinated. Somehow, though, we managed to load up our gear and begin the trek back. I climbed in the driver's seat and drove that huge 25-ton gun back to LZ Woodstock, but honestly, I cannot tell you how. I have no memory of our trip back.

After that, for two more solid weeks, the war raged on with enemy rounds coming in on us and our rounds going out toward them! Bravo Battery was just a few miles up the road from us. They were the closest remaining American armored unit to Laos at that time. One of my good friends in that unit was leaving the field to go back to the rear the next day to go home, his sentence in Hell being completed. So I asked for and received permission to run up to Bravo Battery to say goodbye.

But shortly after it got dark, a loud, ground-shaking massive explosion sounded on Gun Four in Bravo Battery. That was the gun directly next to the guys I was visiting. We knew immediately that this explosion was not a round coming in or one going out! Our first thought being that close to the explosion was that a North Vietnamese round had hit some ammo and caused it to explode. But, in actuality, it was Gun Four, itself, that had exploded!

There had been two guys inside of the gun when it exploded. One was a brand new guy who had only been in-country for less than a month. He had just gotten married before leaving the states to come here to Hell! The other guy was a good friend of mine who only had about a month and a half of time left to serve. The only body parts that were found from these two men combined were a few teeth, part of a jaw bone, and part of a hand with the wrist bone shattered and splintered but with one finger still wearing a new wedding band!

There had been only one man on the outside of the gun that had been throwing the ninety-five pound rounds and the heavy powder bags into the back of the gun. Only three guys had been manning this gun. That is how low the manpower was at that time.

When the gun exploded, the huge heavy breech block, which weighs well in excess of one hundred pounds of solid steel, came blasting straight backwards, tearing through the one-inch thick solid aluminum like it was butter!

That didn't even slow it down! It continued streaking backwards like a flaming bolt of lightning and right into the stomach of the man on the outside! It blasted into him right below his belt line! Again, the man's body did nothing to slow the scalding hot large chunk of metal down, and as it continued on its way, it cut the man completely in half! The lower part of his body, including both legs, flew over thirty feet away!

When the breech hit the man, it was traveling so fast and was of such an extremely hot temperature, that it cut the man in half in a very clean cut! The extreme fiery heat of the metal kind of sutured the blood vessels at the same time as it ripped through them! At first, there was only a small amount of blood that began to pour out of him. But what little remained of his stomach, intestines, and other organs did come pouring out of him! And as he lay there right in the middle of the *Flaming Fires of Hell,* he began screaming, "My legs hurt!!! My legs hurt!!! Oh my God! My legs hurt so bad!"

I was one of the first guys on the scene since we were only about fifty feet away when the gun exploded. The first thing I saw was the guy lying on the ground and missing his legs! I also immediately recognized him as my very good friend, the other half of the Oreo's Dance and Singing Duo, Bad Billy Powers, my hometown 'bro' and the man I had promised to meet up with back in the 'world'!

I ran over to Billy and quickly picked his head up off the ground and gently laid it in my lap. Then, I grabbed both of his arms and held them in my hands. He was trying to reach down and grab for his legs! I didn't want him to know they were blown away and he didn't have any legs anymore! I was sitting on the ground holding his head in my lap and his hands in my hands, and crying every bit as hard and loud as he was! My brother was dying! My friend! My hometown buddy! And I was sitting there hopelessly watching him die!!!

For almost ten minutes, Billy lay there screaming, "My legs hurt!!! My legs hurt!!! Oh God, Jim, my legs hurt so bad!!!" But, He didn't have any legs anymore! Right before he sucked his last ragged breath, he said to me, "Jim, please tell my parents you were with me at this time. They know who you are. I've talked about you a lot in letters. They will appreciate it that you were the one . . . ." He never finished!

I am so proud to have had the short opportunity to have known Billy and to have served with him! I consider it an honor to have been his brother! In fact, we became more than combat brothers that night. We became 'blood brothers'! I was literally covered in his blood! And, I didn't wash it off until it had worn off!

# Chapter 12

About a week after this, our top commanders decided enough was enough. They gave the orders for all American units to prepare to move back to their original locations before this operation began. Because of the South Vietnamese's refusal to fight, Lam Son 719 had been a total failure that resulted in a lot of injured and dead American soldiers, many of them lying unburied inside of Laos! Since Bravo Battery was the closest to Laos at this time, it was the first unit to leave. But during all of this time, the firing of our guns and the incoming of enemy rounds on top of us continued except for only a few brief short intervals.

As Bravo made its way down the road to where they would eventually set up to provide cover for us as we moved out, the North Vietnamese made a huge push to try to isolate and kill as many of us Americans as possible. They knew that if they could kill hundreds of Americans in just a few days' time, the American public would be totally up in arms about it. So, they launched everything they could against us! Because of this, we got cutoff from retreat. There was no way for us to escape. But what was really troubling was that now, there was no way for us to get re-supplied, either. Let me tell you something, being surrounded and cutoff behind enemy lines is an awful lonely feeling! You feel like you're isolated all by yourself and the whole world is against you!

It's now been eight days since the enemy surrounded us. Since then, there has not been any 24-hour stretch of time that we could call a normal day. That day, eight days ago, was the day the light finally came on for all of us in my unit. Eight days ago we all watched in amazement---and hatred---as the last of the South Vietnamese so-called army ran away like little crying cowards and left us totally surrounded and cutoff.

The sudden realization hit us flat in the face like a ton of falling bricks that everything all Americans who had fought, sweated, bled, cried, and died in this place called Hell before me, was for absolutely nothing! Nothing at 'all'!

*'But, no more!'* I thought! *'No more!'* From now on, I'll fight strictly for my own survival and the survival of my combat brothers. That day eight days ago was when we all saw with our own eyes that the last big nail had been hammered into the coffin of this insanely conducted failure of a mission code named, Lam Son 719. It was also the day that the final nails were driven into the coffin of this entire Vietnam War! It would not be long after this mission that the American involvement in this massive mistake of American foreign policy would begin winding down and the hole to bury the coffin of American involvement would be dug!

For these eight days, though, the North Vietnamese have continued to try to blast our unit off the map! For the same number of days and nights continuously without sleep, we have fired our guns back at them. But, without being able to get re-supplied, we finally ran out of the high-explosive ninety-five pound rounds. Without these rounds, we know that it is just a matter of time before the enemy serial killers lock onto our position and blow us away.

We're constantly dodging incoming enemy small arms fire, plus constant bombardment from enemy mortars! It's a never ending, minute by minute, battle just to try to stay alive! Because of the lack of sleep and the ever present tension of trying to stay alive, we're stumbling around like wide eyed, stoned out of our gourds, zombies! So far, though, the casualties have been fairly light. A guy we call 'Grandpa', because he's a decrepit old man of twenty-nine years old, took a lot of shrapnel in his back and legs from a mortar. He's hurt the worst. Several others have also taken some shrapnel, but their wounds are not as bad as Grandpa's. And thank God, no one has died yet! Our two very brave medics are doing a fantastic job of bandaging their wounds and keeping them all alive!

So, right now Mike is yelling at me because we're in the very stressful process of trying our best to survive everything the North Vietnamese enemy is throwing at us until we can manage to escape from their evil tentacles! This is why Mike is yelling for me to get my head down because another large North Vietnamese artillery shell is on it's deadly way and it sounds like it's coming straight towards us! It's either going to kill, maim, and/or, destroy something, or it's going to blast another swimming pool.

"Mike, I'm doing the best I can! If I crawl underneath the gun and it decides to sink down some more into this mud, it'll bury me! And if I duck my head underwater in one of these craters, I'll drown! I can't swim!" I yelled back to him.

"Yeah, man, but what's better? Drowning or being blown apart? ... ... Listen Jim, you don't have a helmet anymore. Remember? If even a tiny little microscopic piece of shrapnel hits you in the head, you're a goner now! Listen; just find some kind of good cover, okay?"

Ah man, I didn't want to have to make that kind of a decision right then. My choices were of whether to crawl down inside of a water filled bomb crater and possible drown, or stay above ground and pray that no pieces of the enemy's 95 lb. killing round hits me. I knew their rounds are basically just like ours. They weigh 95 lbs. just like ours do. And most of all, they also can kill from at least 50-yards away!

I looked over at Mike. All I could see was his head sticking up out of a huge puddle of water. He's dog-paddling inside one of our backyard swimming pools caused by a previous explosion. I decided to go ahead and get curled up underneath our artillery gun. That big monster weighs 25 tons! So, in my opinion, it's going to give me a whole lot more protection than Mike has!

He looked at me, and gave a big smile. I yelled, "How many laps can you do in that thing?"

"Oh, about a hundred, if I need to."

How he learned to swim in the ice-covered frozen lakes in the frigid climate of Minnesota is beyond me, while I grew up in the hellishly hot climate of Arizona and never learned! I laughed. Mike is a really good guy. He's from Minnesota. His dad owns a big dairy farm back there. Under normal conditions if the real world were a nicer place to live and there were no Hells on earth, Mike would be there working side by side with his dad. One day, it will all be Mike's. I kid him about him being a big ole grain fed genuine hunk of prime beef. He retaliates by calling me a 'dirt dwelling desert hot dog'.

Just then at that moment, the enemy artillery round finally burst out of the clouds and exploded! But, it landed about a hundred yards outside of our perimeter. They had the distance correct but their aim was a little off. But, another new swimming pool had been dug.

As the sound of whistling, ricocheting pieces of deadly, flaming steel, screamed through the air, I yelled over at Mike, "Hey Mike, listen, I've had enough of this, man! We don't have any more artillery rounds to shoot back, so instead of just waiting here for the next round to come in that has my name written on it, I'm going to go over to the front perimeter and grab the 60-caliber machine-gun. I'm gonna see if I can do a little gook hunting with it!"

"Your head okay? Can you see straight?"

"Yeah, I'm okay, man. I can see okay, and I can even think straight, too, although, you and the guys probably don't believe that."

"Yeah!" he laughed! "Okay, man. Just be careful over there. ... You do know, Jim, that front area is where they're gonna launch the ground attack against us, don't you?"

"Yeah, of course I do. That's why I want to go over there. I'm really hoping I can see some of those little serial killers pop their skinny little sloped heads up for just long enough for me to get a bead on them.

I want them to know we're not just gonna roll over and die waiting for them to overrun us. I want them to know that when we do die, we're gonna take a lot of them with us! We're not going by ourselves!"

I crawled out from under my gun and began running in a bent over, zigzagging fashion, up to the front area where we have several rolls of concertina wire strung around our entire perimeter. Those strings of razor sharp curled wire are basically the only things separating us from the North Vietnamese sauntering in and killing us all. We do have a few trip wires leading to some claymore mines and other such mean things, but not too many of them.

I knew that it would only be a matter of time before the enemy finds out we have run out of artillery ammo. I also knew that once they do realize this, it would then only be a short period of time before they launch an all-out, full blown, ground attack against us to try to overrun and kill every one of us. I also knew that when the ground attack comes, it will happen in several coordinated waves, one after the other, just like the waves of the ocean coming in! I knew that the first wave of ground troops will come running as fast as they can, naked as Jaybirds, and without any weapons of any kind at all. This first wave will be in a vast suicidal rush. And what is totally spooky and absolutely surreal about it, is that all of these human sacrifices will all be wired so far out of their minds on chemical stimulants and amphetamines, that they will keep on running for a long way even after their bodies are brain dead from being shot and killed!'

I had heard about that happening before but had never experienced it myself. I knew we would have to shoot them in their legs to make them fall instead of taking head or body shots that should have stopped them, but probably wouldn't!

These human sacrifices sole duty is to throw their bodies up on top of the razor sharp, curled concertina wire and then let the weight of their dead bodies smash it down to the ground. Thus, the need for them to keep running until they can get to the wire, and thus, the need for artificial stimulants that will allow a dead body to continue to move even after it's dead! By throwing their bodies on top of the wire, this will allow the following waves of human attackers to use their comrade's naked bodies as human bridges to get across the barrier. If the first wave were wearing clothes, the following waves could get caught in loose clothing and cause them to stumble and fall. Thus, the reason for the first wave to be naked.

My unit still has a lot of small arms ammunition, though, and being that we are well dug in with good fortifications, we will be able to put up a very good flaming wall of solid metal in a firefight that is guaranteed to create a hellishly amount of casualties for the North Vietnamese. The North Vietnamese are well aware of this, too! That's why they're trying to soften us up with all of the mortars, rockets, and artillery rounds they're throwing at us on a continuous basis.

# Chapter 13

I finally made it to the 60-caliber machine-gun nest we had previously dug in along our perimeter. When the enemy does launch a ground attack against us, I'm going to get behind the 60-cal. and begin blasting away at them until their sheer numerical advantage will overwhelm me and send me out of this Hell. But as I arrived at the gun, there were two guys standing next to it. One of them was looking through a pair of binoculars towards the side of a mountain straight out in front of us, about a kilometer away. We knew the enemy artillery forward observer, who was calling in our location back to their guns, had to be somewhere on the side of that mountain. But up until now, no one had spotted him.

Suddenly, I overheard the guy with the binoculars excitedly say, "I see him! I see him! In fact, there's two of them! They're right there about halfway up the mountain near that small bare spot. See 'em'? Do you see 'em'?" he asked.

The other guy kept saying, "Where? I don't see them." But I suddenly did! I yelled to the guy with the binoculars, "I do! I see both of them! Listen, I'm going to try to get them with the 60-cal., okay?"

"You'll never hit them with that. They're over half a mile away! Oh man, I wish we had just one round of HE---(high explosive ammo)---still left."

I yelled at the guy with the binoculars, "I can, too, hit them with the 60-cal.! I'm telling you I can! I'm a good shot, man!". . . . "Listen, what do we have to lose, huh? I'm gonna try, anyway, okay?"

Both of them looked at me for a moment, then shrugged their shoulders and said, "Yeah, what do we have to lose. Go ahead, Daniel Boone! Kill em! Kill them both!" they laughed.

I jumped down behind the gun and began moving around until I got into a comfortable firing position as I settled down behind it. Then, I said to the guy with the binoculars, "Listen, I can still see them but not as well down here. I want you to be my spotter since you have the looking glasses, okay? So, I'm going to pop out just one round. You tell me where it goes, okay?"

With that, I sighted down the sights on top of the barrel. I quickly took into account that I would be firing upwards so the bullet would have to travel farther than if I was firing straight out. I also noticed that there was a slight cross wind blowing where I was, but I had no idea what it may be doing up where the enemy was.

As my mind was computing all of this, I knew that it would probably take a miracle to even get close with this gun. This was in no way whatsoever, a sniper rifle. But, I took a deep cleansing breath and then slowly let it all out. At the same time, I was zeroing in on the targets through the sights on top of the gun barrel as best as I could. As soon as all of the air I had taken in had been expelled, I slowly stopped breathing altogether and held my breath. Then, as soon as I did that, I very gently squeezed off just one round.

Suddenly, the guy with the binoculars yelled, "Man, you almost got them! You're just a little short! Only about ten feet is all. But you're dead straight on them! Aim just a little higher!"

I maneuvered the barrel up to where I thought an extra ten feet would take me. Then, I went through the same routine and squeezed off one more round. This time, there was no doubt as the guy with the binoculars began yelling at the top of his lungs, "You got them! You got them! Keep shooting, man! Keep shooting!"

After that, I didn't hesitate in the least, and began squeezing off a secession of short, three round bursts, right into the heart of where I could barely see them. Suddenly, after about six or seven short 3-round bursts, I stopped shooting and looked over the sights on the gun and watched as two green clad figures suddenly stood part ways up for just a brief second, then topped over head first and began sliding part way down the mountain until their bodies came to rest against some bushes. The guy with the binoculars kept his glasses trained on the bodies until he was sure they were not getting back up. Then, both of the guys suddenly jumped down in the firing pit of the 60-cal. and began slapping me on my back, while yelling, "You got em, man! You just killed the little gooks! Way to go, man! Way to go!"

One of the guys had lived in Texas his whole life before coming to hell. He exclaimed that we now have a new Davie Crockett to go along with our surrounded Alamo, so there was nothing for any of us to be afraid of anymore. I guess he had forgotten that even though the defenders of the Alamo had killed hundreds of Santa Anna's army, 'all' of the defenders of the Alamo had been killed, too!

I replied, "Yeah, man, 'we' got em! I had your help to do it, though! I couldn't have done it without you!"

For the next several hours, the enemy artillery rounds that had been unceasingly coming in on us suddenly slowed way down. A few continued to drop in, but nowhere near as many as before, and they were nowhere near as accurate as they had been. But what we also did not know at that time, was that the deaths of the enemy forward observer and his radioman, had delayed the enemy's planned ground attack against our unit they had planned to launch at around 3 a.m. the next morning. We didn't know it but that extra time would become crucial to our survival and eventual escape.

Because of the slowdown in enemy action, one very brave and courageous Huey helicopter pilot decided to run the gauntlet and bring our unit some very much needed supplies. Before taking off, he told his co-pilot and door-gunner what he planned to do. Then, he told them they did not have to come with him, but, it was their choice if they wanted to. Without any hesitation at all, both immediately said, "Well man, what're we waiting for? Let's roll!"

They had gotten permission to load a bunch of artillery rounds onto a sked that would dangle underneath the chopper by a winch-driven steel cable. They also loaded up the interior of the chopper with more cases of C-Rations, 5-gallon cans of water, and more small arms ammunition. Then, they took off flying at just above tree top level to avoid as much enemy fire as possible, and headed toward LZ Woodstock. Thirty minutes later, they hovered over a small cleared area the guys had made for them to land. It was right outside of our perimeter wire.

They had to hover, though, until the sked could be unloaded before being able to settle down themselves. But the time they spent floating in the same position was enough to give the enemy mortar units time to sight in on the chopper. Several of the guy's in my unit hurriedly ran over and grabbed all of the artillery rounds off the sked just as soon as it made contact with the ground. They then cut the cable lose so the big Huey could itself, lower down and set it's landing skids down on the ground. Then, within mere seconds of those touching down, several more guys ran over and began pulling all of the other supplies off the chopper. Within a couple of minutes they were done and the Huey quickly revved it's rotors back to full power and began to lift off.

Neither Grandpa nor any of the other wounded guys would allow themselves to be evacuated out on the chopper. If their brothers had to stay and fight the enemy with only small arms and then probably die, then "we will all die together!" They said "we have always fought together as a unit, and we will die together as a unit!"

As the chopper began to rise off the ground an enemy mortar round landed directly on top of the chopper's main rotor and instantly blew it into thousands of tiny bits of flying, deadly, spinning pieces of shrapnel all going in a million different directions! The chopper seemed to hang stationary in the air about ten feet off the ground for a brief moment before suddenly tilting towards the co-pilot's side and crashing heavily back to earth.

As it hit the ground half upright and half on it's side, the door gunner standing on the co-pilot's side of the aircraft, went flying head first out of the vacant door, until the straps attached to the inside of the chopper and which were also attached to him, suddenly caught and jerked him to a stop! But that was right at the point where the huge chopper rolled over and landed directly on top of him, crushing and killing him instantly!

When the chopper hit the ground hard on the co-pilot's side, it instantly smashed in the entire side of the chopper where the co-pilot was strapped in his seat. At the same time, the co-pilot's head smashed through the Plexiglas side window. The chopper then rolled over and landed directly on his head, too, smashing it as flat as a road paving roller machine would do. He, too, was killed instantly!

But as the chopper smashed into the ground, it hit hard enough to bounce back up into the air before falling heavily back to the ground once more. This time, it basically settled back upright on the pilot's landing skid that had stayed on despite the crash. The other one on the co-pilot's side had broken off at impact! For no more than a brief instant, I stood there transfixed by what I was seeing. Then, acting on instinct only, I ran over and jumped up inside of the chopper. My only thought was to get the pilot and co-pilot out before a raging inferno exploded and engulfed us. The fuel tank had ruptured and was now leaking gas everywhere!

I already knew the door gunner was probably dead because I had seen the chopper land directly on top of him. But as soon as I jumped inside and took one look at the co-pilot, I realized he was already dead, too. His head was totally crushed! I quickly swung my eyes over to look at the pilot. At the same time, I heard a loud moan escaping from his lips. The pilot was still alive, but unconscious and unable to help himself.

I quickly moved up and reached over and around the pilot to unbuckle his seat straps. At that time, I didn't realize the pilot was taller than me by a good three to four inches, and also outweighed me by at least 40 to 50 pounds. But to me, the pilot was like a leaf floating on the wind, not weighing much of anything! I quickly wrapped my arms around his chest and pulled him over to the open side door. Once there, I jumped down onto the ground, then picked up the 200 plus lbs. of the unconscious pilot, and threw him like a little rag doll over my right shoulder. Then, I began running as far away as possible before the rapidly burning chopper blew up. But, I had not run for more than ten feet, and another enemy mortar round hit the ground and exploded! This one was only about five feet away from me! The explosive concussive blast instantly picked both me and the pilot up, and sent us flying through the air until we landed over ten feet away from where we had just been!

For a moment, it was like déjà vu all over again! I lay there too stunned to move. My head was swimming and my ears were ringing. That was in addition to the solid black wall I was seeing before my eyes! But slowly, I began regaining enough of my senses to remember what had just happened. I remembered hearing the explosion; that had to mean I was still alive! So I quickly began to check myself over to see how many limbs I was missing or were broken.

With a quick thank you to God, I realized that miraculously, I didn't seem to be injured at all other than some bad bumps and bruises that I would not even feel until tomorrow at the earliest. There were not even any pieces of shrapnel embedded in me, either! I wanted to scream halleluiah at the top of my lungs!! But as I turned my attention to the pilot, my euphoria instantly evaporated! One look and I realized that he, too, was now dead, just like his co-pilot and his door-gunner! All three of them had died in a heroic effort to bring us desperately needed supplies!

I looked closer at the pilot. His head was now hanging upside down and facing backwards against his chest, totally against all laws of nature! A large piece of shrapnel had sliced into his neck and had completely severed his entire head except for a small piece of thin muscle and skin that still held it attached to his neck! The pilot's body that had been dangling over my shoulder had absorbed the full impact of the exploding mortar and had undoubtedly, saved my life!

Seeing that was all I could take right then! Huge, gigantic, crocodile tears instantly filled my eyes and began flowing down my cheeks in twin raging rivers, while at the same time, a loud, moaning, animalistic roaring cry reverberated from deep inside my belly and slowly worked it's way up until it finally bellowed out of my ruptured soul in an ear-splitting blast of intense agony!

At the same time, I began screaming, "Why? Why, God? Why did he have to die and not me? He and his crew were the brave guys! They volunteered to bring us supplies! They didn't have to do that! But now, they're all dead! Why? Somebody, anybody, tell me why? Please!"

Let me emphasize this in no uncertain terms, that from that instant on, there are no words to describe the hatred that now blossomed full bore inside all of us towards all of the Vietnamese armies, both North and South! No one could say or do anything to answer me! Some just stood there shaking their heads in knowing sympathy, feeling the exact same way I was. Others quickly turned around, unable to allow their eyes to stay focused on the dead bodies of three very brave American heroes! Still others began running back over to their artillery guns, hoping to get at least one of the artillery rounds these brave heroes had brought in to us. They wanted so much to get some kind of satisfaction to hopefully assuage their raging feelings of revenge and extreme hatred by firing them back at the enemy! They wanted so much to blast all of the evil, murderous, enemy demons straight back into an everlasting fiery inferno called Hell!

Shortly after that, we zipped up the three dead hero's bodies inside of black plastic body bags. Then, with nowhere else to put them, we lay them outside in the 100 degree plus heat. The heat, combined with the 90% percent humidity of a rain-forest jungle environment, made the bodies begin to bask and bake in their own decomposing bodily juices! The hot sun bearing down on the black plastic bags caused the bodies to liquefy and decompose even faster than normal! Every one of us in my entire unit were almost totally overwhelmed and incapacitated by the odor emanating from them! We all knew it would be a smell, and a sight, that we would never be able to forget for the rest of our lives!

# Chapter 14

Soon after this, most of us took up positions around our perimeter again. Because of the helicopter pilots and the door gunner dying, we were really, really praying that the enemy would launch a ground attack against us. If they did, that would give us a chance to get a small measure of revenge!

I had no clue what day it was while all of this was happening. But in Phoenix, it was a Sunday morning. My parents went to church that day like they did every Sunday. But my mom was very troubled! She knew inside of her that something was wrong and I was in a lot of danger. God had placed a burden on her heart that was weighing her down. She went to her best friend and told her that God was letting her know that I was in some kind of trouble and needed immediate prayer. My mom's friend said they needed to go someplace where they could reach the throne of God without disturbing anyone. So, they got in their car and drove over to the friend's house.

Once there, they got down on their knees and began to pray. My mom later told me in a letter I received from her, that the sweet, powerful presence of God descended from Heaven and came into the room. His Presence was so strong that you could actually feel Him! But as they continued praying, my mom's friend began to have a spiritual vision. She began to describe my entire unit right down to the correct location of each of our big cannon guns. She could see the dried dead vegetation surrounding our unit where the intense sprayings of Agent Orange had killed the jungle. But more than that, she could see enemy soldiers advancing towards us through that vegetation. She said there were so many of the enemy coming towards us that they appeared like African Fire Ants that eat and destroy everything in their path! In her vision they appeared as a dark, demonic swarm covering the entire area!

But just then in her vision before these Fire Ants could reach and destroy us, she saw two gigantic hands suddenly reach out and swoop up my entire unit and lift us up out of harm's way!

She later said that it almost looked like the TV commercial that says you're in good hands with some kind of insurance.

As we sat there on our perimeter knowing that we were soon going to die, suddenly, one of the guys from our command bunker came running over to us. He told us they had just received word over the radio that we needed to make a run for it. He said the Air Force was sending some F-4 Phantom jets and a squadron of B-52 bombers to give us support, and also, the Army was sending several Cobra helicopters to help, along with a Puff the Magic Dragon; a C-130 transport aircraft that had been converted into a specially fitted gun-ship that would put fear into even Satan himself. But, we needed to leave now because airborne reconnaissance had spotted thousands of North Vietnamese only a short distance away and moving straight towards us!

It did not take us long! We picked up what little remained of our duffel bags and equipment, threw them inside of our guns, climbed in, revved up the engines and spun the tracks on the guns making our escape! But the odds that we would be able to run the gauntlet were completely against us! We were completely surrounded on all sides by the enemy and they controlled the trail we needed to travel down. But, as we moved down that old carved out jungle trail, not even one single round of any kind came in on us! No mortars! No artillery rounds! Not even any small arms fire!

God had performed a miracle for us! He had picked up my entire unit in His big, gigantic hands and delivered us to safety, at least for the time being! In my Mom's letter telling me all about their prayer meeting and the time that it took place, she described the vision that her friend had that described my unit exactly correct right down to the exact detail. She had everything in their proper locations.

And after having a chance to work out the time difference between Phoenix and where I was, it was the exact same time that our deliverance came through! Yes! God had performed another miracle for us! Don't anyone tell me that prayer doesn't work!!

After passing Bravo Battery we eventually came to the old Khe Sanh military base. Khe Sahn had been abandoned soon after the Tet invasion of 1968. We didn't know how long we were going to be there but we knew we were going to stay at least overnight. Without delay, we got busy setting out perimeter wire, plus trip wires for flares, mines, and claymore projectiles. We also placed sandbags, and other items we were able to scrounge up, over the top of some small dug-out bunkers that we planned on using to sleep in. Finally we felt like we had made a fairly secure area that we would be able to defend ourselves from if we needed to, or to get some well needed sleep in if we were not bothered by the enemy. We still didn't have any artillery ammunition so we knew we didn't have to worry about shooting any fire-missions tonight.

After we finished all of this we still had approximately an hour of daylight left. The four of us on my gun crew decided to pull a little perimeter patrol before it got dark. We began walking across a mostly flat field that had been a bloody battlefield in its not too distant past. Strung all over this old field were all kinds of old military items, including some parts of clothing, boots, belts, canteens, etc.. There were even a couple of old burned out tanks and personnel carriers sitting there deteriorating and rusting in the jungle environment. This old field was also had an abundance of small bushes, plants, and weeds.

The four of us were walking very slowly about five to ten feet apart in roughly a straight line across from each other. I had been looking down at the ground where I was walking, but I suddenly glanced up to where the field ended about 40 to 50 feet in front of me. Up near the edge of where a bunch of trees were growing I spotted a North Vietnamese combat helmet lying on the ground, and it had a bullet hole in it.

For some macabre reason I wanted that helmet for a souvenir. Like a fool, I started walking faster with my eyes fixated on the helmet. But suddenly, out of the blue, a very loud voice yelled, "STOP"! Because of the urgency and the volume of the voice, all four of us stopped instantly. In fact, my right foot was still up in the air. I quickly glanced around thinking that someone had just either spotted a land mine, or had actually stepped on one. At the same time I looked down toward the ground. As I did, I noticed a very thin, almost invisible wire stretched across the top of my left foot. In that instant, my heart almost fell out of my chest! I knew if I just nudged my left foot forward any at all, I would trip that wire, and whatever it was attached to would explode and probably kill all of us!

I began yelling at the guys that my left foot was touching a trip wire and they needed to get out of that field as quickly as possible! I was standing there trembling all over, afraid to even breathe! I squeezed my eyes closed, and waited until they had gotten to safety. Then, I very, very carefully slid my left foot out from underneath the wire. And praise be to God, nothing happened!! From there, I turned around and very slowly and carefully made my way out of the field.

I then found a big rock and threw it towards the wire. With luck—or God's help---the rock hit it. In a blink of an eye, a tremendous explosion sent flaming shrapnel all over the place. It would have killed me for sure, and probably killed or severely wounded all of the other guys, too!

After that, it took a while before our nerves began to calm down. But, I was curious to know who had yelled, "STOP"? I knew that I hadn't and I needed to thank whoever had. Whoever it was had just saved my life, and probably all of the other guys, too! In fact, I didn't even know my foot was under the wire until the word stop had been yelled! Everyone turned and looked at everyone else, but no one was saying anything. We were just kind of staring at each other and shrugging our shoulders. Finally, I said, "None of you yelled? Huh? . . . But, all of you heard the voice yell "STOP", right?"

"Yeah", they heard the voice, but no one knew who yelled it. I know, sounds really weird, huh? But God had just performed another miracle for us!!!!

Later on that night, I was sitting on our perimeter pulling guard duty. It was about 3:30 a.m. in the early morning and it was dark outside. You know the kind of darkness when there is no moon! The spooky kind of night where your imagination hears every demon slithering through the underbrush and your eyes see every ghost floating through the air! The sky was mostly covered with clouds which even blocked out most of the stars. But, I had a night vision starlight scope, and every now and then the clouds would break apart enough so I could get a glimpse through it. During one of those times I was watching the area out in front of the concertina wire. Suddenly, I spotted some unusual movement. Nothing was supposed to be out there! If there was movement, it had to be either some animals, or some demons or ghosts, or the enemy and I was really trying my best to not believe in any of those things right then!

I kept my eyes focused through the scope for a few more seconds trying to see what was out there. Whatever was out there was only about thirty feet or so out in front of me. Finally, just before the clouds covered the entire sky again, I was able to make out what it was. As I did, my heart again dropped right out of my chest! I was looking at six North Vietnamese enemy Sappers, all loaded with explosives and trying to get through our wire. If they managed to do that, each one would then slither over to each of our guns and set the explosives off. They would blow our guns to smithereens, plus most of my sleeping brothers!

I quickly grabbed the M-79 grenade launcher I had next to me. Then, without any hesitation, I began popping out as many rounds as I could, as quickly as I could. From the first round, though, I was directly on target! My grenades began exploding and the Sappers began blowing up. My grenades were also setting off the explosives they were carrying on their bodies! In the blink of an eye, all of the Sappers were blown into tiny bits of plasma!

The next morning at daybreak, I led my guys out to collect what little was left of the bodies and to search them for any intelligence items we might find. There was nothing on them, but we had expected that. That's because there was hardly anything at all left of the bodies! So, we began gathering all of the different little pieces of the bodies that we could find. We put them in some empty sandbags. There wasn't anything left that was larger than about 12" inches long, and there were only a few of those. What was left of the Sappers easily fit inside of about eight or nine sandbags! Soon after that, we dug a shallow common grave and buried the bags in it. They were North Vietnamese soldiers fighting in the cause they believed in, and we gave them an honored funeral.

# Chapter 15

We left Khe Sahn a couple of days later and after about another week and a half, we eventually fought our way back to our old home of Firebase Charlie 2. Man, I tell you, I had never before seen anything more beautiful in my entire lifetime than that old sandbagged, underground, dirt enclosed, caveman style living of Firebase Charlie 2! To us, it looked just like the Taj Mahal! It was 'home'!

About a week after getting back to Charlie 2, I put in for my R & R, which stands for rest and relaxation. It's a two-week leave. The army had just recently begun giving approval that if we wanted, we could go back home to the real world. Up until that time, you were limited to taking your R & R in Thailand, Hawaii, or Australia. I told the paper shufflers to make my orders for Phoenix!

It wasn't long and the day of departure arrived. I flew down to Saigon the day before I was scheduled to leave the country. On the morning I was preparing to leave to go back to the 'world', I decided to go to the airport a little early to have breakfast at a restaurant there. I thought to sit in a restaurant and order food like a real person might make me feel a little bit more normal and civilized since I had been living in a blood soaked, canopied jungle for the last two months.

I walked into the restaurant, sat down in a booth, and placed an order for some over-easy eggs, bacon, and toast. Real food! But, when my order came, sticking up out of one of the yokes were a bunch of little blood vessels and the beginnings of a small beak growing in it. I called the waitress over, who happened to be a Mama-San about sixty years old. I said to her, "Look at my eggs! I can't eat this! There's a beak in my egg!" With a bored look on her face, she glanced down at my food. Then, she looked back up at me with a stern look on her face, "Oh no GI, you eat! But, you pay double! You got egg and chicken both!"

She wasn't kidding. She was serious! During the six months I had been in Hell, I may have become a stone-cold, uncivilized, true menace to society, but there was no way I was going to eat those eggs! I got up from the table, threw down enough military currency script to cover the cost of the meal---toast & eggs only, no chicken---and walked out. In a special way, I was proud of myself for not eating it. I then left the restaurant and ran out to the big old 'Freedom Bird'. After climbing the stairs I quickly found a seat, sat down in it, and mentally prepared myself for the mind-numbing flight back across the Pacific Ocean. Soon after, the plane took off and pointed its nose northeast towards San Francisco. Ah, San Francisco, California, that beautiful, wonderful, glorious, American soil! . . . Or so I thought.

After what seemed like an eternity, the plane came in for a graceful landing. But, I stayed in my seat and waited until just about everyone else was off the plane before I started to leave. I needed to change planes at San Francisco but I had plenty of time to do it. I just didn't know how comfortable I would be around what I presumed were 'normal' people. Also, I had been the only one on the plane wearing camouflaged Army fatigues. The Army wanted us to fly home in our dress green uniforms but I didn't want to. I mean, there was no way I would be able to feel comfortable in a coat and tie after what we had just gone through. But, I didn't know how my camo's were going to be received in the bastion of Hippie-Dom, either!

I finally exited the plane and began walking unhurriedly through the terminal, just taking in the sights and the smells of the place. Suddenly, two very stupid long haired hippies came running up to me. They had noticed the camouflaged fatigues I was wearing. As they reached me, they both began yelling at me and calling me names. The one used most often was that I was a "baby killer".

I tried to ignore them and just push my way on through. As I did, I looked around to see if there might be even one person who may come to my defense and get these jerks away from me. But, no one even seemed to be interested in the least about what was happening. Although, some of the ones standing there were shaking their heads up and down like they were in agreement with the hippies.

As I turned back towards these two very stupid and ignorant individuals, one of them worked up a very large surge of false courage, along with a very large wad of spit, and then leaned towards me and expelled that huge gob right into my face! The next thing I knew, I was being pulled off him by two, very large spit-shined stateside military policemen. Apparently, after the extremely stupid fool spit in my face, I had grabbed the little tweeb by his scrawny little neck, and then had thrown him head first into the solid concrete wall across the aisle. Then, as he bounced back off it, I had picked him up over my head and then body slammed him into the solid concrete floor with enough force to knock the stupid right out of him!

But, I still didn't know what I was doing, so I climbed on top of him and sat down heavily on his chest. At least, as heavily as a 135 lb. person can sit! Then, I again wrapped my hands around his scrawny little neck, where I then gently picked his head up into my soft and caring hands! But then, in that very same instant, Satan must have suddenly entered into my entire body and took complete control over my actions! It was totally his fault, without a doubt, as he made me begin to rapidly smash this stupid idiot's head into the solid concrete floor, "over and over again"; until the MP's showed up and finally pulled me off the fool!

After that, I was taken to a very small interrogation room with a full-bird---totally decorated to the max---Colonel, who had enough jingling and shiny medals and strands of ribbons on his chest that he could have easily been a qualified substitute for a Christmas Tree in the town square if someone had just put lights on him and lit him up. This full-bird Colonel was telling me that the poor little misguided soul just might live and I would not be prosecuted for murder. But, I was still sure to get at least 20 years for assault with a deadly weapon.

I yelled, "What deadly weapon?"

He replied, "Why you, son. You're the deadly weapon! It is an absolute miracle that you didn't kill the guy before we got there to save him. God bless his poor little soul. But son, you are, without a single doubt, a true "menace to society"! We cannot allow stone-cold serial killers like you to come back here to the States and roam around free to create mayhem on our civilized streets!

"This I promise you, either you will spend the next ten to twenty years in prison, or I will personally see that you are sent back to Vietnam where you will then spend the rest of your life on the very front lines of action to assure that you will be killed! This I personally promise you!"

In that instant, I had everything I could do to keep from killing this shiny and jingling imitation of a one-man musical band with my bare hands! "You stupid looking Christmas Tree," I screamed, "with all of your shiny ribbons and jingling medals that makes you sound like a monkey vendor, who do you think you are, King David? You're going to send me to the front lines so I'll get killed? Where do you think I've already been for the last seven months?

"You stupid ignorant fool! You can't send me anywhere closer to the front lines than I already have been! I was on the very front lines of Hell, man! Somewhere you certainly have never been with your spit-shined stupid decorations, that you have never earned a single one of! I outta rip those things off you and make you eat them! Or shove them up your puckered up and scared shut, fat rear-end! You're a 'fraud', man! A fraud!! Do you hear me, fraud-man?

"You swore something to me, man, well this I 'promise' you, Mr. full-bird Colonel, "cur"! I swear that as soon as my combat brothers find out about this, that not only you, but your entire family, are going to die very horrible and painful deaths! Do you hear me? You very stupid fool!!!! I swear we'll break every bone in your entire body while you're begging me to just get it over with and kill you!"

As I was yelling this right into his smooth as baby's bottom silky slick face, every bit of color instantly drained completely out of it! At the same time, his entire body began trembling and shaking like a Parkinson's patient without his medication, or a rap dancer, either one. He quickly glanced away and suddenly reached for a glass of water setting on the table in front of him. But as he tried to pick it up, his hand was shaking so badly that it slipped out of it and the entire contents spilled straight down on top of his beautifully, starched and pressed, stateside khaki pants. Immediately, before the water even had a chance to get him wet, every curse word in the book suddenly began rushing out of his mouth like a raging torrent of vile! To make it worse, I couldn't help but begin laughing at the very top of my voice straight into his very colorless, ghost like face!

But within 30 minutes following this, I was personally escorted onto the plane bound for Phoenix by the same two MP's who had pulled me off the new Einstein candidate for genius. As I took my seat, I thought to myself, "No harm, no foul. I'll let it go this time." ... But, I was very worried about what might happen when I got to my next stop on this very unusual journey of my life.

# Chapter 16

After the plane landed at Phoenix Sky Harbor Airport, I caught a taxi to my home; the place I had dreamed about ever since I had left for Basic Training in what seemed like an entire eternity ago! I spent the evening talking with my folks, but it eventually got late. I got up to go to bed. It sure felt good to be back in my old bedroom. By now, though, my younger brother had moved in and I had to share it with him. But, it was still a bedroom with a real door and with a real doorknob and with a real light switch that you could turn on and off, which I did for about ten minutes straight!

When I woke up the next day, I didn't want to see any of my old friends. That even included the little blonde. I just did not know how I could relate to any of them anymore. So, for the rest of the time I was at home, I mostly just lounged around inside of my house. I never even called the little blonde. What I had thought before being drafted would be a lifetime of love, now didn't even register a blip on my heart! How could it? Where supposed love had once been, now contained nothing but hate!

A huge part of me really, really, missed Vietnam! I don't mean the fighting! The killing! The bloodshed! I mean the camaraderie between the guys in my unit. They were my brothers! In fact, at that time in my life, they were probably even closer to me than my own family. But, another big part of me was saying, "You're stupid, Jim! You're stupid for even wanting to ever go back over there. In fact, you should pack your bags and go to Canada!"

The two weeks passed quickly, and also, at the same time, they seemed to drag on forever. Finally, on the day before I was scheduled to leave, my brother went out of the house to get the newspaper. When he came back inside, he was looking at the front page.

"Hey Jim, have you ever heard of a place called Firebase Charlie 2?" Suddenly, a deep sickening feeling came flooding over me just like a dam bursting! Something terrible had to have happened for my firebase to make the front page! Instantly, my voice rose several octaves and I yelled, "Yeah! That's my firebase. Why?"

My brother suddenly went kind of pale and began trembling! Then, he said, "Uh - Uh", while shaking his head no. He was trying not to believe me. I said, "Yes it is! Why?" Suddenly, tears filled his eyes as he turned the newspaper around and showed it to me. On the front page was a picture of a big mound of dirt that was blown apart and scattered all about. Below the picture, the headlines screamed in big bold type, **"29 Americans Killed in a Rocket Attack at Firebase Charlie 2! Another 33 Wounded!"**

Without reading the article, no one else knew what that big mound of dirt was! But, I did! The big mound of dirt that was blown apart in the picture was the remains of an underground service club on the firebase. I knew that the club was the only place on the firebase where more than five people could be together at any one time. I also knew it was well protected; that it would take a direct hit for anything to happen. Well, a direct hit did just happen and twenty-nine young, innocent, American heroes had just lost their lives!

Tears rapidly filled my entire eyes! I jumped up and ran into the bedroom, and quickly packed my duffel bag. Then, I hurried back into the kitchen, picked up the phone and called the airport to make plans to return to Vietnam as soon as possible. Oh, I felt so guilty inside! Here I was living in the lap of a middle class existence, and twenty-nine of my brothers had just died inside of an old, filthy, underground social club that to the men on that firebase was just like Club 21 in New York City!

# Chapter 17

I was able to catch a flight out that same night that took me back to San Francisco. From there, I was able to hop a Freedom Bird leaving just 45 minutes later to take me back 'home' to Hell. As I was winging my way over the Pacific Ocean, I was thinking that I had just made the biggest mistake of my life by ever going to Phoenix. I should have gone to Australia, or Thailand, or anyplace other than home. I didn't belong to the Real World anymore! Now, I know exactly why that old Sergeant I had met on the plane when I was first going over to Vietnam was going back for his third tour!

Once we touched down at Ton Son Nhut airport in Saigon, I caught the first flight out that was flying up to Da Nang. That flight was leaving within 30 minutes of me landing at Ton Son Nhut. From Da Nang, I caught the first flight up to Quang Tri I could get. I arrived in Quang Tri in the middle of the afternoon. I knew I should stay there overnight. But in my hurry and haste, I stuck out my thumb and caught a ride that took me straight through Dong Ha, and all the way up to the Buddhist grave. But by then, it was after six P.M. and I suddenly realized that the chances would be really slim that I would be able to catch a ride on up to Charlie 2 that night. I was right! No other American military vehicle of any sort came by for the rest of the evening, or the night. So, as thick enveloping darkness descended and began wrapping it's black, scary tentacles around me, I curled myself up into the smallest ball of human flesh I could, and then got right up next to the headstone marker inside of the little stucco fence of the Buddhist grave. I didn't want to be seen by some North Vietnamese sharpshooter.

I also knew I had to stay awake all night so no one could sneak up on me. So, I lay on that cold, old, ground, snuggled up as close as I could get next to the little stucco wall. With the old dead Buddhist sitting next to me, I began thinking that just a day before this; I had been sleeping in my own bed in my own house in a totally different universe!

I had a real mattress. I had a real indoor shower with real hot water. I had real food to eat. I had been driving around in a mostly civilized city in my beautiful Z-28 Camaro enjoying the sights and sounds of Phoenix. I had been in the "real world" where the chances of getting shot and killed were very slim!

But now, I'm lying as flat as I can get right next to an old, dead Buddhist, and I know this is not a bad dream, or a flashback! But it was a nightmare! A very terrifying one! And the odds of me getting shot and killed, or worse, captured, were very, very real!

Every now and again, I slowly poked my head up to see if there was any pink in the eastern sky that would signal the arrival of the coming dawn. Every time I would do this, though, the reality of just exactly where I was would hit me square between the eyes like a brick boulder being thrown at me! The stark surreal reality would bury itself deep down inside of my gut where only paralyzing and agonizing fear can reside!

I was still a very battle-hardened, blood draining, serial killer, I knew! A true 'menace to society' as the MPs at San Francisco had said! But, I was still very scared right then! If I would have had an M-60 machine-gun and hundreds of rounds of ammunition, I wouldn't have felt so bad! But, all I had were two clips of ammo with me. Nowhere near enough to do much damage! And I wanted so badly to kill every one of my enemies!

Suddenly, I heard a rustling sound, and shortly after that, several Vietnamese voices began wafting through the still night air not too far away from me. I know that sound can carry for a long distance at night, so very slowly; I poked my eyes up just enough to clear the little fence to look around. But I couldn't see anyone. And I didn't have a starlight scope with me this time. After a short time, the voices faded away and I finally began to breathe again!

But as all of this was happening, all of my senses suddenly came completely alive and rose to unparalleled heights. I couldn't see any Vietnamese, but I could see just exactly where I was!

"No!" Silently I screamed! "This is not a nightmare! Neither is it surreal! This is reality, man! This is the real world!!! . . . It's my world! . . . And I belong here!"

I ducked my head back down and began thinking. As I did, I began to feel an almost overwhelming hatred for God! I could not understand how God, who is supposed to be so full of love towards us, but yet, He still allows this stupid, insane war to continue on and on and on; just like He has allowed stupid, insane wars to go on throughout the entire existence of mankind! The first killing of one human being of another was one of the first man's---Adam's---own son killing his own brother. Cain killed Abel! And, we humans have been killing each other ever since! For what? For why?

As I lay there, I began thinking about us humans. You know, throw out all of the different nationalities and races of people and what do you have left? Just one race! The Human Race! It just boggled my mind that a human being can be so cruel towards another human being as we were. How can we hate each other so much that we have trained each other, and created weapons of such mass destruction, that allows us to try our best to make our species---our human race---become extinct?

I just could not understand this! And, why did God just sit on the sidelines and allow us to do this? Why did He allow us to try to wipe out the North Vietnamese, and why did He allow them to try to kill all of us? I lay there trying to understand and just was not succeeding at all! Part of me wanted to believe that God did not really exist. That way, if He was not really real, I wouldn't need to have the guilt inside of me that I was feeling for hating Him! As I lay there curled up next to that old dead Buddhist, I pondered on these things all night long. It somehow helped to keep me awake throughout the long night!

Early the next morning around 0630 military time, not long after daylight had broken over the eastern horizon, an American tank came rumbling along. As it approached me, I cautiously poked my head up above the little whitewashed fence and yelled, "American! Don't shoot!"

It startled the driver and his shotgun rider so bad that they did almost shoot me! But, at the last instant, for some unknown reason other than the fact that God was still protecting me despite my hatred of Him, they held up! I then climbed over the wall and jumped up onto the tank. But as I did, they looked at me almost like they were seeing a ghost or something. They just could not believe that I had spent the entire night inside of that little stucco walled grave all by myself. They began to laugh, and then they both said I deserved a medal or something. I replied, "Yeah! One for stupidity for getting stuck out here!"

We soon pulled through the south gate of Charlie 2 and the tank rumbled to a stop. I jumped off, turned around and gave the guys a halfhearted salute, and a smile. Then, I headed over to the Command Bunker. Once inside, our company clerk smiled up at me and said, "Welcome home, Brother!"

I replied, "Yeah! This is my home! And you are my brother!"

I had dreaded the thought of ever coming to Vietnam in the first place, knowing inside that I was probably going to die here. But now that I had come back to Vietnam a second time from my brief foray back to the States I was not real sure that I ever wanted to leave this place again.

I turned to my friend. I needed to know just who had died in the rocket attack at the club, so I kept asking him to tell me the story. To my partial relief, he said that none of our guys in Charlie Battery had been killed. In fact, none of our guys were even over there at the club. The tanks and infantry guys had just returned from the bush after being gone for a while and they wanted the club to themselves for a special party of their own. In fact, the guys had only been back on the base for just a few hours before the attack took place!

Part of me felt real relief that none of my brothers in my own unit had died, but, I was still real sad that 29 young, red blooded, American men would never again be a son, a husband, a brother, or a daddy to someone back home! They died so young, and for what? For a country whose army refuses to fight for themselves?!!

Let me tell you, they certainly didn't die protecting the United States! And they certainly didn't die for South Vietnam, because most of the civilians didn't really care what government was in charge. They just wanted the war to end so they could go back to growing rice. So, what did they die for? . . . They died because 'evil', incarnated as Satan, rules this world! The word of God says, "Satan comes to steal, kill, and destroy"! His sole desire is to kill & destroy every living human being on this earth.

You see, we are made in the exact image of God. So every time Satan looks at us, he sees God, the one he hates more than anything else! So, when he can kill one of us, to him, it is just like killing part of God, too! And, you know what, every time Satan succeeds in killing one of us, to God, it is just like a portion of his own self has died! He created us to be His children. When Satan 'steals' and 'kills' us, to God, one of His children has just died, and it breaks His heart!. . . . 'This' is why they died! Satan stole their lives!

After my buddy finished telling me the story, I hurried up to my artillery gun to put my stuff away. Oh man, when I got up there, it felt so good to be back with my family that I almost began crying. The guys and I spent the rest of the day catching up on what had happened to us. I told them about the 'real world' and they told me about having to help dig bodies out of the collapsed club. In fact, they said, "our gun crew is going back over there again tomorrow and dig some more to see if we can find any more body parts. We don't want to leave any 'part' behind of any American hero over there, no matter how small it could be!"

They said that the rocket that hit the club actually penetrated all the way inside of it before exploding! That meant that all that was left of the people inside of it were just bloody mutilated body 'parts'! They said that, at times, they dug out heads that had been blown off some unfortunate body, and also, just parts of heads with parts of the brain exposed and hanging out of them!

They said they dug out a lot of pieces of flesh with some kinds of bones sticking out of it but they were so mangled they couldn't tell if it was an arm or a leg or whatever! They said they dug out armless, legless, and headless torsos that were so mangled and blasted apart that it was impossible to tell that they had ever even been human! They said that it was the most gruesome sight that any of the guys had seen since being over here, and all of us had seen some really gruesome sights on many occasions before!

All of this just increased my guilt, almost beyond measure! I had been home enjoying TV, the newspaper, real food, real beds, real showers, and all the rest that goes with living in the real world, while my brothers were experiencing all of this insanity that only comes from being smack dab in the middle of the raging fires of Hell!! It was not long after this that I kind of went off the deep-end and completely lost all respect for human life, unless it was of my combat brothers. Satan had completely 'stolen' from me any ability to have any compassion at all for any human beings except my combat brothers!

The next day, we got shovels and went over to the big dirt pile. As we dug, a lot of broken and shattered body parts, including a few more heads, some arms, legs, and some parts that we had no idea what they were came from the pile. The smell was unbelievable! And the gore is indescribable! We put all of these parts and pieces of blown up human beings into bags. They would eventually be shipped to an Army Identification installation where the poor soldiers who worked there would try to put each body back together as much as possible. They didn't want two or three, or even more, parts of bodies put into the same coffin.

I feel real sorry for those poor soldiers whose job this is. Yes, it's very hard on us who dug the bodies out, but it is equally hard on those who have to try to put Humpty Dumpy back together again.

# Chapter 18

Because of the failure of Lam Son 719 to shut off the flow of supplies running down the Ho Chi Ming Trail, and especially because of the refusal of the South Vietnamese Army to fight for it's own country, and because of the 29 Americans killed at Charlie 2, and for fifty-eight thousand other reasons, our leaders in Washington, DC finally decided to begin pulling our American troops out of Vietnam.

The Northern I Core, which consisted of all of Quang Tri Province, were the first American military units to begin leaving South Vietnam. The 5th Mechanized Infantry Division, of which we belong to, was the first to get orders to leave the country. I guess the military higher ups decided to they were going to force South Vietnam to fight for their own country by forcing them to be the sole barrier between North and South Vietnam by protecting the DMZ!

So being that Quang Tri Province is all that separated South Vietnam from North Vietnam, the political and military bigwigs wanted the "Best of the Best" South Vietnamese Army units to occupy the military outposts and firebases we were evacuating. Therefore, the elite South Vietnamese Black Panther Ranger Units were sent up to take our places.

As we were preparing to leave, our leaders decided that if you have sixty days or less left of your sentence in Hell, you could go home with your unit. But, if you have more than sixty days remaining, you were to be transferred to another part of Hell. I had sixty-six days remaining! I got transferred!

Before we actually left Firebase Charlie 2 for the final time, our Top Dog called the one and only military formation we had ever been required to attend. But this time, every member of Charlie Battery was required to be there. Several rear-echelon bigwigs had flown in by helicopter for this formation. To them, it was too dangerous to drive all of the way to Charlie 2. I stood there wondering how they would have felt if they would have had to spend a night in that old Buddhist grave like I had.

I also thought this formation was totally idiotic with all of us standing completely out in the open like we were. If the enemy would launch a rocket at us like the one that blew up the club just a few short weeks ago, it would have killed way more than a hundred American soldiers! Idiocy!!

The formation was called for our Top Dog to tell us how proud he was of us, and how proud he was to have been our 'big brother' to all of us combat brothers! He told us he would remember us for the rest of his life, and he said that he would especially remember all of the ones in our unit who had been either wounded or killed.

He said the upper rank, rear-echelon, desk-hugging, big-butted sissies, wanted to present us with some appreciation awards and medals. He said that when they called out a name, for that person to step forward. It would be in alphabetic order.

The guy whose name was called first stepped forward. Then, the big-butts came up and pinned some medals on his chest while reading off the list of heroics the guy had done. While they were pinning the medals on this guy, another name had been called. This guy stepped forward and the procedure began again.

Then, the next guy whose name was called refused to step forward to accept any medals. He told them in no uncertain terms for them to stick those medals on their bodies exactly where the sun doesn't shine! ---And let me tell you, those rear-echelon, desk hugging, big-butts could block out an awful lot of the sunshine!!!---As the guy was saying this, the other guys who had already received medals suddenly reached up, removed them, and then threw them down on the ground and stepped on them!

Oh man, my name was the next on the list following this. I had a big decision to make. Part of me wanted the medals, which included a Bronze Star. But, a bigger part of me wanted nothing to do with any 'rewards' for being a part of such a stupid and insane reason as fighting a war for a country that didn't want to fight for itself!

I stayed right where I was. I didn't move. One more name was called after mine. He didn't move either. Shortly after that, all of the big wigs got on their helicopters and flew out of our lives. It had been the first time we had ever seen any of them, anyway. And we hoped that it would be the last time that we ever saw them again! To us, they were nothing more than a bunch of rear-echelon, panty wearing sissies! We certainly had never seen any of them up near Laos when the action had been hot and heavy!

The next day, I waved goodbye to several of my brothers as they boarded a plane that would take them to Cam Rahn Bay where they would catch the Freedom Bird home. Just one of my brothers, who just happened to be Mike Stanley, was being transferred with me. He had received the same orders that I had. Several others in my old unit were being assigned to different units in different parts of Hell.

Mike and I got transferred to a place called Chu Lai. It was near the middle of South Vietnam and it sat right on the coast of the South China Sea. When we first saw it, it lifted our spirits a little. "If we can pull our remaining time right here on the coast, we can handle this," we said. It was a very pretty part of hell.

Alas, though, it was not to be. After we processed into headquarters at Chu Lai, we were told that we would be receiving orders to report to a firebase out in the central highlands of Hell. A few days later those orders came through.

We got on a helicopter that flew us out to our new base, which turned out to be a very small firebase sitting on top of a medium-sized hill. But this new base was very different from what we had been used to. The only way in or out was by helicopter. There were no roads coming into the base at all.

As we stepped off the helicopter, there to meet us was a brand spanking new, 'shake and bake', Newbie Officer, fresh out of ROTC. Before flying to this new base, Mike and I had some problems with a stiff-shirted rear-echelon, big-butt, full-bird Colonel in Chu Lai.

He had tried to make us become 'real army' types. We hadn't liked that! So, as we were flying to this new base, the Colonel in Chu Lai had radioed ahead and warned the people at our new base about us.

We turned toward the shake and bake and stuck out our hands to shake his. At that, he suddenly began to turn several shades of fiery red! At the same time, he also was trying to get some words to come out of his mouth, but he was spitting and slobbering all over himself! Finally, something that kind of sounded to us like, "I'm an officer! You're supposed to salute me!" came spluttering out. At least, that is what we thought he was trying to say.

At one time, Mike and I had stared down four North Vietnamese serial killers at a river when we had been trying to take a bath. They had their AKs trained straight at us as we were standing naked in the river. But, we didn't back down then, and we certainly weren't now! A brand new little tweeb just out of officer elementary school certainly was not going to intimidate us in the least!

We said, "Oh, we're sorry!" And, we put up our left hand to our foreheads. At that, he came completely unglued and began to stammer again. As he stood there spitting and stammering, we began to try to help him to get the words out. "You mean" "No, not that" "What" "Something different"

Man, it was real difficult trying to play "What's My Line" with this little spit-shined, fully starched, stut – stut - stuttering idiot. Finally though, we were able to ascertain that he was trying to tell us that we had saluted with the wrong hand. "Oh! What relief!" We were so happy to finally guess the right answer that we reached out and grabbed both of his hands and began to furiously shake them up and down. Then, we began patting him on his back and telling him we would be happy to play some more word games with him some other time but, right now, we needed to go get checked in.

He didn't know what to do. He just stood there looking completely stupid in his freshly starched, bright green, razor sharp creased uniform and his brightly spit shined boots. Seeing him like that, I suddenly had a mental image of him being with us when we had sneaked off LZ Woodstock to go take that bath in the jungle river. If he had been there with us, those North Vietnamese soldiers would have done one of two things for sure. They would have either shot us right then, so they could rid the world of people like him. Or, they would have begun laughing so hard that they would have been rolling around on the ground in the dying cockroach position! Giving him a big smile, we walked away to go find the command hooch.

When we found it, we went inside to meet the Captain of the unit. But instead of him looking like a Top Dog, he looked more like a little Poodle to us. Upon seeing us, he quickly stood up to his full height of 5' nothing, and came out from behind his desk. He took one disgusting look at us, and then told us he had better never see us again until we made ourselves look like 'real army'!

"Whew! What a relief!" we thought as we walked out of there. The Commanding Officer of our new unit had just given us an order to 'never be seen again', because we certainly were never going to look like 'real army'. We went outside and wandered on up to a hooch where there were normal soldiers inside of it. As we ambled through the door, we said "Hi", and then asked the guys if there were a couple of extra cots we could use. They said sure.

But, they sat there just staring at us, almost like they were kind of scared of us. We didn't really have any idea what their problem was! Finally, one guy, in a slow and halting manner, began to speak. He said they had already heard all about us. "Is it really true you guys have been surfing for the last week at Chu Lai?" "Man, did you guys really say you were going to kill that Colonel at Chu Lai?" And, they asked all kinds of other questions. Like, "What does it feel like to be in a firefight?" "How does it feel to kill someone?"

We asked them how they had heard about all of this stuff. They said the shake and bake, LT., took the call from the Colonel down in Chu Lai saying that you guys were on the way up here.

That Colonel had said you guys were totally crazy! He had said that you had probably snapped from what you had gone through up on the DMZ and to be real careful, because, he wouldn't trust you! You really might just kill someone! Then, after that, the shake and bake had gone around telling everyone what all he was going to do to you guys once you got here. "You know, acting like a real big man!"

Upon hearing that, we suddenly smiled real big, and then exclaimed, "Oh yeah? Bring the big boy on!!!"

Well, to put these guys at ease, we assured them that we would never kill any of them. If need be, we would only kill just the shake and bake. "And, that is only if he gives us a hard time," we said. Immediately, though, at that statement, their eyes got real wide with surprise. They glanced up at us, as if just maybe, we really were crazy! But anyway, they began giving us a lot of respect from then on out. In fact, they gave us so much respect that it was kind of fun being looked up to like that.

At that firebase, every morning at 6 A.M., reveille blew and you were expected to attend a formation for roll call by 7 A.M. To let you know how stupid that was, all the enemy had to do would be to drop some mortar rounds in on top of that formation and about sixty to eighty guys would have either died or been wounded! But, the Army wanted to play so-called 'real' Army! Us, not being used to such 'Real Army' games like that, and because the 'Poodle' of this company had already given us permission to not be seen anymore, we just didn't attend any of these formations.

Because of that, the Poodle told the S & B---"shake and bake"---Means a person goes to a school that lasts just a few weeks, and then comes out of it a ready-made officer. Thus, "shake & bake". Throw them in the oven, stir them around, and out they come! ---that he was assigning our rehabilitation to him, and that he expected him to straighten us out.

So, one morning when we did not show up for the formation, the S & B came storming into our hooch. We were still lying in our sleeping bags on top of our cots when he came in. Seeing us like that, he began screaming and yelling at us to get up and come to attention. So, we slowly rolled over and looked at him. Let me tell you, it took all of our will power to keep from laughing out loud as we smiled up real big at him.

Then, very politely, doing our best to not snicker too much, we asked him if he would go down to the mess hooch and get us some coffee, and then, bring it back to us. "Put a little cream in mine, will you?" I asked him. We explained to him that we never did anything before we had our morning coffee. "We just can't get going without our morning coffee," we said.

Up to that point in my life, I had never seen a white man turn that many different colors of red! In fact, his face turned a deep, deep purple! We also really began to fear that his eyeballs were going to pop right out of his face! We know he wanted to talk because he was making some kind of grunting noise, but I think his jaws were welded shut!

Eventually, because of him just standing there trying to talk and not being able to, and with him not really knowing what to do, we rolled back over and told him that if he wasn't going to go get us some coffee, then he needed to leave so we could finish getting our naps out. At that point, he stormed out of our hooch and ran to tell on us to the Poodle!

Soon, the Poodle came running up and stormed into our hooch. "What the _____ do you think you are doing? You _____ better get out of those beds right this instant!"

We rolled back over and faced him. "Hi, TD!" we said. "What time is it, anyway?" His jaw dropped. He didn't know what to do. We were being insubordinate but I think he was actually a little afraid of us. He had heard about his boss, the Colonel in Chu Lai, putting in for a transfer and he believed we had been responsible for it.

It didn't happen too often, but everyone in Vietnam had heard about a thing called 'Fragging!' This is where a grenade has electrical tape wrapped around it and then has the pin pulled. It is then placed in a can of gasoline and put underneath the bed of a bothersome bully of a superior. If he doesn't find it before the tape melts, "BOOM"!!! He dies!

Now, I am not saying we did this or even mentioned it. The only reason I bring it up is I am sure that the TD had this on his mind. He firmly believed we had gone crazy and we were not going to let him think otherwise! He turned around and stormed back out of our hooch. What we didn't know at that time was, another one of our guys from Charlie 2 had been transferred here a few weeks before us and the TD ran to get him. This guy was a real good guy even if he was a lifer Staff Sergeant who had been in the Army for over ten years.

The TD rounded up our old Sarge and brought him into our hooch. We sat up in surprise when we saw him. "Sarge! It's good to see you!" we exclaimed!

He walked over and shook our hands, and then told us to get up. He said that we all needed to have a little talk with each other. He told the TD that we were really good guys, but apparently someone had done something to make us mad. He also told the TD that we had fought a "real" war up north. He said to him that he really should cut us some slack because we had less than 2 months left to go. He then turned back to us and told us to cut the TD some slack.

We said okay, we'll go easy on the TD, but you had better keep that little tweeb, shake and bake LT., away from us. We're not going to take orders from someone who got their stripes in ROTC, and has never even seen any battles. The Sarge laughed and said that the little S & B wouldn't have lasted for thirty minutes up north with us. If the enemy did not shoot him, then one of our guys would have for sure. We all, including the TD, laughed at that.

Because of our talk with the old Sarge we climbed out of bed and stuck out our hands toward the TD to shake his hand. He looked at us for a moment, and then, stuck his hand out and took ours. He said, "I guess I need to get used to not being saluted, huh guys?" We said, "We're sorry, we just never had to do that up north. In fact, none of the officers up there wanted us to salute them. If the enemy were watching and we happened to salute one of them, then the enemy would know whom to target. They didn't want to die! And, if we ever did salute one of them, they then knew that they were in big trouble!"

The TD thought about that for a moment, then said, "That makes sense. Maybe we'll begin that here, no saluting!"

Following that, the Poodle told the S & B that we did not need to attend the roll call formation, but, he wanted him to find us some kind of assignments that would keep us away from the other guys as much as possible so they wouldn't get the idea they could pull the same stunt we were pulling. So, in an attempt to rehabilitate us, we were assigned to pull day guard duty every day on top of the sandbag bunkers surrounding the base. "Heavenly Duty!"

After that, we sat up on top of those bunkers all day long, every day, working real hard on our tans! Also, for something to do to try to have some fun with the little S & B, we began to devise some booby traps with trip wires. We then placed them around the bunker we were on. After doing this, we made sure to tell the guys who were going to pull night guard duty about them. This way, when the little tweeb came around trying to sneak up on the guys to see if they were awake, he would trip the wires.

We had set up a trip wire that would make an illumination flare shoot straight up into the sky from only about three feet away from him. It would then explode up in the sky, light up the entire area, and float back to earth on a parachute. Then, we had also strung a wire right next to it that was attached to a claymore mine. We set it up to face away from our firebase out to shoot its nasty blast of metal ball-bearing out into the vastness of the empty countryside.

Following all of this, it didn't take long, and around 2:30 A.M. that same night, the little idiot came creeping around and tried to sneak up on our bunker. He knew that at 3:00 A.M. is when the next shift came on, and sometimes, guys would fall asleep just before then. So, as he was sneaking up, his foot brushed the wire leading to the illumination flare. Instantly, a loud "whoosh" sounded as it went flying up into the dark night sky! Because of the noise, the little tweeb immediately began screaming, sounding just like a pack of wild hyenas! He also began jumping around like he was on a Pogo Stick! This made him hit the wire leading to the claymore mine. Suddenly, in that same instant, a tremendous "Boom" reverberated and began echoing all over the entire countryside, accented even more by the stillness of the night.

At the same time all of this was going on, the guy on top of the bunker quickly spun around and pointed his M-16 rifle right at the head of the little LT. Then, the two guys who had been sleeping inside of the bunker came running out and immediately jumped on top of the poor little jerk. They quickly threw him to the ground and wrapped him up in a blanket. While all of this was going on, the tweeb was singing the highest notes that have ever been heard on the surface of the earth in the most beautiful soprano voice you have ever heard! Every piece of glass for miles around had to have shattered!

The guys, who knocked him down and were sitting on top of him, finally began to climb off and to take the blanket off his face. They then began to tell him that he was real lucky that they had not killed him. They told him this is a war zone and you should never try to sneak up on someone. All of these things they were saying are what we had told them to say. Then, one of the guys looked down at the tweeb and said, "Ah, LT., you wet your pants! Look at you! You've made a real mess of yourself!" The guy happened to have a camera with him just for this possibility. He quickly pulled it out, and then yelled, "Smile, LT!" At that, the little S & B looked up with the most stunned expression in the world on his face, while at the same time, the front of his pants were totally wet from his waist all of the way down to his feet!

After that, the time went by slowly. Not having anything else to do but sit on top of those bunkers everyday eventually became real drudgery. The little S & B never came around again after that night. In fact, we hardly ever saw him anymore. I guess he finally realized that you just don't play stupid head or power games in a war zone! Too much could accidentally happen!

One day not too long after this, though, the inevitable happened! With a little less than three weeks left until our sentence in hell would be over, our sergeant friend came to our bunker to tell us some bad news. He said that the word coming out of Military Command Headquarters was not verified as of this moment, but apparently, the famed, glorified, stupendous, elite, South Vietnamese 'Black Panther Rangers', had not been able to hold Quang Tri Province. He said that, the word they were hearing as of that moment, all of our old underground haunts at Firebase Charlie 2 were now in the hands of the North Vietnamese. The elite group of the 'best of the best' South Vietnamese soldiers had lost, in just over one month, what us Americans had held onto for years!

Then, he gave us some more, even worse news. He said that since the North Vietnamese had been able to take Quang Tri Province, or were in the process of doing so, they were now headed our way, too. Instantly, I screamed, "No way, man!!!!" . . "Sarge, we only have less than three weeks left! Get us out of here, okay? Get us transferred down to Saigon or even to Cam Rahn Bay, okay? Do something, man, anything!!!"

He said he would have if he could have. But, he said our unit was going to be airlifted out into some virgin valley in the middle of some big mountains. He said that airborne reconnaissance had spotted what appeared to be a division of North Vietnamese troops moving southward. Because of this, he said we were being moved out there to try to stop the advance.

Then, he dropped the bombshell on us. He said, "You two guys, plus me, are the only ones in this entire unit that has ever seen any combat, including the Poodle. And, every one of these guys here look up to you guys as if you were gods or something. So, you two are going to have to go and lead the troops into battle. You two guys are going in on the first wave."

We screamed, again, "No way, man!!!!!" He laughed and said right back, "Yes way, man! Listen; do you want the little S & B leading your friends into battle out there? If not, then you have to do it!" Then he said, "Don't worry, I'll be with you!"

Oh man, that seemed eerily familiar. "Yeah, I had heard something like that once before from a lying Sergeant and that had been when I was the most scared of all of my time in Vietnam!" I thought.

I began shaking my head from side to side, knowing that after eleven months and one week, God was now going to kill me! He had been waiting all along to make me go through absolute hell on earth, and then, He was going to kill me now!

I was so paranoid! In the two days' time that it took to get prepared to move out, I was basically a completely insane person. I really needed to have been put into a rubber room with round corners in it. "The guys think we're gods," I mused. "Well, I certainly am not a god! In fact, I'm so scared that I'm about to drop a load straight into my pants!!!"

On the morning we were preparing to leave, I made sure I was going to get my last shower before we left. I wanted to be clean and be wearing clean underwear when I died. That was something my Mom had always ingrained in me. "Always wear clean underwear because you just never know what may happen," she had always told all of us kids. So, wearing my flax jacket and carrying my M-16 with a big banana clip in it that held thirty rounds, I walked outside to the shower.

Once there, I stripped down to nakedness and opened the door to step in. But just as I was about to put my foot down, I caught a glimpse of movement out of the corner of my eye. I looked down real fast! What I saw just underneath of my foot; that was still hanging in midair, was a huge, 18-inch long by 1-inch thick centipede!

I totally freaked out as I was jumping back real quickly! Then, in a state of absolute paranoia and of almost a full year of extreme pent up emotions, I grabbed my M-16, quickly flipped the lever over to "Rock & Roll," and rapidly, without stopping, put all thirty rounds of ammunition right into the guts of that thousand legged creature that came straight from the lowest pits of hell! But after running out of bullets, I didn't stop there, and I began jabbing the hot smoking barrel of the gun into what little slimy parts I could still find.

Several of the bullets I fired had ricocheted out through the bottom and sides of the shower. It now had peek holes all in it. In fact, with all of the holes around the bottom it was a miracle it was still standing upright!

Everyone on the firebase heard this shooting and almost all of them instantly came running to see what was going on, including the Sarge, the TD, and the little tweeb S & B! "What is going on here?" they all demanded at once.

All I could say was, "I got it! I got it! I got it!", as I kept repeating over and over again for about five minutes straight until my heart finally began returning back to a somewhat normal rate of around 2000 beats a minute.

The Sarge looked at me real hard; then began shaking his head back and forth from side to side in a pitying manner. He then leaned in and looked inside of the shower. As he did he began laughing, "I thought you were a better shot than that. It took you thirty rounds to 'get it'," he said.

Eventually after that, we got everything loaded up and we climbed aboard a helicopter that Mike and I just knew was going to be taking us to our deaths.

It flew us out into the middle of a very large valley that runs for at least a couple of miles in between two mountainous peaks that are completely covered in trees and green vines. As I looked at them, I knew that there were probably a million little slant-eyed gooks hiding in them just waiting until we landed to begin shooting me dead!

But, nothing happened after landing and letting us off. So, the drudgery and exhaustive work of filling sandbag after sandbag began. The first bunker we had to build was to protect all of our artillery ammunition. After that, it was time for us to build sandbag dugouts for ourselves to live in. All of this took most of the first day to do. All of this was after we had set the artillery guns up and made sure they were ready to fire.

During this time Mike and I were filling these sandbags and building us a place to protect us, and just possibly a place for us to sleep in, we were absolutely paranoid! I have no idea at all how our leaders could possibly think that we were 'leading' our unit into battle. What we were actually doing was making them just as paranoid as we were!

After doing all of this activity, it didn't take long for the enemy to realize we had gotten smack dab in the middle of their way! And they were hell-bent on no one slowing down their progress southward toward their ultimate target, Saigon. On the second day in this beautiful green valley, several mortar shells suddenly came flying in on us! At the same time down near the far end of our unit some very nervous combat virgins opened up with their M-16s and 60-caliber machine guns!

Then, a fraction of a second after that, huge, thunderous explosions suddenly began shaking the earth all around us! Thousands of chunks of flaming hot jagged shards of razor sharp shrapnel, along with huge clumps of black dirt and wet sod, exploded up into the sky and filled the air, making it hard to see and to breathe! But in that instant, we knew the enemy also had artillery guns with them, too!

But then, just as soon as the bombardment had started, it suddenly ceased. For the time being, I stayed where I was. I was trying to see if I could feel any pain, or see any blood, where I might have gotten hit. Thank God, though, other than a couple of small scratches across one leg, a deep scratch across my back, and a scratch across the top of one of my hands, I was not hurt.

I quickly crawled out of the blasted up bunker I had been hiding in, and then ran over to the howitzer. Once I got there I began screaming for some of our guys to "get over here and help me shoot this thing!" Four guys began running over immediately. As we got it prepared to shoot, suddenly, it was just like old times. A hot, rushing, flow of adrenaline began running freely throughout my entire being. "Let me have them!" I was screaming inside! Oh man, once again, I wanted to kill as many of the enemy as I possibly could!

In a matter of seconds, we got our cannon ready to fire. Then, we waited for the word to come down telling us the elevation and deflection to shoot. Within a minute or two, we began popping out round after round after round.

Eventually, we were told to stop shooting. A few minutes later the Sarge came hurrying up to Mike and me. He then asked for 'volunteers' to go out on a search mission to see how many dead or wounded enemy soldiers we could count, and to search their bodies. He looked at Mike and me with pleading eyes.

Staring straight back at him, I said with finality in my voice, "No!!! Don't even ask! Send the little S & B!"

Even though I felt God's hand of protection on me that was where I was drawing the line. I had done my part and had served my country honorably. Without a doubt, I had become a real 'menace' to the enemy, and to others. Now, it was someone else's turn. There was no way I was going out on a patrol into enemy territory just to count dead and wounded enemy soldiers and put myself into a position to get killed with just 'days' to go! I was thinking there was no rational reason for me to tempt God to remove His hand off my life!

Following this, Mike and I stayed in the field until we had only four days left. During that time, we had several more skirmishes with the enemy, but all in all, it was not too bad. Actually, being out there in the middle of some action kept my paranoia completely away. I guess it was because I was in a very familiar environment.

Eventually, though, the day came when I shook hands with everyone---including the little shake and bake---and climbed aboard a helicopter that would take Mike and me to Chu Lai. We had to stay at Chu Lai for two days before we were able to get down to Cam Rahn Bay. But for the full four days I spent in the rear waiting to leave Vietnam, I hardly ventured out of the hooches where I was staying, other than to eat and shower. I was not going to take any chances at all!

Finally, October 13, 1971 arrived and I went out into the bright sunshine to begin walking towards the most beautiful sight I had ever seen up to that time, a big, beautiful Freedom Bird that would be taking me home for good! As the plane became airborne, I turned to take one last look out the window at that beautiful South Pacific little country we all called Hell that would forever hold a special place in my heart!

Thus, the most incredibly demanding and demeaning year of my entire life came to an end! But, it's a sad, sad thing to be only twenty years old at the time you had to walk through the raging flames of hell!

This year had been the worst, most heartbreaking, most demanding, most terrible, most awful, most . . . year that I would ever have! But, it had also been the most exciting, most exhilarating, most outstanding, most adrenaline filled year of my life! It was a year that no matter what would ever happen to me from then on for the rest of my life, could ever top! I knew exactly what one of our astronauts had tried to express after returning back from the moon when he had said,---this is paraphrasing---'No matter whatever I do for the rest of my life, no matter what I may accomplish, or even the sum total of it all, could ever equal the excitement and thrill I have just experienced!'

I kind of know exactly what he experienced! Even though I have never walked on the moon, I have walked through The Raging Flames of Hell!!!

# Chapter 19

By the full grace of a very loving and merciful God, I had been able to physically escape the terrors and horrors of Hell with only having received a few bumps, bruises, and scars--- otherwise known as 'burns' from the fires of Hell---on my outer body!

While I was flying home on the beautiful 'Freedom Bird', I had plenty of time to think about some things. One thing; I realized that old preacher of my youth had been wrong about another thing about Hell. He had said no one can ever escape from the clutches of Hell. But, I knew different. I knew, because, I had just escaped from there!

Although I returned home believing at that time that I was physically unharmed, I knew I had come back very mentally and socially disturbed! How do you go from an environment where you are forced for a whole year of your life to kill, or attempt to kill, other human beings just so you can stay alive yourself? How can you do that and then come straight back from there to a seemingly civilized society where the terrifying Hell in Vietnam is basically nothing more than just a byword and an afterthought to most people? For most people, the Hell we went through were only stories they read about in newspapers and listened to on televisions and radios. Nothing more! Nothing less! Just stories!

I've never been able to find an answer to the above question, other than to say, "You can't go through the fires of Hell, and then come out of them without any burns on you! They burn way, way, too hot! It's going to take a long time for those burns to heal, if they ever will! And it's a sure guarantee that the scars from the burns will never heal but will last forever!"

I knew I had burns all over me from the top of my head down to the bottom of my feet! I also knew my insides were fried crisp, too! Especially my seared and scorched mind! Bottom line, I had burns that were so deep I didn't believe I had any kind of a chance of ever healing from them!

For quite a while after arriving home, I again, didn't want anything to do with anybody, especially my former friends. They just seemed so young and immature to me. In fact, to put it bluntly, they just seemed like silly little kids with their silly little kid so-called worries and trials and tribulations! What they thought was fun, I thought was stupid! The idea of excitement for them was stealing a six-pack of beer from the corner food store! "Oh, they chased me and almost caught me!" They had no clue whatsoever of what real 'worries', 'trials', and 'tribulations', were really like! Nor did they care!

But, I didn't want too much to do with my own family, either. I just wanted to be alone, and left alone! I needed time to think! I needed to somehow figure out a way that would allow me to be able to react to, and interact with people! At the time, I had no clue how I was going to do that. What was especially worrying to me was if someone happened to be stupid enough to get in my face, again, how was I going to react to that? Would my finely tuned and extremely sharpened reflexes instinctively take over, again? And if they did, would I violently try to kill that person? I had no idea about anything at all! All I knew was that if I could be alone by myself, the better it would be for not only me, but for everyone else, too!

In addition to my own troubling feelings, I still had several combat brothers who were still over there. At that time, they were still trying their best just to survive for another day without getting burned worse than they already were! I worried about them unceasingly, and prayed for them constantly!

My greatest desire was to be able to go back over there and be with them again! I wanted so much to try to help them survive until the times of their sentences in Hell would be completed and they could be set free, too! I now fully understood why many guys had to return for second and third tours of duty. In the insanity of it all, Vietnam was the only place where we felt 'normal!'

One night, when we were up near Laos, a grizzled and wrinkled looking old man with long, white hair that came down over his shoulders, and which was also falling out in large patches, and who was also spouting a scraggly white and grayish beard on his face, walked right into our unit without even being seen or heard. He came right through the concertina wire, trip flares, mines, and all! When he just suddenly appeared like out of thin air, we just about jumped out of our skins when we suddenly realized he was standing there in the middle of us.

But, that was how good he was in sneaking up on people. You see, he was an American sniper. These guys could be in the bush for months at a time, surviving off nothing but the land. And, they could crawl on their stomachs for miles at a time solely to fire just one bullet. But, that one bullet was the only one that was needed in most cases!

This old man, actually probably only in his early thirties, but looking like he was at least a hundred, told us he was on his fifth tour of Vietnam. His skin was old looking, tough as leather! He probably weighed no more than ninety to ninety-five pounds! He was a white guy but his skin was almost the color of tarnished brass! As he was talking to us, he said he couldn't come home! He said he had tried twice, but he had to come back to Hell each time. It's the only place where he felt normal. His home had become Hell!

I wondered, 'What could he come home to? What kind of a job could he ever get, or especially, hold onto? Could he, or would he, ever be able to fit back into society?' I also wondered, 'Can I myself?' And, the fires I've gone through are nothing compared to the fires that he's gone through.

I longed urgently to go back! But, I couldn't go back and I knew it. Hell was changing! My old unit, Charlie Battery, didn't exist anymore! My old stomping grounds, Firebase Charlie 2, didn't exist anymore! At least, not in the hands of the Americans!

No, Hell was changing! It was being turned over to untrained know-it-all officers fresh out of 'shake and bake' school. They were fresh out of school and thought they knew everything there was to know about how to fight a war and win it! Everything they had learned in all of their school books was all they would ever need, they thought. But let the elusive Charlie Cong or the well trained and well disciplined, professional serial killing soldiers of the North Vietnamese Army engage them a time or two, and all of them would be wetting their pants like little toddlers! Just like the little tweeb did at the firebase outside of Chu Lai! But, the really sad thing is, these school taught so-called 'leaders' would also be sending so many, good, young, extraordinary American soldiers straight to their deaths! You don't learn about war unless you experience war!

Unlike the Poodle at Chu Lai, my old Top Dog up at Charlie 2 knew how to fight a war and how to get the most out of his guys at the same time! His priority was not in how we looked or how we acted. As long as we fiercely engaged the enemy and also survived, that was all that mattered to him! He "cared" about us! He was a 'lifer' in the Army but he was not Army! He was, first and foremost, a 'true' leader! He had to be, because all of us in Charley Battery willingly and faithfully, followed him straight through the wide-open gates of Hell and all of the way straight through the sheer horrors and terrors of it all!

I knew that I couldn't go back to Hell, but, I also knew that I didn't fit into a normal civilized society anymore, either! I couldn't even relate to people. How could I? What could I say to them? What did I possibly have in common with normal people? What did I even know about being 'normal'?

Could I have a conversation with normal people about what it's like to kill other people? No! Although that is exactly what a lot of them wanted to know. Could I talk to normal people about barbecuing steaks? No! But, I certainly could have told them what well-done human flesh smells like after it's been seared and cooked by enemy rockets and mortars and such!

Could I talk about baseball or football scores? No! But I certainly could have told them about kill counts both sides accumulated! . . . As I said, I had nothing at all that I could even talk about to normal people!

Besides, I didn't care about people! In fact, I had so much hatred still remaining on the inside of me that that is the only way I felt about most people. There was an empty hole in my chest where my heart had once been! I seriously wondered if there would ever be a possibility for me to be able to hold 'love' in a place where there is nothing but an empty hole right now and where so much hatred has existed for so long! What is there to 'support' it?

I knew I was extremely sick on the inside, and probably would be for the rest of my life! I missed my family of combat brothers so much! These men really had actually become closer to me than my own actual family members! Oh man, I wanted so much, and needed even more, to return back to Hell again, even if I couldn't!

So, I say again, no one can experience the absolute horrors of the burning hot fires of Hell called war, and come out of it unscathed and unburned! A person who has gone through these horrors sees and hears everything around them, including invisible ghosts that don't even exist. They see every leaf that moves, especially when there is no wind that could be making it move! They hear every sound! Loud noises like a car backfiring will instantly cause a war weary ex-combat soldier to dive to the ground for cover faster than a blink of an eye. A screaming Air Force jet suddenly appearing overhead can sound just like an enemy rocket as it comes diving down on top of you! Again, a quick trip to the ground can instantly happen.

To be able to sleep in a nice, warm, fuzzy bed on real mattresses and to actually sleep in safety was something that was going to take me a lot of time to get used to. To be able to drive down the road, or walk down a street, or to just be out in an open space without fear of being shot was unnerving to me. I was so very jumpy! And, most of all, if I was asleep, no one had better touch me to wake me up!

# Chapter 20

Vietnam was always on my mind all. In fact, it was the first thing I thought about each morning when I woke up and the last thing I thought about before going to sleep. I still had friends over there and I worried about them daily. And, I missed it tremendously!

It took a week after coming home for me to find a job. It was not what I wanted nor was it the type of job I desired. It was only a job. You see, there was no way I was going to find a job I liked or wanted. What I wanted I couldn't have! I wanted something to soothe the intense, gnawing, craving inside of me that demanded excitement. Here I was only twenty-one years old and my excitement fuse had already been completely extinguished over in Vietnam! You see, there just aren't too many jobs available in the United States that can give you the thrill and excitement of being in a life or death situation such as a firefight with the enemy unless maybe you were to become a hitman for the mob.

So, with this craving inside of me going unfulfilled and leaving a huge, unquenchable fire that just wouldn't go out, I finally began hanging around with some of my old friends again. One night, one of them pulled out a joint of marijuana and lit it up. He then handed it to me. Once more, with my conscious decision to inhale an illegal intoxicating weed, I was again ensnared by Satan! Instantly, I fell lock, stock, and barrel right back into his trap all over again! And from that time on, I began to stay high as often as I could. I smoked the dope every chance I got.

I thought by smoking my brain into oblivion with marijuana, it would get rid of the demons from the hell I had gone through that were inside of me. I couldn't see them, but I sure could feel them! They were there, tormenting me every moment of every day and night!

One night I went looking for my friends to see if I could get some dope off them. My friends said they were out of the stuff but they knew where to go to get some more.

So, we climbed into one of their cars and left. There were four of us in the car. I was sitting in the back seat staring straight out the window, feeling like a ten-ton heavy weight was pushing down on top of me.

We found the place where we purchased more dope from some dopes. Then, in the wonderful mentality that all dopers have, we said, "Let's go party somewhere"; which happened to be on the edge of a cotton farmer's field way out in the boonies all by ourselves. ---Doesn't that sound like fun? No girls! No excitement! No nothing, but an old farmer's field! This was normally the way it always was with them, just as it is with most dopers!

A little later on as we sat in the car smoking the dope and filling it full with smoke, we neglected to see some headlights approaching. The car slowly got closer and eventually pulled up right next to us. Then, two of Phoenix's finest blue suited policemen climbed out and peered into our car.

"What are you boys up to?" they demanded, after we had rolled a window down, which allowed a solid white sheet of dope smoke to exit the vehicle. I'm surprised the cop leaning in the window didn't get stoned just from breathing this tainted white air!

"Nothing, sir. Just looking at the stars and admiring God's greatness!" we exclaimed!

"Well, why don't you boy's get out and let us check your car. You got any problems with that?"

We wanted to say, "Yes! We got a problem with that!" But, we didn't. We said go ahead, knowing our certain fate! Within just a few minutes after that, my hands were cuffed behind my back and my nose began itching real bad---Why does that always happen? Why is it when you can't scratch an itch that itch really itches bad? I just don't understand!

Later on that night, I wound up on the top floor of the Fourth Avenue jail in downtown Phoenix. It was in a holding cell with at least twenty others guys. Just a few short months before this, I had been in some very dangerous situations in Vietnam. I had survived all of those and had even felt a secure sense of bravery, or, a certain sense of pride to have faced death and not ran from it. But, looking around at all of the weirdoes, and worse, in that room with me, I was scared! But most of all, I was scared about going to prison for possession of drugs. I had just gotten out of a prison, of sorts---the Army---not too long ago, and now, I was scared about going to another different kind of prison. I knew inside that it was going to be another long night in my wasted lifetime of going without sleep!

I climbed onto a top bunk of one of the bunk beds and lay down to get away from the human trash heap that was occupying the holding cell with me. As I lay down, I began to stare at that stark old ceiling up above me. I wanted, with everything inside of me, to pray and ask God to get me out of another mess. But, I had lied to Him and I knew it. But what really mattered to me was that I knew that He knew it, too! No matter what I had said, or how I had tried to rationalize it, I knew that I had once promised God I would never touch drugs ever again, and I had now lied! I was now in jail because of drugs, and because of lying to God, and I was scared!

But, in total, complete humility, I did quietly cry out to God. I figured I had nothing to lose. I had always heard that God loves you no matter what you have ever done. Well, this was his chance to prove that! So, I said, "This time I really promise you! I promise you that if you will get me out of this mess, it will be the last mess you will ever have to get me out of again---I am sure God either rolled His eyes at that or got a real big laugh, or maybe even both, on that one---Most of all, I promise you, and I really mean it this time, that I will never use drugs ever again!"

Throughout that night, I lay there on that old bunk all night long thinking about how screwed up my life really was! Then, the next morning, I had to do just about the most humiliating thing I have ever done. I had to call my mom to tell her where I was. It broke her heart and I knew it! Man, I felt so bad! I felt so dirty and rotten! I really wanted to die! I even said to God, "Why didn't you let me die in Vietnam and then my parents could have been proud of me, but to be arrested for drugs, this is wrong!

Please let me have a way to make it up to them!"

My mom came down later on that morning and bailed me out. Her big brave war "hero" son couldn't even look her in the face. I felt such embarrassment! As we were driving home, she told me that a nationally known evangelist preacher was in town and holding a meeting that night, and I could make part---albeit a small part---of this up to her by going to the meeting with her.

But, it was a Friday. I was thinking, "There is no way I am going to be in a church service on a Friday night! Fridays are for partying! Besides, what would my friends say if they found out I went to church on a Friday? I would be the laughingstock of Phoenix!" But, I said, "Okay, Mom, I'll go with you. But, do me a favor and don't let any of my friends know about this, okay?"

Later on that evening, my Mom and I got in her car and we drove down to the meeting. It was being held in a large downtown auditorium because of the huge crowds. We walked in and I told her to look for a place to sit on the back row. I wanted to be close to the door in case some religious fanatics came towards me wanting to cast the devil out of me! But, she didn't do that. With her head held high and her shrinking violet son trailing slowly behind, she marched right down about two-thirds of way to the front!

Soon, the preacher began to speak. I don't remember much of his sermon, but whatever he said reached a small portion of my heart. At the end of the service, he asked if there was anyone who wanted to give 'all' of their hearts to Jesus. He said that if so, you needed to get up from your seat and come down to the front and kneel at the altar, and Jesus would meet you there.

He said that it didn't matter what kind of sins you had ever committed, or how many sins you had ever committed; Jesus would still meet you there and forgive you. He added another part, he said that even if there happened to be someone in the auditorium who had even lied to God, Jesus would still meet you there and forgive you.

Part of me wanted to go. I knew that God had told him to add that last part just for me. I knew there was no one else in that service that had ever lied to God, but me! But, I couldn't force myself to go. "What would my friends think? What could I do for fun if I were to become a Christian? How could I ever experience happiness as a Christian? And besides, it's Friday! I could never become a Christian on a Friday! I would just never be able to live that one down!"

I had a million excuses and God was making me use all of them. The best one of all, "I tried this before and failed! I don't have the guts to do it again!"

But, for as long as I could remember, Saturday has always followed Friday. When I got up Saturday morning, I knew immediately, right then, first thing, I was going to go back to that church service that night. There had been something in that meeting that I had never experienced before. I didn't know for sure what it was, but I wanted to feel it one more time.

It was such a good feeling! It had almost felt like "LOVE!!!" Which was a totally foreign concept to me! Even when I had really thought I had loved the little blonde girl, I knew that I had never truly felt love. At least, not this kind of love I was seeing at this meeting! It was something special! This was something I had never felt before, or even knew existed! It seemed to be love for me!

That might not mean too much for most people, but when you have lived your life for the last year with an unbelievable amount of hatred consuming every pore, cell, molecule, and atom of your entire being, and when you know, without a single doubt, that the place in your heart where love is supposed to be held is nothing but an empty tomb with a huge hole in it, the

sheer prospect of finding just a 'nugget' of love means more than millions of dollars to me!

So, I called up one of my best friends and told him everything that had happened. All about going to jail and having to have my mom bail me out, and about going to that church service, and everything. I was right! When I mentioned that I had gone to church the night before, he said, "Man that was on a Friday! You don't go to church on a Friday!" He laughed.

At first, I was humiliated! Then, I started making excuses like, "I know, but my mom bailed me out, so I owed it to her! You know, it wasn't my idea. I was only doing it for her!" Then, I thought, this is stupid!

I said, "Hey man, you know what? This is Saturday, and you know what, you're going to go with me back to that church service tonight, on a *'Saturday night'*! And, if you give me any trouble about it, I'm going to make you sit with me on the front row! Got it?"

Later on that evening, my friend and I hooked up and we headed for the church service. The way the inside of this large auditorium was constructed was as you walked in the doors at the back, you could see a large number of rows of seats on the main floor. These sloped gently downward to a raised stage at the front. Also, along both sides of the auditorium and running parallel to the main floor, were two balconies. As you sat in these, you looked out over the congregation that was seated on the main floor. On the south side balcony is where my friend and I sat for the Saturday night service!

And just like what had happened at the Friday night service, happened again on Saturday night. There was something going on that I didn't know exactly what it was, but I could feel this Presence flowing and moving over the entire congregation! I could sense an awesome feeling of respect and of power in that place! More than anything else though, I could feel a deep feeling of love that was consuming everyone present!

As I gazed out over the congregation from my seat high up along the side, I could see in the people's faces that they had something I wanted. They had something I didn't have, and I wanted it! I didn't know for sure what 'it' was, but I wanted whatever 'it' was. Some of the people were standing there with their heads bowed in deep respect and reverence. Others had their faces lifted skyward with tears flowing down their cheeks. Still, others had their hands lifted up in praise and honor to their Savior, Jesus Christ, and to their God, the Father! And, on all of their faces were glows of radiance and happiness!

Whatever these people had that made them so happy and so much in love, I had to have! I was one miserable puppy with no direction in life! I was searching for something that would satisfy the cravings of my inner being. I had only found that something once and it was a satanic imitation of what these people had. What I had found had been filled with hatred, and with the shedding of blood and death. But, what these people were experiencing, at least it seemed to me, was LIFE and LOVE! And, I wanted it!

But, I was sitting there with one of my best friends and I was too intimidated to do or say anything in front of him. Isn't that just about the most stupid thing you have ever heard? I had stood in the face of incoming bullets and exploding rockets and blasting artillery, and even before four enemy soldiers with their weapons trained right on my heart and I had not surrendered to fear. But, one friend, my best friend, who was probably feeling the same way I was, kept me from going after what these people had!

He did not do anything to stop me. Just his presence there was enough. If I were to go down to the front, I was afraid he would laugh at me. 'Peer pressure'! But, let me emphasize again, he did not do anything to stop me. I was listening to the voice of Satan only. I am sure that if I had been man enough to go down to the front of that auditorium, my friend would have gone with me.

After the service, we walked out and began heading towards my car. At first, we didn't say too much to each other. Finally, I said, "Well, what did you think about it?" He replied, "I don't know. What did you think about it?" I replied, "I don't know, but I asked you first anyway."

You get the picture. Two stupid guys feeling the presence of Almighty God drawing them to Him, and we were too embarrassed or intimidated of each other to say anything.

Then, I did say, "Well, you know what, the final service is at 2:00 o'clock tomorrow afternoon, Sunday. I think I might come back to it. What do you think?"

He replied, "Yeah. You know, maybe I will too. But, we need to get the other guys to come with us, also."

"Yeah! Good idea!" I said.

So, Sunday afternoon, there were four of us sitting up in the balcony in the same area as we had sat the night before. This time, the service was fantastic. I still do not know what the preacher preached about but I know what the Holy Spirit of God was saying to my heart. He was saying, "Son, it's time you now come back home! Come back home to me! I love you! I have never given up on you! I have been patient and have let you go on your own and continue to mess up your life all by yourself. But I have been patiently waiting for you to let me in to help you. I desire to help you if you will only let me! I desire to make you my own son! You are mine! You belong to me but you have lived for the devil for all of these years. Now, give me a chance! Give me a chance to show you what I can do for you. *I have come that you may have life and have it more abundantly!"*

I leaned over to my friend and said, "This is it! I'm doing it! Once and for all, I'm going all the way with God! You coming with me?"

He looked at me real sternly. I could see in his eyes that he wanted to come with me. I could see that he desired to get right with God! But the lurid lures of this world was too strong for him.

I got up from my chair and walked towards the back of the building to get to the stairs to go down to the bottom floor. As I reached the main floor, I could have turned right and went straight out of the door to the outside. Satan tried to get me to do this. In fact, I could feel a satanic hand pushing me to go outside. But, I leaned back against this push. Momentarily, it became a struggle for me. I was pushing to go down to the front and I was being pushed by Satan to go outside! Suddenly, the push gave way and I almost toppled over onto my side. But as I began falling, it made me begin to run to keep from falling, and I ran all of the way down to the front of the place.

By then, I couldn't wait to get to that altar. God had come all the way to the back of the auditorium and had ripped Satan's hands off me. Now, He was leading me by the hand towards my destiny which is salvation through Jesus Christ! With each step I took, the stain and filth of all of the sins I had harbored inside of me began to disappear! By the time I reached the front, tears of joy and of cleansing were washing down my face! I was having an encounter with the Creator of the entire universe and I was overwhelmed!

I had never in my life felt so clean and pure! I had never in my life felt so much joy! I had never in my life felt such peace! But, most of all, I had never in my life felt such love!

I fell totally, absolutely, head over hills in love with Jesus, with God, and with the Holy Spirit! And, I could feel their love for me! I could feel their love for me even more than I could feel my love for them! It didn't matter to God what I had ever done. He no longer cared about my sins! Through Jesus, all of my sins were forgiven! But, not only were they forgiven, in the instant that I had been forgiven, God even forgot them! He removed them from me as far as the east is from the west! As far as He was concerned, it was like I had never even committed any of them! As He was looking at me, it was the same thing as if He were looking at Jesus! Jesus is His Son! Now, so was I!

But would all of my troubles now be over? Would God remove all of the seared burns and scars inside of my tormented mind? Would I now suddenly be 'normal' because of my acceptance of Jesus?

# Part 2
# Chapter 1
# Interlude

During the time I spent in Hell, I had been forced to become a well-trained and dedicated serial killer! This was because our blood thirsty enemies were just as equally trained and dedicated serial killers, too! When I finally escaped out of the flaming hot fires of Hell, I knew I was responsible for a lot of enemy deaths! But, I never felt much remorse for those killings. I always felt, "it's either kill, or be killed!" I survived! Therefore, very little remorse ever existed in my life for these killings! Plus, I rationalized that these killings were of Godless Communists! They were atheists! They didn't believe in God, at least not the true God! So, they were of their father, Satan.

But, it was all of the other things I had gone through in the fires of Hell that bothered me after returning home. As was the norm at the time, there was no distinction whatsoever, between soldiers who were active participants in 'killing', and those who served in rear-echelon mostly safe and secure areas. So, when I returned home, it was like letting my well trained and ferocious guard dog, very aptly named Bear, loose on some home-invaders!

I was turned loose to my home without any counseling or help of any kind from the military! It was like they said, "Here! You've only killed twenty, thirty . . . a hundred or more people in the last year! What's your problem? Can't you just put that behind you and be normal like everyone else? What difference does it make if you held a friend in your arms for the last ten minutes of his life after his entire lower body was completely blown off? What difference does it make if you still hear his screaming cries of, "My legs hurt! My legs hurt!" every stinking night as you close your eyes to go to sleep?

What difference does it make that when you went to tell his parents you were there and that you held his head in your lap while his life forces bled out of him, that it was the hardest thing you had ever done in your whole life? What difference does it make that a heroic helicopter pilot you had just rescued out of his crashed chopper had his head cut off from a large piece of shrapnel while you were carrying him across your shoulder, while that piece of shrapnel was really meant for you? What difference does it make? What difference does it make if you had to help dig the blown apart bodies of twenty-nine heroic American heroes out of an old dirt covered club?

"Huh? What difference does it make? It's just, 'Here you go big boy; come on home and handle things like a man!'"

Every day and night quickly became an on-going continuous battle for the survival of my emotions and my mind. No matter what the Army has said, it will always be a full-fledged battle I'll have to fight. This one will be never ending! The burns from the fires will always be there! They go too deep to ever heal!

Even though I had accepted Jesus Christ into my life, I still had these burns and scars from the fires of Hell to deal with! The Bible says we reap what we sow. That is true in every aspect of our lives! Every experience we go through during our lifespan affects us in some way or another. Again, in the words of the Lord, 'we reap what we sow', whether it is good or bad! So, I still have the reaping to do from what I sowed---or experienced--- while in the flames! And, I always will!

Yes, God in His mercy could take everything away, but if He were to do that, he would have to erase my entire memories. He will not do that. Those memories are a big part of what, and who, I am! But what God does do for us, though, is He steers us to a way that we can find help, in one way or the other.

What He did was to show me a couple of things I could use to try to help put things behind me, and which helps me to survive. The first thing I do is to try to inject some form of humor into most things in life.

To me, humor helps to neutralize and soothe some of the pain I always carry around on the inside. The Holy Bible says in Proverbs 17:22 "A joyful heart is good medicine, but a crushed spirit dries up the bones."

So, I need to smile to survive! I need to laugh to heal! I need to do any and every 'thing' I possibly can to try to forget! Otherwise, my bones will dry up! But, it seems, a lot of the 'humor' I use is tongue-in-cheek sartorial, and many, many people have no idea at all what this is! Where I see humor, they don't! When I laugh, they can't! What I think is funny, they have no clue!

So, this leads me to the other thing I do to try to survive, and that is to totally get as far away from civilization, and thus, 'people', as possible. I do not like most people! I do not enjoy their company! I know the Bible says that we are supposed to 'love' people, but I just can't do that for most of them! There are just too many of them that I would rather get away from than try to love! Hopefully, God understands and forgives me for this! But, my personal feeling about this is, there are just an awful lot of people in this world that only God, Himself, can love!

Even though I have accepted Jesus Christ into my life, I still cannot stand to be around a lot of these people. I don't feel like I fit in. Or to put it more succinctly, I don't even want to try to fit in with them! What their civilization is, is not the same as mine! What their warped and slanted beliefs are, are not mine! I'm not a part of their society, and don't want to be! I'm an outcast, just the way I want it! So, I like to be by myself as much as I possibly can!

To do this, I 'love' to go out into my beloved, Sonoran Desert that surrounds my home in the suburbs of Phoenix, Arizona. I do this as often as I can. I have lived in Phoenix since I moved here with my parents, an older sister, and a younger brother during the summer of 1963. That was also during the summer that I turned 13 years old.

By spending a lot of time out in the desert all by myself, I have often thought that I could live just perfectly fine as an old hermit all by myself without ever having, or needing, the company of another human being. That doesn't make my wife very happy, but she knows where I'm coming from. She has sometimes expressed the same thing, too. She is the only one on this entire earth, other than other combat brothers who have also managed to survive the horrors and terrors of the fires of Hell that really understands and accepts me! She is also the only one who knows most of my darkest secrets! She has been by my side every time I have woken up in the middle of the night dreaming and screaming, "Gooks in the wire!", or, "My legs hurt!", or, "KILL 'em! Kill 'EM!"

But, even so, even with her, unless she has heard me talking in my sleep, I have held a few things back! There are just some things that I can never, and will never, bring forth into the light of day! Or, into the hearing of another person. Because, if I were to, these dark horrors would instantly pierce and wound their soul to the point of no return! They would never be 'normal' again, either, after that! It just would not be fair of me to sear and scorch, and thus, damage forevermore the mind and soul of another person with the worst of the horrors that took place inside the boundaries of Hell! I will not make anyone else live the rest of their lives with some of the unspeakable horrors that took place in there! These memories must stay buried forever inside the dark recesses of my own soul until I have to stand before God on judgment day. At that time, I will either be declared sin free, or I will be declared guilty and returned back to Hell! Heaven or Hell! I'll find out then, just as everyone else who has ever lived will, too!

# Chapter 2

When I had first moved to Phoenix, I immediately fell in love with the place! I became a wide-eyed, open mouthed, wonder-filled youth! Phoenix was a huge city to me with an unlimited amount of things to do and see.

I had moved here from a little town located on the dusty, wind-swept, extremely ugly flat planes of West Texas that had less than 35,000 people in it. My sister and I used to ride our bikes all over that little town in just a few hours' time. We lived on the east side and my grandparents lived on the west side of it, so we would often ride from our home over to our grandparents, and back again easily in a day's time. Phoenix, though, was much, much too large for us to ever ride a bike from one side of it to the other.

To me, the city of Phoenix, the beautiful Sonoran Desert that encompasses it, and the numerous rock-strewn mountains that intersperse and surround what is called, 'The Valley of the Sun', were wild, exotic, and mysterious places. I was young and impressionable and these wild, exotic, and mysterious places called out and drew me in the same way as iron shavings are uncontrollably pulled towards an enormous magnet! I could hardly wait until I turned 16 years old so I could get my driver's license. I could hardly wait until I could go exploring around, over, under, and through them all!

What kind of treasures could I find in those places? What unlimited riches did they hold? What history had happened in them! What had the tall Saguaro Cactus's seen in their lifetimes? The Saguaros live for well in excess of 100 years. In fact, they have to be in the area of around eighty years old before they can even grow an 'arm'. So, when I moved here, many of them had been around since the Civil War was being fought. Many of them were around when Indians were the only inhabitants who lived and traveled in these parts. Some of them may have even been around when Montezuma and the first Spanish Conquistadors marched across the desert.

If these unique and beautiful desert dwellers had a brain and could only talk, what could they tell us of the past? As a teenager, I had to find out! This is Arizona, man! A history full of outlaws and cowboys, of gunfights and deaths, legends and lore's, and most of all, enormous amounts of buried treasures of gold, silver, and copper!!

On the same day that I turned sixteen years of age, I got my driver's license. But also on that same day, something unnatural swooned over and took possession of me. When I woke up that morning, the spirit and drive of the great explorer, Marco Polo, was flowing through my entire mind and body. But now, with a driver's license and an explorer's unlimited drive and energy racing through my being, I had the freedom to go explore these wild, exotic, and mysterious places I had so longingly gazed at every day of my life since the first day I had moved here.

But, the family car was not the best vehicle to go romping through the deeply rutted trails, washed out ravines, and small arroyos with; or even speeding across open desert vistas chasing jack-rabbits. Nor did my parents ever give their explicit approval for their car to be used for those purposes. In fact, if I remember back to those long ago glorious times of yesteryear, I seem to remember my parents giving me their explicit instructions to "NOT" use their vehicle to take into the desert.

So, I saved up my money and I was eventually able to buy an old, beat up, and barely running, 1956 Pontiac, for $25 dollars from an acquaintance of mine. From there, I went to work creating a new masterpiece of space age engineering by converting it from a beat up old car into a wonderful, desert exploring, custom designed sand-buggy, made to go rocking and rolling across the desert in.

After that, with Marco Polo propelling me towards new and great adventures, I was ready to go see the lost world of the desert I so longed to explore! So with canteens of water for me and my buddies, along with our trusty 22-caliber rifles by our sides to protect us from all of the wild, exotic beasts we may occur that live on, above, and under the desert, we drove that old buggy all over the surrounding deserts, and sometimes even up into the pine-tree covered, Bradshaw Mountains, north of Phoenix.

During the few years we explored these places before I was suddenly jerked out of my idyllic lifestyle at the tender age of nineteen to go fight in a very unpopular war in Hell, we found all kinds of exotic and wonderful places! A lot of these places were exciting old abandoned mines. Some of these old mines had tunnels carved out of solid rock and were slanting horizontally way back into the sides of mountains. Others were just deep holes going straight down way into the earth in the middle of the flat desert floor. A few of these old mines had some old wooden shacks that were still partially standing after nearly eighty to one-hundred years where the old miners had taken refuge from the elements in.

Every one of these places was always exciting and fun places to explore. But we never knew if and when, an old miner's ghost would suddenly jump out and grab us. On several occasions, I know we were visited in the middle of the night by some of these apparitions! If not for real, then certainly in our very ripe and vivid imaginations!

Ah, I was so much in love with these rock-strewn, cactus covered mountains that intersperse and surround my home. But most of all, I was deeply in love with the enormous beauty and empty solitaire of my own desert playground!

After returning back home from my journey through Hell, the first thing I did was to head back out into my beloved desert playground. I could hardly wait to get back out into the beauty of the place! But most of all, I could hardly wait just to be able to bask in the serenity and peace that filled the entire place!

Since coming home I have literally spent hours, days, and sometimes, even weeks out in the desert. I'm usually all by myself. I'm out there trying to take my mind away from the inner torments and mental agonies that are continually raging through me! And like I did as a teenager, I do this mostly by exploring old abandoned mines.

Often times when I'm out in my beloved desert playground, I think about people paying thousands of dollars to lay for an hour on a therapist's expensive couch while they supposedly listen to you pouring your heart out to them. I don't need to pay thousands of dollars for that. I have all of the therapist I need only about twenty miles away from my home in the middle of the world's most beautiful desert garden. That is where I have the extreme pleasure to commune with the greatest 'Therapist' of all, the One who originally created it all!

# Chapter 3

It has now been forty some odd years since I spent a full year in the horrors of Hell! But, I wasn't aware that during the first thirty-seven years after leaving Hell, deadly physical attacks were still being launched against me! I thought those deadly attacks were way over with! I thought all I had left to deal with were the scars from the burns I suffered in Hell. But because of our government's reckless actions of spraying huge quantities of Agent Orange---a known health destroyer and killer---over large areas of Hell, this internal war has been continually fighting on the inside of me since that year in Hell.

The accumulated effects from these attacks finally came to a head a few years ago. Unable to prolong the fight any further, my body suddenly took a rapid, almost lethal nosedive face first onto the canvas of life for the full count of ten!

I've now basically become a sixty year old decrepit and disabled old man. During the last three years, I have undergone two major operations; been diagnosed with more major diseases than Webster's Dictionary has room for; taken more medications than the Mexican Drug Cartel has made and distributed; spent eleven months on chemotherapy treatment; been declared disabled by both the Veterans Administration and Social Security; and lost my own profitable business I had created and run for many years!

I had started, owned, and managed my own company business for many years. For most of the time I owned that business, I spent 10 to 14 hours every stinking day, 6, and sometimes even 7 days a week, working to earn a living for my family and myself. And when I lost that business, my wife and I also lost everything the income from that business provided for us, including our beautiful, 5000' sq. ft., luxury home!

But now, I'm finally beginning to feel like doing a few things again. I can, once again, stand on my feet and even walk for certain distances. Although, on most occasions when I do that, I use a cane for support. But basically overall, I finally feel like I'm getting some of my old life back!

I'm sick and tired of doing nothing but lying around the house all day long almost every day. I'm sick and tired of being a burden to my wife! I'm sick and tired of being basically useless! Man, I'm just sick and tired of being 'sick and tired'! So, since I'm feeling somewhat better, I've decided that after a little more than three years of being away, I want to go back out into my favorite place to play. And, that's the great big beautiful Sonoran Desert that surrounds my home here in Phoenix.

Marco Polo's spirit is still inside of me! It has never left me ever since it entered into me on the day I turned sixteen. I have now been totally fascinated with the desert for well over 44 years of my life. So, I told my wife I want to go back out into the desert come the next Saturday. This time, I asked her if she would want to come with me. I told her I had the need to go back to my favorite therapy clinic so I could be closer to God. My youngest daughter, Irma, and her two kids, heard about us going and asked if they could come, too. Her husband, Wyatt, unfortunately has to work and can't make the trip with us.

My wife and youngest daughter, I'm sure, want to keep an eye on me to make sure I don't exert too much energy and effort doing something I shouldn't be doing, or trying to do, yet. I had been so sick for so long, I'm sure they are still very much worried. Besides, I now have diabetes and Parkinson's disease to deal with, along with thyroid problems, etcetera, etcetera, etcetera, all due to the effects of the Agent Orange!

But, through everything, the love and draw of the desert is still in me after all of these years. Every chance I have now as I get better, I want to get away from it all and go back out there and explore. It will take my mind off things! It will get me away from idiot people, too! Plus, there is something new to find every time I go out into the desert! Maybe not gold or silver; I've only found just small traces of those in all of these years. But other treasures; like the best treasure of all and that is just being with my family for the day away from the hustle and bustle and pain and sickness of everyday existence. That, in itself, is the greatest treasure I have ever found!

So, I'm believing that this coming Saturday is going to be a very good day for me! Approximately 19 years ago when I had been out communing with the great Therapist all alone, I had once found and partially explored an old abandoned mine. We're going to try to find that old mine, again. For some reason, I have a deep feeling that there is something of great value that is waiting for me inside of that old mine! It's like I'm being drawn to it or something! I've even had dreams about it that I need to find it again.

# Chapter 4

My wife, Precious, our youngest daughter, Irma, and Irma's two kids, 'Bronco Nagurski', her three year old son, and our little goddess, Venus, her one year old daughter, and I are going to go find the missing pot of gold I have left behind during all of my other expeditions out into the wild Arizona desert.

'Precious' is not my wife's real name. It's Rebecca. But ever since the very first time I laid eyes on her many years ago, I have called her Precious, because that was, and still is, what she is to me! Precious and I have now been married for 38 years and it's just as good now as it was the first time I ever fell in love with her, which was the first time I had laid eyes on her and began calling her Precious!

God blessed Precious and me with five kids. Now, though, they're all grown up, all of them married, and all with kids of their own. Most of the time that leaves just Precious and me alone to care for our three dogs. But not today, Irma and her two little terrors are joining us on a new and exciting adventure into the wilds of the Arizona desert!

Irma is now 24 years old. She is a magnificently beautiful girl who looks remarkably like her mom, Precious. Most of the time, she has beautiful dark auburn hair; that is if she hasn't spoiled it again, by dyeing it some ungodly color, which she does quite often at odd times when she is temporarily, but totally, insane. Along with her dark auburn hair, she has beautiful brown eyes that perfectly accent her high arched cheekbones. She inherited those from my Comanche Indian great-grandma.

Irma, along with every one of our other kids, and especially me, have inherited great things from my Comanche Indian great-grandma; like a wonderfully expressive temper. We can all get very loud and authoritative at certain times. At those times, with Precious' very controlled, organized, and perfection driven German heritage keeping her in perfect peace and harmony, she just rolls her eyes, shakes her head, and waits for the hurricane, or better yet, hurricane(s), to pass.

Now, I know what you're thinking. After that description of Irma, how could I give her a name like Irma? Well, Irma is not my daughter's real name, either. It's Rachael. But I had begun calling Rachael, Irma, when she was just a little toddler, just teasing her. The name just stuck. Rachael hated the name, Irma; still does, but she loves her dad, and thus, she puts up with it.

Now, as I'm sure, you probably also realize that Bronco Nagurski is not my grand-kid's real name, either. His real name is Buzz Lightyear to the Rescue! … … … No, I'm sorry. I just said that until I could remember what his real name really is. Since I don't ever call him by his given name, I couldn't remember it right then. But now I do, it's Wyatt, like his dad's name. But getting back to why I call him Bronco Nagurski, it's because ever since 'Bronco' learned to run---not walk, but run---when he was eight months old, he has 'run' into and over, any and everything, in his way. This is the only way he knows to do it. To run around something is just not part of his makeup. He just lowers his head, puts his right arm out in front of him in a perfect imitation of the Heisman Trophy, and bores his way through any and everything in his path! Thus, I stuck the name of Bronco Nagurski onto my big 'guy', which is in honor of the great old leather-helmeted running back of the old Chicago Bears.

Right now, Bronco is taking more and more after his old 'Papa' as he gets older. I can see it as plain as day. He, too, has been infused with the spirit of Marco Polo. At his tender age of almost three, he already has a full blown rambling and exploring spirit inside of him, and I'm sure that one day, he will take the place of his old Papa and continue the search of the magnificent desert for all of the lost treasure that has remained hidden from me!

Last, but most definitely not least, is the little goddess. And, I'm sure that you'll probably not believe this, but Venus really is the name of our precious little girl goddess. Since she really is a little goddess, no new moniker is needed.

# Chapter 5

In getting ready for our trip, I made a mental note to be sure to bring my guns with me. I have never gone into the desert without my trusty old 22-caliber rifle. But now, I also have a 9-mm pistol. The desert is usually a fun and exciting place to go and explore. But within the last few years, there has been such an invasion of illegal border crossers coming into our state from across our southern border that in many places of the desert, it is no longer safe for us legitimate citizens of our own country to venture out in. So especially, with my family and my precious grand-kids going with me this time, I'm certainly going to try to be prepared for whatever may come our way!

My wife, Precious, will have no problem with me taking my guns when we go. But, she does have a problem with me keeping my 9-mm locked and loaded underneath my pillow on our bed every night. I keep a full magazine in the handle of the gun and another full magazine in the holster I keep the gun in.

Precious just doesn't like the gun being under my pillow. She thinks its overkill in preparedness and I'm just being paranoid! I tell her I'm not being paranoid; I'm just being ready and prepared like I was in Vietnam. When I was over there, my fully locked and loaded M-16 was never more than an arm's reach away from my side. We were under a constant siege then, and I truly believe we are under a constant siege now. Albeit, it's a different kind of siege we're going through at this time. But, it is without a doubt, every bit as dangerous of a siege as it was in Vietnam!

In Vietnam, where I was stationed at along the DMZ that supposedly separated South Vietnam from North Vietnam, we were in a constant battle with what were in effect, illegal border crossers. They were the thousands of North Vietnamese crossing the border of South Vietnam in an illegal invasion. Those illegal border crossers main intentions were to destroy the lifestyles, the economy, and the legally elected government of South Vietnam.

They were trying their best to take the entire country of South Vietnam over and convert it to their own way of life, economy, and government! Which they eventually accomplished because the majority of the people of South Vietnam refused to stand up and put a stop to the invasion no matter what the costs or consequences! This led to untold hardships, agony, and misery for the people of South Vietnam. It also led to an untold number of their deaths, too!

A few years ago, I had the extreme pleasure of meeting a 'legal' immigrant and his wife who were both originally from South Vietnam. These very fine people had been able to immigrate to the United States through the 'legal' mechanism that our government has long had established and in place. I got the opportunity to spend some time to speak with this gentleman and his wife.

When South Vietnam fell to the North in 1975, both the husband and wife were each just twelve years old in their respective families. They didn't know each other then. Both families, though, lived in the area around Saigon. The husband's dad had been a government school teacher under the South Vietnamese regime. The wife's dad was a former South Vietnamese soldier who had been wounded and was disabled.

After the country fell, both sets of parents---husbands and wives---were taken away from their families. They were then put in "Re-Education" camps out in the rural areas of the country. Both sets of parents spent over eight years in these camps before the conquerors decided they had been sufficiently rehabilitated.

After their parents were taken away from the families, both the husband and wife were then left in charge of the remaining members of their families because they were the oldest child at that time. The husband had three younger siblings and the wife had two. All of these kids in both families, plus hundreds of thousands of others just like them throughout the rest of the country, had no other choice than to become thieves and beggars to survive.

But what is really, really sad, is that both had younger sisters who had no other choice but to turn to prostitution to survive or face death through starvation. One of them was nine years old, the other was eight! Prostitutes! How sad! They shouldn't even know about sex at that age!

I could go on and tell you a lot more of what they had told me. But, I won't! As I sat there and listened to them, all of that old hatred I thought had been suppressed and gone, once again instantly began to build up inside of me towards their so-called army soldiers! In fact, tears welled up in my eyes as I thought about that!

Things had not needed to be that way! The South Vietnamese military had every advantage possible in their war with North Vietnam! They had better, and more weapons of every sort than the North Vietnamese had! They had a much larger Air Force and we had trained them to be the best! They had a vast numerical advantage in personnel! They had a much richer and more prosperous economy than the North! In fact, they had everything better! They had everything better, but one thing! That is, they did not have the will to stand up and fight to keep their country free!

They both, being the very polite and well-mannered people that their Asian culture instills in them, saw my tears and asked me why? I tried to explain what I had went through over there and of what I had seen with my own eyes about their soldiers not wanting to fight to keep their country free. I told them that it hadn't needed to be the way it turned out for them! If their soldiers would have only been willing to fight the North could have never defeated the South!

They knew that already! They knew that it was their own country's fault that they fell! They held no blame, whatsoever, towards me or the US! They both told me, "We have no one to blame but ourselves! Our parents never suspected it would be as bad as it became!

"No! We don't blame you! We appreciate everything that you, and all of the other Americans who were over there, did for us!"

But, this is exactly the same thing that is happening in our own country of the United States of America right now! I'm not being paranoid! Let me repeat myself, the exact same thing that happened in South Vietnam is happening in our own country right now!

Specifically, the ones who are most affected by these illegal border crossers are the individual states of California, Arizona, New Mexico, and Texas. All of these are states that border with Mexico. And, all of these states, or portions thereof, were once a part of Mexico.

Let me tell you something you had better believe as the absolute truth, Mexico wants it back! And, whether you believe it or not, the actual government of Mexico is sending untold millions of illegal border crossers across our lawful and legal border to try to accomplish that exact thing, just like North Vietnam did!

But, the majority of these illegal border crossers, instead of using weapons to try to win these states back by violence, are using procreation and our free medical care that our stupid and insane government gives to them to mass produce 'anchor babies' in huge, uncountable quantities, to shift the population to make them the majority! And, when these anchor babies grow up to be legal age, they will then take over our cities, our towns, our states, our governments, and most of all, our way of life!!!

But, this is very, very important! I stated that the 'majority' does not use violence, but there are thousands of them that do! These are the members of the Mexican Drug Cartels and the gang members who walk in goose steps with them! All of these would just as soon kill you as to look at you!

So again, I tell my wife I am not being paranoid, I'm just being ready for the inevitable to happen. All four of these Border States that share a border with Mexico are literally being invaded by human waves of illegal border crossers, just like what happened in South Vietnam. But, this is not just a problem associated with the four Border States only, once these illegal invaders come across our borders, many of them quickly disperse throughout our entire country.

So, with all of these illegal alien border crossers, along with all of the Mexican Drug Cartel drug carriers that on a daily basis are invading our state in the same manner as a North Vietnamese ground attack, the violence associated with them is inevitable! Every stinking day of the year, all we hear about on the news is that these illegals have invaded people's houses! And most of the time, they have used potentially lethal violence in these invasions! If you haven't heard yet, Phoenix is the kidnapping capital of the United States. And, all of that is due to the massive influx of crime that is a direct result of this massive illegal invasion that is taking place in our state!

# Chapter 6

What I am about to say is not a rant, nor is it racial prejudice being spouted from a crazed far right winger like the blue blooded, bleeding heart, biased based, liberal slanted media will scream and declare I am if they see this. But, this is an actual fact, and a fact is something that stands on its own without prejudice! It also is something that cannot be challenged or refuted!

### *A FACT IS A FACT IS A FACT!*

Although, again, the biased based, blue bleeding liberals in our woefully broken society will certainly try to 'twist' the facts of this 'fact' to suit the story in the way they want it slanted! Need I say any more than to go back a few years to give you the perfect example of this phenomenon that only an elitist liberal could actually think up? It was back when an extremely horny sitting President of the United States, who could not keep his own pants pulled up and zipped, tried to confuse the 'facts' of an investigative case against him by trying to get us to focus our attention on what 'is' is? Trying to determine what 'is' is, is the way a bleeding heart, biased based, blue blooded liberal mind works. It is totally unorthodox and without any rhyme or reason or even of common sense! It is a blatant attempt to try any and everything to confuse and deflect 'normal', middle of the road, centrist people from determining what the true 'facts' of a fact are.

Another example; this same horny cowboy of a president wanted all of us very stupid and ignorant Americans to believe that he attempted to smoke marijuana but without inhaling it! First of all, let me ask this question; who in their ever-loving mind would believe that someone would take a lit marijuana joint, bring it up to their lips, suck on it to pull the mind warping synthesizing smoke into your own mouth, and then spit the "stuff" out before inhaling it?

Only a biased based bleeding heart liberal who is narcissistic enough to truly believe that he is smarter than everyone else in the entire country, and therefore, whatever he says will be believed as the gospel truth by everyone who listens to his lies! A person who is not going to inhale the smoke of a joint is not going to put it to their lips in the first place!

But just as Joseph Goebbels, the Nazi Propaganda Minister under Adolf Hitler once declared, 'you can tell any lie you want, no matter how big it is or how blatant it is. But as long as you keep telling it often enough, and with a straight face, people will then begin to believe it'! (Paraphrased)

So, to all of the rest of us so-called, stupid, middle of the road Americans, who actually have the intelligence to think for ourselves and to determine what is truth on our own without the need of a biased based, blue blood bleeding liberal to tell us what manner of truth they want us to believe, the 'fact' of this matter is, I have a friend who works in law enforcement, and this friend has provided me with unimpeachable information of a documented 'fact' that's based on actual booking statements. In other words, this "fact" is in "black & white"! Or, digital!

This fact states that 85% percent of all inmates in the Maricopa County jail complexes are of Hispanic heritage. Maricopa County includes almost all of the entire metropolitan area of Phoenix along with a very large section of the surrounding desert. Let me state this again, all of the county jail complexes combined throughout Maricopa County contain a Hispanic population of 85% percent! But this is in direct contrast to the entire general population of Maricopa County which has a total Hispanic population of less than 35% percent of the entire population.

So let me ask; why is it that 85% percent of the jail population is of Hispanic heritage, while the general population is not quite 35%? Why the great disproportional ratio?

Well, it certainly is not the 'fact' that we have the so-called, self-proclaimed, 'toughest' sheriff in the USA. And it certainly isn't the 'fact' that this sheriff launches publicity raids to round up illegal criminal trespassers, either, just so he can fill up his jails with Hispanic inmates. If you look closely at the number of arrests usually made on these made for reality TV publicity raids, you can usually count them on your two hands! In other words, they don't add up to Jack!

`Recently he appeared on TV to announce his lasted bust. This is after an 8-month investigation. He arrested a total of three people at a restaurant, then said they have another five they're still looking for. It took eight-months to make three arrests!

I believe that he uses these raids in the same manner that former President Bill Clinton used cruise missiles; that is, when he was spending his time 'not' inhaling marijuana joints or trying to figure out what is, is. But, I believe Clinton launched cruise missiles to deflect unwanted---but very much deserved---attention away from Monica Lewinski; who just happens to be the true answer to the question of what 'is' is! In the same manner, our sheriff launches immigration raids when the polls show him losing support or he just needs an intravenous shot of free publicity, his favorite drug of choice!

Another example, to gain what he wants more than anything else in life; and being that he is the world's largest publicity prostitute, our sheriff decided to launch an immigration raid out into our beautiful desert. Again, unfortunately, it is a very true and very sad fact that in many places, our own sovereign and beautiful desert land of our sovereign state of Arizona has been totally taken over by the criminal activities of illegal border crossers. Again, in many places, it is not safe for our own residents of our beautiful state to venture out into our own desert in certain places!

Don't believe me? Let me prove it to you. Instead of sending our National "GUARD" to do what they were created to do, and that is to "GUARD" and protect our own 'Nation' just like their name implies, the spirit of antichrist and wannabe world dictatorial ruler, while sitting on his throne in our nation's capital 'ruling' over all of us little people, decided to pay with taxpayer dollars to have several large billboard signs erected in certain areas of our state that advises all of us 'legitimate' Americans to avoid going into the desert in those particular areas because it is too dangerous to do so! Instead of sending in our National "GUARD" to "GUARD" our own Nation, he erects billboards that tell us Americans to stay out of our own COUNTRY!!! And, some of those very billboards are within 30 miles of the boundaries of Phoenix!

But, getting back to our publicity prostitute of a sheriff; this idiotic response to our country being illegally invaded gives him the perfect opportunity to milk it for the maximum exposure. Our fearlessly brave sheriff launched this raid on the very same day that the first court challenge of our new immigration law was being heard! And, to bring even more exposure to himself, he goes on television the morning of the raid to declare that he and his officers were going to be carrying a 50-caliber machine-gun with them for protection! But, what he was really saying was he was truly hoping he would be able to use that gun not for protection, but for the capture, and/or, deaths of illegal criminals!

Now, at this news conference, a wise and astute reporter from the media---yes, there are a few of them---spoke up and asked the sheriff if he, and/or, any of his deputies had ever shot a gun of that magnitude. His answer was no.

Good Golly Miss Molly! Here he is, a man in his late seventies going out into our desert with his sidekicks; imitating full blown cowboy characters like Wyatt Earp and Doc Holiday, and, they're armed with a gun that shoots bullets that are six inches long! "BUT", neither he, nor his fellow cowboy sidekicks has ever fired it before! I ask you, how stupid is that? No! How insane is that?

I, personally, have fired a 50-caliber machine gun on numerous occasions when I was in the Army. Let me tell you, this gun should never be fired by an idiot amateur who is dead set on grabbing as much publicity as he can! In fact, this gun should never be fired by anyone at all without first being instructed in the techniques of how to use it and then forced to fire it to see exactly how, and what, it can and will do! And, it should never, never, never, be fired by an arrogant, conceited, publicity hound who wants to play cowboy just so he can fill his narcissistic ego with his favorite drug of choice, and that is free publicity!

So, if it isn't the world's so-called toughest sheriff who is to blame for the 85% percent inmate population of Hispanics, then what is the reason? Is it something in their heritage that destines them to be a criminal or makes them commit illegal acts?

Of course not! How ignorant! Not any more so than being white, black, red, or yellow would make a person do anything either 'right' or 'wrong'. An example, me being part Comanche Indian does not destine me to cutting off the noses and ears of my enemies, although I must confess, that thought did enter my mind on occasion during the time I spent in Hell! But, it is not the color of a person's skin, and especially not their ancestral heritage, that makes a person commit criminal activities.

What the plain fact of the matter is, is that the State of Arizona is under an enormous siege of illegal Hispanic border crossers! Our sovereign state is literally being invaded by illegal criminals who are trespassing illegally across our border against our lawfully passed laws! By the unlawful crossing of our sovereign border; that in itself makes them a criminal! It is against Arizona State Law, as well as United States Federal Law to cross our border without proper documentation through a legal mechanism! Now, because of this illegal invasion, our jails are maxed out with these illegal criminals! Thus, the 85% ratio!

The uneducated, uninformed, unlearned, and most of all, un-teachable, biased based bleeding hearts of our society use every word in the world to call these 'criminals' everything except criminals! They call them, 'undocumented workers', 'immigrants', 'aliens', and as our own Federal Forest Service recently came up with, "a displaced foreign traveler"!

But, by legal definition; both federal and state, they are criminals! Again, by the simple fact of crossing our border "illegally", that in itself makes them a criminal!

Now, what I am about to say is probably going to make what are called, Sanctuary People, along with the biased based, blue bleeding hearts little thong panties they all so proudly wear, get all bunched up together into a tightly wound wet filled wad. It is also assured that in their self-inflicted misery, their self-righteous know it all turmoil, and with their anxiety ridden spastic colons fluttering faster than a hummingbird's wings, it is an assured 'fact' that those same little panties will get sucked up so deeply through their puckered up sphincters that it will take a highly trained and highly paid proctologist to get them pulled back out of their rectums. Thus, this explains the highly paid part of it!

Then, they will scream and bellow that these poor little unfortunate people just need a job and a helping hand---does this sound familiar to you---and since the unfortunate and discouraging fact that all of us Americans are vastly overpaid and filthy rich, we owe our savings, our paychecks, and all of our American rights and privileges to these criminals! Plus the fact that since we, ourselves, are a nation founded and built by immigrants, we need to reach out to these poor little unfortunate people by taking money away from our own kids so we can support these poor unfortunates instead!

But what they won't tell you, not even in a whisper, is that these same poor little unfortunate people are, right now, already costing you, me, our kids, and even our grand-kids, millions and millions of dollars every year! Someone please tell me, *"Where does it stop?"*

In most cases, it's not true that these people just need a job and a helping hand! The biased based, blue bleeding hearts know that as well as the rest of us, but due to political pressure being applied by the spirit of antichrist and wannabe world ruler, they will never admit that! The sheer fact of the matter is that most of these people are here only for our services, including free food stamps and welfare payments, our free educational opportunities, and our facilities, including free medical care so they can pop out anchor babies in astronomical proportions! Most of the rest are here to continue the violent activities of the drug cartel gangs!

An example, my wife and I know a person who works in the healthcare field. This person works in the imagining department of a large hospital. This person has told us on numerous occasions about how many Hispanic women come in to their hospital one month using a certain identity. Then, when they come back in for a follow-up appointment, they are using some other identity.

Let me plainly state, this happens all of the time! And, every time it happens, these illegal criminal invaders are using "stolen" identities! This means that not only are these illegal criminal invaders getting free medical care by using stolen IDs, but the people who have had their identities stolen and used illegally are in one gigantic of a big mess! First of all, they now have medical reports in their medical history that is not theirs! How difficult will that be to correct? What if it is a situation where cancer has been put into their report? How is that going to affect their insurance, or possibly even their jobs? And, since the corresponding medical bill is never paid by the illegals, it is usually turned over to collection agencies, whereby, the good people who had their IDs stolen, their credit is now drastically damaged, if not ruined!

As I said, these poor innocent people who have had their identities stolen and then used by illegal criminal border crossers are in a huge mess! It might take them the rest of their lives to straighten everything out! But yet, there is absolutely no remorse by these illegal criminal invaders! And, the sanctuary idiots, and the biased based, blue blood bleeding dumbkofts, cry unceasingly to give these criminals free citizenship where they then, will be free to steal even more identities, plus everything else they can get their grubby hands on!

The main thing is that the vast majority of these illegal criminals have absolutely no loyalty to our country and to us citizens. Thus, to gain whatever they want that they can't get for free from our socialistic governmental agencies, they resort to joining up with criminal drug gangs. From there, they bring their violent crime down on us normal and respectable citizens!

Thus, the inevitable nightly occurrence of home invasions in our cities! Let me ask one more time, is there any who still doubt my need to keep a 9-mm next to me at all times?

If these poor unfortunate criminals really wanted to come here and be productive citizens and work for a living and then pay their taxes and debts, they need to do as all of the other immigrants who have come before them have done! To become a legal citizen of our great nation, a person must swear his/her loyalty and allegiance to the United States of America. But yet, if you look at the news coverage showing the protestors of Arizona's Immigration Law, you cannot help but notice that many, many, many of them are marching through the streets of "our" country with the Mexican flag flying in their hands, or they are decorated with the colors of the Mexican flag on their clothes. Their loyalty and allegiance does not lie with the US, it lies with Mexico!

Many, many, many of these illegal criminals are here only to bring their poisonous dope, and the horrendous violence that goes along with that, into our country. Our own Governor of our great state has gone on record and declared that most of these illegal border crossers are actually drug carrying 'mules'!

And the illegal drugs these 'mules' are carrying are inundating our once great society with death, disease, and destruction!

The vast majority of these 'poor unfortunate "DOPE" carrying 'mules' belong to large organized crime gangs that thrive on unlimited and unimaginable violence! So, if their 'dope' doesn't get you first, their violence certainly will, thus again, .the 'death, disease, and destruction' I stated earlier! Again, if the dope doesn't kill you, there is a real good chance that the crimes associated with it will!

Thus, this is the reason for the 85% percent ratio of Hispanic criminals who sit in our jails as we, the taxpayers, provide three fine meals a day and a nice roof over their heads, albeit, the roof and walls may be made out of canvas.

Please let me emphasize once again; in most cases, these are NOT unfortunate little people just looking for work! Most of them are violent gang members who kill people; who kidnap people; and who break into our homes with mayhem, rape, theft, destruction, and murder on their minds!

All you have to do is watch the local evening news every night and keep a running tally of the heritage of the suspected perpetrators, and also of the arrested perpetrators, and it will burn your cheeks like a fire breathing Chinese dragon that the 85% percent ratio is eerily accurate, or even low!

But one of the real shames here is that long time families of legitimate American citizens of Hispanic heritage are going through Hell themselves by putting up with these unlawful criminals and all of the problems associated with the racial profiling that goes along with it! In most cases, Hispanic American citizens hate this illegal invasion that is going on as much as the rest of us do! They cringe in wariness when they are approached by so-called day laborers, praying that they're not about to get mugged, robbed, raped, or killed! Just like the rest of us do! And they hide behind bolted and locked doors with locked and loaded guns at the ready just like the rest of us do. ... ... *Ah man, "it's just an awful shame!!!!!!!*

So, I may be close to being crazy, but I'm not paranoid even though my diatribe may have sounded like it! Again, I'm just being prepared for the inevitable to happen! Just like it has already happened to thousands of other law abiding citizens of our great state! Just like you see on every newscast every day and every night!

# Chapter 7

With all of this illegal criminal drug gang violence running rampant in our neighborhoods, I keep my guns close to me at all times! My wife knows that if I have to use them for protection for us, I will use them without restraint! I also believe that she is concerned about what will happen when I do! She and the rest of my family already know that I suffer greatly from Post-Traumatic Stress Disorder, and I know they are worried that if I have to use my guns to protect all of us, they have to wonder if it would be enough to push me completely over the edge.

Let me give you an example of why I keep my guns handy. A couple of weekends ago, down the street from where we live is what I have always believed to be a very nice Hispanic couple. They are not overly friendly, and they mostly keep to themselves, but that is just the way it is now days in our society. For the most part, I either keep to myself, or want to, too.

But, they had a party at their house. Quite a few people showed up and it sounded like they were having a nice time. There seemed to be nothing out of the ordinary going on and certainly no reason for any of the rest of us on our street to be concerned, or even to care that they were having a get-together.

All of a sudden, though, one of the attendees walked out of the front door of the house and rambled out to the front yard. He had a cell phone pressed up against his ear. Now, maybe he is hard of hearing, I don't know; but, he was yelling very loudly into the phone in Spanish, "NO! NO POLICÍA! NO POLICÍA! I SAID, POLICÍA!

My wife and I looked at each other. We heard his yelling all of the way inside of our house, which is several houses up the street. "What is 'that' all about?" we wondered!

I'll tell you what it's all about! It's about 'something' illegal that was going on! If it wasn't something illegal, why was he yelling "no policía"? This siege of illegality is everywhere now, including our own neighborhoods; even our nice neighborhoods where I live!

And if something is not done about it very soon, Arizona will soon become just another part of Mexico with violent criminals, unethical judges and court systems, and cops who are in effect, criminals themselves controlling all of us! We'll be afraid to walk down our own streets or even leave our homes. That is, if we're not first deported into "Re-Education" camps! In-addition to everything else, we'll be a nation devoid of a middle class, just like Mexico is today! "Again, is that what we want, people?"

We, the legitimate law abiding citizens of Arizona, are certainly not getting any help from the spirit of antichrist wannabe world dictator that sits on his throne in Washington D.C. ruling over us little people. He will not give us any help; unless and until, he can guarantee that these illegals will help him get re-elected come the next election. Then, if he could guarantee that, he would do something real quick!

What he will probably do anyways, is to go behind our duly elected congressional representatives backs and enter through an illegal 'backdoor' to give them all amnesty and make them all United States citizens in the hope they will appreciate his actions enough to keep him ruling over us insignificant little people.

Don't believe me? Let me ask you this, then? Why are we at war in Libya right now? How did we get there? Our 'Supreme Ruler' never asked Congress for approval! He just used his imperial powers and sent our military into another war! Just like he will do here!

This inappropriate and outrageous action will include the gun toting, drug carrying, violent laden criminals who make up the vast majority of the illegal border crossing invaders! But until that day comes, he will continue to speak with a forked tongue out of both of his two faces, one on his head and the other on his rear-end!

I say this because I heard that the Indonesian doctor who delivered him at birth said that when he slapped his butt to make him cry, it bloodied his nose!

As my wife and I glanced at each other from the yelling down the street, I quickly got my gun. Let me just say, for the rest of the night it did not leave my side! And most of the time now, it sits very ready in a shoulder holster on my body!

"WHY?"

It's because of the wariness that the illegal criminals have put in us! That's why! As I said earlier, we are under siege by illegal border crossers, just like South Vietnam was! I'm a former soldier who is very familiar with combat. I had been under 'siege' numerous times during my time in war. And it's only because of the guns I proficiently used at the different times I was under siege, that I am still alive today. That and the grace of Almighty God! But, if something is not done to seal our border very soon, and to deport these illegal criminals that are already hiding under our rocks, I am so afraid that we will be left to deal with the aftermath of the flowing red tide of bloodshed that engulfs everything and everyone during and after a siege!

Let me emphatically state this "fact"; this country of ours has way too many patriotic former combat soldiers who will take up arms very quickly before they will allow our precious land of "freedom" to fall into the hands of a foreign country! Unlike South Vietnam, a civilian combat force would quickly arise that would be made up of former combat serial killers who are not afraid to pull the trigger if our way of life is threatened!

I pray to God that this will never happen, but with the cowardly power vacuum of socialistic governmental rulers and illegal 'Czars" controlling our country right now, unless God prevails and intervenes, I am so afraid that an armed confrontation will happen very soon! In fact, already an elected representative of our state government has called for a civilian armed militia force to protect our state! I say the sooner the better! If for nothing more, than to keep the fires of Hell from burning our state and the country of Mexico to ashes!

# Chapter 8

Saturday morning has finally arrived. Right now, we're all getting ready to go out into the desert. I have my guns with me but I'm certainly not expecting to have to use them. I'm just hoping I can get some target practicing in somewhere out in the desert if the noise from the guns isn't too loud to scare the kids. Besides, I just have never gone into the desert without, at least, my old trusty .22-cal. rifle. It was just unheard of for me to think otherwise. On more than one occasion, that old .22 has come in real handy out there and I'm not going anywhere in that wild and wooly place without it!

So, all of us are really looking forward to our journey! So far, things are going great! We couldn't have a better day than what this one is starting out to be. It's been a beautiful and glorious morning in the Valley of the Sun.

This morning is the last Saturday of March, in the year of our Lord, 2011. The afternoon temperature for today is predicted to reach up to the mid to high 70's. It comes with a prediction of a scattering of bright white cumulus clouds that will be floating lazily on a serene ocean of a gorgeous, opalescent blue sky. There is, though, a 10% percent chance of rain for after 5 p.m., or some time later in the evening.

All of that depends on whether or not the scattered white cumulus clouds decide to get to 'know' each another by becoming 'one' with each other, in the Biblical sort of way. If they decide to do that, they will begin to grow into huge, billowing and blushing pregnant thunderstorms! Then eventually after that, their pregnant bellies will no longer be able to contain the onset of birth and they will then burst wide open and spill their pent up, life giving water, all over God's great big beautiful world!

A quirky thing in Phoenix, though, is that a 10% percent chance of rain usually means that we will get some. The other quirky thing is that when the chance of rain is 50% percent or higher, it usually means that we will never get any. But when it's lower than that, a lot of times we do.

I have literally spent hundreds of hours thinking about and studying this puzzling matter; probably way too many to be considered a normal study subject, and my thoughts on this are that I truly believe that the wacky weather forecasters in Phoenix must all be drunks and alcoholics who drink on the job, and they can't tell a 10% chance of rain from a 90% percent chance!

But you know, I don't really blame them for being drunk on the job. Being a weather forecaster in Phoenix, Arizona has to be the easiest job in the world, and thus, it must breed absolute boredom to these poor souls! I also believe that their job is so easy that they shouldn't even get paid for what they do! For at least 330 days a year, all they have to do is say; "It's gonna be warm---if it happens to be between November and March---or it's going to be Hellishly hot---if it's between April and October. Now along with the warm or hot temperature, there will also be a bright blue sky above your head, bereft of any clouds at all, or if there are any, they will be so thin they will be invisible to your eyes. So, make sure you keep the sunscreen handy and apply it often."

Now, is that hard? I tell you, again, the job is so easy that they shouldn't even get paid for it, or if they do, they should be paid in vodka so you can't smell it on them! Basically, as easy as it is to tell the weather in Phoenix, my 3 year old grand-kid named Bronco Nagurski, and/or, Buzz Lightyear to the Rescue, could be a highly paid weather forecaster here; that is, if you are fluent in the Egyptian Arabic language, because, I think that is the language he learned last night while he was sleeping and is now speaking most of the time today! I am not really sure about that, though, it could even be a language from another planet as far as I can tell! Ask him to say the word, 'screwdriver', and you will know exactly what I mean!

Anyway, at 9:15 a.m. this morning, as it is right now, the temperature is in the low 60's with a gorgeous, brightly lit, magnificently colored, azure blue sky that flows in vivid glory and splendor all of the way up to Heaven.

That's because, during the dark and lonely hours of the silent night last night, a decent wind had blown all night long out of the west. This is very good because the wind blew almost all of the smog and pollution out of our valley that Los Angeles, California had been so kind to produce and then give to us free of charge. This is so strange because Los Angeles has declared they were going to boycott our great state because of our new immigration law. Well, their smog and pollution is one thing us Phoenicians all wish they would make their top priority to boycott our state with! They can do that by keeping their filthy air inside their own dirty gray skies! Keep it out of here, we don't want it!

Anyway, because we received it free of charge; and being the fact that us Arizonians are such good appreciative people who feel it is our sovereign duty to always pay things forward that we received but did not deserve, it is now our good pleasure to pass this foul tasting, sight robbing, lung-choking, air-borne pollution on forward and give all of it to Albuquerque, New Mexico, or El Paso, Texas, or whoever else wants to claim it. Here, have a piece of Los Angeles via the courtesy of the fine people of Arizona!

By us getting rid of it, we can do as the lyrics of that old song sung by The Who says, "I can see for miles and miles and miles". Right now, if you focus real intently, you can even see the Four Peak Mountains way out on the far reaches of the Valley on the east side of town. The Four Peak Mountains are beautiful looking mountains when we are able to view them without the lung busting, throat choking, disease plaguing, smog and pollution we get from Los Angeles blocking our view. These beautiful mountains are also very appropriately named, Four Peaks, because, they have, "Four Peaks". We don't get fancy out here in Arizona, folks. We just call 'em as we see 'em!

So, as I said, a beautiful, glorious day is unfolding right before our eyes and in the midst of our presence! As I'm putting things into the Tahoe, all of a sudden, that old Rascals song, "It's a Beautiful Morning" just up and popped into my head. Instinctively, as I always do when the spirit comes upon me and produces the inspiration, I opened my mouth and began to let my beautifully loud, annoyingly off key voice make a glorious noise---just like the Word of God says to do---and began singing the old song. Unfortunately, though, the only words I know of the song are, "It's A Beautiful Morning", so those words were all I could sing; over and over and over again! I quickly glanced over at my wife and daughter. Without a doubt, they were suddenly beginning to have second thoughts about going anywhere with me. I couldn't help but smile to myself!

But really, this is a beautiful, glorious, gorgeous day in Phoenix! Days like this are the reason tens of thousands of people flock to the 'Valley of the Sun' every year to either visit or to move here. This beautiful day in the annals of the history of Phoenix, Arizona will go down as a pinup calendar type of day! It absolutely is a Chamber of Commerce day to the max!

At least, this is the way the day is starting out....

# Chapter 9

Like a slow moving almost stagnant river, Irma finally began meandering down the hallway towards the door leading out into the garage. And by the great grace and mercy of God, it took her only two hours and twenty three minutes of meandering to finally be able to travel the entire 20 feet of the long old hallway until she finally reached the doorknob.

"Oh Sweet Mary, Mother of God," I screamed in rapturous happiness! This was a brand new world record for her! She then reached out, twisted the knob, pushed the door open, and finally made her way out into the garage. Oh, I just couldn't help myself! I was so overcome with emotion! In her arms was the goddess, and Bronco was following closely behind her.

Then, miracle of miracles, while it was still daylight outside, Precious came sashaying down the hallway, out through the door, and into the garage. But, oh woe unto me, she was carrying even more unneeded items in her arms that I was going to need to find a place to fit inside of the vehicle somewhere without it blocking my view, and without the stuff becoming deadly missiles if I have to hit my brakes hard. My Chevrolet Tahoe was already stacked to the max with everything she had already figured we would need. Without a miracle from God, there was absolutely no way I was going to find a place to fit anything more into it!

I stood there staring at Precious. "You got to be kidding me", I said. "We're only going to be gone for just a few hours, not for the next two weeks! And, that's only if we get in the car right this moment and get going!"

She stared back at me, unflinchingly calm, cool, and collected; sure of her place in the hierarchy of the universe. And normally, my dogs and I never give her any problem about that. The look on her face and the tone of her voice was, "Just do it! And don't give me a hard time about it! And, besides, it's only 9:45 in the morning right now."

As the dutiful and placating husband that I am, I waddled over and took the items out of her hands. Then, I turned around to make my way to the back of the Tahoe one more time to try to find some place where I could put the stuff. Again, I knew I had only one chance for that to happen and that is only if God were to shower me with His full mercy one more time!

As I was walking in that direction, I earnestly began asking God to please, please, please make a divine miracle of space appear in a place where there was absolutely none now. I also mumbled what I thought was just loud enough for only me to hear, "It's a good thing you weren't married to Moses when they left Egypt. There would not have been enough camels, oxen, donkeys, and carts in all of the entire Middle East to carry the stuff you thought you might need to last you for the next 40 years. It would have stripped Egypt completely bare and left God with nothing to do to provide for them!"

Unfortunately, she heard me. I sometimes forget that I have 'artillery ears' from my combat service in Vietnam many years ago, and I tend to speak louder than what I had intended. This was one of those times.

Behind me, I suddenly heard a loud cough, and then an even louder expression, "EXCUSE ME?"

Her voice had suddenly acquired the same tone, inflection, and volume as you would expect Satan to sound like! In fact, I suddenly thought my old Drill Sergeant from Basic Training had suddenly appeared once again into my life! It immediately stopped me dead cold in my tracks! At the same time, a deathly grip of indescribable fear suddenly engulfed me and filled my entire being just like I had suddenly been enclosed inside of a suffocating coffin filled with below zero nitrogen gas! It is a fear that only a husband can know because he has experienced it before and knows about it intimately!

As this was happening, a cold flowing raging river of icy sweat suddenly broke out from the top of my head all of the way down to my feet! Huge gobs of water began pouring off my forehead like someone had just dowsed me with a 5-gallon bucket of water right in my face! And my crotch area, along with both of my legs, was already bleeding Wrangler blue because I had suddenly lost complete control of my bladder!

Very slowly and fearfully, I glanced over my shoulder back toward her. As my eyes began to work their slow, agonizing way up from the floor towards her stony cold face, she turned her head straight forward away from me while at the same time cocking her eyes to the left towards me. And in that same moment, she gave me an awful little smirky smile that slowly flashed across her mouth. Then, as she made sure that I was making eye contact and watching her, she hit me smack in the middle of my face with an extremely annoying, twitching up and down eyebrow!

I hate that smirky smile! And I get it every time I do something wrong! Even though I had to quickly run back inside the house and change all of my clothes, including my underwear, I soon found out that God was still on my side today, because somehow unbeknownst to me; I actually found a place to put all of the stuff Precious had given me. And, it was a rather safe secure place to boot. I just opened the rear lift-gate of the Tahoe and quickly piled all of it straight on top of everything else that was already in the back. At the same time I jumped up and let all of my beluga whale blubber weight fall down on top of it to try to pack it down. Then, before anything had a chance to fall back out I quickly slammed the door closed.

After that I hurried back to my driver's door, opened it, and quickly climbed in. I slammed the key in the ignition switch, twisted it to the point of almost breaking it off, and fired up the engine all the way into the red zone of the tachometer, all before Precious could say that maybe we might have forgotten something else.

As I was pulling my seat-belt across my supple and ample girth to fasten it, she slowly climbed in the passenger door and sat down in the seat. But, she just sat there staring straight ahead not moving even a muscle. She was doing a perfect imitation of a mime wearing a red costume and with a white painted made up face I'd once seen down by Fisherman's Wharf in San Francisco.

She sat there for a full minute, at least, without moving a muscle and with a concerned look on her face. She was so good at it that I almost reached into my pocket to give her a $.25 cent tip!

But, I knew exactly what that look was. Inside of that beautiful head of hers was the fact that she just knew we had truly forgotten something else. I had no idea what it could possibly be because the entire house had already been loaded into the Tahoe!

Over my shoulder I quickly said to Irma, "You got Bronco and the Goddess strapped in?"

"Yes," she replied.

I said, "Good! We're out of here then! Nothing else is going with us! If we have forgotten anything other than the Goddess's 'Chewpee' (pacifier), we ain't loading it and we ain't going back for it! Do I make myself clear? If you have to pee, pee in your pants! We have to leave some kind of room inside of this vehicle for the 'gold' we're going to find and bring back with us." Out of the corner of my eye I could see both of them snickering and rolling their eyes upwards. Then, in unison I heard, "Yeah sure, dad/honey, we hear you!"

It has always been my dream that one day before I die, or before the desert gets too dangerous to go out in, I would find a huge cache of gold out in the desert. Precious and Irma just smile at each other every time I bring that up to them. They put up with me because they love me!

But today, I have a deep feeling that inside of that old abandoned mine I had once found and was going to try to find again today; will be nuggets of great value! I could hardly wait to get there!

# Chapter 10

I slammed the shift lever into reverse and backed out of the garage onto the driveway, stopping just long enough to reach up and push the button to close the garage door down. I sat there for a brief instant to make sure it closed all of the way and didn't rise back up. Then, I finished backing out into the street and began heading out towards my favorite playground.

For the first time in a couple of years, I'm excited! I can hardly wait until I can go romping across the desert trying to find that old abandoned mine I had once found nineteen years ago! I'm really hoping that we can find it again today. I don't know why, but something inside is really pulling me towards it.


About a half hour later we actually reached the desert. After that, I began going in a direction that was generally heading west but adding just a dash of north to it. The trail we are now bouncing around on is full of deeply gouged ruts so I switched into 4-wheel drive awhile back. Some of the ruts are the size of mass graves, and those are combined with craters the size of backyard swimming pools. It's kind of reminding me of LZ Woodstock, but without the green fauna, flora, and rain!

Already, we have gone through, around, and over countless dry wash beds and rugged water runoff areas. When it rains in the desert, most of the water does not soak into the ground like in most other places of the US. The ground here is too dry, hard, and full of a substance called caliche that is better at holding water than concrete.

So, when rain begins pouring down, the water takes the path of least resistance and begins to flow in a downward direction. The desert may look completely flat but it isn't. Over time, the flowing of these streams of water have created huge carved out washes anywhere from 1' foot deep up to 6' feet deep, or even more in certain places.

And these water runoff washes are full of small stones, large rocks, and huge boulders the size of your vehicle, or even larger. All of these, among other types of loose projectiles, can damage and destroy anything in its path within a matter of a few mere seconds. Plus, it only takes about two feet of rushing water to actually pick your vehicle up and begin to carry it downstream. Two feet sounds like a lot of rain. But, it really isn't here in Arizona. All it normally takes to get a good two feet of water flowing down a wash is approximately ½" inch of rain in a short period of time in a localized area. That happens all of the time!

Sometimes during what is called the Monsoon season, which lasts from June through September, we can get huge thunderstorms that within minutes, drop tremendous quantities of rain over a localized area. Just like the other day, in a span of about thirty minutes, a micro-mini burst located pretty much in a stationary area was plowing rain down at the rate of 5 1/2" inches of rain an hour! When this happens, these washes quickly fill up with raging torrents of water sweeping any and everything out of the way as they cascade over, under, and around all obstacles in its path! If your vehicle happens to get stuck in a wash when it begins to rain, it is totally woe unto you!

Thinking of rain made me quickly glance up through the front of my windshield. When we left the house, there weren't any clouds at all to be seen in the sky. But now, already there are a lot of the beautiful white cumulus clouds floating high above the earth. And unfortunately for us, they look like they may be starting to get attracted to the beauty of each other.

I reminded myself to keep an eye on them and to make sure that any desert wash I come to, I can safely navigate to the other side without getting stuck in the deeply eroded sand and dirt. I also reminded myself that I'm not by myself in my old desert romping sand-buggy right now. I have my wife, my daughter, and two of my very precious grand-kids with me. And as Bronco says, "Papa has to be safe!" At least, that's what I think he said!

Within minutes of this observation, I came to one of those washes. It was six to seven feet deep in the deepest, roughest places, and the bottom was littered with huge boulders that could smash my Tahoe as flat as a dropped potato chip under my size 11 ½ shoe. For sure, the trail ran around and past these vehicle damaging obstacles, but the bottom of it was also covered in deep, loamy, tire grabbing sand that is very similar to quicksand. That deep sand can instantly reach out and put a stranglehold on your truck and quickly pull you to a complete tire sliding stop! I prayed that being in 4-wheel drive, along with the large oversized tires I had on my Tahoe, would be enough to get us through the sand and up to the other side of the crumbling bank. To be stuck in a wash that deep in an Arizona thunderstorm would be sure destruction, and probably death!

With one more glance up towards the quickly darkening sky, I decided to go ahead and take our chances and drive through the wash. With the experience of more than four decades of driving in the desert, I was 99.9999% percent sure we could make it to the other side without any problems.

But as soon as I went down the embankment and my tires made contact with the deep loamy sand, my fairly new Tahoe instantly began struggling under what I was requiring it to do. It began complaining mightily to me by spinning all four tires in different places which caused us to slide sideways, and even made us turn in 90 degree angles a couple of times where and when we didn't want to turn! But with all eight cylinders growling like a roaring hungry lion via a revved up engine under my hood, and with my rear tires spitting dirt and sand out behind my rear bumper like my man-eating guard dog digging a grave to bury a large thigh bone in, I was finally able to get to the other side.

As I pulled up the crumbling sandy banking and was finally able to get safely back on semi-firm ground, I once again began to let my mind begin to wander back to the old mine I wanted so much to find. Ever since the first time I had stumbled upon it way back then, I had often wondered what had been inside of those old rocks that had been carved away.

Could it have been a gold mine at one time? Or, maybe, had it been a silver mine? Or, was it something else? For some reason, though, I just had a feeling inside of me that the old mine had once been full of gold. And I was really, really hoping there would still be some of that wonderful golden stuff still waiting just for me to find inside of it.

"But, what if it is no longer still abandoned?" I suddenly thought. "What if someone in the last 19 years has found the mine and staked a claim on it?" I couldn't walk into someone else's mine and begin digging, I knew.

# Part 3
# Chapter 1
# My Return to the Flames of Hell

*And the Lord said, I have surely seen the affliction on my people . . . and have heard their cry by reason of their slave drivers; for I know their sorrows!*

We continued traveling down the deeply rutted, butt bouncing, back wrenching, rough old trail that was really nothing more than a dirt path carved through the desert by different size tire threads. It wasn't even really a trail as such. It was just something that seemed to ramble in and around various plants and cacti in generally a northwesterly direction.

I once more took a good look at the sky. It was now getting close to 1 o'clock in the afternoon. Even though the drunken weather forecasters had said that rain was not eminent until after 5 p.m., what I was seeing right now was beginning to get me more than a little concerned. The bright blue cloudless sky of the early morning had disappeared a long time ago. That had been replaced with beautiful white cumulus clouds floating lazily above the earth. But now, one glance upwards and you can easily see that those once beautiful, white cumulus clouds, are very definitely on their way to forming into huge monstrosities of water bearing explosive demons! And as I said before, in the desert that can portray instant death and destruction. The formerly beautiful, giant white fluffy clouds are now an ominous, dark gray color with large patches of almost solid black, and they are already covering over half of the sky right now.

I very seriously thought about turning around and abandoning our quest right then. Even if you're on what seems like flat ground when a huge thunderstorm begins its torrential downpour, you, the vehicle you're in, and all of your possessions you have with you can instantly be swept across that seemingly flat ground by rushing walls of water.

And that can happen in a New York minute! One second you're sitting on what you think is safe flat ground. The next second, you're being flung upside down rolling over and across what you had thought had been safe ground.

The area we were presently in was too far away from any cell phone towers to be able to get any reception. If we were to get stuck or be stranded out here; or God forbid, to get tumbled over and across the desert, we would not be able to call for help. That is, if we survived in the first place!

So, naturally, I did not want to get stuck out in the middle of the desert if it started to pour down rain. But, for some reason, I could still feel an unseen, overwhelmingly powerful force pulling me on and on in the pursuit of finding that mine. "It must be the gold that's inside of it, " I thought.

As this thought was running through my head and I was trying to make up my mind about what to do about the weather, I turned my head to the right to glance out Precious' passenger side window. As I did, I happened to notice that there were several sets of tire tracks leading out across the desert perpendicular to the trail we were on. What was unusual about it was that there really wasn't a trail, or a path, that had been worn in at all. It was just a lot of tire marks going across the desert to what was seemingly nowhere at all.

Most of the time in the desert you will see very defined trails, ruts, or even partially maintained dirt roads leading somewhere. They have been formed by excessive vehicle use just like the Chisholm Trail was formed by the iron wheels of huge wagons filled with goods and settlers heading west across the United States. Some of those tracks are still visible to this day running across the vast prairies of Kansas.

But very rarely do you see where vehicles have left the defined areas of the desert and just started out randomly going towards infinity. At least, you don't normally see several tire tracks doing that like what I was seeing now.

This caught my eye right away. There were quite a few tire tracks leading away from the trail that seemed to be going nowhere in particular, except they were running parallel to what looks like a small ridge that extends for several hundred feet, also perpendicular to the trail we are on.

I slowly pulled off the trail and cruised to a stop in front of the ridge. As soon as the Tahoe stopped moving, I reached over and slid the transmission lever up into the Park position, but I left the engine running so I could keep the air conditioner on inside of it for Precious and the kids. I then climbed out and started walking toward the front of my truck. As I did, my wife rolled down her window and yelled at me. "Jim, why did you stop? What are you looking at?"

"I don't know for sure", I replied. "There's something strange going on here, though. You don't normally see tire tracks going across the desert without there being a road, or at least, some kind of a trail leading the way. But, at the same time, it just seems like there is also something really familiar to me about this place right here. It's almost like I could swear I have been here before. As Yogi Berra would say, "Its déjà vu all over again"."

Both of her eyebrows suddenly shot straight up and formed into the cutest little arches you've ever seen over her eyes as the rest of her face gave me a look like I was stupid or something. "What does that mean?" she asked.

With a huge smile on my face, I continued to walk to the front of my truck, not replying, leaving her to figure out that Yogism. In front of me was a rise in the ground higher than the Tahoe is tall. In fact, it's a good eight to ten feet high all along its length. At first glance while sitting inside of the Tahoe, I had assumed that it was a small hill. As I got closer to it, though, I noticed that something wasn't quite right about it. There was something that was just different about it. It was covered in desert floral and basically looked just like the rest of the desert, but as I walked up to it, I suddenly noticed what it was that was different about it.

It wasn't a natural rise in the earth like everything else out here in this part of God's great earth. This rise was man-made.

At first glance you probably wouldn't notice that, like I didn't. But, it extends too far in too straight a line at too much of the same height to be something that God and nature made. If you haven't noticed before in this great big wonderful world that we live in, God likes variety! So, I quickly realized that huge earth moving machines must have been used to pile up all of this dirt and rocks into this huge berm that extends for somewhere in the neighborhood of 250 to 300 feet down the way from the trail we were on. And it wasn't all that long ago, either, that the berm had been formed.

'Man, that had been a lot of dirt to move,' I thought. My ever present conspiratorial mind instantly went into warp drive! Someone had put a lot of time, effort, and money into creating this barrier so you couldn't see what was happening on the other side of it.

'Well, something is on the other side and I'm going to see what it is," I determined. So, I walked over and began trying to climb up the side of the rise. But for every two steps I climbed up, I slid back down at least one. The dirt was still loose and crumbling. So again, I knew the berm had not been there for too long. The sun, wind, and other elements had not yet had time to bake the berm into a natural desert environment, which would normally be about as hard as concrete, even though the creators had tried to camouflage it by planting desert floral all along its path. I had to be very careful to keep from losing my balance and falling or sliding all of the way back down to the bottom of the berm. Or worse, by falling and landing on top of some of the jumping Cholla cactus that had been transplanted on it.

Eventually, though, with much huffing and puffing from my sixty year old rickety legs and lungs, I made it up high enough to get my head above the top of the rise and see what was on the other side. As I did, I suddenly wished I hadn't!

# Chapter 2

Before I began to slide back down, I kicked my feet a couple of times and dug the toes of my boots into the soft dirt of the berm. I was trying to dig a foothold in the hope it would keep me kind of stationary as I looked on the other side of it. It seemed to be working so far, so I once again stuck my head up above the top of the berm. This time I allowed my eyes to take in the view.

I was immediately very glad that only my head was sticking up above the berm. But to be safe, I quickly slid back down a notch or two until just my eyes and the top of my head was still above the ridge.

On the other side of the berm down near where it ends, I could see four really ugly and mean looking men, and all four of them were carrying AK-74 assault rifles in their hands. By looking at the expressions on these men's faces, and by their demeanors, I could tell they knew how to use them, too!

I was also pretty sure that these weapons were the fully automatic kind. On many of my trips out into the desert before today, I had heard automatic weapons being fired way off in the distance. These guns, and the men carrying them, may have been the ones firing before, I didn't know. But no matter what, these very bad boys, including both the men holding the guns, and the guns themselves, could pop out 30 man-killing rounds from the banana style clips that were stuck into the bottom of the guns, in less time than it took to just say this. These were bad guns! And the men holding these guns looked even badder!

An icy cold chill began wrapping around my head and began running wind sprints up and down my spine faster than the water flowing over a broken dam! It totally and completely engulfed me! At the same time, my entire body broke out in a sickly, sticky, sweat that began flowing out of my pores like an Arizona Monsoon thunderstorm in July, while just a fraction of a second later, my ample stomach began doing anxiety induced somersaults, flopping up and down like an Olympic gymnast competing for the gold medal!

What I was seeing was something that the sane part of me wanted nothing to do with! The sane part of me quickly concluded right then that it was time to get out of Dodge, and to do it very, very fast without being seen or heard! But before I could make a move to get back down and out of there, I noticed some more movement in the distance behind these four guys that caught my eye. It was another two men, and they were walking out of a dark, shadowed opening that extended back into the side of a small mountain.

As I saw that, I suddenly stopped and sucked in my breath. "That's the old mine I was looking for", raced through my mind! I instantly recognized it! I knew this was it! Even though it had been nineteen years since I had last seen it, I just knew that it was the same mine I had visited before.

I hadn't seen it while driving across the desert. I couldn't have seen it. Someone had built a huge dirt berm and tried to disguise it to look like it had been made by nature so no one would see the mine, unless that is, they were to climb the berm like I did, or follow the tire tracks down the length of the berm to where it ends. And, if you were to do that, I am sure the guys with the AK-74s in their hands would be very happy to give a very warm welcome to you, and then invite you to stay for the rest of eternity in an unmarked grave!

I was curious, though, what it was these guys were using the mine for. And, "why are they carrying automatic weapons?" I wondered. "What have they found that they need automatic weapons to protect? Have they found a brand new huge vein of gold, and they need to protect it with bad looking bodyguards?"

At that moment, I should have listened to the sane part of my brain and gotten out of there and left them to their own business. Bad looking young men, way less than half my age, and carrying automatic weapons in their hands should have been enough to convince this sixty year old decrepit old man to make like a barren tree and leave. But, I didn't! The insane part of me was overcome with curiosity.

The insane part of me knew these guys were up to no good,

but I wanted to check them out, anyway. And, as it has almost always been the case in my life, my insane persona always wins out! And it's also almost always been, 'oh woe to me', because of it!

Both of my personas, the sane part, and the insane part, have read and watched way too many books and movies about action heroes. The insane part says give me Sylvester Stallone as Rambo, Arnold as the Terminator, Bruce Willis in Die Hard, Dirk Pitt from Clive Cussler, and Richard Marchinko as Rogue Warrior, any day, and I just can't help myself, I'm drawn to action! But the sane part of me is a total rear-echelon, panty wearing wimp, who wants to run from trouble and hide his head in the sand like a big fat ostrich!

So, I flipped a coin to see what I should do. Heads, I'm insane and I stay and check this out. Tails, I'm insane and I stay and check this out. So, with insanity beating the odds and winning the day, I dropped my head just a little lower and watched for a while longer thinking that nobody could see me where I was squatted down behind the berm.

Just then a white Chevrolet Tahoe, very similar to mine, came rolling from around the corner of the mountain on the right side of the opening of the mine. About 20' feet past the opening of the entrance on the right side of it, the mountain slopes to an end and falls away out of sight, at least to my angle of sight. Where I was watching from, I couldn't see past that end of the mountain to know what was back in that direction.

I watched as the Tahoe pulled up in front of the opening of the mine. It stopped and the tailgate popped open and began going up under its own power. As the tailgate was reaching its full upward position, two more bad looking men stepped out of the Tahoe; a driver and a front seat passenger, and began walking down the side of it towards the back end.

At the same time, several scrawny, pale, sickly looking, and very unkempt men began following each other out of the mine. From the distance I was looking at things, it appeared to me each of the scrawny men was carrying in their hands what looked like a heavy sandbag. Each of them, in turn, would carry the sandbag up to the back end of the Tahoe, reach in and stack it in the back cargo area. Then, as soon as they finished stacking the bag, they would turn around and run back into the mine, where eventually, they would return carrying another sandbag, which they would once again pile into the Tahoe. They did this several times until the Tahoe was full and sitting heavily down on its springs from the weight of the bags.

As these scrawny, unkempt men, were carrying the bags out, I noticed that none of them were wearing any shirts, and that the skin on their backs was almost totally black. It looked almost like they had been severely burned or bruised!

All were also wearing old jeans that were no longer blue but were now mostly a filthy brown color. Every set of jeans these fellows had on were ripped full of holes and were very tattered. Some of them were nothing much more than a buttoned waist band with brown strands of fabric hanging down in threads. Most of their covering came from the dirty and stained boxer shorts they all had on. By looking at those, you could easily tell they had not been changed in a long time, either. Plus, not a single one of the men had any shoes on. They were all running in and out of the mine barefoot. That had to be very painful running on the old sharp stones of the excavated mine tunnel!

The two bad looking men that been inside the Tahoe stood on each side of the open tailgate as the laborers were loading it. They were counting the bags as they were being stacked inside of it. But also, they were holding long, leather and metal studded whips, and each time one of the workers would carry a sandbag out of the mine entrance, they would swing these whips down onto the bare backs of these scrawny workers while screaming at them in Spanish what I assumed meant for them to hurry up.

This was just like what you would see in the movies about slave owners beating slaves! They hit them so hard and with such force that I could hear the smacking of leather against bare skin, and the anguished cries and pitiful wails of the beaten men, all of the way to where I was hiding over a hundred yards away. The awful sight and unbearable sound of the beating, combined with the almost unearthly guttural cries of torturous pain screamed by the poor slaves made me even more nauseated! I actually had to turn my head away for a moment to keep from retching!

The bad guys were beating the poor unfortunate men unmercifully! And as they swung those heavy leather whips studded with jagged pieces of metal balls the size of small marbles down onto the bare backs of the poor souls; even from where I was, I could see bright red, gooey, sticky blood instantly begin spurting and spewing out of the cuts that the straps would make! By the time the Tahoe was stacked full, this free flowing blood covered their entire backs in bright red rivers of blood!

My mind was going crazy right then! In fact, it was almost impossible for me to make sense of what my eyes were seeing. I knew what they were seeing, but my mind could not grasp the full import of it, or just did not want to accept it! Either way it was unreal! What my eyes were seeing was out of another time and place! This isn't ancient Rome, and this certainly isn't the time before the Civil War in the US! My mind was screaming, "Not now! Not in this time and age of civilization! Men don't keep slaves now! Not honorable law abiding men, anyway! At least they don't do it in the United States! ... But, this is the United States, so what is happening? This is crazy, man!"

Deep down inside, I knew what my brain was trying to tell me through what my eyes were seeing! What my brain was telling me I was seeing were illegal border crossers that were being used as slaves by what were probably, Mexican drug cartel drug runners; better known as 'mules', as our own Governor has called them. These mules are probably using the old mine as a storage and distribution point for their drugs, and using slave labor as 'workers'.

Thoughts were zipping through my mind. 'Is there any way I can help these poor people? I can't just walk away and leave them here. They probably won't survive much longer. They look like they haven't eaten in days, maybe even weeks. And, you know that the drug runners are not going to let them live to tell what they know.

They will beat them within an inch of their lives and then work them until they fall over dead. And the problem is, just like the Nazi's of World War II used an almost unlimited supply of slave laborers to bring Hell and destruction onto the world, these drug runners also have an almost unlimited supply of slave laborers from all of the illegal border crossers coming across our Arizona border!

"What do I do?" I asked myself. "I have my wife, daughter, and grand-kids with me to think of, too. Their safety must be paramount to me! I cannot, and will not, put them in harm's way! Besides that, I'm only one person. There are at least six bad guys in there, plus the two in the Tahoe. If I turn around and head as fast as I can back to civilization, it will take us at least two hours, or probably even more, to get back to where it may be possible to get cell phone service. Then, it will probably take another three to four hours, at least, to get a SWAT team assembled and get them out here. And, if the weather goes completely bad as it really looks like it may, it will probably be sometime tomorrow, or even later than that if a real mother-of-all-storms bursts loose, before any help could get here.

'Oh man..... .... What do I do?' I wondered. 'God help me to decide. Please!'

# Chapter 3

A person really needs to be careful about what they pray for at times. Most of the time when God answers our prayers, it is in a totally and completely unexpected way than what we would have thought best. Just like He did this time! In fact, the Bible says that "God's ways are not our ways."

I knew I had my guns with me. I also knew that if I had not had my family with me, I would not have been afraid to use them, either. But, in all honesty, what could my little 9-mm pistol and my even smaller, 22-caliber rifle do against, at least, six AK-74 automatic weapons, and at least eight very mean men? And I figured that the other two guys in the Tahoe probably had at least one more, if not two AK-74s, within an arm's reach!

Aw man, where is Cap't Crunch when I need him? Let me lay a couple 155-mm 95-lb. Willie Peter rounds in on top of their heads and that would certainly even up the odds a little. But unfortunately, I don't have my old artillery gun with me right now, and that is just too, too, bad!

Right then, at the same exact moment as my entire being was being torn and ripped from shred to shred about what to do, my sweet, wonderful, and beautiful wife, suddenly made up my mind for me whether or not I should leave and go for help, or stay and figure out a way to do something. She had no idea at all what I was looking at. To her, by the way I was lying on the side of a big dirt hill, it might have looked like I had just decided to take a nice nap and fell asleep.

So, she casually leaned over and placed her hand in a very firm manner right on the center of my steering wheel. This little action by her just happened to allow the horn from the sacrificial altar of Hell to instantly start screaming out a billion decibel blasting sound that could have easily been heard all the way to Pluto! In fact, I am positive without a shadow of a doubt, that the astronomers that man the Zeti observatories 24 hours a day, 7 days a week, every day of the year, listening for the sounds of space aliens, heard that horn and just knew that the first contact with extraterrestrials had just been recorded!

As the sonic blast from Hell suddenly slammed into my head in an atomic explosion of intense noise and drastic pain in less time than it takes to blink an eye, both of my ear drums instantaneously exploded right out of the openings of my ears in a gooey bloody mess. At the same time as that was happening I just about jumped completely out of my skin and flew all of the way back home to Alpha Centauri without a space ship! And at the same time as that was happening, I also lost my tenuous grip on the side of the berm and began sliding down it feet first. But in my haste to try to grab a hold of anything that may save my life, I misjudged and suddenly flipped over and began tumbling uncontrollably head over heels in a somersault fashion all of the way to the bottom of the berm! I can assure you that this was not a good thing for a sixty year old soft, flabby, sickly couch potato of a man to have happen to him!

Finally, after what seemed like an eternity of time to reach the bottom of the Royal Gorge of falls and spills, I suddenly landed on solid ground with a big, painful THUD, by landing flat on my back! In that very instant, the lifesaving oxygenated air that had previously been flowing freely and unrestricted in my lungs suddenly escaped out of my poor, wretched body in a loud screeching, whooshing sound! Otherwise, I would have let out a scream of pain that would have surely equaled the tortured cries of the tormented souls spending eternity in Hell!!

Since I couldn't scream out loud in pain, and since I was too stunned to move, I lay there perfectly still, not moving at all. I was afraid that if I did make any movement my entire body would suddenly erupt in an unearthly amount of torment!

Eventually though, after what seemed like an hour but was in actuality only about a full minute or so, a fuzzy realization that I was still alive entered into my consciousness. And, miracle of miracles, as a little more time passed, I suddenly realized that I didn't have any broken bones, or even any major injuries other than a lot of bumps and quickly developing bruises.

As soon as I realized this, I tried to jump back up to my feet so I could get back in my car and get out of Dodge as quickly as possible before the mean boy's posse arrived to capture us! Without a doubt, they had to hear the horn! But unfortunately, being that I am a sixty year old broken down and disabled man who had just taken a rolling tumble down the south side of the Grand Canyon, it took me about five minutes to make that jump back up to my feet.

As I was able to eventually stagger back onto my feet, I was looking more like a bent over knuckle dragging Neanderthal than a human being. But as fast as I was able to, I turned around and quickly began hopping back towards my truck, albeit, my left leg was dragging behind me in the soft dirt which was making a wriggling groove eerily similar to that of a Sidewinder rattlesnake's crooked trail.

I also was finally able to get a little air back into my lungs that had been so rudely squished out of them from the tumble down the steep hillside. So, in a strained, stretched, and painfully pitched voice that sounded like an almost perfect imitation of Tiny Tim singing 'Tip Toe Thru The Tulips', I started yelling towards my wife, "Don't do that! I mean it! There are some really bad guys on the other side of this berm and we certainly don't want them to know we're here!" But even as I was saying this, I knew if space aliens at the edge of the universe 13 billion light years away had heard the horn honk, then these very bad men certainly had, too!

My wonderful wife and daughter were sitting in the truck watching all of my tumbling trials and tribulations unfolding right before their eyes, and were laughing their silly rear-ends off at the same time! In a voice barely under control from a spasmodic episode of undeniable hilarity, my wonderful and caring wife said to me, "Well, why didn't you say something to let us know? We thought you had fallen asleep lying up there on the side of the hill. We had no idea what you were doing or what you were looking at!" Then, after another sudden bout of unrestrained laughter, she replied, "Well, hurry up then. Let's get out of here."

But before I had the time to make it all of the way back over to my truck, the white, drug laden Tahoe, came screeching around the berm billowing a huge plume of dirt and dust into the air behind it, and straight towards my family and me. I had no chance to make it back to my Tahoe. We had no chance to escape anywhere! They were on us too fast! And in a very mean and threatening manner, they had brought their bad boy AK-74 automatic guns with them. As they screeched to a halt right in front of us, they trained those bad boys right at us, just itching to pull their triggers to prove they had recently passed from puberty into manhood!

# Chapter 4

"Alto!" (Stop), they yelled, "or we'll shoot!" At least, that's what I think they said. They were speaking Spanish.

I came to a quick halt and then slowly and painfully lifted my hands up above my head. The one riding in the passenger's seat quickly jumped out of the Tahoe and started screaming something at me in very rapid fire Spanish as he was running over towards me.

I can read Spanish better than I can understand it spoken, and that's not saying much. To be completely honest, for the most part, I can't read or understand it hardly at all, either way! Being that I have lived most my life in Texas and Arizona, I really wish I could understand and speak it. I should be able to, but unfortunately, I can't. All I can usually understand is a small smattering of individual Spanish words when it is spoken in a clear and concise, very slow manner. Like the word 'alto', I knew it means 'stop'.

Sometimes I can make out what is being spoken by putting the few words I can figure out together with the ones I have no idea what they are. It is like playing word games or something like that. But with the way this guy was screaming at me in a machine-gun staccato, I had absolutely no idea what he was saying. So, I just stood there with my hands up in the air above my head.

As he came running over to me, he got right up in my face, and then pointed down at the ground. As he was doing this, he was still screaming at me in Spanish! I looked at him with a totally blank expression on my face while raising my shoulders slightly trying to let him know that I didn't have any idea what he was saying. This must have upset him dearly that I didn't understand Spanish in my English speaking country, because, he instantly took the barrel of his gun, reared it back, and then swung it forward as hard as he could straight into my solar plexus!

In that instant, all of the air in my entire body, including the oxygen that had already mixed with my red blood cells inside of my bloodstream, suddenly and completely exploded out of me in a gagging, puking, coughing, spitting, choking, explosion! But, before I collapsed and died, I immediately started telling myself that it could have been worse! "It could have been worse! He could have shot me instead of just stabbing me!" For some reason, though, I was wondering why I hadn't noticed the bayonet on the front of the gun before he stabbed me!

By some kind of a miracle; or "not", I never completely lost consciousness. But, my brain immediately became severely oxygen deprived. All of the brain cells I had in my head died except for two very weak and sick ones! This caused me to begin wobbling very unsteadily back and forth on my feet. I still didn't fall down to the ground, but I should have! That was what the unfriendly fool wanted me to do in the first place---This is another perfect reason why immigrants; both legal and illegal, should have to learn our language if they are going to be in our country. If this pushy and cruel fool would have known how to speak our language, I would have gladly done exactly what he wanted me to do and avoided all of the pain and agony I was about to go through!

He pointed down at the ground again with the barrel of his gun as he continued screaming at me in his native tongue. For some reason, instead of looking at his face, I glanced down at the bayonet on the front of his gun. I guess I wanted to see how much of my blood was dripping off it. But, to my complete surprise, there wasn't a bayonet, and there wasn't any blood either. 'Then, how can I be in so much pain?' I wondered.

By now, I was completely doubled over in unbelievable pain and agony! My head was hanging so far down between my legs that I could have easily kissed my butt if I had been so inclined! But, I was gasping for air right then, and it had nothing to do with my butt, either! I was gasping for air that I had never even fully regained after getting it knocked out of me from my tumble down the side of the berm.

As my body slowly began sinking to the ground and blackness began sweeping in from the sides and enveloping over my eyes, I thought right then that my soul was leaving my body and entering into a blessed eternity!

I was now almost to the point of complete unconsciousness and my body was already on its way down towards the ground! But as soon as my collapsing knees hit the ground, this ugly animal suddenly reared back and kicked me as hard as he could right in the middle of my back. What small amount of air I had somehow regained in my lungs instantly escaped out of them, again, in a loud, hissing, moaning sound as I tumbled face first onto the hard packed dirt. Without a doubt, my two remaining brain cells told me for sure I had just died!

Unfortunately, though, I hadn't died! But, I couldn't breathe, nor could I move any part of my body as severe shooting and burning spasms of indescribable pain instantly erupted throughout my entire being! In that instant, I knew that the idea of my soul leaving my body and entering eternity was only a very wishful fantasy right then! As I lay there gasping, gagging, coughing, twitching, and retching, he reached down and brought one of my arms around behind my back while taking his foot, putting it on the back of my head, and kicking my face down against the hard concrete like earth! This caused an ostrich sized egg shaped knot to begin growing right in the middle of my forehead. It also caused a large cut right in the center of the knot, along with busting my nose, and blood began flowing freely out of my entire face.

He then slapped a plastic locking cord around my wrist. Then, he grabbed my other arm and brought it behind my back. With no arms or hands to support my body, this forced my face to again, slam against the ground, which this time split both my lips and increased the amount of blood coming from my nose! Also, the large bluish-blackish egg shaped knot continued growing, and bleeding in the middle of my forehead! Blood was spilling everywhere from my face, but he didn't care!

The crueler, the better, as far as he was concerned. As he jerked my other arm behind my back, he took another plastic locking cord and tied my two hands together.

I couldn't move any part of my body because of the beating I had received and from my hands being handcuffed behind my back. In fact, I began to worry that maybe I had been paralyzed! There was nothing at all I could do, even though my entire mind and body was crying out for me to do something, anything, to protect my family, and for me to get revenge!

"Revenge is mine, saith the Lord!" Well Lord, I'm sorry to disappoint you, but tonight, someway, somehow, with your help, revenge is gonna be Jim Cooley's!!!! ... But at that moment, all I could do was lie there and try to get my breathing back as close to normal as possible. I was also praying very fervently that I wasn't permanently paralyzed.

While the one bad guy had jumped out of the Tahoe and was knocking me around and down, the other bad guy had jumped out and run straight over to my Tahoe. He then quickly forced my wife and daughter out of the truck and down onto the ground. They complied more quickly than I had, although my daughter put up a running scream about her two kids still being in the car.

There are not too many people in the entire world who can out talk my daughter! She gets that from her mother. She also gets a lot of her mothering instinct to protect her brood from any and all harm from her mother. As that thought coursed through my mind, it actually made part of me pity these two fools if my daughter and wife were ever released and they could get their hands on them. They would be ripped apart limb by limb and then made to eat ... ... Well; let's say that my revenge would be nothing in comparison to theirs!!

I was looking over at my wife and daughter as they were being manhandled down onto the ground. Oh, I wanted so much to rip these scum of the earth animals apart with my bare hands! These walking upright apes were not human! They were animals! But, they had me hog tied and bound. At the moment, there was nothing any of us could do.

I also knew we were on very dangerous ground right then and that we didn't need to inflame the situation any worse than it already was. By now, I had finally been able to catch a small portion of my breath again. So I glanced over to my wife and daughter, and spit the words out to them the best I was able to; especially to my daughter, "Hey! Listen to me! Now is not the time to antagonize these guys any more than we already have! Just lie quietly and do what they say to do for the time being! We'll get our turn later; that I promise you from the bottom of my heart! But for now, they haven't killed us yet so we still have a chance to get out of here. OK?"

I didn't know if these fools knew any English or not. Right then, I didn't really care! All I cared about was finding a way to get these cuffs off me and then get my hands on one of their AKs. "Give me an AK, and even though I haven't used an automatic rifle in 40 years, I guarantee the odds will have suddenly swung in my favor, you stupid fools!" I thought! "I, too, know exactly how to use those kinds of guns!

Reluctantly, my wife and daughter quieted down some. They're just like all women when they get worked up; it's really hard to shut them up. But for the most part, they did.

For some reason, the bad boys began to realize that the women probably needed their hands to hold the babies. So, they tied their hands together in front of them but in a way that would allow them to hold the kids. Then, they picked them up off the ground and stood them back on their feet. They then motioned for them to reach in our Tahoe and get the kids out of it. Rachael stepped up inside and unstrapped both of the kids.

I was really wishing right then that she knew about my guns hidden in the compartment in the rear under the stuff back there. But, there was no way she could have gotten to them without the bad guys seeing her. Also, there was no way I would have put her in the position to have to shoot and kill someone. That's a real hard thing to do if you have never done it before, no matter how much bravado someone might spout beforehand.

So, I kept my mouth shut and allowed her to hand Venus out to Mamma. She then took Bronco by the hand and led him outside. As I watched that cute little Arabic speaking grandson of mine jump down out of my truck, I begged God with all of my heart to please give me the opportunity to save not only his, but all of our lives!

After Irma got the kids out, the bad guys pointed their weapons at them, and then marched them back over to their own Tahoe. Once there, they opened the rear passenger door and made them get in the seats. My wife and daughter were told to hold the kids on their laps.

Once they got them settled in, both of the bad guys came back over to me. They reached down, one on each side of me, and very roughly grabbed me by my shoulders, and then jerked me up to my feet. I thought to myself, 'Can't they see I'm an old guy with major physical problems?' There was so much blood on my face that I was virtually blind! 'They don't need to be so rough!'

Once my feet touched the ground, though, I knew in that instant that I wasn't paralyzed. "Oh, Thank You God!" I so much wanted to scream right then! I could feel the ground through my feet and legs!

But I wasn't given the chance to shout that because they both jabbed the barrels of their rifles hard against my back and shoved me over to the passenger door that was still open. Once there, they both lifted me up off the ground, swung me backwards in the air, and then bodily threw me into the Tahoe onto the floorboard on top of the women's feet. Then, in Spanish, they yelled for us not to move or they would kill the babies!

At least, we assumed that is what they said! We recognized the words 'matar' and 'bebés' that we took to mean murder and babies.

Naturally, we all either sat there, or lay there in my case, very quietly! Bronco, though, looked down at me lying on the floor, and asked, "Why is Papa laying down there, Mama?"

"Shush, Honey. Don't say anything right now. Just be a good boy, okay? Papa's okay."

"But Mama, Papa has a big booboo on his face. He's got blood all over his face!"

"I know, Honey. But Papa is okay. He's not hurt. I promise you! Now, be quiet for a moment!"

Irma looked over at her mother and mouthed the words, "These guys are in big trouble when dad gets loose." Precious shook her head knowingly.

The bad guys climbed back in the front seats of their Tahoe and started it up. Then, they made a loop to turn around to go back in the direction they had come from, back over to the opening of the mine. I lay there not knowing what the future held. But, if God allows me just one opportunity to avenge Bronco's concerns, these demonic subhuman animals are going to be paying big time for this! That much I knew!

# Chapter 5

Once we got over to the mine entrance, they climbed out and opened the back passenger door. They then reached in and grabbed me by my feet and jerked me out. Again, because my hands were tied behind my back, I landed face first on the old, hard, rock strewn ground! Again, that busted my lips and bloodied my nose; possibly even breaking it this time. Blood, again, began spewing freely down my face, dropping onto my neck, and began to flow on to my shirt!

I lay there for a minute, trying to catch enough of my breath so I could gain enough strength and energy to roll over onto my side and sit up. I didn't want to choke on my own blood.

They didn't do anything to stop me, or even seem to give much notice to me. They just left me sitting on the ground, bleeding profusely, while they reached back in and made the ladies climb out.

Then, they pointed their weapons toward the entrance of the mine and made us understand with much gesturing and unintelligible words, that we needed to start walking in that direction. The other four bad guys with automatic weapons I had seen earlier now stood there with their guns pointed right at us, too. And just like the others, they were just daring us to do or say anything. The looks on all of their faces were as hard and cold as arctic glaciers used to be before Al Gore's carbon footprint made them begin to melt! You could see it in their expressions they really were just itching to pull their triggers and blow our brains out!

I thanked God neither Precious nor Irma said or did anything right then. And both of the kids were being good and not making any fuss as of yet. We all knew that wouldn't last too much longer, though, and we were dreading what the consequences could be. A one year old and a three year old just cannot sit still for too long.

For some reason, a toddler always has ants in their pants! Because of that, their attention span just doesn't last that long. And with Bronco wanting to put on his best imitation of the old leather helmeted running back; well let's just say it wouldn't be long before he would want to run over and through everything in his path. I knew I had to think of something and do it fast!

They jerked me to my feet, and then made us begin walking all of the way down the tunnel to where it suddenly veers off to the right. This was the part of the tunnel I had been in nineteen years before, but I had never been past the point where it veers off. My flashlight had gone dead and I had turned around and followed the light from the mine opening back outside.

I wanted to turn around and look at the opening again. But the bad guys did not let us stop at that point. They quickly came up behind us gibbering something totally unintelligible and pushed us hard in the middle of our backs. Then, they pointed down the tunnel veering off to the right and jutting the rifles down that direction. Being the bright, intelligent people my wife and daughter are; and with my new found ability to suddenly begin learning what their signals meant, we rightly assumed they wanted us to go in that direction.

The tunnels were brightly lit with overhead fluorescent light tubes. One no longer needed a flashlight anymore to see where you were going. In fact, the further into the mine we went, we realized that the entire mine was brightly lit with the same fluorescent tubes. Somewhere way in the background, we could hear the muffled noise of a gas powered generator humming along and providing the power to keep these lights shining brightly.

This tunnel we were now walking down looked like it extended back into the dark recesses of the mountain for about one hundred or so feet. It had very little, if any slope to it. The width of the tunnel was at least five feet wide, and it was between eight to nine feet high.

As we got closer to the end of the tunnel, we saw that it opened up into a fairly large room that measured probably about thirty feet square with a ceiling about ten to twelve feet tall. We also saw that at least one half of the room was stacked almost full from floor to ceiling with the same type of sandbags that I had seen being loaded earlier into the back of the Tahoe.

We also noticed that there were eleven other men inside of the room besides us. I quickly counted them as my eyes roamed over them. These were the same poor men who had been beaten bloody while loading up the Tahoe. They were now sitting in a row with their backs up against a wall, or slumped forward with their heads hanging down against their chests and their knees pulled up in front of them. Several of them were moaning in deep pain. One looked like he was on the very verge of death! He was slumped over, and you could see that he was barely breathing. What few breaths he did take, were very ragged and raspy!

A few of these men glanced up at us as we entered into the room. But, you could see in their expressions that their eyes were glazed over. They were unable to focus clearly because of the intense pain they were all suffering. Also, the entire wall behind them where they were sitting looked like a thick coat of paint had been applied to it, but it was actually stained a deep reddish brown or almost black color from the blood that had poured out of their backs onto it.

Each of the eleven men now had an ankle cuff around one of their ankles. A large metal chain was fastened through the cuff and then the chain was fastened to the guy next to him until it got to the end of all of them. At that point, it made a complete loop and was chained back to the wall. This insured there was no chance of one of them being able to escape; at least not while they were chained inside of this mine. Maybe there might be an opportunity when they were unchained and made to load the vehicles, I thought.

I would have to find out, because, we were now just like them. There was no way we would ever be allowed to leave this place alive unless I could figure something out! And, I certainly did not want my wife, daughter, and myself to die there as slaves, let alone the horror of what may happen to little Venus and Bronco!

I began to wonder why I had felt such a drawing; such a pulling, to find this mine again! Was it the demonic powers of absolute evil emanating everywhere in and out of this mine that I had felt and been drawn to it for some reason? As I looked around the place, I thought that this was as close to Hell as a person could get without actually going there! "Maybe Satan is planning on getting even with me after all of these years because I had been able to escape from that other Hell he had created!", I wondered.

One of the bad guys turned to his compatriot, and what I assume, said for him to keep us covered with his gun. He then told us in very broken English to sit down against the wall next to the chained men and to not move until their leader got here.

We did as he said without hesitation. But I was really hoping that their leader would get there real quick before Bronco or the baby began acting up. I did not want to attempt to kill the guy with my hands tied behind my back. But, before I would let any one of them hurt one of my grand-babies, I would surely give it everything I had!

# Chapter 6

The other bad guy that had led us to the back of the mine returned shortly with a rough looking nylon rope in his hand. With this, he quickly tied all of us up, including putting a loop around Bronco's waist. Whether it was a brief act of humanity or just an oversight on his part, he did leave the baby loose, though. When he had us all secured to his satisfaction, he then tied the rope to a large attachment that was itself attached in the wall. It was also holding the chain that held the poor scrawny slaves.

After that, I guess they felt like we could not do any harm or damage or escape, so they walked out of the room and down the tunnel, where they continued walking on out of the mine.

I looked over at my wife and Irma, and said, "Listen to me! Please look at me right now and listen! Okay? I know you're real scared and you can't even hardly think straight, but believe me when I tell you that we are going to get out of here alive! We are! I don't how or when right at this moment, but we will! I know that in my heart, and I promise you that somehow, someway, we will get out of here alive and be free! Listen; in all of my years of living, when this feeling of 'knowing' is inside of me, like it is now, it always works out exactly like I knew it would! This 'feeling' comes from God!

"But, listen to me real closely, whatever I say or do from this point on, you must not interrupt me or interject anything into it. Do you understand? I have always been able to talk my way out of, or into, anything. I was often told that I could have even sold ice to Eskimos. So, let me sell this boss man who is coming to see us, and I promise you, with God's help, I'll get us out of here."

"Dad?" Irma said.

"Yeah?"

"Dad, why don't you pull one of your crazy Vietnam things on them? Maybe you'll scare them enough to release us, or maybe they'll feel sorry for us. I don't know! ... Just get us out of here! Okay, Dad?" she cried.

"Honey, listen to me. I will get us out of here, and I'll do it without us getting harmed in any way whatsoever; or harmed any more than we already are. But, you have to trust me! You must! Okay? … … and if I have to pull a Vietnam thingy on them, as you say, believe me, I certainly will! And let me say this, if I do that, oh man, it will certainly be woe unto them!"

She nodded her head up and down while huge alligator tears were continuing rolling down her cheeks. I know she wanted so much to believe me! But, our situation looked completely hopeless to her at the same time. Bronco looked at his mom in bewilderment and confusion. Finally, with tears welling up in his own eyes, he said, "Mama, why are you crying?"

"It's okay, honey. It's OK! I know your Papa is going to get us out of here!"

I smiled at them the best I could with blood caked and cracked lips, while at the same time, trying my best to not wrinkle my forehead in the least. My forehead felt like I had a two foot long unicorn's spear sticking out it from the huge knot that was still growing on it. It had finally stopped bleeding, and I was afraid if it were to begin again, the blood would flow down into my eyes, and then, I wouldn't be able to see.

I turned my head from looking at my family and looked toward the poor slaves. In a very low voice, I asked, "¿Habla inglés? Do any of you speak English?"

The one who was actually sitting closest to me slowly lifted his head up off his knees where he had tried to rest it, and looked in my direction. I instantly noticed that he had such sad, defeated, pain-filled eyes! There was an actual glaze covering over them from the intense pain and deep agony he was in! As I looked at him, I wondered just how much more strength he had left before he just gave up and allowed himself to die.

In a barely audible voice that was more like a hoarse croaking sound, he mumbled, "I do. At least I speak some."

"What is going on here? What are these people doing? I saw them beating you! I thought they were going to beat all of you guys to death!" I said.

He took a deep breath and then looked at me with a very pained and hurtful expression. Then, he slowly said in low drawn out words, "We are undocumented workers. All of us each paid two thousand five hundred American dollars to be brought across the border by people who are associated with these people here. We had been promised by the people we paid the money to that we would have jobs waiting for us once we got inside of the United States.

"That is all we wanted; just a job. It doesn't matter what kind of a job, either. Any job here in the US is 'mucho grande' than anything we can find and do down in Mexico. We are not trying to take legitimate jobs away from Americans. We only want to do the jobs Americans don't want to do. We are just trying to put food on our family's tables and a roof over our heads! That's all! We are not criminals. We just want jobs.

"But look around you;" he said with unmistakable bitterness and a sudden deep hatred in his voice, "these are the jobs they promised us.

"These are not jobs! They lied to us and stole our money at the same time! Once they got us here, they turned us into 'slaves'!!! There were twenty five of us when we crossed the border a month and a half ago. Now, there are only the eleven of us left. The others have passed on. One or two of us pass on almost every other day! Just look over there at that man who is slumped over. He will be dead by tomorrow morning. Then, these cabrón will take him away and we will never know what they do with his body!"

You mean, he will die?"

"Si. Yes, die."

"How? Why? Do they kill you guys, or work you to death?"

"Si. They are killing us by working and beating us to death. Again, these are not jobs! We are nothing but slaves to them. We do not get paid for any work we do! They do not feed us anything except one small uncooked frozen meal a day that is less than a dog would eat. The food doesn't even have any protein in it. It is just fatty processed carbohydrates.

Also, they only give us one small bottle of water to last us all day long. It is 90 - 100 degrees inside of this mine, and they give us just one bottle of water a day! On top of that, they beat us with those leather whips that have metal studs embedded in them! They beat us without any mercy and without any provocation whatsoever; no matter how hard we try to please them!"

"Who are these people that are doing this to you? What is this place?" I asked.

"They are a part of a huge Mexican drug cartel. They bring their drugs across the border on the backs of illegal 'mules'; which are uneducated Mexican lowlifes and violent gangsters who cross the border, not to come to America and find jobs to work so they can feed their families back home, but to bring the dope across and make mucho money from doing that. They have no loyalty to the United States. And they don't care that the drugs are killing thousands of children, teens, and adults in the US! All they care about is getting rich from the drug trade!

"But once these bad people get their drugs across the border, they somehow get it to this place. From here, they make us load the vehicles and they then send them out for distribution from this old abandoned mine. They have two different Chevy Tahoe's. One is a white color, the other is black. See all of those bags over there? Those are all full of dope! And they send that stuff all over the United States from here."

It was exactly what I had suspected. I turned back to the speaker, "Have you tried to escape from here? I mean, is it possible?"

"No, Senor, not me or any of the ones left here. But, one of the original twenty five who came with us tried to. But, they caught him real quick. He barely even made it out of the mine before they caught him. Then, they made all of us watch as they made an example and punished him. Oh, I tell you, it was terrible!

"First of all, they stripped him completely naked. They then took his arms, tied them together at the elbows, and then again at the wrists. They used duct tape to do this.

Then they stretched his arms way up above his head, and tied his arms to the loading bucket on a front-end loader. After that, they raised the tractor bucket up until he was stretched completely off the ground with his feet hanging at least two feet in the air. You could actually hear the bones in his arms and his shoulders snapping and cracking as they popped out of their sockets! Oh amigo, he was screaming and crying and pleading! He was in so much agony! To this day, I still hear his screams inside of my head all of the time!

But then, an even worse thing happened! El Supremo Diablo took a knife he keeps strapped to his thigh. It is about 10" inches long and it has a serrated edge on it like one you would use to scrape scales off fish. He then began at my compadres right foot and began to cut and peel this poor fellow's skin right off him while he was still alive!

"Yes! I tell you the truth! It took El Supremo Diablo over two hours to cut his entire skin off him just like you would skin a rabbit or a deer! And up until right near the end, the poor amigo was still alive, too! Every time he would pass out, they would throw water on him to revive him! And El Supremo Diablo made us stand and watch the whole entire thing!

"I tell you, my ears have never heard such screaming and agony! Nor have my eyes ever seen such brutality and torture! This happened a week ago and my mind still cannot comprehend such cruelty! I never knew monsters like these men here even existed! These men here are very bad people! They are all el Diablo's! They are devils! They are not Mexicans! They have dishonored our race and our country by their deeds and their actions! And I can see by looking at your face that they have treated you very badly, too!"

I nodded my head, then said, "Yes, they hurt me, but it is nothing compared to what they have done to you guys here, or to the other poor people who have died at their hands!"

As I looked this poor fellow right in his sadden, pain-filled eyes, I instantly felt a huge bond of brotherhood with these men! What they had gone through would stay with them the rest of their lives. That is, if they can somehow survive and live to tell about it! This bond I'm feeling is very much the same type of feeling I felt about the other men in my unit when I had been in combat in Vietnam! I felt like we were all combat brothers!

At the same time, a deep pang of guilt swept through me. I suddenly realized just how calloused and prejudiced I had previously been towards people like this man and the other ones! Yes, there are many, many questions and enormous problems associated with people crossing our border illegally. There are the ones who come across purposely intent on taking advantage of our generosity and intent on stealing from us. I'm not talking about the drug mules, either. There are thousands who come across our border just for the financial benefits they can gain by stealing our identities, and also, by the use of our facilities including free medical care and schooling! These illegal moochers cost our state billions of dollars every year because of the costs associated with welfare and food payments, educational expenses, stolen identities~(big time expense), not paying taxes, and the huge costs associated with the incarceration of the flagrant criminals, plus many, many other expenses. These are just to name a few.

But, these men here were different. I believed what the man was telling me. I truly believed that all they really wanted were jobs! Any jobs! Other than being slaves!

This is where the need for comprehensive immigration reform is most needed in our country! I truly believe in a guest worker program. Always have. If people want to come across our border strictly for work, then I say, let's give them a job! This is the United States, for God's sake! We are the richest country on the face of the earth, or was before the last two administrations, including the current one, have almost broke us. But, we can still afford to give many immigrants a job!

But, if we do, we must make sure first of all, that we are not taking a job from a legal resident or citizen of the US who wants to work that particular job. If no legal resident wants the job, then hire the one who is willing to work it.

Next; and this is every bit, or even more, important as giving them a job, they must be paid a fair and honest wage! Many, many employers hire illegal immigrants because they know they can get away with paying them wages that are far below the market rate. This act alone costs the states and the federal government millions of dollars in lost tax revenue; not to say in the least of what it does to demean, humiliate, and discriminate against the workers who are basically subjected to the role of sharecroppers at the most.

Because of these men who really have been subjected to the horror of being slaves, I quickly asked God to forgive me for my bigotry and the hatred I had harbored towards all of the illegal border crossers! In my confused and convoluted feelings, I had combined all border crossers together without any mercy or distinction and made them all illegal criminals! I could see now that not all of them were that way, even if they have broken our law by coming across our border illegally.

Tears welled up into my eyes. I couldn't help it! I turned my head real quick so this guy could not see me while I tried to blink them dry, but the guilt of my bigotry remained inside of my heart! I determined at that moment that I was going to ask this brave man and the other men to forgive me as soon as we made it out of here!

At the same time, all of this just increased my determination that I was going to find a way to get all of us out of this hellhole, and once I accomplished that, I was then going to kill every one of these 'El Diablo's'! And I was going to relish it as they died! Very slowly and very painfully, I hoped!

A woman has an internal instinct to protect her brood from danger at any and all costs. But a man's internal instinct to protect his family far exceeds that of any woman. Maybe it's because he believes he has the ability to succeed at it.

At that exact moment, my internal instinct of protecting my brood from the danger we were in kicked into complete overdrive and it also included this man and the other men!

Inside of me, I determined that somehow, someway, with God's help, I was going to find a way to get out of here and not only save my wife and family, but I was going to save these men too! All thoughts of three years of sickness and chemotherapy were vanished!

I looked around the room; trying to see if I could spot anything that could be used as a weapon. I didn't see much, though, other than the huge cache of dope. So, I figured that the best weapon I had available to use at this particular time was my powerful mouth. At one time, I had been a very successful sales representative, and I had always prided myself on my ability to talk just about anyone into anything, even if they were adamant they didn't want what I was selling. Many of my peers in selling had often told me I could have sold fire to firemen. I don't know about that, but I do know that I am going to use everything I can think of to try to get free so I can have time to develop a plan and a strategy to free all of us.

I looked back over at the poor slave and said, "Amigo, my name is Jim. What is yours?"

"Juan."

"Well Juan, let me tell you something, my friend, we're going to get out of here. All of us! You, these other men, and my family! Believe me when I say this! You must trust me, though! Do not give up hope! And, tell these other guys what I said. But, I'm serious, do not lose hope!

"But most of all do not think I am abandoning you by what I'm going to tell their leader. I have to do what I have to do to get myself free first. OK? I can't do anything while I'm cooped up and bound in here. But please, Juan, do not take what I say to their leader as the truth, either. It is just my way of getting us out of here. Again, OK?

"One more thing, I was a combat soldier many years ago in Vietnam. During that time, I was in many serious predicaments on many different occasions. One time, my entire unit got cut off from our other forces and from being able to get any supplies whatsoever delivered to us.

During that time we were totally surrounded and outnumbered by the enemy by at least a 100 to 1 ratio. That siege lasted for over a week before we were finally able to escape out of the trap. But, because of God helping us, we did it then! And, we will do the same thing now, my friend! I killed several men during that siege and during that war. I did so to stay alive. And I promise you this; I will do the same thing again here in this hellish place very soon so we all can go free!"

"Si, y amigo!" He gave me a smile but I could see by the expression on his face that he thought I was probably just blowing smoke. Who could blame him? In his eyes, all he could see was an old man who had walked in here with a very pronounced limp, and who also was shaking like a rag doll from the effects of Parkinson's disease. But, in the old man's favor though, he did seem to have a big mouth. I also knew most importantly, he did not want to see me skinned alive!

It didn't matter to me right then what thoughts were going through Juan's mind, just as long as he keeps his mouth shut when I begin my sales pitch. But, later on, I may need his help, and that of his compatriots, too. So, I hoped he would not take the words I was going to say to heart, but to just trust me!

# Chapter 7

Just then, we heard several footsteps echoing down the tunnel. The sound they were making suddenly reminded me of the old war movies of black shirted, German SS Gestapo troops goose-stepping in formation. An ungodly evil spell of satanically induced terror swept over me, and my heart and bravery faltered badly! My heart began pounding harder in my chest with fear and anxiety than it had in the last 40 years! I slowly lifted my eyes up to see who it was that was coming into our room.

At the same time, I heard a collective sigh, along with several moans and groans coming from the poor slaves sitting next to me. They quickly pulled their legs up into as small of a ball as they could and pressed their backs hard against the wall. If they could have, they would have curled all of the way up into the fetal position. All of them wanted to turn invisible if that were possible! Most of them did not lift their heads up to see who it was, either. They knew who it was by the sound of the footsteps. It was the spirit of Adolph Hitler reincarnated inside of an antichrist demonic being they called, 'El Diablo Supremo'! They kept their eyes focused down on the floor, or just kept them shut as tightly as they could, hoping and praying all of the Diablos would leave them alone and not beat them anymore.

I assumed that one of the three men who had just walked in was the leader of this group. Two of them looked vaguely familiar to me. The one in the middle who was walking a half step ahead of the others had to be their leader. I had not noticed him when my eyes roamed over the faces of the others.

I was right. 'El Supremo Diablo came swaggering in to our holding cell very reminiscent of the evil one whose spirit he embodied! The one thing noticeably different in looks, though, was the half mustache of Hitler. This one's mustache was wide like Wyatt Earp's had been.

But one look at him and I knew immediately that if not the actual spirit of Hitler had entered the room, then the devil himself had just walked into my presence! I could also swear that the temperature in the room suddenly went down several degrees cooler than it had just been. It seemed like a cold evil wind had suddenly blown into this inner sanctum we were in. Without a doubt, I instantly knew inside that if this was not the devil himself, he certainly was a living representation possessed by him!

This supreme devil (El Diablo Supremo) was a very ugly, very bad looking dude with tattoos engraved all over every inch of skin I could see! And to complete the look, he even had little red and orange horns tattooed on top of his forehead! His face, in addition to having several tattoos on it, also had several large, angry looking, red scars rippling and weaving in different directions across it.

As he came up to me, he bent down and leaned in towards me until he was within an inch of touching his face to my face. The other two stopped a step or two back behind him. As they did, I suddenly had a mental picture of them yelling, 'Heil Hitler', while raising their right arms up high above them in a Nazi salute!

These two demonic beings had the same automatic weapons in their hands the others had, and like the other Diablo's, these guys were ready, itching, and just waiting for an excuse to use them. You could see it in their eyes! These guys thrived on the smell of blood and the stink of death! They feasted on it! They loved it! It convinced them of their passage into manhood!

El Supremo Diablo stood about five foot eleven inches tall and probably weighed about one hundred and ninety pounds with not a sign of an ounce of fat anywhere on his muscular body. His arms were rippling with bulging muscles that looked like oaken tree limbs. They were hanging down on each side of a huge muscular chest that would have made many women envious. Both of his legs looked like huge California Redwood tree trunks supporting his massive frame!

I knew by looking at him he had either spent a lot of time working out in a gym or acquired those muscles by being incarcerated in a prison for a long time sometime during his life. By the looks of him, he was someone I was not looking forward to tangling with. Not in a physical confrontation, anyway. I knew in that regard I wouldn't stand much of a chance.

Actually, though, we're about the same height and weight. But, where he has muscles, I have flab. Where he has youth, I have old age. Where he is in great shape, I am mostly a couch potato. Where he has the movements of a lioness on the hunt, I have the shakes and moves of a rap star, or a Parkinson's patient, either one. At that instant, I was really wishing right then, again, that I still had access to my old Cap't Crunch artillery gun! A 95-lb. bullet dropped on top of his head would certainly, at the very least, put a dent in his oblong, bald-headed, scarred up moon face!

But, there is one thing that I am far superior to him in. In that very moment, a sudden surge of heavenly sent strength and courage blasted through me like a nuclear bomb blast! I suddenly had a complete lack of fear in his presence! I knew that where he has false courage and flimsy strength because of the incarnation of Satan inside of him, I have 'El Shaddai', the Almighty God, indwelling me, and my family! And that gives me complete access to all of the forces of Heaven! What's a measly 100 to 1 ratio when you have God fighting for you? There was not a doubt in my mind that someway or other, I will eventually tangle with this demon! And without a doubt with God's unlimited help, I will find a way to kill him! I have to kill him! There is no other way to free my family other than to go through him!

I think he could suddenly see that in my eyes! By now, I had totally regained my composure and courage. This 'devil' was not going to intimidate me to make me cower and cry like a little baby over spilled milk! If he couldn't see anything else at this moment, I know he could see that there was absolutely no fear at all in my eyes toward him.

I also know that a man like him respects that. Men who kill other men respect men who die with honor and without fear! The worst thing a killer hates is a crying, begging, wimpy little coward too afraid to stand up like a man and die honorably. I wasn't afraid to die; probably because I somehow knew on the inside of me that I was going to be the one coming out on top and all of these other Diablo's were the ones who were soon going to be dead.

But, that didn't stop him from trying to intimidate me. He stared at me with eyes as cold and hard as stolen, frozen blood diamonds without blinking or wavering. As he did, I swear I could actually see little red and orange flickering flames of fire reflecting off the cold hard ice in those dead expressionless irises that are set high and far apart on his ugly, scarred, tattooed, and pimply face! Without any fear or awe at all, I thought, 'He really is El Diablo in person!'

He continued staring at me for what seemed like an eternity. Then, in a surprisingly high pitched voice that did not seem to belong to someone of his size, and especially, his shape, he spoke to me, "Who are you, and why have you intruded onto my turf?"

At that moment, because of his high pitched little girl like voice, I so much wanted to ask him if he had gone through puberty, yet! But, with all of the willpower I could muster up, I didn't! And, with a strength I never knew I possessed, I also did not laugh at his little high pitched soprano voice. So, I stared right back at him, never blinking nor taking my eyes from his, just like he was doing to me. But at the same time I allowed a friendly looking little smile to wrap across my face as I replied, "My name is Jim." Pointing toward my wife with my head since my hands were tied behind my back, I said, "This is my wife, Rebecca, but we call her Precious." Leaning out and again pointing with my head toward Rachael, I continued, "And this is my youngest daughter, Rachael. The two children are Rachael's kids and our beautiful grand-kids. The little boy is Bronco Nagurski and the gorgeous baby girl is our little goddess, Venus."

I mentioned all of this on purpose to personalize them to him. It is the reason I gave my daughter, my wife, my grand-kids, and my name to him. My way of thinking is that unless a person is totally void of any kind of a conscience or has absolutely no humanity inside of their demented and hardened souls, it is much harder for them to hurt, and/or, kill someone who has become more than an 'it' to you! By personalizing my family to him, they are becoming living, breathing, human beings with names to him! It might not mean much to a hardened killer like El Diablo, but every little bit helps, I hoped!

This is why when a salesperson is trying to sell a client; he always gets very personal with him, or her, by using the person's name over and over and over again. It is so much harder for someone to say 'no' to an offer to buy from someone who has become a 'friend' to them instead of a sleazy salesperson.

I turned my eyes back to face him and once again locked them on his. I still had the friendly smile on my face even though my bloody and cracked lips were splitting open again and beginning to drip blood down my chin once more. I tried to ignore the pain associated with that the best I could, then continued speaking, "Nineteen years ago, I was out here in the desert trying to find and explore old mines. One day, believe it or not, I actually stumbled upon this very same mine right here, and I tried to explore it just to see what was in it. I thought that maybe I could find some gold or something valuable like that, inside of it. I've always believed that one day; I was going to find a pirate's treasure inside one of these old mines!"

As I said that, he let a loud squealing snort squirt out of his nose that sounded just like a hungry rooting pig makes! That was followed immediately by a very high pitched sounding, little grade school playground girly type laugh! He couldn't help himself. And it was exactly what I was hoping for!

At the same time, a small chunk of greenish spittle fell out of his mouth and landed on his horribly scarred up chin. But, even though his face brightened and his mouth formed into a smile, never once did his eyes show the least little bit of humor! They were still as cold as an Antarctic iceberg!

I didn't let any of this deter me in the least, and I continued, "Unfortunately, at that time, though, I was only able to make it back to where the entrance tunnel branches off to the right because my flashlight batteries went dead. I never saw this room or was even able to enter the tunnel leading into it.

"For these past nineteen years ever since I was first here, I have always wanted to come back to this mine again and finish exploring it. Something has always stopped me from being able to do that, though, until today. But, I never knew, or even suspected, that someone may have filed a claim on it and was already using it. That never even entered my mind."

He continued looking hard at me, not saying anything now. His laughter had long ago died down. But I could tell he was still going to allow me to finish my story. I could see a little curiosity that was showing through on his face right then.

I knew right then that it was now or never! If I was going to be able to talk us out of this place, I had to say something to get into his confidence, because I knew he was never going to let us leave here alive unless I could win him over with my deceit. To allow us to walk out of there would be insane by any standards, including my own if I had been in his shoes. He knew the first thing we would do would be to go to the authorities and blow his operation. So, I opened my mouth again, "Sir, would you mind telling me what your name is? I would really like to know who I am talking with. As I'm sure you are already aware of, you have absolutely nothing to fear by giving me your name." I said this in a laughing voice and manner. This was another blatant attempt by me to personalize our blossoming one-sided relationship.

He thought for a second. Then, I guess he figured it wouldn't matter anyhow. Like I had already said; as far as he was concerned, we were already dead to him. So, he said, "My name is Tomas."

I said, "Do you mind if I call you Tomas?"

"No. Now tell me what you have to say. Get it over with and make it fast! Do you comprende?"

"Yes, Tomas, of course I 'understand'." By me using an English word instead of repeating the Spanish word for understanding was a direct ploy of mine. I planned on using this and others like it, a little later on. "But what I am about to say is going to be a big surprise to you."

With that, I hesitated for a brief second to let that sink in; then continued, "Tomas, I am really, really glad we found this mine again today. And especially, I am really glad that we have been able to have the pleasure and honor of meeting you today." A huge look of surprise instantly ran across his face. Without him being able to help himself, both of his eyebrows rose up in curved arches and his eyes softened just a little.

Before he could react I quickly continued on, "I say this will surprise you because I know that your plans are probably to kill Rachael, Bronco, Venus, Rebecca, and myself. And after you kill us, I also know you will get rid of our bodies so no one will ever find us again. Am I correct?" Again, without giving him a chance to answer, I hurried on, "And, if I was in your shoes, I would do the same exact thing! So, Tomas, I ask you to tell me why I am glad to be here and to meet you?"

My wife and daughter just about had a heart attack and died right then when I mentioned about killing us and hiding our bodies. The looks of astonishment, surprise, and even some red cheeked anger swept across their faces like rolling thunder! But, I was praying they would keep their mouths shut and not say anything! I just needed them to continue to trust me!

El Diablo didn't say anything right then. Maybe he didn't know what to say, I don't know. The smile had long ago vanished from his face but the surprise of my words was still etched on it. Without knowing what to say or do right then, he just kept staring directly into my eyes. This went on for what seemed like an eternity. But, I never blinked and neither did he. We were like two mean pit-bulldogs in a life or death stare-down trying to find out who the biggest alpha dog was and who was going to come out on top.

Eventually, though, a small smile began to crease across his face once again. This time, his eyes seemed to soften just a little more, although that was still almost imperceptible for anyone else to notice but me. Finally, in a very slow and drawn out voice, he began to speak, "I don't have any idea why you would be glad to meet me. As these other men who are chained here beside you rightfully know and can attest to you, I am El Diablo Supremo Muerte; the supreme devil of death! So, my soon to be dead amigo, why don't you tell me why you're glad to meet me?"

I didn't let his threat or his bad bully boy bluster spoken in his little girly voice deter me in the least. I continued on like he had said nothing at all. "Tomas, you need me, that's why I'm glad to meet you! And" … … At that moment, Tomas threw his hands up in the air and started to interrupt me, so I hurried on. "Don't laugh or get yourself worked up, my friend! Let me finish, okay? You hold all of the cards right now. Our lives are in your hands. So what do you have to lose by letting me finish talking to you? … … … Okay, I say that 'you' need me, and I will soon tell you why! But first, as you already know, I also say I need you, too," I said the last part in a loud and authoritative voice!

A look of incredulity raced across his expressions. "Why do I need you? And why do you need me? I am going to kill you, man! I am your executioner! Don't you understand that?"

Again, my wife and daughter just about shriveled up and died at that moment from fear! They both instantly and involuntarily sucked in their breaths which seemed to echo all around the room! As little Bronco heard this noise he turned to his Mama and said, "Mama, why are you afraid? Why are you crying, Mama?" as uncontrollable tears quickly overwhelmed her eyes and began rushing down her cheeks like ocean waves blowing in a hurricane!

The fear they were both feeling was so strong in them right then that you could have easily cut it with a knife. But, I wasn't afraid no matter what this El Diablo was saying! Or at least, I wasn't going to let him see me that way!

In my mind, I was thinking that I already had this guy! To me, he was as done as a Thanksgiving turkey that's been basting in the oven for several hours. You could stick a fork in him and feed him to the vultures, which I planned on doing later on! I knew inside that I already had him reaching for his wallet to buy the bull I was selling to him even if it was against his best judgment!

Of course, I couldn't communicate that to my wife and daughter at that particular moment to let them know to calm down and let me handle this.

"Look, Tomas, I am not a fool. I can see what is going on here. It is very simple; you are using this mine to distribute illicit drugs inside of my country." I emphasized the words, 'my country'.

"I can also see that by looking at you and talking with you, you are not a fool, either. So, as two intelligent men speaking soberly and clearly with each other, I ask you, Tomas, who are the drivers that you use to distribute these drugs? Are they dark skinned Mexicans like you? Are they the same ugly looking men who captured us a while ago?"

He didn't answer me. But his face suddenly took on a very dark look as anger only a serial killer can know suddenly filled his spirit! His eyes instantly returned to frozen solid ice, but this time, they had bloody red daggers in them to go along with the orange flames of fire! I knew he thought I was being racist and putting Mexicans down. In a way, I was. But, to get the point I needed for him to understand at that moment, I had to be. I also knew this was putting me on very thin ice right then. In fact, the ice might be so thin that it only had one side to it! But, I was already on dangerous ground! I had nothing more to lose, other than maybe being skinned alive instead of a short fast death. But, I had to make sure I got my point across in a very plain and blunt, "English" language so he could understand me real good.

"Listen, Tomas, I only ask this question to you because, as you already know, Arizona has the toughest anti-immigration law in the United States. And whether or not anyone will admit it, being a dark, brown skinned Mexican like you and your drivers is a sure way to be spotted by the cops!

"Then, in many, many cases, without you even being suspected of doing anything wrong; once you are spotted by the cops while driving a very nice new Tahoe, without a doubt, you will be pulled over and stopped! And after that, again, even if you have done nothing at all to warrant it, all of you are very likely to be arrested!

"Am I right, man? Call it racial profiling, or call it anything else you want! But, you know it as well as I do that the simple fact you and your drivers are Mexicans here in Arizona have placed big red targets right over your hearts.

"Listen to me, Tomas; I know what I'm talking about! I know a guy who is friends with a guard at one of the county jails here in Phoenix. He tells me that at least 85% of all inmates locked up behind those bars are either Mexicans or other Hispanic people. I believe him! And let me tell you, amigo, you should believe him to! They're looking for you guys!"

I paused for effect and took a deep breath like a very patient professor getting ready to give his top student the answer to his problem! "Tomas, why do you think it is that the ratio of inmates is mostly Hispanic?"

Again, without waiting for an answer, I hurried on.

"Let me give you the answer, okay? It is because they are targeting you, man! To them, basically every Hispanic; whether you are legal or illegal doesn't matter to them in the least, to them all of you are illegal criminal border crossing drug carrying mules intent on raping our women, stealing our identities, committing home invasions, and murdering our citizens, plus every other bit of mayhem and anarchy you can think of! By arresting you, whether or not you have done anything wrong, it takes another Mexican off the streets! And, in addition to that, it helps them make their arrest quotas. That makes them look real good to their superiors, and especially, it makes them look like real big men to their fellow officers!

Again, it doesn't matter if you haven't done anything wrong. As I'm sure you well know and can attest to, the policía can manufacture evidence of a crime faster than a Las Vegas magician can pull a duck out of his sleeve, or quicker than you can blink an eye! Am I right?

"So Tomas, let me ask you; how much money is a full load of drugs worth like what is now loaded inside of your Tahoe?"

Again, he didn't answer me. He just continued giving me an evil glare. But, I could see that the glare was mixed with something else; might be a little confusion, or it may be an awareness of a partial answer to a major problem the Mexican drug cartel has. It's also the same problem Al Qaeda has in the US. His glare was nowhere near as strong as it was at first. He had even moved his face back away from me about a foot and was now sitting back on his haunches on top of his heels. I could tell that he was trying to figure out exactly where I was going with this.

"Listen, it doesn't matter to me what it costs. It's none of my business, anyway. But, I bet it is worth a whole lot of money! I would guess that it is probably in the high six figures, or even into the sevens, huh? One load! Either way, man, it's a lot of money!

"Look, again, it doesn't matter to me how much it is worth. I don't care! But, I know without a doubt that it sure matters to you! And I'll bet it especially matters to your superiors if you lose a load of this stuff to the cops! Not only you, but I'll bet your superiors get really, really angry; and this is as they should! Don't they? Have you ever lost a load, Tomas? If you have, have they ever threatened you over it? ... Don't answer that! It's none of my business!

"Look, Tomas, when the cops stop you, you not only lose a load of drugs which are worth a ton of money, but you lose two more soldiers who will sit rotting in jail for a long time! I know this has to put severe crimps into your operation! Especially if your drivers were to cut a deal and rat you and your operation out! Huh?

"Anyway, Tomas, what I am getting at is that you need a new type of driver to make your deliveries! It needs to be someone who the cops won't ever be targeting, or even be looking at. It needs to be someone who would be the absolute last person the cops would ever think to look for! Someone totally anonymous and basically invisible in society! Someone who is as American as mother's apple pie, baseball, and 'white bread'!"

I hesitated for a brief moment as I let all of that sink in. I had to make sure that he was catching the gist of what I was saying! I was leading up to the most important part of my escape plan!

The look on his face told me he was beginning to see where I was going with this, so, I continued, "Look at me, Tomas. I am a sixty year old 'white man', not a Hispanic. I look old because I am old. In the last three years, I have undergone two major operations in my body. I am also a former US Army combat soldier who participated in a lot of combat skirmishes in Vietnam. As a combat soldier, I have killed at least twenty other human beings. I say that not to brag but to let you know that I would not be afraid to use force to protect your goods and operation.

"While over there in Vietnam, I was sprayed with Agent Orange defoliant on three different occasions. Because of that, I now have several physical diseases that classify me as disabled. I recently completed eleven months of chemotherapy to treat one of those diseases. I got that one from being covered on many occasions with the blood of my enemies over there. I almost died from that disease! I also almost died from the treatment itself! This chemo-treatment is the exact same treatment that is used to treat cancer. Right now, I am being treated for Parkinson's disease, which is another disease caused by exposure to Agent Orange. I take so many different medications that I don't have enough room on my vanity to keep them all! In fact, my supply of drugs is probably almost as large as yours!"

A brief, almost imperceptible little smile flickered across his face. He was beginning to like me as a person! I knew right then and there that I was 'selling' him big time! I had him locked up solid! He had his checkbook in his hands and he was ready to sign on the bottom line!

I also knew that almost everything I had told him had been nothing but lies! All of Arizona's local and state law enforcement officers are the absolute best in the entire US. This I am absolutely sure of! I am acquainted with several law enforcement officers in different departments and jurisdictions, and I firmly believe not a single officer in our entire state has ever arrested someone just because he racially profiled that person.

Because of our tough immigration laws and the sometimes radical enforcement policies by our sheriff, all of our officers are under the hugely magnified microscope of intense public observation and liberal media scrutiny. If even one of our officers were to target someone because of their race or the color of their skin, every news outlet in the entire country would descend like the filthy vultures they are and blast Arizona to pieces!

That is exactly what they are waiting, looking, and hoping for; the big illegitimate bust! In fact, I am sure that big bucks have already been offered for 'proof' that would show discrimination, and/or, profiling! But to this day, nothing; not even one shred of evidence has been produced that can show either. But, at this particular moment, I was saying and doing everything I could possibly think of to get the bonds of restraint off me so I could do something to free my family and the other good men held in bondage with us!

"Tomas, three years ago when I got sick, I lost everything I had ever accumulated over the years. Before I got sick I had owned my own business that I had started with my own calloused and bare hands, along with my ingenuity, and my ambition. I was living the American Dream, and I say that to let you know I am not afraid to work hard and long if that is what it takes!

Back then, I was living in a 5000 square foot house and I had plenty of money in my pocket to do just about anything we wanted to do. Now, my wife and I are trying just to survive with her working at least 50 hours a week every week, while I get a puny little government disability payment every month. Let me tell you, that payment is an absolute joke compared to what I used to make! And to say I am bitter is not an understatement in the least!"

I slowly tilted my head down and did not look at him for a moment. Then, in a firm and forceful voice, I quickly lifted my head back up and stared him right in his eyes with eyes almost as hard as his own. I said, "So, what I am saying is that you really do need me, Tomas! You need me to be your new driver to deliver your 'product'. To me, that is all it is, a product. And you know I'm not going to steal any of it from you! I have my own stash of drugs!

But look, man, again, I am a white, sixty year old man, who has a disability placard on his license plate! I am also a former combat veteran who normally wears an Army hat to show his patriotism and to keep cops away from me. I am the absolute last person on this earth that the cops would ever pull over, even if I were speeding. And, on top of all of this, I figure that the money we will make from you will certainly be a lot more than we are making now with my wife busting her rear-end every stinking day!

Also Tomas, my government did this to me! They turned me into the decrepit old man that I've become! The way I feel about it is that they owe me big time! But, all I get is an embarrassing little pittance in return for what I gave to them! I have no more allegiance to my country! And, I certainly have no qualms whatsoever to helping you out!

"So, amigo, what do you say? Am I hired, or what?"

# Chapter 8

This was the last thing in the world that El Diablo Supremo ever expected to be presented to him. It was also the last thing my wife and daughter ever expected to hear come out of my mouth. They had no idea where I was coming from. They knew me as a staunch conservative who abhors drugs, crime, most politicians, and big government in equal amounts! They knew me as staunchly patriotic and very pro-American! They knew me as the guy who has tears running down his face as the National Anthem is being played! So, at this time, they were really confused as they had no idea if I was being serious or not. And, if I was serious, then they didn't really know me at all! But, for the time being, they were still trusting me enough to continue to keep their mouths closed.

While El Diablo Supremo was still too stunned to say anything yet, I took a chance and glanced over at Juan. I wanted to see how he was handling the things I had just said. His face said it all, though! He had a look of pure, unadulterated hatred covering his entire face, and he was not trying to hide it from me in the least. I could understand his frustration. I know from what he had just heard from me sounded like a complete betrayal to him and his friends. But, I was hoping that he would continue to keep his own mouth shut and just let things play out. I had to get free before I could do anything else to try to help anyone else, so I was using the only weapon I had available; my big mouth!

Tomas was clearly confused, I could tell! But, he leaned forward towards me and again put his nose right up against mine. As he did, suddenly a huge, loud, smelly, stinky burp that lasted for an entire two minutes and thirty nine seconds erupted from out of the deepest and furthermost chambers of the inner sanctums of his stretched and distorted colon and then came boiling all of the way up inside of his body, until it finally came blasting out of his mouth like a belching sulfuric volcano that easily rivaled that of Mt. St Helens in intensity!

The double meat and cheese enchilada with green hot sauce

and extremely strong onions with wild miniature avocados he had eaten for lunch was so strong that it almost made me puke right back into his face! It took every bit of the willpower I never even knew I had and could muster up in that moment, to keep from barfing right back at him. But, I didn't really think that would have made a real good impression on him, although, he seemed to get a big kick out of my obvious and apparent discomfort from his gastric eruption.

But, it was very apparent that humor does not play a very big, or often, part of the man's life, as after a short period of time, his amusement waned and he once again began staring an unbelievably hard look right into my eyes. How anyone could change that fast was beyond me! I could swear his eyes once again had burning fiery flames in them, but, I could also detect a look of something else, too. A look that said that maybe I was on to something; a look that said that maybe what I had said could be as great as finding the missing link in the fossil chain, although he himself came close to that distinction! All he would have needed to do to discover that would have been to just look in the mirror!

I stared right back at him, never even blinking; trying my best to be the most ornery person, but also, most entirely capable person, he had ever met. I didn't have far to go to reach being the orneriest person. But, I needed to convince him that I was also the most capable! I did not, and could not; allow him to see any fear in me! He had to know that I was as tough and mean as he was, and that I had meant every word I had said!

After what seemed like an eternity, Tomas finally leaned over and said to me, "Man, I swear, if you are bull-sh-e-e-e-ting me, I will cut you into a million little pieces and make your wife and daughter eat your body parts raw like human sushi! Do you hear what I am saying?"

He took what I am sure was the same knife he had used to cut all of the skin off the other poor fellow who had tried to escape, and pointed it right at my throat for emphasis.

But, I didn't flinch or even seem to be bothered! I just gave him a nonchalant shrug of my shoulders as I said, "Of course I hear you!" I replied. "And I believe you, too! But, you know what, Tomas; you have nothing to fear from me, or my wife or daughter. Just give me a job and we'll all be as happy as pigs in a mud sty! I'll prove to you just how good I am, and at the same time, you can prove to your superiors just how great you are by having recruited me!" I gave him my best used car salesman's smile that I always keep held back in reserve only for the enraptured fools who just bought into my sales spiels like he just did!

He turned around and said something in Spanish to one of the others standing there. I couldn't understand a word of it. But, one of the demons standing there walked back out of the mine to go get something. The other went over and unsnapped the ankle cuff that was attached to the slave who looked like he was already almost dead.

Shortly after that, the demon that had walked out of the mine came sauntering back in to where we were. In his hand was a two foot long machete. He handed it to El Supremo Diablo Muerte. At the same time, the other Diablo had hauled the poor sick slave up to his feet and dragged him over and made him kneel on the floor of the mine only about one-foot away from my face and my lap where I was sitting.

From there, they pushed him over and down where he was sitting on his knees and bracing himself up with his hands. This made his neck stick straight out. In that very instant, as Juan, and all of the other poor slaves began yelling and screaming, and as Precious, Irma, and I looked on in complete horror, El Supremo Diablo Muerte, brought the machete up high above his head. Then, for the briefest of an instant, he paused before swinging the murderous weapon down with all of the force and power he had in his muscular arms!

Then suddenly, a loud *"THRACK"* exploded throughout the entire mine and blasted into everyone's ears! In that same instant, the machete sliced right through the poor guy's neck! As it did, his head toppled off and fell right into my lap splattering blood and gore all over me!

Precious and Irma both fainted! Almost all of the slaves began puking up what little food they had in their stomachs! I sat there unable to move, or to even hardly react! I was stunned! Paralyzed! In that very instant, I knew without a doubt, that I was right back in Hell in the very presence of Satan himself!

Then, El Supremo Diablo Muerte leaned in real close to me again. He stopped when he was only an inch away from touching my nose! Then, he stared straight into my eyes with absolute hatred and death in his own eyes, and with murder dripping from his voice, he said, "If you screw me, man that will be what will happen to your wife, your daughter, and your grand-kids! Do you understand me, man? I will make you watch me cut their heads off before I kill you, too!"

He turned to the guy who had brought the slave over in front of me. He told him to untie me. He also said to untie my daughter so she could take care of the kids. My wife, he would keep tied up for now as insurance that I would do as I promised, but she was free to use her hands to hold the kids.

One of the El Diablo's came around behind me and untied the rope and plastic cords that were binding me. Then, he motioned for me to stand up. I started to get up, but it took me a while to do so because my legs had severely cramped up, and because I was needing to take a pill right then for my Parkinson's. I was also very weak and ill from what I had just seen!

When I was finally able to get to my feet, I was very wobbly and unsteady on them. This worked even more to my advantage, though! It gave El Supremo a big visual sight of the extent of my physical ailments.

At that moment, by seeing me tottering on my feet, he thought there was no way the cops would ever bother me even if they did stop me, and also, he believed right then that he had absolutely nothing to worry about from me in a physical sense.

To him, I was nothing more than an invisible, harmless, crippled up weak old man!

But I was now completely determined to prove him wrong! And, I was determined to make sure this would be his final fatal mistake!

# Chapter 9

The guard who untied me made some kind of a guttural noise that kind of reminded me of a big bad mama grizzly bear who is about to tear apart and consume an unfortunate soul who has innocently wandered into her cub's play area! He then motioned with his AK-74 for me to follow his boss down the tunnel and out of the mine. By this time, I had gotten pretty good about interpreting these gun signals and what they meant!

Inside, even though I was feeling sick and horrified about what had just happened, I was also doing somersaults! At my age and with my disabilities, the only way I can do flips and somersaults are inside of my mind, or tumbling head first down a big berm. But I was free, though! And that's what mattered!

Now, I had to figure out a way to get the rest of my family out of there, plus the other remaining ten men held in bondage before the supreme devil of death killed all of them, too! I also needed to think of a way to get my guns out of the back of my Tahoe so I could then take on the persona of a deranged workplace killer, and kill all of these devils of the desert before I ran out of bullets.

Before I left the room to follow Tomas, I quickly glanced over at Precious and Irma. They had regained consciousness from their fainting spell, but they were unresponsive, totally paralyzed with fear and horror! I mouthed, "I love you", to them, along with a painful wink of my left eye. I then turned and began hurrying to catch up with Tomas to go out of the mine.

We walked out of the mine and into only a partially blue sky that was now mostly covered with dark, thunderstorm looking clouds. He stopped and turned towards me one more time. As I came to a stop next to him, he moved up and got right in my face again. El Diablo and I stand almost eye to eye in height, so his rancid, less than half digested, gastric enchilada fumes were again almost gagging me, but I still didn't flinch or even bat my eyes!

There was no way on earth I was going to let him know that he intimidated me in anyway at all! I may die from lack of oxygen because of his poisonous gastric breath blowing in my face, but I refuse to let him know I am uncomfortable in any way whatsoever!

As he faced me, he began to scream at me, again, sounding even more like a little school girl, "Listen to me, white bread cracker man, I swear I will kill you if you cheat me or double-cross me in any way whatsoever! Do you hear me? But first of all before I kill you, I will make you watch as I first kill your grand-kids. Then, I will make you watch as all of my men rape your wife and daughter so many times that they will beg to be killed themselves. Then, I will kill you; but I will do it so slowly that it will take two weeks for you to finally die!"

Again, he screamed even louder in his high pitched voice that would have made Bobby Hatfield of the Righteous Brothers very envious and my dogs yelp with intense pain, "Do you hear what I am saying?"

I said in a very firm and controlled voice that I purposely lowered several octaves just to try to make him feel silly, "Sure, Tomas, I hear you. But you listen to me, too; look at me, man, I am a sixty year old disabled man. Surely you can see that with your own eyes! Can't you? And by looking at me, you must know that you have nothing to fear from me. What could I do to you and your men? Huh? Again, I am a decrepit old man who just wants to make some money so it will be easier on my wife and me. I am not going to cheat you.

"Look at me, man, I'm an old man! And most of all, amigo, my government did this to me! They have abandoned me with only a little tiny fraction of what I used to earn", I screamed back at him!

He nodded his head at me as if he finally understood. By me getting right back in his face and screaming back at him, he knew I was as tough inside as I had been making out that I was. He knew he had an old ornery man that he thought he could trust; otherwise, this old man had to be a total fool to try such a stunt!

He figured only an old combat veteran who had killed men before in his life would either be brave enough to get back in his face, or stupid enough to want to die! He chose to believe that I was more brave than stupid. I wasn't too sure, though!

He allowed a small smile to cross his face; then said, "This man here is named Gerardo. He speaks good English. He grew up here in the US. He is going to go with you to make this delivery we have already loaded up. You will drive and go where he tells you to go. You will not say anything unless Gerardo tells you to. And if you try anything at all, he will tell me, and I promise you that I will do just as I have said I would!"

He pointed over to the Tahoe. "The keys are in the ignition."

I gave him a big smile and stuck out my hand to shake his. I wanted him to shake my hand so he would become familiar with the feel of the man who was going to kill him later on this evening! But he just stared at me while totally ignoring my hand. Then, he turned his head to the side and let lose a huge gob of green colored spit. "Just do what I said, and don't give me no trouble, cracker man!"

I quickly turned around and began to wobble over to the truck. But before I did, I thought I would push his buttons just one more time. I looked back over my shoulder and said, "Hey Tomas, maybe this is not a good time to ask what my pay will be? HUH?" Then, I let loose a huge, ground shaking laugh. In spite of himself, a small smile briefly crossed his face, too, but it was a smile nonetheless.

# Chapter 10

I turned around and hurried over to the truck. Once there, I opened the driver's door and quickly climbed in. Then, I reached down, turned the key, and started the engine. After that, I glanced over at Gerardo and said, "OK, amigo, where do we go?"

He pointed straight ahead. "I'll tell you where to turn. Just drive!" Friendly fellow, I thought.

I wondered if I was going to be able to somehow get near my Tahoe, and if I could, what kind of excuse I could use to retrieve my guns. I had no idea so I decided I was just going to have to play it by ear and let God handle it.

I knew that God had gotten me free. I also knew that God never has just a 'partial' plan in place for us! He says, "I know the "plans" I have for you." So, I put my complete trust in Him to do exactly what His Word declares! Someway or other, He would work things out for me.

I pulled the gear lever down into the drive position. Then, I took my right foot off the brake, moved it over to the accelerator pedal and began to lightly press on it. At the same time, I let my left hand fall down inside of the storage panel on the driver's door without Gerardo noticing me. I was hoping I could find something that I could use as a weapon down inside of it in case I couldn't get to my guns.

I glanced over at Gerardo to see if he was looking at me. I noticed he's a pretty big guy. He stands probably around six feet one inch tall and probably weighs somewhere around two hundred and twenty pounds. If I find something to use as a weapon, 'it had better be something good,' I thought.

I was hoping that Gerardo would be the first one of the El Diablo's that I could put out of his miserable existence. I wasn't for sure that he considered his life a miserable existence, but as a drug runner and a member of the Mexican drug cartel who is responsible for the deaths and destruction of thousands and thousands of lives, plus being a part of this particular group who has already killed fifteen illegal border crossers they had first forced to be slaves, and who is also now holding my family as hostages threatening to kill them, too, he is sure miserable to me, and that is all that mattered. So, I have no qualms at all about killing him if I can find a way to do it.

I have killed before. I was twenty years old at the time, though. I was, also, in very good shape back then due to lifting a lot of 95-lb. bullets every day and night. I was pretty much as strong as an ox. I had never had any guilt or second thoughts about ever pulling the trigger to take another human life! The enemy was either going to kill me, or kill one of my combat brothers. To our minds and most definitely in reality, it really was, kill or be killed!

I was rationalizing that this was the same thing as Vietnam. Like then, I am right now in a position to either kill or be killed. And worse than that, I am in a position to either kill, or watch my wife and daughter be repeatedly raped without mercy, and then killed, along with my two beautiful grand-babies being killed! I cannot allow this to happen!

Man, I tell you, at this moment, this ornery old man is having absolutely no qualms at all about ending the lives of several demons incarnating themselves as human beings! In fact, where there normally should have been anxiety and fear, along with shaking hands and an acid filled upset stomach, I was having to force myself to keep from bursting out laughing! I was reveling in the warm fuzzy feeling I was feeling inside! I knew that God had helped me get free, and that He was going to help me rid His beautiful earth of this garbage that was polluting it! I could hardly wait to find a weapon that I could use to dispatch this enemy of mine that is sitting in the passenger seat next to me! "Oh, I want so much to send this Diablo straight back to Hell where all El Diablo's (devils) belong!" I mumbled under my breath!

# Chapter 11

By now, we had traveled a little over two miles away from the mine. We could no longer see it, nor could they see us because of the twists and turns of the trail we were traveling on. It was a different trail than the one I had come in on; this one was much smoother and faster.

The time was now a little after six o'clock in the evening. The sun was almost all of the way down but there was still a little streak of yellow tinted light emanating from it way out on the western horizon. Also, the huge cumulus clouds had now all gathered together and had formed into huge rain bearing dark gray monsters that were now covering the entire sky. The smell of rain was everywhere. It was very apparent by now that they were just begging God to allow them to release their pent up torrents of water and hurricane force winds down onto the earth. At the same time bright flashes of lightning were shooting crazily throughout the sky. These were followed shortly afterward by loud rumbles of thunder. Within minutes of all of that, small droplets of sprinkles began falling onto the windshield.

As I looked up at the sky, I saw the bright flashes of lightning shooting down that were coming directly from God's own eyes! I also heard the thunder of his awesome voice echoing throughout the earthly atmosphere! I knew inside that God had stood up from His throne and had stepped up to the podium to warm up the orchestra of heaven for the climax of judgment He was going to allow me to bring to these satanic evil beings!

All the while, I surreptitiously continued to rummage around in the side pocket of the driver's door with my left hand. It seemed to be full of nothing but papers and other junk. But, just then, my fingers tightened around a ball point pen. Through my fingers, I thought it felt like it was the fat expensive kind that is made out of metal.

At least, that's how it felt in my hand. Anyway, it was a weapon! It was not my first choice of one but it would have to do.

And, with God's help, it would serve that purpose!

I say with God's help, because to me, I just couldn't imagine God being willing to allow these Diablo's to continue their killing of innocent border crossers who they first turn into slaves; nor their killing of thousands of others through their dope and drugs and violence. I also could not imagine God allowing them to kill my grand-kids, and rape and then kill my wife and daughter! So, to me, I knew just like I did in Vietnam, that God was on my side!

Gerardo was not paying any attention to me at all. With his youth and his strength, I was the last person he would have ever suspected to make a move to hurt him! He had his head turned to the right and was staring out his passenger window. He only turned his head to look out the windshield only now and then to tell me where to turn.

Suddenly, though, he turned all the way so he could look at me. He said, "Hey man, look right over there." He began pointing out his side window off into the near distant. "You see that little dirt mound over there? Behind it is a deep mine shaft going straight down into the earth at least a hundred feet." He paused for a second and started laughing.

Eventually, he continued, "That is where we throw the immigrant scum who die inside of our mine. We throw them down the shaft and no one will ever find them! It is also where we will bury you, and your wife and daughter and grand-kids, if you screw us man! You hear me?"

I glanced over at him with a look of disgust on my face! Then, in a very slow and clear voice, I said, "Yeah, Gerardo, I hear you. But, let me ask you something; are you and your boss so hard of hearing yourselves that you can't hear me? I mean, this job is something that I have dreamed about! It's something that will allow my wife and me to eventually retire and then travel the world! Don't worry about me, OK?"

After I said that I could see him relax all the way. He began to take me at my word. The tension in his shoulders melted away. That allowed them to slightly fall forward. His breathing also seemed to be more regular and less forced.

I was watching him out of the corner of my eye. 'This is doom on you, fool! Enjoy the rest of eternity in Hell, the place God created especially for "all" devils!' I thought!

He didn't say anything more to me but turned his head back to stare again at the mine shaft out of his side window. He chuckling as his eyes focused on the death chamber again. I quickly moved the ball point pen from my left hand over into my right hand. I made sure that the point was facing backwards toward the heel of my hand and that my thumb was on the push lever on the top of it that makes the tip come out. I quickly glanced down to get a quick peek to make sure I had it in my hand correctly and that it would do what I intended it to do. I knew I would probably only have this one chance to make this work, and if I failed, well... ... ... I preferred not to think about that right then! But, the pen did appear to be very sturdy to me, and it was made out of some kind of metal; probably pig metal from China, but metal, nonetheless.

I glanced back at Gerardo. He was still focused on the mine shaft out his window. "It's now or never!" I thought! So, I suddenly stomped on the gas. This caused us both to be flung back into our seats. But, it also gave me much more acceleration and momentum to swing my arm that much harder.

Before I stomped on the accelerator, I had taken my right arm and lifted it up into a horizontal sideways position with it cocked at the elbow. My hand was near my chest with the pen pointing straight away from me. Then, as soon as I stomped on the gas, I swung my arm outwards as hard as I could and straight towards his neck! I didn't actually see what happened next because I was swinging my eyes back and forth. I was looking at him for a second, and then back at the road in front of me.

But, I knew that I had done real good because I felt the pen make contact and instantly penetrate deeply into the soft skin of his neck! Also, I could feel the heel of my hand slam hard into his Adams Apple, which actually crushed his larynx! At that same moment, I suddenly stomped on the brake which threw his body forward and at the same time, it helped me to insert the pen even deeper into his neck!

Instantly, in a blink of an eye, he brought both of his hands up and tried to grab his neck! At the same time, he began gagging and spiting and coughing as his blood began spewing all down the front of his shirt and onto his pants! Again, I knew I had caught him real good when I saw it was spewing and spurting blood out of it for at least a foot in long angling arches with every beat of his heart. I knew I had hit his carotid artery! I also knew he would be dead in less than a minute.

As he reached for his neck, though, I quickly pulled the pen back out, but as I did, I jabbed it sideways in the hope that I could tear his carotid artery completely out of his neck. I knew I had nailed him real good, but as big as he was, I wanted to make sure he died real quick. So as soon as I pulled the pen out of his neck, I reared back and once again swung my arm as hard as I could towards him. This time, the pen went straight through his left eyeball that was already protruding out of his face part ways because of lack of air from swallowing and choking on his Adam's Apple!

With a loud smack as the side of my hand hit his face, the pen penetrated all of the way back into his brain. He died instantly, unless he was already dead from his carotid artery being torn apart! But to make sure, though, I took my hand off the pen for a brief second. It was just hanging there in a very grotesque way sticking about an inch and a half out of his ruptured eye. I quickly stomped on the brakes and brought the truck to a complete stop. Then, I used the flat palm of my hand and swung my arm one more time and slammed the pen all of the way back inside of his brain until it was completely buried out of sight inside of his head!

The force of my blow made his head bounce hard against the back of the seat. Then, he fell forward until his seat straps wouldn't let him go any further. He wasn't moving and the blood had ceased to spurt from his neck! He was dead!

I wanted to shout hallelujah! "This was one Diablo down, just a few more to go!" I thought! Inside, I was now even more totally stoked and elated! At sixty years old, I had just killed a devil that was less than half my age and that was much larger and stronger than me!

I leaned over and looked past Gerardo out his side window. Seeing him sitting there did absolutely nothing to me except boost my emotions with glee! I was filled to the brim with absolute disgust and hatred towards these demons---demons that could cut heads off innocent sickly men like it was nothing more than taking candy from a baby! So their deaths were my newly acquired job as a way to earn my families', the poor slaves, and my continued ability to live!

I let my foot ease off the brake and began turning the steering wheel to the right to move over to the vertical mine shaft he had pointed out to me. It was going to be his burial place, too. I was going to let the ghosts of the poor slaves, who were in the deep hole torment this devil for eternity!

I pulled the Tahoe up close to the shaft with the passenger door next to it. I then reached over and turned off the engine and removed the key. Even if Gerardo was dead, I wasn't taking any chances!

I opened my door and walked around behind the Tahoe over to the passenger side, keeping an eye on Gerardo the entire time. He didn't move, as I expected. When I got to his door and opened it, though, he instantly slumped out of the door towards me until his seat-belt finally caught and restrained him. To tell you the truth, in that very instant, I almost died myself from fright! I thought this devil had somehow come back to life and was coming after me!

But, as I said, he was dead. After my heart finally settled back into a more normal rhythm of about 2000 beats per minute from about a million beats a minute, I was able to rationally realize that! So, I reached in, unbuckled his seat belt, and removed it from around his body. As I did, his dead weight caused him to tumble sideways out of the vehicle and fall down to the ground head first. As it hit the old hard ground, it sounded like a ripe watermelon plopping open. He quickly came to a stop and quit moving, so I took my foot and rolled him over onto his back. Then, I again took my foot and kicked his legs and arms straight out from his body.

He still wasn't moving. So, I bent down and began to check him for weapons. Underneath his non-tucked shirt was a holster pressed against the middle of his back. In it was a 9-mm pistol just like mine. I set it aside for a moment and continued checking him. I found strapped along his left thigh, a 10" inch long serrated killing knife in a scabbard. I removed it and set it aside, too. Finally, strapped on his right ankle was a 38-caliber snub-nose pistol. I removed it, too.

After getting all of his weapons, I began going through his pockets to see what I could find in them. In his wallet was a thick stack of hundred dollar bills. I didn't take the time to count them, so I didn't know how much was there. I just shoved them in my pocket. That was my pay for killing him! In his left front pocket was another big roll of money with rubber bands around it. Again, I didn't take the time to count it; I also shoved it into my pocket.

After that, I began rolling him over towards the mine shaft. Once I had him teetering on the edge, I stared down at him. A big wad of burning bile rushed up into my throat. It wasn't because I had killed him. It was because of the unbelievable amount of complete disgust and hatred I was feeling for him and the other Diablo's!

I don't normally curse, which is probably funny to you. I know what you're thinking; I can kill other living beings without any qualms, but I don't use curse words! I agree it is weird! But it just isn't part of my makeup. At least, it hasn't been since I left Vietnam. My mama didn't curse, and if she would have ever caught me cursing, well, let's just say that I would rather have fought the real devil in a face to face, life or death combat than facing her! That would have been much less painful than a beating on my bare legs with a huge switch she would have made me bring her after she forced me to cut it off the big Willow tree in our backyard.

But, I just couldn't help myself this time. I yelled at him, "I hope you're burning in Hell right now, you filthy bastard!

"My only regret is that you died too quickly! I should have made you suffer and feel the pain you have been giving to those poor slaves!" With that, I brought my right leg back and then swung it forward as hard as I could, right into the middle of his back. For a brief second he balanced on the edge of the drop; then, he went tumbling head over heels straight down to the bottom of the shaft where I eventually heard him hit with a splat. Oh, how I wish it had been deeper than it was!

# Chapter 12

I took the 9-mm and tucked it in the front of my pants under my T-shirt. I had already popped the magazine out of it and counted the shells. As I figured, there were 20 rounds in it. I popped the magazine back in place, then pulled back the slide and chambered a round. I also put the spare magazine with 20 more rounds in my front pocket where I would be able to get to it real easily. Before tucking it in my waist band, though, I made sure that the safety was on. I certainly did not want a freak accident to cause a round to fire out of the gun in the direction the barrel was pointed even if my days of having kids are far behind me!

I also took the knife and strapped it to my right thigh. I wanted it up high where if I needed it, I could get to it real fast. The little .38-cal., I put in my right rear pocket. Again, I made sure the safety was on. Again, I did not want a wild freaky accident to cause a round to fire in the direction the barrel was pointing, either. If it were to, I would probably never have to squat to take a dump again. A bag hanging on my side would do the job just fine.

After that, I got back in the Tahoe, started it up, and moved it around so the rear-end of the Tahoe was backed up close to the mine shaft. I then shut off the engine, but this time I left the keys in it. Then, I got out and walked around to the rear of the vehicle.

Once there, I reached out and popped the tailgate up. Then, I pulled one of the sandbags towards me that was full of destructive, life destroying dope that had been destined for our American streets. I took the hunting knife I had taken from Gerardo and made several large rips right down the middle of the bag. Then, I turned around and let the off-white colored contents inside of the bag fall to the bottom of the shaft. It reminded me of an open bag of flour being dumped down into a garbage bin. I then reached in, grabbed another one, and did the same thing as before.

After that, I continued cutting up and emptying every bag in the truck down into the mine shaft. Almost an hour later, I finally finished the job. "No more lives are going to be destroyed by these drugs!" I said.

When I had gotten down to the last layer of bags and began removing them, I noticed something was hidden underneath a small canvas sheet that was under the bags of dope. The dope had been sitting on top of the sheet.

As I lifted the sheet up to see what it was, my heart began to flutter with gladness and hope! I almost let another shout of Hallelujah rip out of my lungs right then. Underneath the sheet was another one of those AK-74 automatic rifles fully locked and loaded with two extra full magazines of 30 rounds each lying next to it. And, another thing I quickly noticed was that there was a big round soup can looking attachment screwed onto the front end of the barrel. This time, I just couldn't help myself and I did let loose with a reserved, but still enthusiastic, "Hallelujah! This beautiful automatic weapon has a silencer on it!"

I picked up the gun and fell instantly in love with it. I had owned my old 22-caliber rifle for a lot of years and I was still in love with it. But, this new powerful little man-killing baby was just flat out beautiful! I leaned over and slowly and lovingly brought it up to my lips. This weapon was going to save my family and the slave's lives!

"The tide has just turned in my favor, El Supremo Diablo, Tomas! You are a walking dead man, and what's great about that is, you don't even know it yet! But by sunup tomorrow morning, you, and all the rest of your Diablo's, will be back in Hell where you somehow escaped and where you belong again!"

Just then, an enormously bright streak of lightning flashed across the entire sky! Less than two seconds later, it was followed by a huge blast of rolling thunder. I have always heard that you can tell the distance lightning is from you by counting the seconds after the flash until you hear the thunder. The number of seconds equals the approximate number of miles away that the lightning is from you.

I don't know if that is true or not, but I knew from the loud sound of the thunder that it was close. I also believed the lightning and thunder was God congratulating me on a job well done! One more of Satan's demons returned back to Hell!

Even though it had not started to rain yet, other than a few sprinkles now and then, I expected it to begin coming down in huge torrents any minute now. I didn't want to get wet right then, so I hurried back around to the driver's seat and climbed back in. But, I knew the lightning and thunder would be perfect for me later on when I get back to the mine. The thunder will help drown out any sound I may make and the lightning will light my path through the evil bowels of Hell I have to travel again.

I reached over and started up the truck. But, before I could put it into gear to go, I happened to glance up through the windshield. Up ahead of me in the distance I noticed some headlights from another vehicle coming towards me. The headlights were on the same trail Gerardo and I had been on, but whereas we had been heading towards town, these lights were coming towards me from town. I was hoping it was just some young fools out driving through the desert at night temping God and nature not to get killed by the weather, or someone else other than more Diablo's.

# Chapter 13

I quickly turned the engine back off. I hadn't yet turned on my own headlights so I figured that whoever it was, had not had an opportunity to see me. At least I was hoping they hadn't! Where I was at the vertical mine shaft, was about 200 yards off the main trail and partially hidden behind some large desert floral.

I gently opened my door and climbed back out, pulling the AK-74 off the front seat as I did. Again, I quickly made sure that a round was chambered and it was ready to fire. It was. For the time being, though, I left it on safety.

I began making my way on foot back across the desert over to the trail I had been traveling on my way to town. The trail is the same one the car will be on if he stays on the same course he is now traveling. I stayed down low and tried to keep behind any desert bushes and floral as I made my way back over towards the road. Whoever this was, I didn't want them to see me.

In fact, I had no intention of ever letting anyone even know about what happened out here! That is especially true for any law enforcement authorities of our state or federal government. That is why I threw Gerardo's body down the mine shaft and took his identification from him. If anyone were to find out who I am and what I have done, without a doubt, my name and all of my family's names would be plastered all over every news outlet in the western hemisphere, and possibly even around the entire world. We would certainly have our 15 minutes of fame! But that's all it would last, because then, my entire family would be the 'walking dead'! It would only be just a short period of time before we stopped walking and then lay perfectly still inside a container with six feet of desert dirt piled on top of us!

I knew that the amount of dope that had been inside of the Tahoe, and the amount that is still inside of the mine, has to be worth several millions dollars at the very least. Any idiot would be able to tell that.

So, I knew that the drug cartel that owns all of this dope is not going to take it lightly that I am going to kill a lot of their soldiers, destroy millions of dollars of their drugs, and most of all, ruin a very large and so far, successful, distribution system of theirs! If they ever find out who had done that to them, torture and death would be sweeping down on all of us to consume and burn us beyond recognition like a raging, unstoppable, out of control, lake of fire! That's why I had to check out the vehicle that was coming towards me!

I finally made my way over to the road. Next to it were several large bushes. I moved over and hid behind them for a brief moment so I could get a better look around and at the oncoming vehicle. I quickly estimated that at the speed it was coming towards me, I would have about two to three minutes to get ready for it. That was plenty enough time to get hidden.

I noticed a large, almost round boulder about 4' high and at least the same width but had a fairly flat top on it. It was only about ten feet off the path. To me, the boulder was like a Godsend! It would give me a very good view of the oncoming vehicle, and if need be, a very good firing angle at whoever was in it. Plus, the size of it would give me a lot of protection from any return fire if I missed and got into a firefight. I was praying so much that wouldn't happen because of the noise it would generate. But the great thing about the boulder is I could use it as protection for myself, and also, as a place to steady and aim the rifle by laying it on top of the rock.

As the vehicle got closer, I saw that it was another Chevrolet Tahoe like Gerardo and I had been in. But, the different between the one I had been driving and this one, is that this one is black in color; just as Juan had told me. He had said they use two Tahoe's to deliver the drugs in; one white and one black. Well, I had the white one; this had to be the black one.

I don't know why, but sometimes at very weird times, out of nowhere songs just seem to burst out in full glory into my mind. I guess it's because I love music! It happened right then. Just as soon as I saw the 'black' Tahoe, the old Rolling Stones song, "Paint It Black", flooded into my mind!

Maybe it was just the color of the Tahoe that made the song

come into my thoughts. Or maybe it was the 'black' situation I was playing a big role in right then. I didn't know, or care. But, the song began running through my mind over and over again.

As it got near to me I looked hard into the Tahoe to see who was in it. At that very instant, a very fortunate bright bolt of lightning flashed all the way across the sky searing its way from the eastern sky all the way across to the western sky. And for a brief instant, it lit up the entire desert just like it was the middle of the day. It was just enough light and just enough time to provide me with a perfect view to see the inside of the Tahoe. And what I could see sent chills running up and down my spine! Inside of it were two very ugly, very bad looking, dark skinned Hispanic guys in the front seats. And both of them had tattoos covering all of the parts of their bodies that I could see. These were not chills of fear, though. They were chills of joy and excitement! I was going to be able to dispatch two more Diablo's straight back to the Hell they had escaped out of and into our world.

I knew, without question, these two bad dudes were part of the drug gang at the mine! I also knew that I needed to stop them right then and there, too! I couldn't allow them to reach the mine. If they were to get back to the mine, they would add that much more to the amount of concentrated firepower and manpower they would be able to throw against me. I was already vastly outnumbered! I didn't need to face more of them back there! And, I certainly did not want any more of them to be around my family that were being held prisoners inside of it!

So, I slowly raised my beautiful new rifle and gently laid it on top of the boulder. I tilted my head and laid my cheek against the stock of the gun so I could look straight down the barrel. I then moved the gun into position so I could point it straight at the driver. I had to get him first so the vehicle would come to a stop. I didn't want to shoot the passenger and then have the driver stomp on the gas and get away from me. He would certainly tell them back at the mine what was happening, and if that were to happen, my family would die horrible, painful deaths!

I sent up a very quick prayer to God that the gun had been sighted in, and thus, would shoot exactly where I aimed it.

As I looked down the barrel, I also thanked God that both the driver and the passenger's side windows were open all of the way. It had not yet begun to rain any more than a few drops now and again, so they must have been enjoying the beautiful smell of the soon to arrive rain and the cool nighttime temperature. This was good. Shattered glass makes a real mess. Plus, the shattering of glass being hit by a bullet moving at supersonic speed was surely going to make a very loud noise. I knew that where I was had to be at least two miles away from the mine, but I also knew that sound carries a long way at nighttime; especially when a sky is full of low hanging thick clouds. I certainly did not want to raise any suspicion back at the mine if they were to hear something that sounded odd to them. I, again, quickly thanked God that this beautiful new weapon had a beautiful silencer on the end of it!

I continued looking down the barrel of the gun. They were getting closer to me; soon to be in perfect, can't miss, range. The vehicle was cruising very slowly, probably not going any more than 5 to 10 miles per hour. They weren't in any hurry to get back to the mine, I guess.

The interior of the Tahoe was glowing from the lights on the dash. It cast a strong defused light onto the two demons! I could not only see them very well now, but I could also hear their confident sounding voices coming from inside of the truck. They were laughing and having a good ole jolly time right then! They were speaking Spanish but I heard one of them say something about what I thought was a million US dollars. I didn't know what he meant, but I was going to make sure they had absolutely no chance of enjoying any part of a million US dollars!

If I had needed anymore confirmation, this was it! It confirmed to me these two guys were two more of the drug smuggling Diablo's! I slid my finger over and silently moved the safety switch to the off position. I also gently moved the firing lever to single shot from fully automatic. Then, I took a deep breath and slowly exhaled.

The truck was cruising up slowly right in front of me. As it did, the driver suddenly turned his head to the left to look out his side window. He seemed to look right at me. At the same time, though, the last remnants of air emptied out of my lungs and I slowly sucked in my breath and held it. I then made a very slight adjustment and placed the sights on the barrel right in the middle of the driver's forehead right between his eyes. I didn't know if he saw me or not but he made no moves like he did. I didn't care either way!

'Taking out the driver will be an easy shot if the gun is sighted in', I thought! At the same time I gave the trigger a very gentle squeeze! A soft muffled poof echoed a brief fraction of a second later. In what seemed to be the same instant, his head snapped straight backwards as a round red hole suddenly appeared right in the middle of his forehead, right where I had aimed! At the same time as the round red hole appeared in his forehead, the entire back of his head suddenly exploded!

A brief instant after that, the truck suddenly veered off the road to the left. Out of reflex action the driver must have jerked the steering wheel to the left. The truck had not been going very fast to begin with, but it now began to lose all of its momentum and to slow down. But, it still had just enough speed to continue to roll in a complete 360 degree loop right in front of me.

'Miracles do happen', I thought. As the truck was making the circle, it put the passenger directly into my gun sights! He had not yet, had enough time to digest what had just happened. All his brain could do was tell him he had suddenly heard a slight muffled poof sound. Then, before he even had time to blink his eyes, he saw the back of his friend's head explode like a huge splat of bird droppings falling on a concrete floor! And in that same instant, blood and brains and gore splattered all over his face and began to burn and sting his eyes and make him temporarily blind!

Before he had any chance to react, I gently squeezed off another round and watched as a brief second later, his head exploded, too!

What little was left of it went flying straight backwards and slammed into the headrest mounted on the back of the seat. For the briefest fraction of a second it stayed there, and then came flying forward where it bounced twice against his chest before finally coming to a complete rest. The entire back of his head was missing; blown off! He had died instantly, just like the driver had.

The truck continued to roll slowly around in an ever increasing oblong circle until it eventually stopped as it slowly bumped into a huge Saguaro cactus. The huge cactus was as strong as a steel gate and it made sure that the Tahoe was stopped dead in its tracks. I ran over to it, all of the time keeping my gun pointed right at the men inside just in case there may be more bad guys hiding in the back seats. There weren't any, and the two bad guys in the front seats were not making any moves at all. They, too, just like Gerardo, were stone cold dead!

I reached in the truck through the driver's side window past the slumped over driver, grabbed hold of the keys and turned the engine off. I then opened the door. As I did the dead driver made a sudden move over towards me. This time, though, I didn't even budge. I again glanced at the round red hole in the center of his forehead right between his eyes. I also got a very close up look to see that the entire back of his head was blown almost completely away. There was no way he could still be alive. His brains were completely gone; most of them onto his friend in the passenger seat!

I also saw as I looked across the driver's body at his passenger that he, too, had a round red hole in his forehead, and that the back of his head was also missing. I, again, almost shouted for joy! This meant that my new favorite gun was perfectly sighted in; which meant that the remaining Diablo's at the mine were, without a doubt, now for sure, walking dead men not even aware that later on tonight, they too, would all be dead! This was the last night they would ever be alive on this earth! In just a matter of a few hours, they would all be back in their normal abode where fire and brimstone, gnashing of teeth, screams and crying, and absolute total darkness will surround them for all of eternity!

Again, I had absolutely no regrets about killing these human impersonators who are nothing more than demons who have escaped from the boundaries of Hell! That's all they are! They're not human! They're devils! "Diablo's!" They even call themselves that!

But I'm sure; some bleeding hearts will probably say that I killed them in cold blooded murder, that I didn't even give them a chance. Well, I say, so what!!! These demons have already killed fifteen slaves in the last month and a half! One by skinning him alive! Another by cutting his head off! Who knows how many they have killed before they kidnapped this bunch of illegal immigrants? And now, they're threatening to rape and kill my wife, my daughter, and two of my precious grand-kids, and you want me to look for the good inside of them, and forgive them?!! You are absolutely crazy if you think that! It's for God to forgive! It's for me to free my family and these poor slaves! And, I will do whatever it takes to do just that! I tell you, I will kill every one of these demons without an ounce of regret and the world will be a better place because of it!

These two demonic Diablo's would certainly have killed me if I had given them any kind of a chance! Or, if I would have let them go back to the mine, they surely would have loved participating in the raping, torture, and killing of my wife, daughter, and grand-kids! To me, it is kill or be killed! My only regret was that I killed them too quickly, just like Gerardo! A true fitting death for them would have been one that lasted for hours on end, or until sunup at least.

I reached in and unbuckled the driver's seat-belt and pushed him over as far as I could towards his passenger. Once I got him scooted over enough to give me room, I climbed in the driver's seat, reached down to the keys, turned them on and started it back up. I then put the truck in reverse so I could back away from the Saguaro Cactus far enough to go forward and drive around it.

I then pulled the lever down into drive and turned the steering wheel in the direction to take us back over to the vertical mine shaft. I had two more bodies to unload down that shaft! Unfortunately, though, all of the drugs were already gone. They're already on the streets of "my country" getting ready to poison and kill!

As I was driving over to the vertical mine shaft, I laughed out loud. I thought that at this rate, that old vertical mine shaft would soon be completely full of dead bodies before too much longer. I also thought that the song, 'Paint It Black' was so appropriate for tonight as I continued to hum the tune to it! I just couldn't seem to get the song out of my mind!

I pulled up to the mine shaft and again got as close as I possibly could without actually driving into it. I didn't want to have to drag these bodies too far. Even though I wasn't feeling any pain, I am still a sixty year old disabled and decrepit old man with many medical problems, and I knew I didn't have a lot of extra physical strength. If you have never lifted a dead body, let me tell you, they are heavy no matter how much, or how little, they weighed when alive. Bodies are 'dead weight' when they are dead. (Yogi would probably be proud of that one) Again, I couldn't help but laugh as that thought ran through my mind.

I was still laughing as I walked around to the passenger door. So far, the night was going absolutely fabulous! It couldn't be any better than it was so far, except getting my family and the slaves free, and that would happen very soon! There were a few more Diablo's back at the mine I still needed to dispatch into a fiery lake of a Hellish eternity, but at least, there were now three of them already in that fiery lake discovering it's total terror first hand!

As I walked up to the passenger door, I reached out and took hold of the door handle and pulled it open. I then reached in and unlatched the seat-belt holding the passenger in the vehicle. As it popped loose, he, too, started to fall out towards me, but I quickly reached out and grabbed hold of him to stop his fall.

I turned him kind of sideways to where I could get my hands under his shoulders and then took a deep breath and heaved him out of the truck. As he came sliding out I let go of him and let him drop hard down to the ground right next to the shaft.

Then, I began searching him, too, and just like with Gerardo, I found several weapons attached and strapped to his body. I removed those and then took his wallet out and everything else in his pockets from him. I then gave him a hefty kick and sent him flying over the abyss. "I hope you're already burning in Hell, you slimy snake!" I yelled at him!

I reached in the truck again and grabbed the guy who had been driving. I pulled him out and let him fall down onto the ground next to the shaft. I then began to search him, too. Again, I found some weapons. I removed those along with his wallet and the contents of his pockets.

I walked back over to the truck and laid all of the weapons on the seat right next to where I will be sitting in the driver's seat. I now had three 9-mm pistols with several extra magazines, plus two more knives. I also had two of the little .38-caliber snub-nose midnight special guns. I wanted everything close to me just in case I ran into any more traffic on my way back to the mine.

Before I began to walk to the back of the Tahoe, I took the contents I had taken out of their pockets and laid them on the front floorboard. There were again, several rolls of US dollars wrapped up by rubber bands. I did not take the time to count any of the money. None of it would make any difference, anyway, if I did not succeed in killing all of the rest of the bad guys and freeing my family!

I closed the passenger door and then walked around to the back of the Tahoe where I reached over and opened up the lift-gate. As the gate moved up and completed its rise to the fully opened position, my eyes instantly fell on another beautiful and fully loaded AK-74 automatic assault rifle lying there, along with two more fully loaded 30 round magazines.

This AK also had a silencer on the end of its barrel, too. "Oh man, this is wonderful! It's absolutely better than any Christmas I have ever had!" I shouted in a very happy but low voice.

Naturally, though, there was no more dope inside of the vehicle. They had already made their delivery. The dope was now headed somewhere to the mean streets of America where it will soon be ingested into the dilapidated veins of the scum of our country! I thought, 'Let the Sanctuary and Bleeding Heart Do-Gooder fools, who believe there is good in everyone, take care of the scum-bucket addicts'!

Me? I'd give them three chances to break the habit and make something of themselves. If they 'struck out' as in three strikes you're out, I'd cut out all help of every sort and then tell them, "Either help yourself or die because we're through with you. You've cost us thousands of dollars and continued to be useless to society. So either straighten yourself out or you will starve to death!"

Harsh? You bet! Cruel? NO! Some people will just keep relying on others to support and help them until the helpers are bled completely dry! I know about this first hand by trying over and over and over and over to help a family member who kept bleeding me until I finally had nothing left to bleed! The only way to help these kind of people is to let them hit total bottom by themselves where the reality of death by starvation stares them flat in their faces, and then many will finally pull themselves up by their bootstraps and become a productive member of society! Or they will die and society will be better off anyway!

Before I closed the tailgate, I continued looking inside of the truck just to see what other goodies may still be there. I noticed a large black duffel bag stuck up right behind the driver's seat It was a cube with the length of it about 4' ft. feet long and about 24" inches tall and wide. It was very evident that it was crammed full of something because the sides and the top were pushed out to their limits. I figured it wasn't full of dope. But, I am not stupid, either. I assumed it was the million dollar payment for the dope that had been delivered.

A big smile swept across my face as I reached in and took the AK out of the back-end of the truck. I then reached up and grabbed hold of the lift-gate, pulled it down, and shut it. With my beautiful new rifle in my hands, I walked up to the front seat where I reached across and laid it where I would be able to get to it in a hurry if I needed to.

I then climbed inside and sat down on the driver's seat. As I got comfortable, I reached down and pulled the seat-belt across my body and buckled it up. I didn't want to be thrown all over the inside of the Tahoe when I went over bumps and ruts and washes on my way back to the mine. Then, I reached over and closed the door. Not once did it occur to me that I was sitting in a pile of brains, blood, and gore. But even if it would have, it wouldn't have bothered me in the least. I was on a hunting trip, and the blood and gore are just a natural part of my mission! To me, it was nothing more than gutting a deer would be!

I reached down, turned the keys in the ignition, and started it up. Before I put it in gear to drive away from there, though, I thought I had better try to come up with some kind of a plan for when I got back to the mine. That was my next stop on this hunting trip and six or more very bad El Diablo's were still my prey! I needed to be prepared!

# Chapter 14

Just then, another huge streak of lightning flashed across the sky. It was followed almost instantaneously by a huge clap of thunder. This time, it was so close that it actually shook the earth under the Tahoe and would have hurt my ears if I didn't have artillery ear syndrome! Without a doubt, I knew God was very angry at the 'demons' still remaining alive! I also knew He was on this mission with me to rid His beautiful earth of this dung scum who were polluting it! He was going before me and preparing my way! He was fighting on my side! *If God be for you, "who" can stand against you?"*

Barely a brief second later, several more tremendous streaks of lightning flashed throughout the sky, which were again followed almost immediately by huge booms of thunder. The thunder was booming and blasting and rocking and rolling so loud and powerful that this time, it actually did hurt my ears as it continued shaking the ground! To me, it was almost like old home week. I felt just like I was back in Vietnam with the North Vietnamese artillery rounds exploding all around me the way the ground was shaking and the noise the thunder was making! And, unfortunately, the blood, gore, and death that I was having to play a huge role in again was just like it had been over there! Without a doubt, I was very much right back in Hell! Irma had been right. I had needed to do a Vietnam 'thingy' one more time!

Right then, in that moment, it started to rain. But this was not just any rain; this was one of those famous Arizona thunderstorms that can easily drop several inches of solid sheets of driving, blinding, machine-gun-bullet like rain within a very short period of time over a very localized area. The drunken weather newscasters call them micro-bursts! And, believe it or not, they had gotten the forecast correct. With only a 10% percent chance of rain predicted for some time after 5 p.m., it was now pouring huge sheets down onto the hard-packed desert surface at around 7:30 p.m., or thereabouts.

At first, I was kind of disappointed by the rain. But after just a moment of further consideration, I thought that this was probably a Godsend! 'Those fools back over at the mine were not going to be out walking about in this kind of weather', I figured. If they were, I knew that without a doubt, they would all quickly melt and wash completely away being the fact that their entire beings were made out of pure, unadulterated, dog turds! 'That would certainly solve my problem pretty fast,' I thought. But, it would also take away all of the fun I was going to have in flushing this dog breath dog doo down into the wide open toilet lid of Hell! I also thought the rain was a very good way to wash all of the blood and gore off me, along with allowing me to wash some of the inside of the trucks out as well as I could.

I figured with the Diablo's back at the mine being holed up either inside of it or somewhere else close by, it meant I could drive this black Tahoe back over close to the mine without being heard or seen. That way, I would not need to do too much hiking across open ground in dangerous weather to get there. I didn't want them to see me, at least not yet, and I certainly didn't want them to hear me. But, I figured I could drive at least as close as my own personal Tahoe was to the mine. I knew my Tahoe had been left where they had captured us. That was in front of the high wall of dirt they had piled up to hide the mine. I also figured there was so much lightning flashing through the sky that I could see to drive the black Tahoe back over there without turning the lights on if I went slowly.

This is what I decided to do. I would get as close to the mine as I could without taking the chance of being seen. Then, the rest of my plans I would leave up to God. Those would be determined anyway, by what I found when I got there. I had a lot of firepower with me. I just needed the chance to use it. As I said, that part of it was in God's hands! So, I pulled the lever on the transmission down into the Drive position, placed my foot on the accelerator, and gave it a gentle push. I then turned the steering wheel to move back over to the dirt trail I had come from that would lead me back to my Tahoe.

# Chapter 15

I made it back to my Tahoe without any trouble. There was so much lightning that it almost made the sky as bright as day at times. I also didn't have to worry about being heard because there was so much thunder shaking the earth and blasting eardrums that the smooth quite running of the Chevrolet Tahoe was drowned completely out.

I pulled over next to my Tahoe. I then shifted the transmission lever up into the Park position so I could sit there for a minute to think of what else I was going to do right then. The first thing I noticed, though, was that the front window of my Tahoe on Precious' side was still rolled down and rain was now pouring in through it. That was not good for my beautiful, light-gray colored, soft leather heated seats.

I reached down and turned the ignition off. I quickly opened my door, jumped out and then ran around to the driver's side of my own Tahoe and jumped in. Before I even had a chance to settle down, I quickly reached down and turned the ignition switch over until I could get power to roll up the window. The keys had been left inside of it when they had captured it. Precious had been able to turn off the ignition but had not been able to get the keys out before they pulled her out. I didn't start it up, though. I only turned the key to the accessory position that allowed the power window switches to work.

I jumped back out and headed back over to the black Tahoe. As I was running through the rain and puddles to get there, I suddenly remembered the big duffel bag stuck up behind the driver's seat.

I moved over to the back door behind the driver's seat, reached for the handle and pulled the door open. I then reached in, grabbed hold of the bag and began to pull. 'Man, this thing is heavy', I thought. It barely moved at all with only my right hand pulling on it. So, I reached in with both of my hands and pulled harder.

This time it came sliding out, but very slowly. As soon as the bag fell out of the door, the weight of it made me drop it down to the ground. I didn't know a million dollars of paper money could be so heavy! As it slipped out of my hands and fell, it just happened to land in a large puddle of muddy water which created a huge splash which instantly covered me from head to toe. I didn't mind though, the mud and water mixed perfectly with the blood and gore to just add to my camouflage.

I left the bag sitting in the puddle for a moment as I ran over to the rear lift-gate of my Tahoe. I popped it open, but one glance inside and I quickly realized there was no way anything else was going to fit in there because of Precious' insistence on us bringing the entire GNP of Egypt with us.

I quickly slammed it back down before anything could fall out. I also didn't bother to try to get to my own guns underneath all of that stuff. I figured if I didn't already have enough firepower to do the job I needed to do, I would be dead a long time before I could ever get to fire my own guns.

I hurried over to the back door behind the passenger seat and swung it open wide. Then, I hurried back over to the duffel bag. Again, it was very heavy; this time even more so with the added weight of water that had soaked into it! So, I kind of carried it and drug it, all at the same time, over to my open door. Once there, I managed to manhandle it up onto the floorboard between the front seats and the middle seats. Irma would just have to put up with it and sit with her feet on top of it once I busted them out of the Hell they were bound in. I also wasn't concerned about the mud and water getting all over the inside of my truck. I figured a million dollars would buy a very nice detail job once I got back to town.

I then closed the door quietly, hurried back over and climbed in the open driver's door on the black Tahoe. I didn't bother to buckle my seat-belt this time. If I needed to get out of the vehicle in a hurry I didn't want anything holding me back. I also only had about a hundred yards to creep down the side of the berm before stopping and getting back out.

By now, a furious thunderstorm was raging all around me. The wind was blowing and gusting probably somewhere in the neighborhood of 50 to 75 miles an hour! In all of the years I have lived in Arizona, this was one of the worst---or best--- thunderstorms I had ever been in.

I had once gone through a typhoon over in Vietnam. In countries south of the equator and over the Pacific Ocean, hurricanes are called typhoons. They are the exact same storms, but just called by a different name.

At the time I had the unenviable presence of having to go through that typhoon, I had been inside a small bunker that was made entirely out of sandbags. The bunker was about seven feet across the front of it, by five feet on both sides, by about six and a half feet high inside of it. Along the front and sides were open gaps that substituted for open windows. The side gaps were about one foot tall and three feet wide. The front gap was only about six inches high and five feet wide. The front faced the way the enemy would approach us from if they decided to attack us. That's why the height of it was so small. It was basically just a firing slot to shoot at the enemy while having a means of protection behind heavy, dirt-filled, sandbags.

Through the entire night the wind had howled and blown so ferociously that I actually wondered if the sandbags might collapse and let the plywood roof that was covered in three layers of sandbags; fall down on top of me. The rain that was coming down in almost solid sheets was actually flying almost horizontally because of the strength of the wind! Where this bunker was located was only about 20 to 30 miles inland from the South China Sea where the storm was blasting in from. Therefore, the speed of the howling winds had to be somewhere in the neighborhood of 100 to 130 miles an hour!

By the time the morning finally arrived in a very dark gray dawn of heavy, thick, cloud covered, defused light, there was over two feet of water in the bottom of the bunker. I had needed to stand up all night long to keep from drowning. It almost came up to my knees. I thanked God that the wind, rain, and standing water were not too cold or unbearable!

During the night I was supposed to be on guard duty inside of that bunker. I was supposed to keep a sharp eye out through the front firing slit to make sure that no enemy soldiers approached us. And, if they did, I was supposed to put them out of their miserable lives with the 60-caliber machine-gun I had resting on a firing shelf pointing out their way. But, I knew there were no enemy soldiers out there that night. Where I was, inside of a bunker, I was totally miserable, and I, at least, had some protection from the typhoon; at least from the brunt of the wind and some of the driving force of the rain. That driving, blowing rain felt like sharp knives stabbing you as it hit!

The protection I had was not much, but it was much better than what the enemy would have had. The enemy, if he was out there, had nothing but the cover of the land for protection. In other words, the enemy had no cover at all. So, I knew they would not be out in it trying to sneak in and kill me. It just wasn't going to happen that night! They would have probably died from the storm long before they would have gotten close enough so I could have killed them.

That is almost the way it is tonight. This is not a typhoon, but it is an Arizona thunderstorm, and that's bad enough! I sat there inside of the black Tahoe listening to the pounding, machinegun like, drumming of the rain beating down against the roof, along with the whistling roar of the ferocious wind as it rocked the vehicle back and forth and tried to put some kind of a plan together in my mind.

# Chapter 16

The first thing I decided to do was to ride out the storm for a while; at least until about 3:00 o'clock in the morning. That was the time I decided I was going to hit them. It's the time when a person is normally in their deepest sleep, or at least, their drowsiest state. Hitting the enemy very early in the morning is a typical military maneuver used for the maximum surprise effect.

I figured they would not be too concerned about the two guys in the black Tahoe coming back to the mine tonight. With this weather, only a fool would be trying to drive in it, and that would be on paved streets. Trying to drive in the desert in this weather would be just plain ludicrous!

Also, I didn't think any of the bad guys at the mine would be stupid enough to be waiting outside of the mine in this weather watching for it to arrive. I thought they would probably assume that the guys in the black Tahoe would spend the night in town instead of tempting fate by coming back in this weather. I also assumed that if someone was up and looking for the black Tahoe to arrive at the mine, they wouldn't recognize that it was me driving it at first, so I would still have some element of surprise on my side. I also figured that my wife and daughter and grand-kids were still safe right now. I didn't believe that anything would happen to them until I got back from my delivery. So, I decided that I would get some rest before I actually had to begin running through the flames of Hell!

I was also thinking that even if I had made the delivery for them and everything went fine, there was still no way they were going to release my family. What if they released my daughter and she was to tell someone about this, their operation would be ruined and they would all go to jail. So, I knew that my entire family, and myself, were eventually going to die inside of that old mine! That is, unless I killed all of them first, and this is exactly what I planned on doing!

I pulled my cell phone out of my pocket. They hadn't bothered to take it from me because they knew there was no cell service out there in the desert. I wasn't going to use it to try to make a call; I just wanted to set the built-in alarm clock on the phone, which I set for 2:15 a.m. That would give me enough time to roust myself up and to get mentally prepared to go kill a bunch more people.

"No! Not people! These were not people!" They were not even up to the level of animals! To me, again, they were nothing more than a bunch of demonic beings impersonating humans and they needed to be vanquished back to Hell where they belong!

I leaned my head back against the seat and closed my eyes. My thoughts immediately went to my wife, my daughter, and my precious grand-kids. "Oh God, please keep them safe. Please don't let anything happen to them. And, please keep the ten slaves safe, too. Ease their pain and calm their nerves. I thank you so much!"

It was now only 9 p.m., but I suddenly felt like I hadn't slept in days, or even weeks. I was totally exhausted! That was no surprise to me being what I had just gone through so far tonight. But, part of it could still be the lingering effects of the chemotherapy I had suffered through for eleven months, and just recently completed! My eyes suddenly grew heavy and slowly closed. The next thing I remember, my alarm is alerting me that it's now 2:15 a.m.

"Okay, time to get up and get myself ready." I noticed that it's still raining; not as hard as it had been, but it was still coming down at a good clip. That's good! I knew it would help me. I still figured that only a fool would be stupid enough to be outside in it, so I thought I could drive the black Tahoe all of the way down to the mine.

I wanted to get it as close to the mine as I could so I would have access to the rest of the guns I had taken off the dead Diablo's I had already killed. I also figured, again, that even if someone did happen to see me, they wouldn't think too much about it because the black Tahoe was due back tonight.

I was hoping that if someone did spot me, I would have enough time to pop a round into them before they could alert anyone else.

During the rest of the time before I drove down to the mine and launched my attack, I double and triple checked both of the AK-74s. I also made sure I had all of the extra clips stuck in my pockets for easy access. I made sure, too, that the 9-millimeters were ready to fire. I strapped two of those on my belt going around my waist, one on each side of my body. Plus, I strapped another serrated killing knife on my left thigh.

Finally, it was time to go. My cell said it was 2:45 a.m... "It's time for me to go play cowboy like our brave sheriff!" I thought. At the least, I looked like a cowboy with the guns on my hip. I only hoped that this cowboy would be the one still standing after the gunfight at the old formerly abandoned mine was done!

# Chapter 17

I reached over and took hold of the ignition key. As I felt it slip into the palm of my hand, I glanced down to look at it. I expected my hand to be shaking but it was as steady as a mannequins'. I knew that if it wasn't shaking from nervousness, it certainly should have been shaking because of the Parkinson's disease that has taken a tenuous grip on my body. But, my hand was rock solid! There was not even a glimmer of movement! I couldn't help but smile. This was just another sign to me that God was on my side, and everything was gonna be alright!

I turned the key to the right. Immediately, the Tahoe kicked over and started right up. At the same time, a loud bolt of thunder exploded throughout the heavens that once again, shook the foundation of the earth and probably broke windows somewhere. It definitely shattered the sound barrier just as loud as any Air Force jet would.

"Thank you, God!" I said. Because of the thunder, there was no way anybody heard the Tahoe start up, even if they were stupid enough to be somewhere outside the mine and listening for it.

I pulled the transmission lever down into Drive, eased my foot onto the accelerator, and took a deep cleansing breath. Then, I lightly pushed down on it and began moving along the dirt berm directly towards the mine opening at only about 2 miles an hour. I was just creeping along. I did not turn the lights on, either. But, I could still see perfectly fine because of the flashing lightning blazing throughout the sky and lighting my way.

When I got within about a hundred feet from the end of the berm, I punched the accelerator a little harder to make the truck speed up. Then, I reached down and quickly turned the engine off. At the same time, I also moved the transmission lever up into the neutral position.

I then allowed the truck to coast from there until it finally slowed and came to a stop only about 5' feet from the end of the berm. That was good because I was still hidden behind it, and I hadn't needed to use my brakes to come to a stop. If I would have needed to, my brake lights would have come on and possibly alerted someone by the bright red glow that would have emanated from them. By stopping about 5' feet from the end of the berm, if anyone happened to be standing in the mine opening, there was no way they would have seen me, and they probably didn't hear me, either.

I slid the transmission lever up into Park. Then, I slowly and very quietly opened my door. As quietly as I could, I climbed out of my seat and stepped down outside. During the extra time between 2:15 a.m. and 2:45 a.m. when I left to drive towards the mine opening, I had lifted the hood and found the fuse box. Then, I looked until I found the fuse that controlled all of the interior lights inside of the Tahoe. I removed it and put it in the side panel of the driver's door. I was very glad that I had thought of that because I certainly didn't want any lights to come on when I opened the door of the vehicle so it could alert someone. It would have been as bad as brake lights coming on.

As my feet settled onto solid ground, I turned back toward the interior of the truck and reached across the driver's seat so I could grab one of the AK-74s. I then pulled it towards me. After I got it out of the truck I tilted the butt down and leaned it against the side of the truck. Let me assure you the safety was now off! The gun had a round in the chamber and it was ready and raring to light up the night sky like a bolt of lightning by spitting 30 rounds out of it in about the length of a heartbeat! It was fully set to sing heavy metal Guns and Roses!

After I had laid the gun against the side of the Tahoe, I reached back in and pulled the other AK out towards me. When I got it out, I took the sling that was hanging on the gun, stretched it out taut, then slung the gun up and over my head. As it settled around my neck, I pushed it around to where it would hang across my back. Now I was ready! I slowly and quietly closed my door.

But right then as I did that, my heart suddenly decided to pretend it was a top fuel dragster racing down a ¼ mile asphalt strip at over 300 miles per hour, and began beating a million times a second. For some reason, at that exact moment, it just then ripped through my mind that I was only one man; and a beaten up disabled sixty year old man at that, going up against six or more, Diablo's, by myself! And who knows what else the powers of Hell may have in store for me?

"Nah!" I thought. "I know that I have almighty God, 'El Shaddai' himself, and all of His unrivaled power including the full and entire armies of Heaven, on my side tonight! Hasn't He already proven that to me time after time after time already?" I also believed that in addition to having God going into battle with me, I also had the huge advantage of surprise. I was wide awake and I was really hoping they were all sleeping very soundly.

"So, how can anything go wrong?"

I took a deep cleansing breath and let it slowly ease out. My mind instantly became much clearer and my heart quickly returned back to normal; maybe even less than normal. In that same instant, I somehow became more focused and alert than at any time since I had come home from Vietnam. In fact, all of my senses, including my sixth sense, were on full alert power just like they had been in Vietnam. My old artillery ears had suddenly been healed, because I could now hear a pin drop from a hundred yards away! My eyesight had suddenly reached to the point of almost having x-ray vision! And without a doubt, the adrenaline rush plowing through my veins just then was just like the time I had popped the two North Vietnamese artillery observers off the side of that old jungle covered mountain many years ago!

I took the AK I had leaned against the side of the truck in my hands and pointed it out in front of me. I had the firing lever set on fully automatic but I was hoping that I still had the ability to blast out just three round bursts at a time. That is how you maintain control of your weapon.

Firing a 30 round clip on full auto will cause the gun to jump upwards and move at least a foot. No matter what it looks like in movies, it is impossible to keep a gun aimed where you want it when you are firing it on full auto. But, if you blast out only three rounds at a time in short bursts, it will allow you to keep the gun down, aimed where you want it to shoot, and able to move it in any direction you want. I knew that, I was hoping the Diablo's didn't if they were to shoot back at me!

I eased over close to the side of the berm and began to move along it toward the mine opening. I was using it for cover in case someone did start to shoot at me, and also, to hide behind. But no one saw or heard me.

I approached the end of the berm and squatted down onto one knee so I could lean over and peer around the end of it. As I peeked around the corner my breath suddenly caught in my throat! Standing right inside of the mine entrance was one of the Diablo's'! He was thoroughly enjoying emptying his over-filled bladder right out of the opening of it. I guess he didn't want to come all of the way outside and get wet standing in the rain, so he was standing back inside about a foot from the front. But, he had a real healthy stream of urine flowing right out of him; plenty enough to make it all of the way out of the opening and beyond where it was quickly washed away with the rain.

I took the real good steady stream as a good sign thinking that maybe they had all consumed a lot of alcohol before falling asleep. It would be fantastic if they were all blasted out of their minds with tequila, or some other mind altering, liver destroying, reaction numbing, devilish concoction! That would just absolutely be the icing on the cake! It would certainly make my task so much easier to literally 'blast them the rest of the way out of their minds' if they are drunk or stoned!

I decided to not take any chances or to assume anything, though. I needed to stay completely alert and ready for anything! So, I quickly glanced past the guy standing in the mine opening to look down the tunnel as far as I could see. I wanted to see if there were any more of them standing back inside somewhere.

Right then, I was so very thankful for the bright lights of the fluorescent tubes shining brightly and lighting up the tunnel just like Christmas. It allowed me to see all of the way down the tunnel almost to the place where the other one veers off. I couldn't see anyone else standing inside the mine, though. I then quickly glanced around outside of the mine, too, just to see if there might be someone stupid enough to be out in these elements. But, I didn't see anyone else anywhere.

*"THANK YOU, GOD!!!"* I mumbled under my breath.

I slowly brought the AK up and pointed the barrel right at him. He was so close to me I didn't even need to aim. I quietly slipped the firing lever over to a single shot from full automatic at the same time as he was just finishing and beginning to pull his zipper up. Without aiming at all, I pointed it at the center of his chest and squeezed the trigger. He didn't even have time to hear the 'poof' before the bullet hit him dead center in his heart, immediately ending his life and sending him back to the fiery Hell he belonged in.

As the bullet struck him, he went sprawling straight backwards down onto the ground with his arms and legs splaying out at awkwardly angles. The loudest sound that anyone could have heard was his head cracking open as it hit the solid rock wall behind him. The silencer on the AK worked to perfection.

But at that moment, I was not completely sure if I had killed him by hitting him in the chest. I also didn't know if maybe he might be wearing body armor and all I had done was stun him. The way he was sprawled on the ground with his head smashed against the mine wall left the top of his head pointing straight at me. This time, I looked down the barrel and took much better aim as I pulled the trigger one more time. In a New York second, his head totally exploded like someone had put a firecracker inside of a pecan and blew it to smithereens!

I waited where I was for a good two minutes without moving. I wanted to see if anyone else may have heard any noise and may show up. But no one did.

Even though my chronological clock was sixty years old, I was now feeling like I was twenty years old again; just like the way I felt in Vietnam. I had no pain anywhere in my body, which was a miracle in itself. My old creaky, stiff joints were moving like they were part of a well-trained, muscle bound, thoroughbred race horse! But in any case, I never would have known if I was hurting somewhere in my body with the amount of adrenalin that was pumping through me! It was stronger than any drug or dope these lousy fools could ever concoct and distribute.

I moved with the catlike graceful movements and cloaking invisibility of a beautiful black panther, combined with the speed of a mama cheetah chasing down dinner for her little cubs; over to the guy I had just killed. As soon as I got to him, I reached down and grabbed a hold of his feet and began pulling him out of the mine. As soon as I cleared the opening, I pulled him over around to the left side of it and dropped him down into a puddle of water. The water was deep enough to hide a good portion of his body, plus, it was also in a very dark place. No one should be able to see him until the morning light, and by then, either all of the bad guys will be dead or my family and I will be.

I leaned my head back around the edge of the mine opening and peered down through it, at least to where it veered off. There was still no one around. But before heading down the tunnel, I decided to make a quick reconnaissance around the right side of the mine.

On the left side of the mine opening was a semi-recessed area that only extended back about six feet before the mountain began again. But on the right side of the opening, the mountain continued for about twenty feet past the opening and then came to a corner that went backwards. I wanted to see what was back in that direction. I thought that was where the gas generator was located that I heard running. I also wanted to see if there was anything else; like maybe a shed or a small house, where some of the Diablo's might be sleeping. If not, then they were all inside of the mine right now. Bottom line, I had to know where and how many, demon devils I was up against!

So, I dashed across the mine opening over to the right side of it. Then, pressing my back up against the mountain, I quickly shuffled sideways across those twenty feet as quickly and as quietly as I could manage. As I reached the end, I slowly turned around and faced the wall. Then, I moved my head over to the right just far enough so I could peer around the edge. I was surprised by what I saw. Only about ten feet away from me was a large metal shipping container sitting on the ground. It was sitting kind of at a sideways angle of around 45 degrees to where I was standing with the front side of it facing towards me.

The container is the same kind that you see loaded on huge freighter ships that ply the oceans, or see riding on the backs of flat-bed railroad cars traveling across country. It was about 40' feet long, by 10' feet wide, by eight feet high. On the front side of the container is a single wide entry door mounted in the frame. And to my great enjoyment and pleasure, the door is located at the far left end of the container with only about two to three feet of the wall showing past it.

Along with the door are two windows on the front side that I guessed to be about 4' feet wide by 2' feet high. There's also a smaller vertical window on the right end of the container that's nearest to me. It has an air conditioning unit mounted in it taking up the entire window. Even with the rain and the time of year it is, the AC unit is turned on and blasting air into the metal building, and it's making enough noise to almost wake the dead. With that kind of noise, I knew there's no way anyone inside of the container is going to hear anything that happens out here, or especially, down inside of the mine. That was how loud the air conditioner was. Actually, I couldn't imagine how they could even sleep with that much noise, if in fact; this is where the Diablo's are sleeping.

Again, *"THANK YOU, GOD!!!"*

I slowly began to make my way over to the container being ever vigilant for any sign of movement or any kind of unnatural noise. I needed to look on the other side of it to see if there was another door, or any other way for them to escape out of the unit from that side when I start shooting.

There wasn't another door but there were two more windows that matched the ones on the front side, just as I had assumed. Every one of these converted shipping containers I had ever seen only had the one door coming out of it. In an emergency, people could escape out of the windows on the sides of the unit if they needed to. But if these Diablo's were to try that, I would pop them off just like I was at a shooting gallery at a carnival show.

I sent off a quick prayer that none of them inside of the container would wake up before I got back. My first concern was freeing my family from any more guards that may be in the mine. I didn't think that Tomas would leave just one guard inside of it to keep everybody guarded.

I also didn't know if he was militarily dedicated enough to make sure he always had at least one guard awake to keep an eye open for any escape attempt. Then again, maybe the guard I had already sent packing back to Hell had been the one assigned to stay awake at this time.

I moved swiftly back over to the mine opening. As soon as I reached it, I stopped right next to it and slowly moved my head just enough to be able to look inside. Again, there was no one there. So, I slipped around the corner and began moving slowly and very quietly down the tunnel. I was very thankful I was wearing rubber soled shoes that made almost no noise at all. Also, as I was moving down the tunnel, I moved my index finger over and once again switched the firing lever on the gun back to the full auto mark just in case there were several of the Diablo's inside and they happened to still be awake. I wanted my gun to be ready to spit the judgment of heaven out of it if I needed it to!

When I reached where the other tunnel branches off to the right, I stopped for a brief moment and then moved my head to peer around the corner. Again, there was no one there, either.

I now pressed my back up against the wall on the left side of the tunnel as I began creeping sideways down it. If anyone were to walk out of the big room, being on the left side of the tunnel would give me the best firing angle to cut them down.

I had the AK tucked up against my right shoulder and pointing straight ahead of me with my finger resting heavily on the trigger. I was moving without making any sound at all. Even my breathing was slow and normal!

As I got close to where the tunnel opened up into the large room, I could hear snoring, lots of it. It was exactly what I was hoping for! I was so much hoping that everyone would be asleep, including my wife, daughter, and grand-kids. So like a wary, vigilant, and very much experienced lioness sneaking up on a sleeping prey, I continued on moving towards the large room, again without making any sound at all.

As I got to the edge of the room, I could see my wife still bound to the opposite wall across from me; but she was slumped over asleep. That was good! I also saw my daughter and grand-kids curled up on the floor and lying on their sides next to each other. They, too, were sound asleep. That was also good! Very good!

As my eyes continued sweeping the room, I saw the ten 'slaves' either with their backs leaning up against the wall where they were chained to it, or were slumped over still in a sitting position with their heads hanging down against their chests. All of them, too, were asleep.

Then, I saw what I was looking for; one more Diablo. He was the only other one in the mine which meant all of the others should be asleep inside of the metal container outside. All of this was, again, very, very good!

The demonic evil creature that's impersonating a human being was lying on a soft air mattress on his side with his face turned straight towards me. *"P E R F E C T!"* I whispered to myself! Without another thought, I used my finger and quickly switched the lever back to the single shot position while lifting the barrel so it was pointed straight at the demon's forehead. This time, I took careful aim. I wanted a quick shot that would kill instantly!

I looked down the sights, slowly exhaled very quietly and then held my breath. I then gave the trigger a gentle tender squeeze. As I did, a poof came out of the end of the gun that in the confined quarters of the mine, sounded a lot louder than it had outside! But, before the sound even had time to reach my ears, the 5.45-mm bullet spit flaming metallic fire out of the front of the gun, and what was close to being equal to the speed of light, the back of the devil's head instantly exploded, looking like a cracked coconut while only a little red hole suddenly appeared in the center of his ugly face.

The poof sound the silencer made was just loud enough to wake up Juan and a few of the other slaves. Their nerves were so shot to pieces that any sound at all that was out of the ordinary was enough to send them into a wide ranging, full blown, anxiety ridden panic attack! As the low explosive sound of the gun suddenly echoed throughout the confined room, and then swiftly reached their ears, and from there, instantly blasted full blown straight into their scared and tortured brains, their eyes instantly popped wide open in a perfect caricature of the Chicken Little cartoon character! Then, within a nanosecond following that, all of their eyes quickly and fearfully began racing around the room until they finally focused on the dead Diablo who was missing a very large portion of his head!

As they saw the blood, the gore, the reddish gray brain matter, and the chunks and splinters of bone fragments spewed out everywhere behind the demon's head in a large oblong circle, several of them immediately began to audibly retch and dry heave! The remaining few who were not doing that began trying their best to try to stand up so they could run away from the horror and absolute terror they were seeing! But, their chains held them tight and restricted!

Shortly after that, several of them finally moved their fearfully blood shot eyes over to me. As they did, another perfect caricature of a horror filled movie villain jumped out of the solid rock walls of the mine and straight towards them!

What they saw was a bloody looking, gore covered, rain drenched, human apparition of a long, stringy, white haired, and white bearded, old decrepit man standing partially bent over in front of them with a smoking rifle in his hands!

My face was a grotesque mess! My nose was swollen to more than twice its normal size and was lying sideways, broken, against my left cheek. My lips were cracked and dripping dried blood from the corners. And most fearsome looking of all was the huge black and blue colored, bleeding red knot coming straight out of the front of my forehead looking just like a Klingon warrior! Add that with all of the blood and gore smeared on me from the dead Diablo's I had already killed, and I had to look like some kind of a frightening angel of death apparition come to personally take them into the dimension of death with me!

In less time than it takes to blink an eye, all of them who had woken up began shuttering and shaking like dried leaves blowing in a hurricane! They also immediately began mumbling and groaning in some kind of an unintelligible language, while trying their best to find enough of their voices so they could begin screaming at the top of their lungs! But I couldn't allow that to happen!

Who knows, the other Diablo's inside of the container may hear them and wake all of the rest of them up! If that were to happen, I would be in deep doggie doo doo; enough to completely cover over and bury this 5' ft. 11' inch old man alive!!! So, I quickly raised my finger up to my mouth signaling for them to stay quiet and to not say anything, or even to move. I then said in a whisper, "Juan, it's me, Jim! Stay very quiet, and make sure your men stay quiet, too! Don't any of you say anything or make any sound at all! Just nod your head, yes or no, and listen to me, okay?"

He was shaking and trembling so badly I swear I could hear his bones creaking and rattling just like a living skeleton! At that instant, he was too stunned to do or say anything just yet.

His eyes were bulging out of his face looking just like a big, bug eyed toad! All he could do was just continue to stare up at me with an astonished look of incredulity and disbelief all over his face!

For what seemed like a long time, but was probably no more

than a full minute, he continued staring at me. Then, he slowly lowered and moved his eyes back over to the demon that was missing the entire back side of his head. Then, with another instant flash of terrified horror sweeping across his face, he quickly looked back up at me again.

But as Juan's eyes once more settled back on me, he seemed from somewhere deep inside of his heart, to suddenly muster up and gather together a huge surge of courage and hope! Then, as a look of fearful determination slowly began to creep across his face, he sucked in his breath and began to slowly shake his head up and down, meaning "OK", he understood what I was saying and doing. At the same time, he also quickly let loose a very quiet blast of rapid fire Spanish that I assumed was telling them all to be absolutely quiet and not to make any noise at all.

I kept looking at every one of them to make sure they were calming down and able to get their senses back about them. Then I said, "Do any of you amigo's know how to use a gun? Like one of these automatic assault weapons?" I lifted the gun up so they could get a good look at it. Juan shook his head 'no', but interpreted for me to the other guys.

A second passed as my eyes wandered over them, looking from face to face. Then, I heard a deep sounding voice speak up in perfect English, "I do."

I glanced over at the guy who had spoken, "You do?" I whispered.

He nodded his head, 'yes'. At the same time, it just struck me right then that he had spoken English when he said 'I do'. So I said, "Do you speak English, also?" Again, he nodded his head up and down. I thought, apparently he doesn't speak too much of it with him just nodding his head.

Anyway, I said, "How do you know about firing a gun like this?" I certainly did not want to put a gun into the hands of a former cartel member or a hardened criminal who might turn and use it against us.

He then spoke again in almost perfect English with just barely a hint of an accent, "I was once in the US Army's 5th

Mechanized Infantry Division. I spent a year in Iraq, and another six months in Afghanistan as a sniper infantryman. I've used a gun like that on many occasions!"

I was flabbergasted "You were in our Army; the US Army? Then why were you trying to cross the border illegally? You should already be a citizen of the US because of your service."

"No, being in the Army does not automatically make you a citizen of the US. But, the reason I was crossing the border with these people is because I got kicked out of the Army and then deported."

For a brief instant, he glanced down at the ground. Then, with a look of defiance on his face, he looked right back up at me and stared directly into my eyes. "Listen man, according to the Army I did something wrong. What I did was, I pulled the trigger against a woman in Afghanistan and killed her. She had just killed my best friend and ammo carrier! So, I didn't care, I blew her away! But the Army said I should have brought her in instead of killing her! ... ... Aw man, you wouldn't understand! You've never been to war to know what it's really like! No one knows what war is really like unless you have been there!" He dropped his head down and would not look up at me.

Again, my heart went out to another one of these men! I suddenly realized that of all of them that had woken up, he was the only one who was not shaking and trembling with fear. For him, what had happened had just happened! It just meant that one of the Diablo's had just bought the bacon and that was all! I looked right into his eyes and said in a quiet voice, "Amigo, look at me. Tell me, por favor, what is your name?"

He didn't want to look up at me. But finally, he said, "Jose".

"Well, Jose, let me tell you something, I do know what war is all about! I have been there! I spent a year in Hell in what stateside sissies called Vietnam. And, I was not a rear-echelon, panty wearing, pencil pushing, paper shuffling, butt sniffing, brown nosing, shake and bake officer, either. I was a ground grunting cannon-cocker in an artillery battery!

"I spent that year in Hell in almost continuous combat along the Demilitarized Zone separating South Vietnam from North Vietnam. I also spent a couple of months of that time along the Laotian border. And on two or three different occasions, we actually crossed the border and went into Laos so we could save the retched cowardly rear-ends of the South Vietnamese ground grunts. I have pulled the trigger many, many times, my friend. I have much blood on my hands from that time in my life, including that of a woman who had a six year old child with her."

At that, he quickly looked up! "You did? You actually shot a woman with a kid?"

"I shot the woman, not the kid. The woman had just thrown a grenade into one of our jeeps that had a lieutenant and a private sitting in it. I, too, almost got in trouble for killing her. They wanted to Article 15 me, and then give me a dishonorable discharge! But, you know what? She deserved to die! She killed two of my combat brothers! I did what I did and I have absolutely no regrets! So, my friend, do not tell me I don't understand about war! Without a doubt, man, War is Hell!"

This time, he looked at me with new found respect as a huge smile raced across his face. I said, "Would you be willing to take one of these AKs and go play soldier boy with me one more time, because Jose, we are at war again tonight! I've entered into the realm of Hell once again! Already tonight, I have killed five of these Diablo's that have imprisoned you guys, including that one lying over there with his head almost blown off. But, there are several more of these devils still alive and breathing our air. They should not be doing that. They should all be dead and I could really use some help in shutting off their air supply for all of eternity!"

He laughed with an unadulterated glee in his voice, "It will be my absolute pleasure and honor, amigo. Mucho Gracias!"

I laughed, too, and then reached over and slapped him on the shoulder. "You're very welcome, my amigo!"

I then stood back up, turned around, and began walking back over to the dead guard. Once I got there, I knelt down and began rummaging through his pockets. Finally, I turned my head back towards Juan and said in a loud whisper, "Juan, do you know where the keys are for that lock that has you guys chained?"

"It's on a hook hanging from his belt on his left side. Its hanging on a quick connect loop."

I rolled the guy over. Sure enough, there they were. I pressed the loop and pulled the keys off it. Then, I hurried back over to Juan, bent down, and inserted the key and unlocked him. Then, I handed the key to him and told him to unlock the rest of his guys, but to unlock the former Army hero first. I needed him to quickly get outside of the mine to protect us from any intruders with a gun in their hand. I also told Juan to make sure the men stay right here and make absolutely no noise at all after he unlocks them!

He quickly stood up and moved over to my new combat brother. He reached down, grabbed the chain, and unlocked it. Then, as Jose scrambled up to his feet and out of the way, Juan continued going man to man to the rest of them, unlocking them all. At the same time, he whispered to them to keep quiet and to not say anything or make any noise at all and especially, to stay right where they were until I told them what to do.

By this time, because of the whispering that was going on and the unavoidable noise the chain was making as it fell loose off the men, Precious had woken up. She looked up and saw me standing in front of her. Her eyes grew as large as 1875 silver dollars! Her face instantly froze with an incredulous look plastered on it and her mouth was as wide open as it could possibly get.

She knew by my old looking unshaven and wrinkled face who I was. She also knew deep down inside of her that she was married to me. But, at the same time, she had no idea who this guy was that was staring back at her and who was wearing her husband's face on top of his shoulders. He had the same face and the same body as her husband, but he also had an evil looking assault rifle strapped over his back, another one in his hands, two pistols strapped around his waist with one on each side, and two large hunting knives strapped to both thighs. She also saw a lot of reddish brown colored blood splatter that was all over me and my clothes.

I saw the look on her face and I thought she was just about to scream as her eyes suddenly moved from me over to the almost headless dead guard! Again, I quickly put my finger over my mouth signaling to her to not say anything while furiously shaking my head from side to side. With a speed and agility I didn't know I still possessed, I quickly moved over and squatted next to her. I reached out, put my arms around her and began pulling her towards me. At first, she resisted and pulled back away from me, not wanting to get any of the blood and gore on her that was on me. Plus, I think a big part of her still wasn't too sure if it was really me, or some kind of an outlandish incarnation of me that a demon had assumed!

I took my hand and brought one of the knives out of its scabbard and started to move it around her to cut the rope away that was binding her. But, as she saw the knife and me moving towards her, her eyes got as wide as saucers, again, and she gasped in a loud echoing voice, "NO!"

"Honey, look, it's me! Don't worry! All I'm doing is cutting the rope off that's around you, okay?"

I guess at that point, by hearing my voice, she finally realized that it really was me. So, in that very same instant, she turned back into my very sweet and wonderful wife! She immediately began badgering me, "Where have you been? What have you….." I put my hand over her mouth.

"Not now! I will tell you everything when we are free and a long ways from this place. But, there are still at least another four, five, or six really bad guys who will kill all of us if I don't go and kill them first. So again, don't ask me anything yet. I'll tell you everything just as soon as I can!"

Once again, her eyes grew as wide as saucers and her mouth, again, began hanging wide open! Thank God there were no big bugs flying around. She looked at me for a long, hard, minute with a huge mixture of confusion, fear, and maybe a little trust, too that was beginning to slowly gain a hold over her. After a moment, she looked me straight in the eye, and then said, "Do what you have to do … but… … be careful, my darling! And, I …. … love you … … and I really do trust you!"

I said, "I love you, too. And we will have time for a lot of that in just a little while, okay? But right now, I have some more very important work to take care of. But first, listen to me; I want you to get Rachael and the kids up. Then, I want all of you to follow me back down the tunnel and out of the mine. But please, please, please, do not let the kids make any noise at all! If you have to put your hands over their mouths, do it! Under no conditions are they to make any noise, okay? As I said, there are still at least four, and possibly six, more Diablo's I have to take care of before we're all safe."

She didn't know what the word Diablo meant, but she nodded her head up and down. At that same moment, Rachael suddenly woke up and blinked her eyes open. As she did, she quickly glanced around the room until they suddenly focused on me. She immediately saw the assault rifle on my back and the other one in my hands. She also saw all of the other weapons and knives strapped to me. But most of all, she saw the blood staining my clothes and basically covering me from head to toe. A very scared and terrified look instantly flashed across her face! In a sudden movement, she sat straight up and exclaimed, "Dad, what are you doing? You're not having a flashback of Vietnam, are you?"

I quickly put my finger in front of my mouth again. Then I whispered to her, "Yes, I am, honey, and I decided to bring the hell of Vietnam back over here! Now, keep your mouth shut and do what I tell you to do, okay? But don't, don't, don't, make any noise at all! I have already taken care of five of these demons but there are at least another four still left for me to send back to Hell where they belong. Jose over there, and I, are going to go play soldier boy and finish this job. But, we need you to keep the kids and yourself absolutely quite! We need the element of surprise for only the two of us to take on the rest of these demons. So, again, keep quite! Do you understand?"

She slowly nodded her head. All of her life she had heard comical stories that her dad would get up in the middle of the night and wander the neighborhood in his olive drab underwear with a stick in his hands thinking it was an M-16 and dreaming he was chasing gooks. None of it was true, other than a few wild and wooly dreams of the same sort, where I really did cry out, "Gooks in the wire! Gooks in the wire!" But now, right in front of her eyes, her ornery, jaded, and decrepit old dad, had somehow instantly transformed into a twenty year old killing machine that some MPs at the San Francisco Airport had once labeled as a 'menace to society'!

I turned around and hurried back over to Juan and my war hero buddy, Jose. I said, "Listen up, Juan; you can interpret for me to these other guys. There are still at least four, and probably six, el Diablo's still left. I believe they are sleeping in a converted shipping container outside around the right corner of the mine."

I looked at them real hard as Juan interpreted for me. Then, I continued, "Jose and me are going to go kill them all! Do you understand me? Not one of them will be left alive, okay?"

Again, Juan told them what I had said. Jose had a big grin on his face! He was just itching to get started! He had revenge on his mind! I looked back at the rest of the men with a hard look still on my face. I needed them to believe what Juan was telling them! Every one of them looked right back at me with some finally beginning to show me some teeth, at least the ones who had some, with small grins.

Most of their faces suddenly began to lighten up with unrestrained relief as the realization that their desperate prayers had been heard by God, and they would soon be free from this Hellish place they had been held captive in, swept over them! They knew I was right. They might be trembling and totally scared out of their shorts but they could not help but give me a smile!

I turned to Juan one more time, "Juan, to assure them I mean what I say, tell them I have already killed five of these Diablo's, including the two that were driving a black Tahoe."

As I mentioned the black Tahoe, his eyes got real wide. "You killed those two, too?"

"Yes! And that is what we are going to do with the rest of these punk pukes!"

"Yes, Senor! Oh yes!"

I turned to the Army veteran, and said, "Okay, Jose, this is what I want you to do. I want you to take this AK-74 and make your way outside. Find some cover out there that you can keep an eye on the mine and both sides of the shipping container at the same time. If you see anyone anywhere, except us, 'kill them'! OK?"

He nodded his head.

I looked at him, "Amigo, have you ever shot one of these AK-74s?"

He said, "No, not one of those, but I've definitely used an M-16, plus many other weapons."

I said, "This is much better than an M-16! Use it with pride!", as I handed it to him.

He looked at me with an incredulous look. How could I, an American, say a Russian made gun was better than an American made one? He wondered.

I said to him, "Listen, I tell it like it is. This is a fabulous gun! And, it is already sighted in for at least 50 yards. If you need to shoot at a further distance, aim for the chest, OK?"

He nodded.

"Also, that big round thing on the end of the barrel is a silencer. Unscrew it and take it off. I want you to get outside as quickly as possible to give us cover as we come out. But, I want to be able to hear if you get in trouble. I wouldn't be able to hear with the silencer on. But, if you begin shooting with it uncorked, I'll know, and I promise you I'll be there in just a couple of seconds to join you in the fun, okay? I can't allow you to have all of the enjoyment, amigo."

I looked at him with a small smile on my painfully swollen and cracked lips. He was looking back at me with a huge smile on his face. I nodded my head towards him, then lifted it back up and gave him a big wink with one eye!

I thought he was going to burst out roaring with laughter! So, I quickly put my finger over my mouth, again!

He took the gun out of my hands and lifted it up to see it better. He, then, partially pulled the lever back to make sure a round was already chambered. After that, he turned it over to see where the lever was that controlled single shot from full auto fire. He flipped it to auto. He then checked where the safety was located and made sure it was switched off. I also reached in my pocket and handed him another full clip of 30 more rounds just in case he needed it. But, being that he was a former sniper, I figured he could probably kill two of these demonic birds with only one round!

As Jose hurried out of the mine, I turned back to Juan and said, "I want all of your guys to follow you and me out of the mine. I want them behind us and in front of the women and kids, okay? I want the women and kids to be the last ones out of the place just in case we run into any trouble?" He nodded. "Then, when we get outside, I want your guys to sneak around to the other side of the berm. The black Tahoe is sitting over there. There's a 9 mm pistol sitting on the front seat. When the men get to it, I want all but two of them to quietly get inside of it without making any noise at all.

The other two men, I want them to take the 9 mm, plus one of these here I have on my hip, along with them, and then, I want them to guide my wife and daughter and grand-kids down the length of the berm until they come to my Tahoe that is sitting down there. Do you understand me so far?"

"Si, Senor. No problema."

"Okay, now while they are all doing that, you and I have another job to do. I want you to sneak around to the back side of the shipping container along with Jose. I want you and him to find a place to take cover back there, okay?

I want you to take this other 9 mm with you. And if anyone tries to come out of one of the windows on that side of the container, I want you and Jose to shoot them. Look at me, Juan! Do not hesitate even for one second. You aim and shoot! You comprende? Listen, man, they have already killed fifteen of your compadres when they turned all of you into slaves. Now, it's your turn to turn them into slaves! Slaves of Hell!!! Do you comprende?

"I am going to the front side of the unit and shoot them as they come out the front door. Or, if the door is unlocked, I'm going to sneak inside and blast them straight to Hell from there. Either way, not a single one of the Diablo's will be alive within another ten minutes!"

He nodded his head. I could see a transformation come over his face and in his eyes. It was a hardness! A determination! I knew at that moment no one was going to get by him.

I stood up and stretched my legs. Then, I turned to look at Precious and Rachael, "Did you hear what I said to Juan?" They nodded their heads. I said, "You are to go with two of these men to our Tahoe. Once you get there, you get in it and start it up; and then get ready to fly out of here. If I, or any of these men right here, do not come and get you within twenty minutes, I want you to put the pedal to the metal and get the heck out of Dodge as fast as you can! Rachael, you drive, okay? Then, you head straight for a police station and tell them where I am and what is going on!"

They both started to protest. "Honey/dad, we can't leave you here! We'll wait for you to come get us."

I looked them square in the eyes, "Listen, if no one comes to get you within the next ten to twenty minutes, it means I am dead! So, you get out of here and save yourselves and my precious grand-kids! And, don't hesitate! I mean it! You must give my grand-babies the chance to live a full life!

"Also, be very, very careful crossing washes and stream beds! We have had a ton of rain tonight and many of them may still be flowing full of water! If there is any water at all in the bottom of these washes, DO NOT enter into them! That is as sure of a death as it would be by El Supremo Diablo murdering you!"

They both broke down and started crying. I said, "Look, God has been on my side so far tonight. I don't believe He is going to forsake me now. You must believe that, too!"

I then turned to everyone else, "Okay everyone? Are we ready to go?" Everyone shook their heads up and down.

# Chapter 18

With Jose was on the outside providing cover for us I had absolutely no fear. I knew that if any of the Diablo's showed their face, they were as good as dead! So, I turned around and began to lead everyone out of the mine with Juan walking confidently and assuredly by my side, carrying the pistol just like an expert. I glanced over at him and caught him looking at me. I nodded my head and gave him a smile. "It's gonna be alright, Juan, my friend! Trust me!" Then, I winked at him, too.

I thought he was going to burst out laughing, too, but he caught himself. He hesitated for a moment while a sober look suddenly came across his face. Then, he said, "You know, Jim, after what you said to Tomas, I hated you. I had believed what you had told me. But, I listened to what you were saying to him and I believed that you had been just lying to me. ... ... I'm sorry!"

"It's okay, amigo. What I was saying to Tomas is what is called, 'selling the prospect'. I used to be very good at it."

This time, he did laugh, "You still are very good at it! You not only sold Tomas, but I think you sold everyone else in the mine, too, including your own wife and daughter. None of us knew where you were going with things!"

I laughed, too. "All of you will just have to get over it! It got me free, though, didn't it? And now, here we are with only a few more demons left to dispatch back to Hell and all of us will be free, once more!"

As soon as we got to the mine entrance I stopped and signaled for everyone else to do the same. So far, everything was going good. Even the kids were still asleep. I leaned my head out and looked around the corner. No one was in sight and I couldn't hear anything that would alert me that someone was up and moving around. I also looked to see where Jose was, but he was very well hidden. "Just like a perfect sniper!" I thought! I trusted him. I knew he had our backs!

I moved forward over to the edge of the berm. I then turned

around and signaled for Juan to move over to a place where he could keep the front door of the container covered. I whispered to him, "If anyone comes out that door, pull the trigger and keep pulling it! Just keep shooting in that direction until you run out of bullets, okay? I'll take over from there."

He nodded and squatted down with the pistol pointed right at the door. I then signaled for everyone else to come hurrying over and around the berm. As Precious came up next to me, I leaned over and whispered to her, "Two of these guys are going to go with you to our Tahoe. When you get there, you do what I already said. You get Rachael to start it up and turn it around so we can make a fast exit if we have to. But listen, Baby; don't honk the horn this time, okay? Bad things happen when you honk horns. You let a bunch of demons escape out of the clutches of Hell the last time you honked it!"

I leaned over real quick and gave her a kiss on her cheek as she tried her best to smile at me. "I love you!" I whispered.

"I love you, too. Please be careful, my Darling!"

"I will. But, it doesn't hurt to say a little prayer for us, you know."

She smiled. "I know, and I will."

"Go now. Hurry!"

She turned and began hurrying down the pathway towards our Tahoe with big boy Bronco in her arms. He had his head on her right shoulder still sleeping just like an innocent little baby, which he still was, and I pray that he always will be! Rachael was right on Precious' steps carrying Venus. But before Rachael left, she turned to me and said, "I love you, Dad. Stay in your Vietnam mode until you get them all. You came back from Vietnam! So ... you come back this time, too, okay?"

"I promise you I will."

"I love you, dad."

"I love you, too, "IRMA". And don't forget, you once were a '4-wheeling mama'. You went up the side of a huge mountain with your old dad one time! That earned you that name of 4 wheeling mama. So, if you have to, you do it again tonight, you hear? Get the kids, your Mom, and yourself out of here as far as possible! But, do it safely!" She put on a very brave smile while nodding her head up and down.

Finally, all of the others moved away from us and it was just Juan and me left. I turned to try to find Jose, but I still couldn't locate him. But as I turned back to look at Juan, Jose just suddenly appeared out of seemingly nowhere by our sides with a big smile on his face.

Just like a sniper, he never made a sound at all and was totally invisible to us until he wanted us to see him! The spirit of antichrist wannabe world ruler made a huge mistake in allowing this great and brave man to get kicked out of our armed forces! This kind of man is who has helped our country stay free since its independence! We need more just like him!

I reached out and put my arm on his shoulder and smiled back. Then, I said, "Jose, you and Juan sneak around to the back side over there and get into a position to shoot anyone who tries to come out of the windows, okay?" They shook their heads up and down and began moving out. I stood where I was and waited until they got in position. Then, I popped out the magazine cartridge I had in my gun and inserted a fresh full one in. I put the partially used one in my pocket for use later if I needed it. Then, I moved like my outdoor kitty cat named, Charlie, who kills at least one unsuspecting bird a week, over to the front door of the container. I was also hoping and praying that I would have nine lives like Charlie, too, if needed!

As I silently got there, I leaned my head forward and placed my ear against it. The only sound I could hear was a lot of heavy snoring coming from inside. That was a very good sign, so I slowly reached down for the doorknob and gave it a slight turn. It wasn't locked. For about the hundredth time tonight, I silently cried out inside, "Thank you, God!!!"

The door was at the far end of the unit which was perfect. If it had been in the middle of the container, I would have had to go in the door and fire first in one direction and then turn and fire in the other hoping that I could get them all before one of them would be able to get off a shot and kill me first. With the door being at the end, all I had to do was go through the door and begin blasting. This time, I had the gun set on fully automatic and I intended to shoot all thirty rounds until the magazine was empty. Then, I intended to jump back outside and slam another clip in and wait for any survivors to come out.

That was my plan at least.

I twisted the knob once again and leaned into the door. It began to open without making any noise at all. This was good; very good! The hinges must have been oiled real good.

The door opened all of the way, but I stayed where I was and listened to see if I could hear any movement or of someone stirring. There still wasn't any noise at all except the snoring. So, I leaned my head around the door and looked in. A dim night light was glowing from an outlet on one wall. It was just enough light to allow me to see everything, and everyone, inside of the place. As I quickly glanced around the room I saw there were five Diablo's; all of them probably sound asleep in a drunken stupor, I thought. At least, I was hoping and praying that was the way they were.

Two Diablo's were sleeping on military cots on the right side of the room and two more were on cots on the left. All of them were aligned sideways against the walls, one above the other. El Diablo Supremo was asleep on a cot in the middle between both sides. His cot was directly underneath the air conditioner but his was sticking straight out into the room towards me. At the moment, he was lying flat on his back. His legs were splayed out sideways with his feet hanging almost off the cot. Both of his arms were curled and draped over his chest and stomach. But what was really wonderful to me was, he was lying on top of the sheets with nothing covering over him. Plus, he was wearing only saggy, dirty looking, loose fitting boxer shorts. His feet were closest to me with his ugly round head at the top of the cot.

All of a sudden, I wanted so much to take him alive, at least for the time being. So, I quietly switched the firing lever back to single shot. Then, I took careful aim at the guy on the right that was the farthest away from me. I gently squeezed off a round and watched as it hit him square in the middle of his chest. Without any hesitation at all, I quickly moved my aim down to the next guy and fired a quick shot. It, too, hit him square in the chest.

Then, I quickly moved the gun sight and lined up on El Diablo Supremo. As I did, I quickly took aim for it to be the perfect shot! I squeezed the trigger and it smashed into him directly in the middle of his groin!

Without any hesitation at all, I quickly moved my gun over to the left side and pulled the trigger two more quick times. Both of the Diablo's on that side had begun to stir and sit up, especially when they heard El Supremo begin screaming such a beautiful and lyrical soprano concerto at the very top of his wonderfully operatic little elementary school girl voice. But before their tequila infused brains even had a chance to realize what was happening, they were slammed back onto their beds as dead as an Egyptian mummy, with burgeoning round red bleeding holes in their chests. But to make sure they were dead, I aimed again and fired a shot into each of their heads, along with the other two demons lying on the right of Tomas. For the moment, I left him alive, screaming at the very top noise spectrum that a human being can make.

I then reached over and turned on the full interior lights while keeping my gun aimed directly at Tomas. He was in way too much pain to try to grab his own AK-74 weapon that was lying on the floor next to his cot. He was screaming at the top, glass shattering, high octaves of his soprano voice just like a little girl while both of his hands were grasping and holding what little was left of his unrealized manhood! It couldn't have been much to begin with what with his little voice never having changed during puberty.

I laughed at him as loud and as crude as I possibly could! Then, I screamed at him even louder than he was screaming, "Look at me, you stupid, gullible, ignorant fool!

"Did you really think I would betray my family and my own country, by allowing you to hold them hostage and to bring drugs into it?"

I then walked over to a window and opened it, while still keeping my gun trained right on Tomas. But as I threw open the window, I kept my head down just in case Juan and Jose got trigger happy and thought I was a bad guy trying to escape. As it swung open, I yelled through it, "Hey Juan, Jose, both of you come on in right now. Everything's alright and under control!"

I then turned towards the door and waited until they came in. At the same time, I also continued to keep an eye on El Supremo Diablo. But, I also wanted to make sure that Juan had his gun pointed away from me when he came in. By Jose being in the Army, I trusted him to know better.

Juan cautiously first pointed his gun into the room, and then slowly followed with his head. I said, "Juan, point your gun down towards the ground. It's okay! Everyone's dead except for Tomas. I left him for you and Jose to finish off, my friends. After what you have been through, you guys definitely deserve the honor of that!"

After I said that, they both walked on into the room. They first looked at me, then at the dead bodies, then at Tomas. He was still screaming and squirming and begging to be killed! A visible shiver ran all of the way up and down Juan's body as his eyes settled on Tomas. I could see it. I knew he really believed he was actually staring right into the eyes of the real Diablo who occupies a toilet lid throne in Hell!

Juan quickly raised his gun to shoot him. I yelled, "Juan, wait! Don't you want some payback for what he did to all of your friends? Especially the one he skinned alive?"

He stood stock still for at least a full minute, not moving a single muscle. I could tell that he was trying to decide what to do. Finally, he turned towards me and lowered his gun at the same time. "Amigo, thank you for leaving him for me, but, I am not a killer. I cannot kill him no matter what he has done!

"I am a simple farmer who was looking to put food on my family's table. No, I cannot kill him."

"Okay. I understand." But before I had the chance to do or say anything else, Jose quickly stepped forward and raised the barrel of his rifle. He pointed it right at the center of Tomas' chest. Then, looking right into his eyes with his own eyes as hard and cold as more stolen blood diamonds, he screamed every bit as loud as El Diablo Supremo, "BURN IN HELL!!!!" At the same time he jerked the trigger as hard as he could and kept it there until all 30 rounds of the large banana clip magazine was empty and the barrel was smoking red hot!

I stood there for a few seconds just staring. Tomas deserved everything he had just gotten, and more! Much, much MORE!!!! His body was literally cut in half, both ways; across and up and down! Then, I turned to Juan and Jose, and said, "He died too easy! You should have made him suffer a lot longer!"

Jose shook his head that, yes, he understood. But then he said, "I shot him 30 times. Are you going to report me to the authorities?"

He was clearly worried! If he had gotten kicked out of the Army for shooting one person who deserved it, he was now thinking that he was in really BIG trouble for cutting a man in half with 30 bullets. I smiled, then walked over to him and put my arm around his shoulder. "It's okay, amigo, you did good! Very, very good! Mucho Good!"

I then said to them, "Listen to me, guys; first of all, no, Jose, I am certainly not going to report you to any authorities! You are my hero, amigo! And, as far as I'm concerned, you got screwed big time by the Army and by our political oppressors in Washington D.C.! Okay?

"But secondly, I want all of us to destroy everything in this entire place! That includes the mine and everything in it, too. It includes this container and the bodies in here. I want this entire place destroyed so no trace of any of us can ever be found!

"I don't want a single sniff of any drugs left! I want to hurt the drug owners where it hurts the worst, in their pockets!

"And, I want to keep all of that murderous, mind altering, body destroying stuff off the streets of our country! And especially this; look, my friends, and listen very closely. If the authorities find out about any of us, and especially what we have done by killing all of these Diablos and destroying their drugs; well, with the politicians we have running our country and the crazy liberal judges ruling over us, all of us may be going to go to jail for a very long time! But what would be even worse than us going to jail is if anyone at all; no matter who they are, ever finds out about us! If anyone finds out what happened out here, and especially, who we are, all of our names would be plastered all across every newspaper, every television station, every radio newscast; in fact, every type of media in the world!

So let me ask you, my friends, do you think if the demonic drug cartels know who we are, they're going to let us live? Absolutely not! They will not only kill all of us, but they will kill all of our families, too! That's our kids, our wives, our parents, our aunts and uncles ~ everybody!!! So amigos, let's totally destroy this entire place and everything that could link any of us to it, okay?"

The reality of what had actually happened tonight suddenly rocked them all of the way down to their inner cores like a bolt of lightning splitting a gigantic redwood tree in half; and it plunged into the inner reaches of their brains like a hot knife slicing through butter! They stood there for a moment actually wobbling back and forth on their feet! At the same time, the blood in their heads rapidly drained out of it and they were on the verge of fainting!

For a brief time, they were even unable to put two rational thoughts together! It had hit them big time! "We are now free from being slaves at this mine, but at what cost? And for how long? Are we going to be marked men for the rest of our lives? And are our families now going to have to suffer for us gaining our freedom?" ... ... They both slowly crumpled to the floor and began to suck in huge gobs of air as a loud sob suddenly erupted out of the throat of Juan, followed quickly by one bellowing out of Jose!

I looked on both of them with a heart overflowing with pity. I knew exactly what they were going through. I had experienced the same feeling earlier that night while waiting for my cell phone alarm to go off.

"Yes! Everyone who was in this mine, including my wife, daughter, and grand-kids, will be targets for the rest of our lives." I knew!

But, there is a big way to either neutralize that threat or to delay it infinitely. So, I turned to Juan and Jose and said, "Listen to me, my amigos; yes, you, me, and everyone else who has been in this mine tonight will be marked people for the rest of our lives. But, we can overcome that if we work together. What we have to do is totally destroy everything in this place! We have to eliminate everything that could leave any trace at all of who we are! The drug cartel doesn't know who has already died and who has remained alive. If they know anything at all, all they know is twenty five people came across the border on such and such a date. They may also know that 15 of you died already and 10 still remain alive. But I guarantee you that if they do have even this much knowledge, which I personally doubt, they have absolutely no idea who has died and who is still alive!

"So, listen to me, they have no idea that Juan is alive! They have no idea that Jose is alive! They have no idea who I am or who my family is, or even that we exist! My amigos, we have to keep it this way for all the rest of our lives for us, and our families, to be safe! So, let's look around and see what's in here. Let's see what we can find to use so we can totally destroy everything here, okay?"

I had to get them up off the floor and get their minds free from their fears and back full of courage again! So, I looked away from them and began acting like if I had to, I would do all of the destroying of this place by myself! I had to do something to get them out of their pity party!

I walked away from them and began looking around inside of the place. My eyes suddenly settled on a dining table over against the far corner of the room. But there was no food on it.

Instead, stacked on top of it were tall bundles of green colored paper banded together with big rubber bands. I turned and walked back over to Juan and Jose. Then, I reached out and took them both by the arm lifting them up. In a strong and firm voice, I said, "Get up! Both of you! Stop this pity party right now! Do you hear me? Look, the answer to our dilemma is right here!"

I literally pulled them up off the floor. Then, I pulled them over to the table. On it was just what I thought it was; a very large amount of American paper money all banded together in nice even stacks.

We looked at each other, stunned with the amount of money that was stacked there. It was more than any of us had ever seen with our own eyes! At that very moment, the doom and gloom suddenly lifted off them like the sun burning a dark fog away and leaving nothing but brilliant sunshine in its place! You could actually feel the spirit of defeat packing its bags and moving out!

We again looked at each other. Then, big smiles wrapped their way across all three of our faces from ear to ear! Without a doubt, we looked just like the Jack in the Box character describing one of his newest concoctions!

With no rhyme, reason, or provocation, suddenly all three of us quickly reached down and picked up a stack of the bills and began to count the money in it. Each stack was bundled in used, $100 dollar bills, and each stack contained a total of $10,000 thousand American dollars. We quickly figured out that all of the rest of the stacks held the same amount, so we began counting the number of stacks. Altogether, the money equaled to $1,000,000 (million) American dollars; all in $100 dollar bills.

I reached down and began separating the money into ten separate stacks of one hundred thousand dollars. After that, I separated two stacks from the others. Then, I turned to Juan and Jose, "Juan, Jose, this money right here is yours. The other stacks are for the other eight men with you. This is $100,000 (thousand) dollars for all of you." I smiled at him.

Juan quickly turned his face to look up at me. "Oh no, Senor! I, we, none of us, can accept this money! It is not ours."

"It is now, Juan." I replied.

"No, Senor, we can't! You don't understand. This is dirty money. It is from drugs. It has blood and death on it! ... My apologies, Senor, but you take it," I didn't take the time right then to think about what his implication meant about me, and why I would be able to accept it instead. I allowed it to go over my head.

"Okay, Juan, I'll take it." I said. I then reached out and pulled all of the stacks of money towards me. Then, I looked back at him. "Okay, Juan. This money is now mine. I own it, you see? So, because it is now my money, it is no longer dirty because it belongs to me. So now, since it is no longer dirty, I give it to you and to your friends."

With that, I pushed the stacks of money back towards them. Juan continued to look at me like he was undecided. "But, Senor, this is not fair. You did all of the work tonight to release us. This money really does belong to you."

"Juan, as I said, I give it to you! If anybody deserves it, it's you and your friends. My God, man, think about the suffering you and your guys have gone through! You have been slaves now for how long? Just think of this money as being the wages owed to you for the work and beatings they have demanded of you!"

With that, he couldn't help it and a huge smile wrapped itself around his face. $100,000 thousand dollars was more than he would have ever made in his entire lifetime working for sixty years down in Mexico. This was a fortune to him.

I said to him, "Juan, listen to me, and listen real good, this money is now yours. But, the drug cartel who owns this operation believes that it still belongs to them. You must be very careful how you, and all of the rest of your men, handle this money.

"Voices have a way of traveling long distances! Large luxury purchases paid in cash have a way of traveling long distances! So, you and your friends must keep your mouths closed completely shut, and your purchases very discreet.

"Never tell anyone about what happened out here. Never tell anyone that you were turned into slaves. And, only spend small amounts of money at a time.

"Now, I want all of you to go back to Mexico. Only tell your wives what happened to you but only if you trust her to keep her mouth shut, too. Then, you don't stay there in Mexico, you hear? You pack her up and bring her back here to the US. I don't know how to tell you to do it. But, I would not trust anyone, again, to bring you back across the border. Maybe you could use some money to make a very roundabout way back here by going to some South American country first. Spend some time there and then make your way back here if you still want to come here.

"But I'm telling you, Juan, if you stay in Mexico, the drug cartel will find you. Then, they will cut your heart out after they rape and kill your wife in front of you.

"You make sure you tell this to all of the others, too! I'm trusting you, too. You see, if any word gets out about who did this, then I am a dead man, too, along with my entire family. So, everyone must keep their mouths shut tight forever!

"One last thing, even though I feel a very deep bond of friendship and brotherhood with you guys, for the safety of all of our lives, we must never try to find each other ever again. Okay?"

I could tell that the gravity of the situation was still shaking him all of the way down to his core. But, I believed that he would do as I said. I just hoped and prayed the others would, too!

I said, "I'm going to go outside and see what I can find out there to destroy the dope inside of the mine. You go get the other men to come get their money. But, send one of them down to tell my wife everything is all right and to drive my truck back down here so she can pick me up."

He nodded. But then, he said, "Amigo, you must take a share of this money! We cannot take all of it. I refuse!"

I once again reached over and put my arm around him. "Amigo Juan, you gave this money to me, remember? All of it! Well, I gave all of it back to you and to your friends. Again, remember? It was mine. Now, it's yours!"

He looked at me as tears began to fill his eyes. "Thank you, amigo! Mucho gracias, my dearest friend!" he said.

"You're welcome, my dear friend!" I said. "But, you need to thank God, too. He is the one who really did the work of setting all of us free!"

"Oh yes! We all will surely thank God for His goodness and His grace!" Then, he looked me right in my eyes and said, "You do know, amigo that God sent you here so you could rescue us. It was in answer to our prayers that God would send someone to save us. And, He did! He sent you just for that purpose!"

This time, big tears instantly welled up in my eyes. I couldn't help it! But, I continued looking at him the best I could through the big wet tears that were rolling down my face. At the same time, I suddenly remembered the prayer I had prayed asking God what I should do to help these men. I could plainly see how God oftentimes answers our prayers in a totally unexpected way?

Then, in a voice heavily choked with emotion, I said, "I am not so sure about that Juan. But, I appreciate that you were kind enough to say this to me. One thing I am sure of, though, is that God also rescued me tonight. He taught me a lot about the good in people like you, Juan, and the rest of your friends.

I previously slammed all of you who came across our border as illegal criminals and threw all of you into one large group who deserved no pity, but much punishment! Please forgive me, Juan! I am truly, truly, sorry!!!"

# Chapter 19

A moment later, with tears still stinging my eyes, I turned around and walked outside to go try to find something to use to destroy the contents of the mine. Juan and Jose went over to tell their friends to come inside of the storage unit to get their gift. They also sent one guy down to tell Precious everything was alright and to come and pick me up.

While this was going on, I walked over to the large gasoline powered generator that was still humming along in perfect harmony. It was located partially back behind the container. Next to it was a large aluminum storage shed that was unlocked. I pushed the sliding doors apart and peered inside. With wet tears once again swiftly filling my eyes, I saw six large five gallon gasoline cans filled to the brim and one 55-gallon drum of gasoline about half full. Also, there were several large packages stacked on top of each other that were labeled, "Danger! Dynamite!"

Again, "Thank you, God!!!" I yelled!

I grabbed one of the cans and went back over to the storage unit. Juan and his friends were still there. I said, "Get your money and hurry and get out. I'm going to set this place on fire. Also, Juan, there are five more of these cans of gas and several packages of dynamite over next to that generator in a storage shed. Send some of your guys over there and get all of that stuff. And then, tell them to take them inside of the mine down to where the dope is. Tell them to soak all of the dope real good with the gasoline. We will set it on fire after we place the dynamite so it will blow up and collapse the entire mine. That will completely destroy the entire place, I'm sure! Then, tell them to come back and refill the cans once more from the 55-gallon drum that's also inside of the shed."

After I had soaked the inside of the storage unit with the gas I had with me I followed the guys back down into the mine. But, I did not set the container on fire just yet. I wanted to make sure that was the last thing we did before we left the area. I wanted the inside of the mine to be destroyed first!

Once down in the mine, all the men climbed up and over all of the drugs making sure we were soaking all of it by pouring twenty full gallons of gasoline all over that large stack of dope. Juan, Jose, and I stood there waiting until the others had made their way back out of the mine. We then took several crates of dynamite and placed it where we thought it would make the ceiling collapse. Then, we took the last of the cans of gas and began pouring a fuse back out to the front entrance. There was exactly enough to complete that task. But by then, I had no doubts that it would be.

I turned to Juan, "Anyone got a match?" He reached in his pocket and pulled out a waterproof camping match, then, handed it to me.

I then reached inside the door of the mine and struck the match against the wall. It flickered for a brief second and then flamed up high with a steady yellow and bluish flame. I turned to all of the ones standing there and said, "I'm going to create my own version of Hell right now. I only wish I could throw all of the rest of the entire members of this evil demonic drug cartel into it."

I then threw the match down on the gas fuse trail we had made. In a brilliant flash of light and heat, it instantly caught on fire and began racing down the tunnel towards the back of the mine much faster than a man could run.

I then walked with Juan and Jose back over to the shipping container that held five dead bodies but was now completely empty of cash. For a reason known only to God, it had now stopped raining. I quickly glanced up at the sky. The heavy, thick, rain bearing clouds were clearing out and a quarter-moon was beginning to break through what remained of them. I yelled, "Juan, look up at the sky. God is smiling at us!"

A big smile, equal to the one God was showing, crossed his face as he looked up to see the partially round smile of God on the face of the moon hanging serenely in his heaven. Then, he reached down, lit the match and threw it inside of the unit.

Immediately, the container blazed into a roaring inferno of Hellish proportions! Without a doubt, Hell in all of its fiery fury had just come for El Diablo Supremo and the other devils inside of it!

Juan, Jose, and I looked at each other. Then, we all leaned forward at the same time and wrapped our arms around each other. "Take care, my Brothers!" I said. "You take care, too, my Bambino!" Juan replied. I laughed! But then said, "May this be the last time any of us ever have to experience the horrors of Hell!"

We turned around and began to walk back over to the two Tahoe's; me to my white one, and Juan to the black one. Right at that exact moment, the dynamite inside of the mine suddenly exploded and the mountain seemed to tremble for a brief instant before suddenly falling down and totally collapsing on top of itself! We all let out a huge smile along with a big sigh of relief.

I then turned to Juan once again, and said, "Juan, there are a lot of you in that one vehicle. If the cops see you, they are going to suspect you are illegals, and they are going to stop you. I am also sure that there is still a lot of blood and gore in it. And that will be very hard for you to explain!

"Listen, when we get about two miles down the road from here, I am going to point for you to go off the road. About two hundred yards away over there is a very deep vertical mine shaft. Unfortunately, that shaft contains the bodies of the other fifteen people who came over here with you. That is where these Diablo's disposed of the bodies in there.

"Well, that shaft now contains something else. Tonight, I threw another three of the Diablo's in there, too, along with all of the dope that was in that white Tahoe. But, next to that mine shaft is where the white Tahoe I originally left in still is. Drive over to it, and then have some of your friends get in it and disappear. Okay?

Also, on the front floor board is some more rolls of money. Split that up between you and the guys, too!

"Finally, take the cans of gasoline and what's left of the dynamite, with you. Open the lids on them so all of the gas will spill out. Then, throw those cans down inside of the mine shaft along with the dynamite, too. I know it is a terrible thing to do, but we cannot allow the drug cartel to know who is dead and who survived. If they somehow pulled the bodies out of the mine, they would find out you and your friends are still alive. Do you see what I mean? So, you have to totally burn the entire contents inside of that shaft beyond any recognition whatsoever! And hopefully, the dynamite will make the shaft collapse on itself like this mine! Oh, and one more thing, when you decide to ditch these vehicles, make sure you wipe all of your fingerprints completely away. Maybe you can find a way to set them on fire, too, so any DNA that might be in them will also be destroyed!"

He looked at me with huge, unashamed tears rolling down his cheeks. Again he said, "You are an angel that God sent to rescue us. Without you, we would have had no idea to do the things you have told us to do! You do know that don't you?"

I smiled back at him and said, "I'm not sure about that, Juan. But I do know God rescued all of us tonight! Without Him, we would have stood no chance at all!" I remembered what I had prayed and I remembered how much I had been drawn to come back to this mine. I thought that God may have used me as His earthly agent to rescue these poor men, but I also knew in a very powerful and wonderful way that God had rescued me, too! He had rescued me from a life of bigotry and hatred!

We climbed in our vehicles and began driving away with me leading the way. When we reached the place for me to show Juan where to turn to go over to the white Tahoe, I also happened to hit a big rut in the road that made the heavy duffel bag bounce up and hit Irma in her shin. She let out a big yell, then said, "Dad, what is in this big bag on the floor back here?"

I turned my head to look at her, then at Precious, then I said, "Uh, its gold! I finally found my fortune out here in the desert! But, it's not yellow gold that's in it! It's green gold. Oh, and it's probably somewhere in the neighborhood of $1,000,000 million dollars." They both let out a beautiful imitation of Tomas' screaming, then, they fainted!

# Epilog

I was way off in my estimation of what was in the duffel bag. Actually, it contained $10,000,000 (ten million American dollars) in stacked piles of one hundred dollar bills stuffed into it; ten times what I had originally guessed! I could not help but laugh and tease my wife and Irma, because after 40 some odd years of going out into the desert to look for gold, I had actually finally found it. No, it was not the yellow metal type, but it was a fortune nonetheless, even if it was made out of green paper.

My biggest concern first of all, with that much cash, was how to hide it; and then second, how to spend it without raising suspicions. I was sure that the cartels had their tentacles out everywhere looking and listening for anyone who may make a large purchase with cash. I am not street wise enough, and especially not Wall Street crook wise enough, to know how to launder money. So, Precious and I make weekly deposits into our checking accounts of anywhere from $1000 dollars up to $7500 dollars. We do have a business account that we use most of the time to make these deposits in. If anyone asks, we just tell them we have a home-based internet business, which we really do. Thank God very few have ever asked, though.

Precious and I also make deposits of $4000 dollars a month into the banking accounts of all five of our kids. Plus, we give them another $4000 a month in cash. We have not said anything to them about where the money comes from, other than to tell them we are making some pretty good money from our internet business, and we just want to share the profits instead of letting our socialist federal government leaders 'spread the wealth' to undeserving lazy mutants who were stupid enough in the first place to vote them into power!

Precious and I have not gone on any huge spending sprees. She kept the job she was working but has cut back on the number of hours she works. We do not need a lot of money for us to have a good time. We both opened up several secured credit cards with cash deposits.

Each of those cards has at least a $5000, (five thousand dollar), line of credit. A couple have $10,000, (ten thousand dollar), lines of credit. We have used those to take a couple of well-deserved cruises, then quickly paid off the balances.

We feel that Irma deserves more than the other kids are getting, due to the fact of what she and her kids went through. She and the kids, because of me and my undying love of the desert, had to experience the terrible horrors of Hell out in our supposedly safe rural areas of Arizona! And through no fault of her own other than wanting to spend time with her dad and mom, she would never have had to experience that horrible trauma.

So, again, we believe that Irma deserves a little more. But, with her mother's fierce, unalterable, and stubborn determination bred in her, she absolutely refuses to take any more than the other kids get. But, she is also the only one who knows where the money really comes from, and thus, she knows that if she ever needed more for some reason, she could get it, as could any of the other kids.

But since Irma knows where the money comes from, and because little Bronco was old enough to remember certain horrors himself; like his Papa having blood streaming down his face from split lips and a huge cut from a bleeding bump on his forehead, he was able to tell his daddy about those horrors. This necessitated Irma into having to eventually tell Wyatt about everything that happened. But instead of him getting upset about the kidnapping and the killings, he was mostly bothered that he wasn't there to help me dispatch the demons back to Hell! I could have really used his help, too! And, I would have been very appreciative of it!

But now that Wyatt also knows about everything, Irma has threatened him with the torturous pain and complete humiliation of receiving an unwanted 'total' body makeover by becoming a really ugly woman with a flat hairy chest, instead of staying a fine looking man, if he ever mentions even one word about our experiences to anyone.

In other words, if he wants to keep his manhood until he dies of old age, he had better keep his mouth shut!

As I said, if our other kids ever needed any more money for any reason, they would get all they wanted, too! But, we do not feel that we should tell them where the money actually comes from. That would probably scare the steaming hot elephant dung right out of them! And, it would also probably leave them constantly looking over their shoulders for the rest of their lives.

That would be no way to live! Precious and I can tell you that first hand! The difference is, she knows that I will use my several new wonderful automatic rifles with several beautiful silencers on the ends of them, without any hesitation whatsoever, to protect all of us with! But, by the way that we do things concerning our kids other than Irma, they all get to enjoy the benefit of the money without the fear of a sudden death destroying that! So, we break the money down into weekly and monthly contributions in varying quantities between cash and checks to all of the kids. This basically keeps it from the suspicions of the IRS and allows them to enjoy life free from financial problems.

For the next several weeks after our ordeal had ended, Irma and Precious both kept looking at me in kind of a weird way. I don't know what they were expecting me to do or of what they expected me to turn into, but I never did anything to make any of their fears or suspicions become a reality. One day, they both approached me and asked how I could kill all of those men like I did, and never act any different than I had ever done. They told me that if it had been them, that would be all they would be able to think about all of the time. They wouldn't be able to eat, sleep, or God forbid, even go shopping! But, I never acted any differently than I did before this all happened. "WHY?" They wanted to know!

I didn't tell them much of anything. I couldn't! All I basically could say was that this wasn't the first rodeo I had ridden in, and because of that, you have to ride the same horse you first learned how to ride in every rodeo you have to go through in life! I don't know if this made any sense to them, but Yogi would probably be proud of it!

You just have to learn to live with things. You can't internalize them! If I would have let all of the things I have gone through in my life stay inside of me, well, without a doubt, I would have been standing in my yard howling and baying even at a partial moon, instead of only at a full one, a long time ago! But the bottom line is; it's like Jose had said, only a person who has experienced the horrors and trauma of war can know what war is all about! I also say that only a person who has gone to Hell can actually know what Hell really is like! I've been in both places! I know what they are like!

But, never in my wildest dreams would I have ever thought that once again, at the old age of sixty years old, I would be forced to return to Hell and become once more, a killing machine. Or, as those sissy stateside, panty wearing Military Policemen who were stationed at the San Francisco Airport had once said of me, "a menace to society"! Because, that is exactly what War and Hell does to you! You are no longer a normal human being! Instead, you transform into a machine, a well-oiled killing machine! And then, you become an absolute menace to society, or at least, you do to the Mexican drug cartels!

But, not once have I ever had any regrets about killing those demons and taking their money! In fact, I was very happy that I had been able to cleanse the earth of several air breathing demons and send them back to their fiery underground lairs they had escaped from! I was also very happy to keep the money out of the filthy bloody hands of international gangsters and killers!

I was also very, very happy when I heard on the news a few days after the inferno at the mine that an estimated $50,000,000 to $60,000,000 million dollars' worth of dope had been consumed in a huge fiery inferno at a supposedly abandoned mine in the desert north of Phoenix. It had been determined that the mine was being used as a main distribution center for the Mexican drug cartels to import, and then send their poisonous concoctions throughout all of North America. It also made mention that as of yet, the cause of the fire had not been determined. They were assuming an accident had taken place with gasoline and dynamite being stored together down inside of the mine. Plus, to my great relief, there wasn't any mention of any dead bodies found anywhere. The fiery inferno inside of the container had totally burned the corpses to a crisp before totally melting the entire container down to the ground!

I knew that the loss of the dope, plus the $10,000,000 (ten million dollars) we had, plus the other $1,000,000 (one million) Juan and his guys had, put a hurt in the cartel's wallets, but it was far from putting them out of business. Yes, it was a setback, but it was not devastating to them. They would soon regroup and be back in business like nothing had ever happened; maybe even in another supposedly abandoned mine out in 'our' desert.

If there is, unless God specifically comes to me and tells me face to face, or at the very least, through a burning bush, to go and destroy it, I ain't going! Yes, my desert-dwelling, dirt-romping, butt-bouncing, berm-jumping, air-gathering days are finally over. No longer will I go back-wrenching, head-spinning, pin-stripping, delirious out in the desert! In a way, this is sad to me! But, the time has come for me to finally realize I am truly old. Much, much too old to ever have to return to Hell again!

What happened that day and night confirmed to me that God rescued me, too, every bit as much as He had rescued Juan and his men. But, in addition to rescuing me physically, He also rescued me internally. I still have an ornery streak in me as you can tell from my little rant about socialist government leaders and wannabe world dictators who inhabit the spirit of antichrist inside of themselves.

And, I still get upset about all of the crime that is committed by illegal border crossers. But, I now have a different perspective about some things.

I used to pile all of the illegals into a big bag and draw the string tight around it to bind them all together. To me, all illegal border crossers were the same thing, criminals! But, after Juan,

Jose, and the other eight men with those two, I no longer can do that. There are 'some' of the border crossers who really desire nothing more than a better life for them and their families. These are the ones we need to somehow separate and encourage to come into our country legally. The Bible calls it "separating the wheat from the chaff", Juan, Jose, and the other men are definitely wheat!

I don't have the answer for how to do that, but if we could somehow allow the good ones to come here, they, most definitely, would add tremendously to our diverse society, our financial futures, and especially, our gene pool!

Maybe one test of who is allowed into our country could be in how they view the US. Do they see us as only a place to come and make money while their loyalty lies with Mexico, or other Central and South American countries? If so, let them have a green card while they are working, and then they need to go back home.

Or, are they willing to come here and be patriotic American citizens of the United States? If so, then they need to put away the Mexican flag and all of the other flags from the other countries they have come from, and honor our flag and our country! It is alright for them to fly their flag to celebrate some cultural heritage or holiday, but to march in protests inside of the United States carrying the flag of another country like so many do, is an affront and a disgrace to us citizens of our great country. And, if confronted, there are definitely those here who will defend our country to the limit, even if our elected leaders will not. So, I say, come here if your desires and loyalties lay here with us citizens of the United States. But, if they lie under other colors, I say come here and rot in jail!

But, I pray every day and night that Juan, Jose, and his cohorts have somehow been able to come back here to the good ole US of A! I know without a doubt that if they are here, and if God blesses them with little Juan's, Jose's, and others, then our gene pool in the US is already greatly increased and blessed. Without a doubt, they are very good people!

I pray unceasingly that God keeps all of them safe and under His care and grace. If anyone in the world deserves it, after what they have been through, these men do! And, I pray for my family's safety, too! One word, one purchase, one action done in the wrong place at the wrong time could set the cartel on us.

Finally, as I've already stated, I don't think we are ever going to go exploring in the desert anytime soon. In fact, we probably never will venture off a paved road again. It is no longer a beautiful playground for people to go and see and interact with the vast wonders of God's diverse creation. Due to the invasion and siege of illegal border crossers that are intent only on creating violence and mayhem, and living a life of crime, the beautiful, exotic, and mysterious desert of southern and central Arizona is now a very dangerous place to be! Due to the complete inaction and political infighting of our own federal government, parts our own country are unsafe for us American citizens to visit. As one of Arizona's sheriffs, whose area of responsibility encompasses the war zones of our desert, said recently, "Our own federal government is now our enemy!"

And until all of our existing cowardly federal government so-called leaders, who are so severely lacking in the testosterone and estrogen areas due to the simple fact that they have never grown a pair either between their legs, or on their chests, decide to stand up and once again protect our own country, I dare say that God's beautiful desert in Arizona will remain a place too dangerous for the citizens of our own country to visit!

These impotent, sissified, so-called leaders must either grow a pair between their legs or on their chests, and then cleanse our country of these invaders, or we need to vote new men and women into those offices who were born with the testosterone and estrogen needed to stand up and say, *"ENOUGH IS ENOUGH"!!!*

# 2 Years Later

I was back in my favorite persona of impersonating a couch potato by lying on my sofa watching a football game on TV. Just as I was about to dose off for one of my twice daily 2 hour naps that I need to stay in shape and keep healthy, I heard my doorbell ring.

"Now who is that? Don't they see the 'No Soliciting' sign?" I growled!

By now, the Parkinson's has progressed even more and I am having more trouble walking. Most of the time, I use a cane to try to steady myself. I reached over and grabbed it, and then brought it close to use in helping me to stand up.

Finally, after much effort, I made it to my feet and began the slow shuffle to get to the front door. By that time, it had begun to ring again, and again, and again, almost constantly without stopping.

I yelled, "Knock it off! I'm coming as fast as I can!"

Finally, I shuffled up to the door and leaned forward to peer through the little eye piece mounted in the middle of it. I could make out two shadowy figures. Without opening the door, I yelled through it, "Who are you and what do you want?"

One of them turned straight towards the door and began to reply. But before he did, I instantly recognized who it was. As I did, my heart immediately jumped right out of my chest, fell straight down through my stomach, then raced down my legs until it finally bounced off the floor about a foot high once it exited through my bare feet!

"Juan! It's Juan! What is he doing here? … … … Oh man, I'm dead! I'm dead! And, my entire family is dead, too!"

I jerked the door open! There stood Juan, and Jose was standing right next to him! Neither was smiling!

# Author's Bio

**"Hell Comes Again"** was the first novel to come out of the
imagination of T W Manes,
followed soon by a book that is sure to go viral,
**"The Seed - The Tree - The Cross"**
The next book, **"Ezekiel's War"** is in production and
should be available by December 2011
T W's love for writing began from a class writing assignment in
the 7th grade. He wrote a story based on the
Robert Frost poem, "The Road Not Taken"
Not only did he get an "A" on the story,
but he won the writing contest, too.
Thus, the love for writing began. Only took 48 years to come to
pass! Ha!
He lives in Phoenix, AZ with his wife and 3 dogs.

For more information, please visit
**www.twmanes.com**

Made in the USA
Charleston, SC
28 July 2011